20

Zo

[*a novel*]

XANDER MILLER

 ALFRED A. KNOPF | NEW YORK | 2020

THIS IS A BORZOI BOOK
PUBLISHED BY ALFRED A. KNOPF

Copyright © 2020 by Xander Miller

All rights reserved. Published in the United States by Alfred A. Knopf,
a division of Penguin Random House LLC, New York, and distributed
in Canada by Penguin Random House Canada Limited, Toronto.

www.aaknopf.com

Knopf, Borzoi Books, and the colophon
are registered trademarks of Penguin Random House LLC.

Library of Congress Cataloging-in-Publication Data
Names: Miller, Xander, author.
Title: Zo : a novel / Xander Miller.
Description: First edition. | New York : Knopf, 2020.
Identifiers: LCCN 2016009324 (print) | LCCN 2015045682 (ebook) |
ISBN 9781101874127 (hardback) | ISBN 9781101874134 (ebook)
Subjects: LCSH: Poor men—Fiction. | Fathers and daughters—Fiction. | Haitians—Fiction. |
Haiti Earthquake, Haiti, 2010—Fiction. | Haiti—Fiction. | BISAC: FICTION / Cultural
Heritage. | FICTION / Literary. | GSAFD: Love stories.
Classification: LCC PS3613.I56257 Z9 2016 (ebook) | LCC PS3613.I56257 (print) |
DDC 813/.6—dc23
LC record available at https://lccn.loc.gov/2016009324

Jacket images: (palm and sea) Jasmina007/Getty images; (woman) Hello World/Getty Images
Jacket design by Janet Hansen

Map by Joe LeMonnier

Manufactured in the United States of America

First Edition

For Naomi

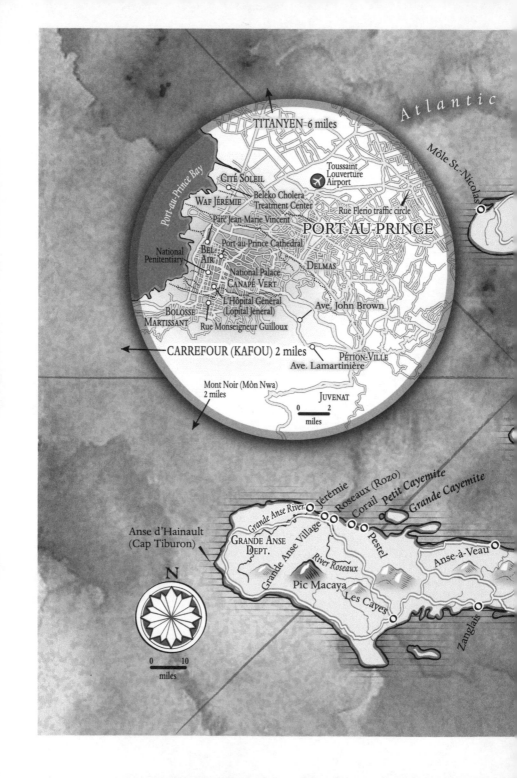

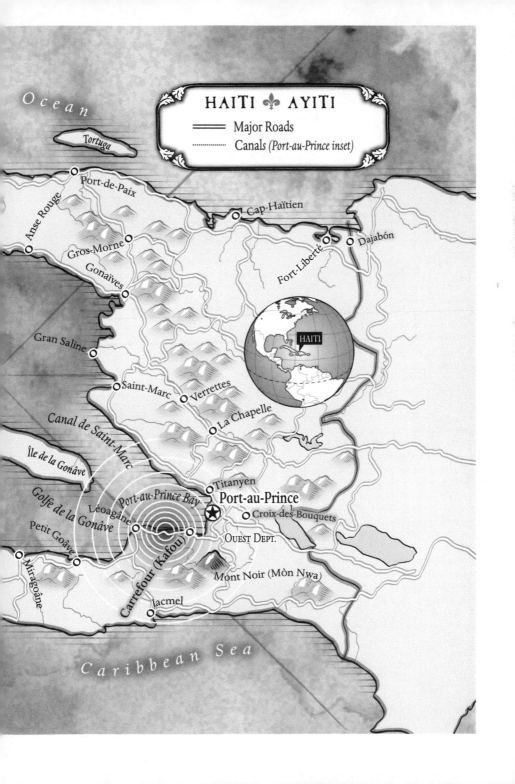

• Book One •

1

ZO GREW UP in the fishing village of Grande Anse on the Caribbean Sea, where he taught himself to swim at great peril. A spear fisherman called Bully once pulled him drowning from the surf to find he had tied five-pound rocks to his wrists like the divers who hunted abalone off the reefs.

"There are easier ways off the island," Bully told him. He instructed Zo in the rudiments of stroke by comparing everything to his own daily labors. "Make your hand into a harpoon, good and sharp. Drive it into the water and spear the fish." He lunged forward. "Bring it to your belt and wipe the guts."

Zo stood up the beach and practiced in the sun until the sweat stung his eyes and then he practiced in the water. He placed an empty gallon barrel under his stomach and set himself adrift. Like this he mastered the rhythm of the front crawl. He learned to open his eyes in the salt water and turn his face to breathe.

Zo was an orphan in a town without an orphanage, and the cool sea was one of the few joys of his childhood. At five years old he could float on his back and see the strand and the high white church and the smoking mangrove coast at dawn. At seven he could hold his breath long enough to go diving.

Zo knew the tides and the boats of the fishermen who plied them. He knew who was likely to throw him sardines from their leftover baits, and he always made sure to wait on these beaches when the tide came in. When the nurses came each year to dispense chewable vermicide tablets, Zo waited in line two times and savored them like candies.

Though he never attended class or stood for an exam, as the close apprentice to poverty Zo learned everything worth knowing. Food is hard to come by, but very few people starve to death. You can sleep anywhere if you just close your eyes. It is better to steal one banana from the bunch than the whole bunch at once.

The town of Grande Anse lay on a golden beach under the mountain. It was marked to the west by the picturesque prison in the hill and to the east by the river and the mangrove forest. No one lived in the forest, and only the shrimpers and lobstermen ever spent the night. Bully told Zo stories about the gloomy alligator who lived there.

"He's old as a dinosaur," Bully said. "The last of his kind on the island."

He installed Zo in his leaky canoe and took him out to sea.

"You're my bilge pumps," Bully said, "and must not stop bailing water."

But no matter how fast Zo worked, the ship sank away beneath them until they arrived standing in water to their knees with Zo bailing out the whole ocean.

They visited the sandbar off Petit Cayemite where Bully's people lived all spring, salting the fish they'd sell in Port-au-Prince through Lent. It was the farthest Zo had ever been from the mainland, and he asked Bully if they would soon reach that other country.

Bully had joined the Rastafarian church and, observing the sacraments of his faith, he puffed a fat spliff at twilight. "Look at that," he said, blowing off the smoke. "You see that yellow line?"

Windward, far out to sea, a golden island sparkled in the sunshine.

"The fishermen will tell you it is a beach of crushed pearl," Bully said, "or the island where the black pirate Caesar stashed his stolen gold. But they're wrong." A cloud of blue smoke trailed from his mouth. "That is the edge of *Amerik*. If you could only reach it, you'd become a millionaire."

Zo was nine years old when he heard that. It was 1993 and the embargo was starving him to death. He was sleeping on the gallery of the government school, in cardboard bedsheets. One afternoon not long after his trip with Bully, Zo found the geography professor in his classroom.

"How long would it take to swim to America?" he asked.

The professor had stayed late to grade papers. Something about the boy's question and the earnestness with which he'd asked it struck his professional interest. He put the pencil in his mouth and drew down the wall map. "Can you show me where you live?"

Zo had never seen a map before and he said so.

The professor showed him their island in its blue sea. "We are surrounded by water," he said. "Here the Caribbean, there the Atlantic. Ours is the poorest nation in the Western Hemisphere," he said. "And you yourself are quite possibly the poorest citizen therein." He took Zo's shoulder and looked him in the eye. "Do you know what that makes you?"

Zo did not.

"The poorest man in the Western world," the professor said.

That evening Zo went to bed without dinner. But he felt somehow altered, almost proud, and studied his hands in the dark. "The poorest man in the Western world," he said. He put a pinch of salt under his tongue and drank two cups of water as the best cure against hunger. Then he walked out to the end of the island.

The current was running out under the stars. Zo stepped out

of his underwear, set it in the sand, and walked into the sea like he meant to face it down, like it was his first enemy and stood for all those to come, and he'd vanquish it naked and malnourished even at the end of the earth. The professor had never mentioned scale, and Zo remembered the narrow sliver of blue sea from the map. He waded in to where the swells reached his neck. The water was warm and smooth like bedsheets. He looked once at the yellow half-moon lying over the east. Then he pushed off the sand and began his stroke, with an even kick and his face in the water, as Bully had taught him.

"Spear the fish, bring it to your belt, wipe the guts," he chanted to himself as he swam.

Zo did not panic when a cold longshore drift cast him down-coast. He swam through it, breathing every third stroke with the poise of an Olympian in the medley. When he finally arrived on that fabled reef he spit up a briny mouthful of ocean. He put his hands on his wet flanks and looked back at where he'd come from. The town of Grande Anse lay on a golden beach under the mountain. The mangroves smoked under the stars.

Zo sweated whole autumns in the almond orchards, where the women laid linen in the roots of the trees and the men beat the trunks with great rubber mallets called *el martillos*. The mallets came from Cuba and the orchards were relics from plantation days. The children waited under the trees and swept the nuts into five-gallon buckets while they fell from the leaves like rain. Zo worked among them until he turned thirteen.

That year they gave him *el martillo* and he went to work beating the trunks of trees like enemies. His work was steady and long among the black trunks. He was not large, but there was method and a secret violence about him, so they took him to try boxing.

They fought him Sundays at a gas station laid down in the end-less banana, where foreign money was changed and *zouk* music blared from a megaphone strapped to a lightpole. There was cock-fighting on Saturdays, and they boxed him in the same ring of chickenshit and clay, behind a small cinder block market that sold gas and beer in all the miles of cane and bush and somewhere out there the blue coast.

The cane-cutters walked Zo out after church, rubbing the blood down his arms and talking like experts. This was just after Mackenson Laforge, the pugilist from Gonaïves, had won the Caribbean Boxing Federation bantamweight title and the whole island was mad for boxing. "Always follows through," they told him, "one hand after the other. Winner takes all."

They bought him beer before the fighting and Zo learned to like the taste of it cold on Sunday mornings. When they finally put him in the ring he fought like he worked in the almonds, bare-foot and passionless, with a ready violence that had no source. He danced in the heat and dust. The worst of the bettors cursed him to his face when he lost, but when he won they'd buy him ice cream out of the winnings.

Dried fish was Yiyi's business. She walked the streets every day singing, *"Aransò! Aransèl!"* That was all Zo knew about her. Sometimes he saw her haggling over the piles of anchovies in the morning. She was small and fierce, and her prominent underbite reminded Zo of the barracuda he saw sometimes swimming in the seagrass close to shore.

Pulling Zo aside one afternoon, she asked, "How would you like to live with me, at my house?"

Zo was thirteen years old and had figured no one would ever take him home. He didn't think that Yiyi even knew who he was, and here she was about to adopt him. But he soon found out that it wasn't exactly an adoption as much as it was a business proposition. Yiyi took him home, stood him in her kitchen, and explained the venture.

The plan was simple: she would make a fortune selling cold drinks. No one had electricity during the embargo, and a cold beverage couldn't be had anywhere in the *arrondissement*. She'd overheard important men saying they'd kill for an icy cola. But Yiyi knew where she could find a steady supply of ice. The brilliance of her idea—what set it apart from all the other ingenious little plans to sell cold drinks at that time—was that she would buy her ice from the government morgue. The only problem was the distance to the morgue. It was far, and the ice was heavy. The trail was bad and the hills were steep. She needed Zo to cart the ice.

He started his labors with a simple cooler, carrying it overhead from Grande Anse, filling it with ice at the morgue, and running it back again on the same trail. The people living along the route came to recognize him; they called out and cheered him on, especially in the bottom of the wide, misty valley where a pair of beautiful sisters sold cookies and biscuits.

Yiyi soon presented him with a wheelbarrow, which Zo loved inordinately. He washed it with soap and water, maintained the wheel bearings with castor oil, and patched the tire with rubber plugs when it was punctured by the hard gray rocks that studded the trail. Each morning, Zo would go to the morgue, put the block ice into Yiyi's cooler, and then push it in the wheelbarrow back to her stall at the covered marketplace.

Yiyi refused to sell the ice, not even a chip for a toothache. "If you want cold, you better buy a drink," she'd say.

Yiyi's calculations had been correct: it proved to be a profitable business, but disastrous for her health. Selling ice-cold drinks exacerbated her ulcers. Salt fish lasted weeks in any weather, but the ice was always melting. On hot days she'd shout herself hoarse drumming up customers.

Yiyi suffered from indigestion, kidney stones, and gastric ulcers. She had a bad habit of scratching her back with the long kitchen knife she used as an ice pick. But she was capable of incredible generosity, especially after church services on Sunday, when Zo could expect to eat meat.

It was Yiyi who made him believe that a woman was a type of magic. Just by touching him she could cure his fear of the dark. Zo had no parents, and that touch was the one thing that eased his cold orphanhood. It was the only thing he ever wanted more of. For three years, he regarded Yiyi as his protector and her daughters as his closest companions.

Yiyi's daughters called him *kabrit* because he slept in the kitchen shed like a goat. They kissed him there one night while he sat up on his cardboard bedsheets, all three of them one after the other as if they were waiting in line to try. It was dark, and Zo tried to match their kisses to their temperaments. At twenty-one, Terez was the oldest and most mature. She went first and had the dry, perfunctory kiss of a matron. Next was Merline, the innocent middle daughter. Zo found that she had the dull, wet kiss of a simpleton. Only the youngest, fifteen-year-old Darlene, had any style. Her tongue did rare tricks in Zo's mouth. But when he asked if she loved him Darlene laughed.

"Don't be silly, *kabrit*," she said. "It's only practice."

The electricity had been restored by then and Yiyi couldn't compete with the refrigerators of the professionals. She had gone back to selling dried fish, and needed Zo less and less. "He's become handsome and lazy," Yiyi told her friends. "A dangerous combination for a woman with three daughters."

Taking Zo aside, she told him something he'd never forget.

"People will help you once," she said. "But the next day you've got to fend for yourself."

With that she arranged for him to be delivered by boat to her cousin in Jérémie.

Zo had seen the city once before, but only from the sea. He was amazed by the high balconies and the size of the highway trucks.

When the Panamanian freighter *Dread Wilna* made port, he sat
and watched the stevedores unload cargo all night long.

Zo went to work for Yiyi's cousin, who was a businesswoman
just like Yiyi except she sold bread instead of salted fish. It was a
subscription bakery business, and Zo took the loaves door-to-door
in the morning with a wheeled cart that kept them hot. He was
asked inside one morning by an older woman while they stood in
her doorway, and he had gone just to see the inside of her house.
She was a widow and there were many delicate things of porcelain
and pictures of children older than he.

Zo made love to her there on the cool tile of the front hall in
the late morning, with the city just beyond the door. He was seventeen and she thought of him like a young horse and coaxed him
fittingly. "There now," she said, "*dousman*. Slowly." She praised his
chest and mentioned his power and said it came from there and
from his stomach. She kept her skirt and panties on like hiding a
secret even while she picked him naked.

Zo finished inside her because it was his first time and he
knew no better. Afterward, she cradled his head on her breasts
and called him sweet names, saying there was no danger any longer from that. She left him lying dazed and naked on the tiles at
noon to fix a plate of white rice and *sos pwa,* and then she fed him
one spoonful at a time. She bought more loaves of bread than she
could possibly eat and gave him more than they cost.

Zo was useless all afternoon. The bread went stale while he
sat on the seawall regarding the twilit sea, haunted by the melancholy he'd picked up from the widow like a bad rash. He had tried
to give her what she wanted, which was a forlorn love rooted in
grief and smelling of her dead husband's aftershave. He realized
that to be a good lover was not to be forceful and obstinate, as he
had thought from listening to the raucous stories the men told on
the cane plantation. It was to love the woman in the way she most
wanted to be loved, even if she never asked for it and didn't have
the words to describe it herself.

II

Zo began his wanderings as a mendicant lover of the Greater Antilles armed with nothing but his workman's boots and his poor man's habits, and the abstract idea that it was possible to repay women with physical love for the tenderness they had shown him in his youth.

He left Grande Anse and the sea-level flats and worked all the ranges of the plateau country. He hauled scrap tailings in an open bauxite mine in Artibonite under one hundred days of blue sky. He stopped at a lunch cart for a plate of *bannann fri* and ended up making love to the chef. He hadn't meant to do it but she served him and then pursued. While he drank beer and ate the fried plantains under the trees off the park, she came and stood before him barefoot in the grass. She asked if he would keep quiet all day or if he was going to say something.

"What do you want me to say?" he asked.

Zo had the forearms of a fighter and black stubble flecked his jaw, but his strength and good looks were tempered by a resignation so complete it bordered on submission. It was as if he'd been waiting for her to come along, pick him up, and put him to her uses. She'd been ravaged before her time by the twin trials of childbirth and poverty, but Zo admired the directness of her approach. He liked the way she knelt in the grass and brought her mouth against his ear.

"All I want is for you to ask nicely," she said.

She led him into the hills beyond the last mine shacks, and there, choking with desire in a field of hot grass, she turned and commanded him to undress. She appraised him mercilessly in the white heat of afternoon.

"Turn around," she said.

Then she guided him through the minutiae of their lovemaking as though she had studied for and was now completing the operation of a particular machine, telling him how she wanted to be held and how to position himself across her body and what to say once they began.

"Take my throat," she ordered. "Call me your bird."

Zo cut cane in the cane-cutting season. He bore a cane-cutter's scars and sang his songs: "The cane hook cuts the cane but gets no profit, the cane hook clears the road but goes no place." No matter how many times he bathed, he could never get clean. The dirt from the fields wound up in his dinners.

Zo learned to read in a library at Les Cayes, on the south coast. It was funded by the charity wing of the French Teachers' Union and staffed periodically by a retired schoolteacher who traveled in the islands. She read a story every evening at six o'clock, and Zo came straight from the fields to sit among the school-age children. The teacher's voice made him drowsy, and Zo often fell asleep in the middle of her readings. Then she cast him long looks while she went among the aisles of children's books before closing.

One night she woke him. "You're a little old for children's stories," she said.

Zo rubbed his eyes.

She took a book down and opened it. "What does this say?"

"I only look at the pictures," he said.

"*Voulez-vous apprendre à lire?*" she asked.

Her glasses were so fogged by the heat and humidity Zo couldn't see her eyes. He told her with tremendous sincerity that learning to read was the thing he wanted most in the world.

They began on Monday, with the alphabet, and made love after their first lesson in the empty library. Zo sucked her long pink nipples among the reference works. She put her head back and knocked a dictionary from its shelf. They fucked on the desk amid the stacked volumes in the back office where she kept the daily returns. Zo worked her slowly and steadily with brutal detail, pushing the volumes off the desk and holding her hips like a mechanic to his daily machine. Like this he brought her to climax.

The librarian was forty-seven. Her skin smelled of suntan oil. She told Zo that her husband had left her for a younger woman. "He made love the same way he went tackle fishing," she said. "He would just cast his line into the sea and wait. But you . . ." She took Zo's head in her hands. "You work and sweat at it."

Alongside his reading lessons, she taught him the complex art of oral sex as it was practiced in Europe, comparing each of her orgasms to an animal of different size and gait and ferocity so that Zo came to think of a woman's pleasure as either a cat or an elephant or a running gazelle. They went on like this through the cyclone season, when the wind came off the sea and blew the smoke from the charcoal cook fires. Zo's joints ached in the rain and his fevers spiked with the regularity of clockwork. When he peed bright red one morning, he was afraid he would die if he didn't get out of the cane.

Before Zo left, the librarian gave him his first book. It was the volume on animals she'd used to explain the intensity of her orgasms, and he kept it packed among his things like an obscure reference manual. Besides that book he had two pairs of pants, five shirts, and a collection of ragged underwear. His boots were stamped MADE IN AMERICA, and he figured they would last forever.

Zo woke in the sun on a beach beside a harbor. A pair of fishermen stood above him.

"Where did you come from?" the younger one asked.

Zo was sickly with the ravages of malaria. He had the cloudy eyes and languid habits of his disease. *"Mon yo,"* he said, wiping the sand from his hair. "The mountains."

The fishermen exchanged a look. They were a father-and-son team who worked together in the same boat. The senior was called Daniel, and his son, Daniello, was a near replica of the old man. They had the same build and complexion and gap-toothed smile, the same lines in their palms from barehanding fishline all their lives.

Daniello invited Zo to sail with them in the sixteen-foot knockabout sloop they called the *Tribulation*. It was double-ended like a whaleboat, with a long, curved keel running underneath. The single sail was stepped forward and furled; the body was painted red and blue like the colors of the national flag.

"My father's a real patriot," Daniello explained. "The *Tribulation* is his pride and joy."

"The only protection against wood rot is a good paint properly applied," Daniel said.

The fishermen hauled the *Tribulation* into the surf and Zo climbed aboard. Daniel took his post at the tiller, while Daniello fitted the oars into the oarlocks and set about the heavy work of driving them through the breakers. They swung about finally and cruised on easy seas with the sun setting behind them. The long coastline drew clear out of the haze.

The white cliffs in the sun, the shipwrecks in the reefs, the charcoal fires burning in the forests—they all seemed so familiar. Zo had been plucked from his wayward life, malarial and hopeless, and taken by sunset cruise down the beloved coast of his childhood. He knew every cove and hawk and mangrove root. He recognized the bottom of the sea. The fishermen were taking him back to Grande Anse.

It was the first return of Zo's life, and though he didn't have parents or anyone to return to, it was still grand and he would remember it forever. They cleared the cape and Zo saw Grande Anse for the first time in years: the red roofs under the green mountain, the white beach at the sea. "It's just as I remember it," he said.

A single bonita tossed itself from the swells and the fishermen grew solemn and demure. Daniel released the tiller and Daniello stilled the oars. The water around them boiled with hundreds of fish, rolling on their backs and flashing their silver bellies in the dusk. Daniello slammed Zo on the back.

"You may not be a fisherman," he said, "but you brought us good luck!"

Then they went to work. Daniel dropped the boat motor over the flat transom and they raced over the swells, their faces bright with the chase and the pure beauty of catching their own dinner. They made five passes through the school of fish, trailing their lines behind, the father at the helm and his son drawing the line barehanded. With every pass Daniello hooked a bonita and sometimes two. He pulled the fish from the surf and broke their throats with his thumb and forefinger and clubbed their skulls with a piece of iron rebar kept handy just for that purpose. Then he threw them in the prow at Zo's feet.

As they coasted home, Daniello talked of the meals they would make from those fish. "Bonita fried in lime sauce. Bonita in sour soup with yam and watercress. Bonita salted and served cold with cabbage salad . . ."

Zo helped haul the *Tribulation* up the beach and sat beside it in the sand. He was exhausted and still a little seasick.

"What's next?" Daniello asked.

"*Mw razè*," Zo said. "I'm broke."

"Where will you go?"

"This is it," Zo said, raking his fingertips through the sand. "I grew up on this beach. I was here when Bully brought in his eight-foot marlin."

"That must have been a long time ago," Daniello said. "No one's caught a marlin in years."

Daniello's father washed the fish in the sea and wrapped them in newspaper. Coming across the beach, he gave Zo one from the catch. "Take it," he said. "The meat is good for ailments of the blood."

Zo took the fish and went looking for Yiyi's house. The town hadn't changed much since he last saw it, but the fever confused his way. The old river bridge had been replaced by one with iron trusses. The wharf was wrecked in the sea. He found Yiyi's house on Avenue Gaston but she didn't live there anymore.

"They don't call her Yiyi anymore, either," the new tenant said.

"What do they call her now?"

"Gran Yi," the tenant said. "You'll know why when you see her. She sells corn up the highway." He pointed. "Follow the sound of the trucks."

Zo tucked the fish under his arm and walked a wide sandy track through a banana plantation. The highway was new—a wide black line running straight against the coast. There were no markings of any kind to mar the perfect pavement, and Zo walked dead center with the sea to one side and the mountains to the other. He reached the crossroad and saw, under the lone light, the merchants at their corners: the rum shop, the lotto, the fried egg stand, and there, against the seawall, the old lady roasting corn.

Zo crossed the highway and called out to her. *"Tant mwen.* Auntie."

"A cob for five *gourdes*," she said.

Zo crouched across the fire. "Yiyi," he said gently, "don't you remember me?"

When she stuck her face over the flames to turn the cobs, he saw that there could be no mistake. Her teeth were wasted from chewing thread and corn all her life, and her eyes were milked across with cataracts, but Zo recognized the woman who had raised him.

"I slept in your kitchen," he continued. "I grew up with your girls." He came around the fire and squatted at her feet like her long-lost son. "Yiyi," he pleaded, "don't you recognize me?" He took her hand and placed the dry palm against his face. "I used to work for you. We sold iced drinks in the marketplace. They fought me at the *stade gager,*" he said, "after the roosters."

Yiyi's face never changed. She didn't even blink.

"No discounts," she said. "A cob for five *gourdes*."

At the center of his endless fever, Zo saw that he was without origin, like the wind. He'd blown through Grande Anse without leaving a trace, and the woman roasting corn at the night market was not the closest thing he had ever had to a mother but a stranger whose face he had once caressed in passing. He let go of her and looked down the road, to where it disappeared in the dark.

"I'll give you half this fish if you cook it in your fire," he said.

Yiyi reached out and he placed the bonita in her hand. She smelled it through the paper, unwrapped it, and drove a stick down its throat. It hissed and popped in the flames.

They ate the fish half cooked in the skin, with a side of roasted corn on the cob, while Gran Yi told him her recurring dream of two white dogs that were not dogs fighting on a hillside in the moonlight, with the thunder sounding deep downcoast and lightning in the stars.

Zo woke on a bench at the roadside eatery. Yiyi was gone, and even the bones of the fish had been dragged out of the cold ashes of the fire. Last night might have been a fantasy if his stomach weren't full. Then a voice called him by a name he hadn't heard in years.

"*Kabrit*," it said. "I never thought I'd see you again."

Zo rubbed his eyes and opened them. There was Yiyi's eldest daughter, Terez. She was fatter and darker than he remembered, but she had the same deep-set eyes and the little rock-hard mouth he'd once kissed for practice.

"*Ou sonje mwen?*" he asked. "You remember me?"

"It's been a hard life," she said, "but I can still remember my first kiss."

It turned out Yiyi and Terez worked the same crossroad in shifts. The elder sold corn on the highway at night, and Terez opened her coffee shop there in the morning. Zo saw the hand-painted sign: TEREZ'S CLOTH FILTERED. It referred to her brew method. She put the grounds into a cloth cut and sewn over an iron hanger and poured boiling water through until the brew had the desired cast and flavor. The whole shop consisted of a fire pit, a cauldron, a wooden stand, and that old iron hanger.

Terez ladled a measure of boiling coffee into an enamel cup and, coming around the fire, passed it to Zo. "Don't mind Yi," she said. "She's blind as a bat and can't remember anything."

"She was like a mother to me," Zo said, sitting up. He took the cup and, smelling the steam, he said, "It's just like she used to make."

Terez clapped. "The nose doesn't lie! I use the same berries and roast them just like Yi did." Then, while he dipped a sweet roll and drank the hot brew, she told him the story of her life and how she'd tried to escape to the Bahamas.

"We set sail from Au Cap under Captain Simak. Twenty-seven of us at sea for three days in one of those wooden parcel boats," she said. "Simak had two tricks: a handkerchief, which he claimed would make us invisible to the coast guard, and a *kalbas* gourd full of wind. All he had to do was take the top off and *whoosh*." She puffed her cheeks and blew. "We reached Inagua island all right but were later found at a house in Matthew Town. That was our mistake," she added. "We stayed together." Terez braided hair for two months in a Bahamian prison before they sent her home in an airplane.

"You've been in an airplane?"

"I've been living my life, *kabrit*. What have you been doing?"

Terez's first customers were farmers and fishermen; they came before sunrise. Then it was the drivers and shop owners and women on their way to market. One of her early customers wore jeans, boots, and a hard hat. The tape measure he wore on his belt was prominent as a badge. It gave his rank and station.

"Foreman," Zo said. "Boss. Are you looking for a hand?"

The foreman was missing some teeth and had to turn his roll
this way and that to get purchase. "What do you do?" he asked.

"I've worked in the cane and cotton. The gravel at Borde. The
sand in Hinche."

"He worked for Yiyi during the embargo," Terez said.

The foreman told him to stand up. "Have you ever been
convicted?"

"Of what?"

"Anything."

"No."

The foreman regarded Zo's posture, the ready way he stood
leaning into the present as if he'd throttle it, and decided it didn't
matter. "Consider this your interview," he said. "We start at seven
o'clock." He looked at his wristwatch. "You're already late."

Terez wrapped a fried egg sandwich in newspaper and came
around the table. "You never asked about wages," she said.

"I don't want to know," Zo said.

"You better hurry," she said. "It's a long way on foot."

"How do I get there?"

"Follow the signs for the Grande Anse commons."

Zo hopped the seawall and did his morning toilet in the salt
water. He rubbed the cool sea on his face and scraped a dry tooth-
brush across his teeth. Then he headed down the highway in good
spirits. The iron-rich fish had fortified his blood and the hot coffee
had dispelled last night's melancholy. He had a job and a lunch to
eat at noon. Terez remembered him and his kiss.

The road was new, but the countryside was just as he remembered it. To the south, on his left, were the green foothills of the
Massif de la Hotte, the high heart of the Tiburon Peninsula. To the
north, the Caribbean stretched away to Florida.

He came to a sign along the highway. It advertised the Grande
Anse Commons, to include a schoolhouse, medical clinic, and
Fishermen's Union. Farther down the road, closer to the work site,
he saw a sign for the Fishermen's Union. The slogan was "OUR

POVERTY IS OUR FORTITUDE." The last sign had been professionally made and was posted at the work site. It described a joint project of the Departments of Health and Education, made possible with money from something called the Global Fund.

A clearing had been cut from the cane and banana wilds along the highway. And Zo found the crew there singing Christian songs while the foreman sat in the shade.

> Ak Jezi m ap marche sou wout la
> De viktwa en viktwa
> Lanme wouj pa ka bare m
> Dyab rasyal pap ka bare m.

"You're late," the foreman said when he saw him. "Go join Bos-T in the pit."

Bos-T-Bos, or Little Boss Man, had scoliosis of the spine. He walked like someone playing catch with himself, swinging his left hip wide around and throwing his right shoulder after it. He was barefoot, too, and used the flat of his foot as a mixing trowel.

"It's hard work bending down all the time," he said.

They spent the day in a pit of white birdlime, stirring the cement to keep it from setting in the heat. Bos-T confessed before noon that he'd never been with a woman before and claimed to be waiting for marriage. "I'm too ugly for anything else," he said.

"It has nothing to do with how you look, or what you say, or how you move," Zo said. "It's about knowing what kind of love she wants and giving it to her." He began to instruct Bos-T in the art of seduction while they sat in the sunshine eating lunch. Then they went back to the birdlime and worked until dusk. At the end of the day, Boss Paul gave Zo a pair of gloves and pay that amounted to $1.60 U.S.

The laborers slept together in the partially completed schoolhouse. They moved their pallets into the classrooms after the children left for the day. Zo was assigned a berth in the sixth class, with Bos-T-Bos, Tiken, and Sonson. The first thing he did was unroll the wall map and show them their island in its wide blue sea.

"I don't believe it," Sonson said. "It's too small."

"It's not much," Zo agreed.

He lay down and passed a fitful night on the schoolhouse floor, his fevers breaking into cold sweats and mounting back to fevers again.

In his wild young manhood of always work, Zo had slept in the orchid jungles of the Pic Macaya. He'd made love to a retired French schoolteacher in the library at Les Cayes. He had played a game called *bourik* where he carried heavy loads down out of the mountains like a donkey and poor farmers paid him poorly. But he'd never ridden in an elevator, or had a hot-water shower, or been inside of a bank. He had never had a vaccination or been paid for his intellect, and he had never been in love.

2

HE FIRST SAW HER in the morning and he was in love with her by noon. All she had done was climb out of a truck and sip sour cherry juice from a glass, but that had been enough. Until then it had been an unremarkable weekday at the work site. A course of block had been raised at the clinic. Edson was cutting rebar with a handsaw. Zo was still in the mortar when the white Land Cruiser pulled into the yard. They'd seen it before, with tinted windows and government plates. It belonged to one of the deputy ministers from the Department of Public Health.

The laborers stopped working to watch the passengers descend.

"That's *Dokte* Dady Malebranche," Tiken said. "The director general himself. He's eighty-two years old." Malebranche seemed a kindly old physician, with a walking cane and a white goatee clipped neatly against his mouth.

"Who are the others?" Sonson asked.

"His deputies," Tiken said.

They were four altogether, the director general and three depu-

ties. Two of them wore long white medical coats. The third, who'd
been driving, wore a business suit. The building plans were rolled
under his arm.

"That's Dr. Leconte," Tiken said. "The real boss, and no mistake. It's his signature on all the checks."

Leconte was the biggest among them, tall and wide. The weight
of his stomach seemed to pull his shoulders forward in the shirt.
His face was oval, widest from ear to ear. He pulled the sunglasses
down over his eyes and bellowed for Boss Paul. His voice was rich
and confident.

"But what I want to know," Bos-T said, "is who she is."

She climbed out of the back seat like a revelation, a woman in
her early twenties with skin the color of burnt honey.

"Probably some rich man's wife," Sonson said.

"Or the queen of a goddamn kingdom," Bos-T added.

Afterward, while the officials followed Paul through the work
site, she stood under the spreading mango in the schoolyard sipping sour cherry juice from a tall, clear glass.

Bos-T was afraid to look. "What's she doing now?" he asked.

"Just standing there, sipping that juice," Sonson said.

Zo speared his shovel into the gravel and left it quivering.
"Someone should get her a chair," he said. The workmen asked
what he was about to do, but even Bos-T, who'd become Zo's con-
fidant, couldn't guess. He disappeared into the schoolhouse and
reappeared a moment later carrying a school desk overhead. Not
a single desk but a picnic table, with two benches on either side of
a long tabletop.

"That imbecile is going to get himself fired," Tiken said.

Zo carried the bench down into the grass. He held it upside
down, gripping it by the long benches. He couldn't see her through
the sunshine, but once under the shade of the mango he saw her
quite clearly. Her skin was smooth and bright with a brightness
that had nothing to do with the daylight, like she would lie glow-
ing in a room at night.

She had seen Zo coming and prepared herself accordingly, assuming a posture simultaneously so aggressive and nonchalant it seemed impossible. The entire time that Zo struggled to set the bench evenly in the grass she sipped her juice patiently, and only when he was done did she take her mouth off the straw.

"*Se ki es?*" she asked. "Who are you?"

"I work with Bos-T-Bos," he said, "in the birdlime."

"Which one is Bos-T-Bos?"

Zo pointed out the stunted laborer where he pretended to be working.

"Do you know who I am?" she asked.

Up close, she seemed to be the purpose of the island, its fruit and culmination, but Zo didn't say so. She was dressed in the uniform of the government nursing school—a blue gingham shirt under a white apron—and her smell of hospitals reminded him of being sick with worms.

"*Ou se enfimye,*" he said. "You're a nurse."

Paul shouted for Edson to lay off the vibrating soil compactor and there was a deafening quiet. No bird sang in all that jungle. She sucked the red juice up the straw and looked at him with such a frankly appraising stare that he felt unsteady.

"I have these fevers," he said, holding his forehead. "They are much worse at night."

"Everyone on this island has a fever of one kind or another," she said. She put her glass down on the table and asked for his hand. "Give it to me." She placed two fingers at the base of his thumb and they were cold from the icy juice. They spent a moment in the secrecy of the shade while she measured his pulse. The wind blew the hard green mangoes in their leaves.

Then she inquired about his breathing, his appetite, and the color of his urine.

"*Eskize m?*"

"*Ki koulè pise w ye?*" she asked.

"Yellow," he said.

"Yellow or red yellow?"

Not wanting to say either red or yellow, Zo said orange. How could she possibly know about his red urine in the cane fields? He'd begun to sweat even in the shade. But when he tried to take his hand from her she held tighter to it. It was so still they could hear the cooing of the mourning doves in the leaves above them.

"They're watching us," she said.

Zo looked over his shoulder. The laborers idled over their shovels, pretending not to watch. The director general and his three deputies, who'd been following Paul through the work site, were standing in the half-finished clinic, not even pretending.

She let go of his hand, and Zo fought the sensation that he was drowning.

"I'm only a third-year nursing student," she said, "but you don't have to be an expert in tropical diseases to know that if you have intermittent fevers and blood in your urine, you most likely have malaria and need to be treated."

He called her "miss" and gave an odd bow he would regret for days. Then he resumed his post, took his shovel from the gravel, and tried desperately not to look at her again.

"What did she say?" Bos-T asked.

Zo shook his head as if he couldn't believe it himself. "She said that I have malaria."

Though he had suffered through the high fevers and night sweats of chronic malaria, this love was much worse. A common fever could be eased with seawater and ice, but this lovesickness had no remedy. The symptoms were protracted and unpredictable. Zo drank because it had a taste in his mouth. He walked the streets like a paranoid with his mind in other places. He spoke about it to anyone who would listen. He told Sonson, Tiken, and Bos-T-Bos. Then one evening he told Boss Paul, who heard him out until the end.

"It's simple," Paul said. "You sleep on a pallet in this school-house. She sleeps in that pretty little house over the sea." He turned and pointed up the darkening coast. The stars had come out along the bluffs, and the workmen could see the homes of the wealthy perched across the water on the white cliffs of Chabanne.

"Which one is hers?"

The foreman squinted, took the hat off his head, and wiped his brow. "I can't tell at this distance," he said. "And even if I could, I wouldn't tell you."

"Why not?"

"I don't want them to shoot you for climbing in the windows," Paul said. Putting a hand on Zo's shoulder, he added, "Pigs don't sleep in the trees."

Tiken translated that roughly as "You will never, ever, ever fuck her, Zo."

But then, the next afternoon at the work site, Zo suddenly speared his shovel into the sand and stood beside it and spoke to Tiken as if the conversation of last night had never ended, as if they'd not all gone off to sleep and woken again and taken care of their morning toilet and put in a half day's labor on top of that.

"I don't want to fuck her," he said. "I want to love her until I am old."

Sonson didn't like the sound of that. He thought Zo should find himself a rich widow and sleep happily in her big bed.

"But a widow doesn't love right, Son," Zo said. "She wants you to love like the dead man."

"That's no problem for Son," Bos-T called. "He already fucks like a dead man."

"I'll bet you never even get into that house," Tiken said. "Even if your name is Zwazo Delalun. Even if you have fucked half the women on the island, including the Dominican side. Even if your cock is a masterpiece and you always know how to use it and just what to say."

But then Zo did get into that house, even if it wasn't on invita-tion from the girl. It was from her father.

One evening Boss Paul called the crew together and commended their workmanship. "You boys are doing a good job," he said, "and I want you to keep it up. Our present employer is so pleased, he's offered us a second account." It sounded like a great victory, and the crewmen cheered. Boss Paul explained that Vincent Leconte had decided to have a patio put into his backyard. "He wants a slab overlooking the sea, wide enough to accommodate a gazebo. And from there, a staircase to reach the strand in no more than twelve steps. He thinks we are the ones to do it." They still had to work through the week on the clinic and would have to give up their Sundays.

He asked for volunteers and every man raised his hand.

They began the first Sunday in March, renting a *taptap* and filling it with shovels and wheelbarrows and trowels from the work site. They took apart the old pouring forms and stacked the wood to make new ones. They bought cement mix in the market at the market price and purchased a half load of white sand from the mine. Then they drove north from Roseaux, crossing the Guinaudee and then the Grande Anse River on the highway bridge.

Leconte lived in a lush neighborhood of ocean-side villas, where the houses were perched like pastel castles on the high white cliffs. Wild bougainvillea vine grew under the grand mango trees in the yards. The doctor had a two-story bungalow with a broad front porch and a balcony that came off the second floor at the back half of the house, commanding a long view of the sea. The workmen took to calling it *Kay Touni*, Naked House, because a man standing at the front windows could gaze clear through to the backyard and the sea. There were leather couches inside and full-length mirrors, an upright refrigerator in the kitchen and African art on the walls.

Zo was put on the heavy-lifting crew, and by afternoon he was all that was left, shouldering eighty-pound bags of mix to the back of the house. He stacked his bags in the grass and returned for more, finally unloading, hauling, and stacking by himself 3,200 pounds of National brand cement mix before noon.

He stopped for a brief lunch and twice to drink water from a hose, and then he labored on into the afternoon. He took his shirt off in the rising heat and worked without rest, in blue jeans tied to his hips with an old electrical cord. He worked with such intention that when Leconte and his daughter finally came back from wherever they had been all day and stopped in the yard to regard Boss Paul and his crew and their progress, Leconte took special notice.

"Look at that," he said. "How much weight is he carrying?"

Zo was just then in the pose of a weightlifter, his arms thrown about his head, only his weights were bags of cement and the powder swirled about him. He had three bags on each shoulder.

"Six bags of Nasyonal brand, at eighty pounds each," Paul calculated, "makes four hundred eighty pounds."

"*Li se yon bourik!*" Leconte marveled, using the country term to call Zo a donkey. "Where did you find him?"

"Jérémie," Paul said, "with the others."

"He doesn't look like the others."

The crew stood in various poses of exhaustion. Sonson hammered stakes into the grass, while Tiken placed the pouring forms, singing:

> *Work, work with your head and your heart*
> *Never mind the sickness and the heat*
> *The time will come*
> *When you can enjoy your lady*
> *If you only put your shoulder to the wheel.*

"They can all work," Paul said.

"But do they work *hard*?" Leconte asked.

"Hard work is what made me a foreman," Paul said.

"He'll be a foreman one day, too," Leconte's daughter said.

Zo reappeared shouldering 480 more pounds of National cement mix across the yard against the declining sun. He did not shamble or bend but went on like the pumping of machine pistons in the cool off the sea. There was a fierceness in his gait that couldn't be placed, whether from anger at his station, a fixless ache over a woman, or a true devotion to the task at hand.

"It takes more than hard work to make something of yourself in this country," Leconte said. "You need this." He touched a finger to his skull.

"I'm sure he's smart, Papa."

Dr. Leconte turned to Paul. "Just tell me one thing, Boss. Can he read?"

Paul was offended without knowing why. "Of course he can read," he said. "Just like a deacon. Why, he reads to the others."

"What are they reading?" The doctor laughed. "Diderot? Racine?" But then he had to shut his mouth.

His daughter left them standing in the shade of the house and made her way across the littered work site. She had a way of moving that was more like devastation, and watching her approach, Zo was devastated. For the first time that day the cement grew heavy across his shoulders. He felt the weight in his hips and a hunger in his stomach.

"*Travayè*," she said, "how are your fevers?"

Zo felt like a carnival clown. Cement dust had whited half his face and he was black again where the sweat had run through it. His mouth looked very red in contrast. "Hotter every night," he said.

Her aspect was incongruent with her face. She looked twenty years old but had a coolness drawn from beyond her experience, as if every man wanted to sleep with her and she pretended not to know it. "I'm Anaya," she said. "At school they call me Miss Leconte."

She stood in his path like a flower in the path of a bull, so close that he could smell her perfume.

"My name is Zo," he said, squinting. "They call me Zo."

At dusk, the workmen stood among their buckets and cast-off shovels and watched the sun settle into the sea. Then they went about packing the essential things back into the truck. When

Bos-T-Bos went to fetch the last of it, he found Zo perched at the bluff edge, a cigarette burning down to his lip and the smoke curling up his face.

Zo had put his shirt back on. It hung like a tattered flag across his shoulders, and he seemed like a monument to the poorest men of the world and their pride. The first stars were out over the headland. Bos-T-Bos stood next to Zo and asked what she had said to him this time.

"*Kiyes?*" Zo said.

"The girl," Bos-T said. "The fucking engineer's daughter."

"He's a doctor."

"What did she say?"

"She said, 'You can take more bags than that.'"

"*Ki sa?*"

"She told me I could take more cement than what I carried. She said, 'With a body like that, I'd think you could take ten bags at once.'"

Bos-T multiplied on his hands. He carried the tens and hundreds. "That's eight thousand pounds," he said. "Not even a donkey could do it."

"Eight hundred," Zo said, smoking while the surf rose beneath them. "But the math isn't the important thing."

It sounded so strange to Bos-T-Bos that later, as they walked across the lawn bearing the last of the supplies, he asked Zo if it had really happened just like that.

"Exactly."

"But what did you say?" Bos-T was hoping for the best, but Zo didn't give it.

"Nothing," he said. "I took the cement to Sonson."

Bos-T shook his head. "Fucking Sonson."

They rode the loaded truck out of the wealthy neighborhood and onto the bad roads of the lowland, and Zo didn't say another word—not about the girl, or the day's labor, or even Sonson's joke about a *lougawou* flying into a bedroom window because it had never heard of glass. Zo didn't talk while he brushed his teeth or completed his nightly toilet. But then, when they had all lain down to sleep on their separate pallets on the schoolhouse floor, Tiken spoke.

"That old bastard will never let you in the house," he said.

"That's why he's got to do it in the banana." Bos-T-Bos spoke like he had been considering it all night long. "Standing up if you have to."

"Standing up is better," Sonson offered. "You got to give it to her so she can't forget. You'll probably have only one chance."

"You think a girl like that fucks in the banana?" Tiken said. "She only does it in hotels, on Labadee. A girl like that probably doesn't fuck at all."

"No." Zo shook his head. "That's the thing. They all do at one time or another."

None of them could argue with that. Zo had learned love the way other men learn a trade. He had apprenticed himself to women all across the country. He knew that to make love well was to make love slowly and with purpose. He was the only man among them who could successfully make love to two women at once. He was the only one who had tried. In Jacmel he'd had his life threatened by a jealous suitor and a gun brandished in his face. But though he knew how to make love to women of every body type and temperament, though he understood the power of a steady hand across her belly, Zo had never been in love until now.

3

It was payday in a poor country before they finally understood the magnitude of Zo's illness, and then it was not the malaria they were worried about.

They poured the floors that afternoon in the festive atmosphere of eighteen men getting paid in cash that night. They took their boots off and went barefoot in the wet cement like press men at a winery, stomping the lumps from the mix. Zo was on the manual mixer and turned the rumbling barrel all day long, while Tiken and Bos-T worked first and second shovel, tossing the fresh cement to the crewmen who raked it flat before it set under the tropic sun.

Bos-T-Bos was in a rare humor and gave bizarre orders all afternoon. "I'm the master of all you fools, so shut your mouths and swing your tools." At quitting time, while they waited for Boss Paul to pass out their wages, he postulated on his love for big women: *"Plis tete, plis bouda, plis vant."* He held forth like a mathematician working measurements. "More breast, more ass, more belly. It's like making up for lost time."

"More is better," Tiken seconded. "They cannot be big enough."

Edson was serious and married and Christian. He was the machine specialist, and they joked that he held on to the gasoline jackhammer the same way he held on to his wife. "What about you, Zo?" he asked. "What kind of women do you prefer?"

Zo squatted in the yard and spoke gravely. "I used to like them all," he said. "Any age, any weight, any color. But this girl is in me like a cane hook in the cane. There are only the two of us and I don't stand a chance."

Zo's admission shocked the good spirits right out of them. They sat quietly afterward and waited to be called into the schoolhouse to receive their pay. Boss Paul's office was a classroom for primary-school students. The foreman sat like a behemoth behind a desk designed for a six-year-old, his knees pressed up to the underside of the writing surface, and passed their wages by kerosene gaslight, like a first mate paying the sailors on his ship.

Edson went first and came out again, counting his money. "I'm pretty sure the old man stiffed me fifty," he said. "Those glasses are falling off his head in there. He only wears them on payday anyway."

"That's because it's the only time the big boss really cares if he makes a mistake," Tiken said.

Bos-T-Bos took his pay, rolled the bills into a tight flute, and played his remarkable payday tune while Sonson danced in the yard. Zo went in, took his money, and counted it. Then he went behind the schoolhouse, stripped naked, and took his bucket bath. There was a sliver of blue Fitso soap in the box, and he scrubbed the sweat from his body and rinsed off among the banana and stood there naked in the cool.

By the time he'd dressed and mounted a motorcycle taxi bound for Jérémie, the sun was falling down the mountains. It was the beginning of the vetiver harvest, and the fresh-cut grass lay in fragrant piles along the road. The highway crossed the rich bottomland and came out along the sea. Zo could see the provincial capital down the staggered coastline. The white churches towered in the neighborhoods and the wharf stuck out into the sea. Farther out, beyond the swells, the blue Gulf Stream ran swiftly under the last sunshine.

Zo dismounted at the *komisseriat*. The police were playing *tou kay* and smoking cigarettes in their uniforms. Schoolgirls with miraculous posture carried buckets of water on their heads. The early vetiver was packed in the warehouses and the whole market was awash in the rich balsam smell.

Because of its position as the most westerly of all the ports in Haiti, Jérémie was oriented toward Jamaica and the Caymans. Belizean junks were docked at the wharf. Zo bought the leather belt he'd wanted for weeks and a brand-new shirt still in the plastic wrap. The salesman told him it had just come on the ship from Belize and showed him the decorated interior of the cuff and collar. He showed Zo how to roll the sleeve back to reveal the colorful pattern. Then Zo visited the stationer in her stall, where he was talked into purchasing an expensive journal with a plated lock and key and scented pages. He unwrapped the package, sniffed the book, and knew he had to have it. Then he started back to Grande Anse on foot, broke and regretting it.

He avoided the new highway in favor of the old dirt track that threaded the coast, passing through the fishermen's quarter at Roseaux. The houses were built of coral and seashell, like habitations floated from the depths, but the fishermen and their families lived like vacationers at a resort. They drank green coconuts with their feet in the sea, ate barbecued fish, and made love on the beach.

Zo found the *kleren* salesman at his usual post behind the church. He was called Medsen Fèy, Dr. Leaf, because of the potions he peddled, of which it was said, "What doesn't cure you gets you drunk." Medsen Fèy produced the rum himself from raw sugarcane juice. It was turned into cane wine and the water was burned off by long boiling, leaving the strong, clear agricultural rum called *kleren*. Finally, Fèy infused the raw liquor with herbs he brought from the mountains.

Fèy was regarded as a fastidious chemist: if not generous with his measures, he was skilled with his potions. He dressed like a doctor, in a long white lab coat, and diagnosed conditions from frenzy to venereal disease based on the odor of the patients' breath, the color of their urine, and the stories they told about themselves. Then he wrote a prescription and filled it, too.

When Zo appeared with his packages, Fèy asked how he wanted it. "Hot or sweet or neat or clean?"

"What makes you think I need one of your potions?"

Fèy laughed. "I know a customer when I see one," he said.

"It's these fevers," Zo said. "It's getting so I can hardly sleep at night."

Fèy folded his arms across his chest. "Don't tell me," he said. "It's a girl. And she doesn't love you back."

Zo tucked the packages under his arm. "I'm not a rich man," he said.

"You think those purchases will help?"

Zo didn't answer.

"I can't take her out to fancy places."

"Bravo." Fèy clapped. "Bravo. You are beginning to understand your limits. It means you're growing up. Can I make a suggestion?" He took two bottles down from the shelf and combined the contents. Zo could hear them fizzle and pop. "Save those things for another woman." He pointed to the packages. "Preferably one who'll love you back."

"The woman is not the hard thing," Zo said.

Fèy looked pleased. "Oh?" he said. "You're the first to say that."

"I can see you spend all your time selling rum from this cart, so I'll tell you how it is."

"How is it?"

"A woman wants to love that thing in a man that is hard and fixed," Zo said.

"His cock when it is at attention?"

Zo shook his head. "His heart, Fèy, when he knows what it wants."

"A heart like a stone, then," Fèy said. "Something that sinks." He stirred Zo's drink with a cane swizzle. "*Byen, dako*. What about us?" he asked, passing it across. "What does a man want to love?"

"A man loves those things in a woman that are soft," Zo said, taking the drink, "that can be reached."

"Ha!" Fèy clapped again. "Now I understand. Her *koko* when it is wet and ready." He wiped the counter with a rag. "You are not wrong on everything, my friend."

"*Granmoun mon cher,*" Zo said affectionately. "It seems you've been drinking too much of your own *kleren*."

Fèy thrust his face under the light so Zo could see the scars of an ancient pox. "You think women like what they see?"

"You shouldn't have to convince her. It's not about your looks or the things you say," Zo said.

"Let me make it easy on you," Fèy said. "Don't tell me what *men* want to love. Just tell me what *you* want to love."

"I've known that since I was seven years old."

Fèy leaned across the cart with exaggerated fascination.

"I love the things in a woman that make her cry," Zo said.

The rum dealer slapped his forehead and reached across the cart. "Oh, you really had me going! You really did. But you're more confused than I am. Listen to me, *travayè*. Let me tell you something. A man loves that which stays skinny and stays home." He made a slicing motion with his hand. "Find yourself a girl with a flat stomach and she will make you happy." Then he offered Zo the cure. "No credit, though," he said. "I'm afraid you're a fatal case."

"What will it do?"

"Cure you."

"Of what?"

"Your stupid love."

Medsen Fèy passed him the bottle. Zo opened it and sniffed the potion.

"Take it somewhere dark, where you can be alone. Hold your nose and drink the whole thing at once, without taking your mouth off the bottle."

Zo reached the riverbank and followed it to the sea. He waded into the lagoon. It was just as Medsen Fèy had prescribed, a dark and lonely place. Then he took the bottle from his pocket and held it up in the dark to eye the contents. A bundle of herbs had sunk to the bottom. He tore the stopper out and sniffed the liquid again. It was even more caustic there, under the wide half-moon with the sound of the sea, than it had been at Fèy's cart. He held his nose, inclined his head, and drained the bottle, while the wind climbed across the river and a fire surged in his throat. He drank the whole thing without taking his lips from the bottle. Then the earth tilted and he dry-heaved in the muck.

All the drink gave him was diarrhea and a strange, hallucinatory drunkenness and, the next day, a hangover that felt like death. He woke with a pounding head and heart palpitations. He couldn't speak because his spit was like ashes. He was still in love with the doctor's daughter. Not only was the condition unimproved, but it had grown more serious than ever.

When Bos-T saw his face, he ran to see Terez and brought her back to the work site.

She fixed a pot of her boldest brew and had Zo drink it black. He moaned from the far side of his hangover, but Terez took no pity. She wiped his face with a wet cloth. "Finish it," she said. Then she poured him a second cup. "It looks like you have it pretty bad. Let me tell you about the girl."

Anaya Leconte was the only daughter of Dr. Vincent Leconte, a physician who had been elevated into politics after his levelheaded response to Hurricane Gilbert in '88. "The man had water stockpiled *before* the disaster," Terez said. "Imagine the foresight." In that way, Jérémie had avoided the outbreak of typhoid that killed more people than the hurricane in Les Cayes. Word was that Leconte was most likely to succeed Malebranche when the old man retired from the Ministry of Health, and then he'd be the director general himself. "Well?" Terez said.

"You haven't told me anything about the girl," Zo said, holding his head in his hands.

"Didn't you hear?" Bos-T said. "Her father's going to be the *direktè jeneral*. We're just laborers on his patio. What more do you need to know?"

"Does she have brothers? Sisters? What about her mother? Tell me everything, Terez."

"Her mother is dead," Terez said. "She was a nurse at St. Antoine's. That girl is the only child."

"It's just the two of them alone in that big house?" Zo asked.

"Exactly," Terez said. "Now you understand? That girl is all he has in the world."

Zo worked through the following week like a prisoner on a penitentiary farm, without opinions and without humor. One afternoon, just as the laborers were quitting for the day at the clinic work site, the St. Antoine Hospital ambulance pulled into the yard. The double doors opened and Anaya Leconte climbed out, accompanied by a pair of nurses from the city hospital. Miss Leconte was wearing her school uniform, the white apron and the checkered blouse of the École d'Infirmières Notre Dame du Perpétuel Secours.

"If I woke up in the hospital with her standing over me, I'd think I had died and gone to heaven," Bos-T said.

By now the laborers knew of Zo's love for the girl and they made strange calls in his favor. "Zo can really lift," they whispered. "Zo can pull and push."

Zo himself only doubled his shovel loads and worked as if he were trying to die. They did not see him look up from his labor once during her tour of the work site. He quit with the rest of them and went to collect his cold-water bath bucket. He went behind the schoolhouse, stripped naked, and poured the water over his shoulders, and that was exactly how she found him: standing naked by the pump shack, soapy-thighed and dick out among the yellow flowers and purple eggplants.

Zo didn't know how long she'd been watching or which of them was more surprised. He, naked and steaming, with his sudsy loins hanging over the grass; or she, watching from behind the barred windows of the schoolroom. He could see the blood beat in her jugular vein as she gripped the window bars. She looked so directly and cleanly at him that he almost said something in apology or explanation. She appraised him from toes to soapy scrotum and then drove home a long, hard look in his eyes before turning around like she'd seen better, and Zo thought maybe she had.

Later she came back into the schoolhouse, where the workmen were eating red beans and rice, sitting at children's desks or along the walls beneath the drawings of ten-year-olds. In that room of little furniture they seemed men of mythic size. They heard her heeled shoes in the hallway long before she appeared at the door, and by then they had already assumed the distance and fatigue of employees before the boss.

"What can you tell me about *filaryoz?*" she asked.

The workmen hovered over their food like penitents.

"Some of you probably have it right now," she said, "living inside you."

They stopped eating.

"It's a stomach parasite, a roundworm endemic to Haiti." She had their attention now. "It enters your bloodstream through the pores of your bare feet."

"That's why we wear shoes," Tiken said.

"Not everyone is so lucky. There are plenty of children in this neighborhood who can't afford them."

"What do you want us to do about it?" Tiken asked.

"The hospital is sponsoring a clinic here tomorrow afternoon," she said. "But the yard isn't safe. The piles of block and gravel. The iron rebar. We need a clear, safe place where the children can wait in line, and we can distribute the medication."

"That would take all night," Tiken said. "What about the wages?"

"The treatment is free," she said. "Come get cured."

Some of the laborers started eating again.

"I never had a vaccine in my life," Sonson boasted.

"It's not a vaccine," she said. "Just a pill. And I wish I could pay you, but there's no money for it. St. Antoine's is giving up its nurses. The students are volunteering their time. Even the pills are a gift, from the World Health Organization." She held the doorframe with both hands and leaned into the classroom. "I'm asking for your help," she said. "For the children."

"I don't work for the children," Tiken said. "I work for cash. Besides," he added, under his breath, "I bet you know how to handle a shovel."

Zo rose from his place against the wall and sent his plate clattering onto the floor. "Show me where you need it," he said. "I'll do the work."

They teased him when he walked out after her in his overalls. "I know where she needs it," Tiken said. Sonson asked if he was going to carry her home on his back like a *bourik*. Bos-T wanted to know if he was going to finish his beans.

Zo took a shovel and wheelbarrow from the gallery and followed her into the yard. She took a dozen steps and then wheeled around to face him. One of her braids had fallen forward over her eye and, obscured like that in the moonlit yard, full of justice and passion, she was more beautiful than ever.

"*Filaryoz* is a serious problem," she said. "It can stunt a child's growth and cause anemia or even heart failure. And the cure is so simple! Just one single pill." She looked at him. "Do you know what albendazole is?"

Zo held the wheelbarrow with both hands. "I guess I had worms often enough as a child to know what the cure is."

She crossed her arms over her chest and Zo saw the tops of her breasts in the dark and the gold chain that fell down between them. "I was hoping you'd be the one to help," she said.

"Why?" he asked. "Because you've seen me naked?"

She showed her small, clean teeth. "Because I've seen how well you carry furniture out into the grass."

"Is that what I'm to do?"

Anaya was in her third year of nursing school, doing a dual major in nursing and public health. She told him that distribution of vermicidal tablets to schoolchildren was her capstone project, her thesis. What she needed was a clear, safe place in that littered work yard where she could pitch a couple of tents and distribute medication to a thousand schoolkids without worrying about them contracting tetanus.

He surveyed the yard and saw it was a long job. The construction materials were everywhere. Piles of gravel, bundles of rebar, a load of white sand from the river, the stacked mixing forms. But he didn't say anything about it. He was afraid to look her in the eye. Hitching the overalls over his shoulder and squaring up against the gravel, he dove his shovel in past the blade.

He went on dragging his rake in the dark until the dirt was flat and smooth and there was nothing left to be cleared, no stone or stick or piece of trash in all that wide yard. Then he went into the schoolhouse and started emptying the classrooms of their furniture. The crew woke in the middle of the night and watched him placing the chairs in neat rows under the mango tree. Bos-T was the first to lend a hand, wiping his eyes and coming out in his underwear. Then Sonson stumbled out with a pair of chairs. Tiken stood in the doorway with his arms crossed and called them idiots.

They placed the last chair at four that morning. At six, when the tents arrived via flatbed truck, Zo had a team ready with guy ropes and hammers. The tents were already pitched and the first patients were sitting on benches under the tree when the nurses arrived by bus. The distribution started early and went all day. It was Saturday, and the workers spent the morning on the gallery drinking coffee. Anaya approached them at lunch, and Zo had to concentrate to keep himself from trembling. She used his name for the first time.

"Zo," she called. "*Vin ba lo.*"

The workmen were struck dumb. They didn't make any jokes at all when Zo got up and followed her around the back of the school. They passed the pump house and waded into the banana grove, where the hot air smelled of decaying leaves.

"I've been thinking about your fevers." She produced a rapid malaria diagnostic test kit from her purse and, breaking the seal, took out a clean lancet. "Give me your hand."

Zo hesitated.

"Don't tell me you're scared of the needle."

"Who isn't?"

In one practiced motion she bit the cover off the needle and pricked his finger. She squeezed his blood onto the test strip and waved it back and forth.

"Why did you leave the city to come work for my father?" she asked.

"I didn't come from the city," Zo said. "I came from the hills."

The level of his voice, the way he stood straight under the banana, the power of him in the daylight—Anaya thought it would be thrilling to lie in his arms.

"You see these two red lines?" She showed him the malaria test. "It's positive."

Zo held the test strip with both hands, like a drowning man holds the rope cast out to save him. "What do I do?" he asked.

"Tomorrow," she said. "*Nan* Chabanne. The beach beneath my father's house. But don't miss it," she warned. "I'm the only one who can cure you now."

Zo didn't say it was exactly the other way around, that she was the very thing making him sick.

4

ZO SET OUT to compose a love letter but ended up listing the diseases of his youth and comparing them to love. Like that he managed to fill half a sheet. "I wish I hadn't bought so many pages," he said. "I wouldn't have this much to say in a lifetime."

Terez read the first draft and pronounced it a disaster. "Malaria, typhoid fever, amoebic dysentery. What is this, Zo? Are you wooing a virus or a woman? No," she said. "The best thing about this letter is the scented paper."

Zo argued that she was a nurse and would understand him.

"This girl is from Haiti," Terez said. "She knows all about parasites and typhoid fever. You've got to tell her something unexpected, something beautiful."

Zo took the letter back and tore it in two. Then they sat brainstorming another draft. Tiken thought Zo might write of his work in the mines and cane fields, but Terez said absolutely not. Bos-T-Bos thought Zo should tell her about some of the women he'd been with, and how happy he'd made them, but Terez said that was even worse.

"Tell her something special, Zo. Something only you would know. What can you give her that no one else can give her?"

Zo told them the story of the boat trip he'd made once around the western edge of the island. "Just Bully and I, in his open boat. From Jérémie to Les Cayes." But the thing he remembered most—what he could never forget—was the sunset in Anse d'Hainault. "Anse d'Hainault is the westernmost town on the island," he said. "When you're there, you see the last sunset over Hispaniola."

"That's it," Terez said. "Write about that and you just might get your chance."

Zo took a fresh sheet and started again. He described the slopes, bare and green, and the water clear as air. *You can see the lobsters on the seafloor.* He told her how he had sailed there in Bully's open boat, and how Bully had taught him to swim. He described the house he dreamed of building—three rooms, French doors, and a porch with a view of the sea. He wrote for twenty minutes, sweating over every word and placing every period with the precision and intention of a carpenter with a nail.

Terez took the revised letter and read it, alternately sucking her teeth and breaking into hoots of loud laughter. "You might as well promise her control of the bank account and the right to name your children." She slapped the letter and asked, "Are you a husband or a loyal dog?" But Zo never had a chance to answer. "It's perfect," she said. "Loyalty is exactly what she wants."

With the letter finished and folded away into the matching envelope, Zo turned to his toilet. Terez made a shampoo from the leaves of neighborhood trees and washed his hair while he squatted at her feet like one of her own sons. She rinsed him and rubbed the lemon-smelling suds across his chest. She cleaned his ears with a chicken feather and pared his nails. When it was over, and he was dressed in his new shirt and scented with vetiver, Terez pronounced him beautiful.

Zo asked if it was too early to leave.

"If you don't go now and make it happen," she said, "it never will."

The schoolyard where Zo and the other laborers slept was four kilometers downcoast from Leconte's bungalow in Chabanne. Zo took the whole thing by foot. The slim jungle paths turned into the foot trails of the banana plantations, and the banana plantations gave over to the wide vetiver fields of the growers' cooperative. The fragrant green grass grew into the hillsides.

It would have been more direct to walk along the national highway, but the road was loud and crowded, and Zo wanted to be alone with his intentions. He approached lovemaking much as he approached a fistfight, visualizing the encounter blow by blow. In this case it was Anaya, her desires, and the potential routes to her pleasure. For that kind of work he preferred the tranquility of the coast, which took him behind the city without interference. He passed into the fishermen's quarter and out again at the delta of the Guinedee River, where he had once drunk a potion designed to rid him of his stupid love. A woman grazed her cow on grass at the abandoned sugar mill, and an old man with cataracts and a backache hauled cane. Medsen Fèy had his shop open at the bend of the coastal road, where it came within sight of the sea, and he called out when Zo passed.

"Zo!" he cried. "Where are you headed?"

"Where do you think?"

Fèy laughed. "How is it now?"

"Even worse than before."

"My drink didn't work for you?"

"I felt like I slept in your *kleren*," the laborer said. "Even my teeth were spinning. Now I want her more."

"Ah." The old man tossed a hand. "You need more than a strong drink."

"What do I need?"

The rum dealer took a long time regarding Zo against the sea in the growing dark. "The one thing you'll never have," he said. "Money."

Zo dug in his pocket and came up with a few crumpled bills. He laid them over Medsen Fèy's cart. "Give me something to make me brave," he said.

Medsen Fèy didn't take the money. He mixed a drink and passed it across. "This one's on the house," he said.

Anaya and Zo had made plans to meet under the cover of darkness, but he was early. A blue light still lingered over the coast. He found a patch of wild star anise and chewed the licorice-tasting leaves for sweet breath, waiting until the last light went off around the cape and the wharf came alive under the electric lights. He could hear the stevedores singing galley songs while unloading the ships' wares by night.

Only then did he venture out along the final stretch of beach, passing behind the courthouse and beneath the government school until he reached the wealthy neighborhood where the houses backed up to the sea. The steps behind Dr. Leconte's yard were partially complete; the forms had been laid, the iron grid set and filled with compacted gravel, but no cement had been poured. Zo climbed them halfway and sat contemplating the sea.

It was April. The days were hot and brief and the twilights cool and lingering. A white-tailed tropic bird coursed the shore and disappeared in the dark. Zo imagined her feet on the stairs so often that when she finally came he had to fortify himself against looking. She smelled of the lemon and vanilla soap that gave her the aura of a clean child. Standing behind him, she ran her hands through his hair, and he leaned his head against her bare legs.

"If you left this beach," Zo said, pointing at the sea, "and swam straight across, if you kept kicking and breathing long enough, you would reach the coast of Florida."

"It would be easier to fly," she said.

Her fingers moved in his hair while the lazy surf struck the shore.

"I've never been on a plane," Zo admitted. "I've never been off the island."

She sat beside him on the step and unscrewed the cap on the most expensive-looking bottle of rum Zo had ever seen. "You make it sound like a prison." She fitted her lips to the bottle mouth and took a sip without taking her eyes from the water.

"It is a prison," he said, "with coconut palms and cockfighting." He reached across and wiped a drop of rum from the corner of her lip. "And beautiful women."

"Why don't you go, then? Why stay here and work for my father?"

Zo took the bottle from her and had a long drink in the dark. He wiped his mouth with the back of his wrist. "I stay for the rum," he said seriously, "and the women."

"Don't you think there is more to life than that?"

"Than what?"

"Rum and women. Working for a dollar a day. Waiting to die of typhoid or tuberculosis."

"They haven't killed me yet."

"What about malaria?" She wrested the bottle back from him as if to prove a point. "What about your fevers at night?"

Zo took her left hand up from where it lay in her lap and held it against his forehead. "They are getting worse," he said.

Anaya took a small packet from where she had been hiding it in the elastic waistband of her skirt and started to break the little white pills from their foil.

"What are those?" Zo asked.

"Do you trust me?"

He said that he did.

"Open your mouth," she said. Zo was an obedient patient and she placed four pills on his tongue. She took the bottle and tipped the rum into his mouth. "Swallow." When it was done, she told him that it was chloroquine, and only the first dose. "If you don't get rid of it now, you'll go blind. Or die. Do you know the life expectancy in Haiti is just sixty-one years?"

Zo took the bottle up and raised it to the horizon. "To midlife," he joked.

They took turns swigging straight from the bottle like pirates, watching the salt roll in the distance. The rum was smooth and sweet and burned in the chest. They drank three times without speaking and then Zo proposed a toast.

"To the most beautiful woman in the Antilles."

"Can we toast to something else?" she asked.

He surveyed the strand as if he'd find something worthy among the seagrass and trash. "Nothing comes close," he said, and something in his voice kept her from disagreeing.

She turned to face him for the first time and was unsettled. The sincerity of Zo's expression and the vulnerability in his gaze were the exact antithesis of his frank and brutal physicality.

"Are you married?" she asked.

"No."

"You have children?"

He shook his head.

Anaya lifted the bottle and took a long swig of the raw liquor but didn't swallow. She took Zo by the back of the head and brought their mouths together, and slowly, in the heat of their mingled tongues, she spit the burning drink into his mouth and he swallowed. Afterward, he looked about the world like a man in a daze.

"That was the best drink I ever had," he said.

They made love on the staircase with a fabulous thirst in both their throats and the surf pounding all about them under the stars. First with him sitting, and she straddled across him with her back to the sea and her ass in his hands. He moved her with his thighs and watched her face rise and fall against the horizon. Then with her on her side, and he squatted to get at her center, with one leg wide and high on the upper step and the other below, lunging like a champion of gymnastics. Finally with her knees on his shirt on the stairs, and he behind her, more serious at his work than either the sea or the stars with theirs. As she grew tired, Zo's efforts doubled. He dropped between her legs and worked with his tongue and lips and even, Anaya swore, his teeth. She orgasmed in the middle of things and once at the very end, just as they heard the mournful horn of a ship adrift.

It took everything Zo had ever learned from his wanderer's life to love her right. How to hold his breath when he dove for pearls, and why one did it with the eyes closed; how to swing *el martillo* in the heat; even fistfighting for cash behind the gas station of Grande Anse—it was all just preparation, so that when the time finally came he could give her the love she needed. Anaya had been too long intact; she wanted to be shattered and left in pieces.

The beautiful hour passed. She left him drained and breathless. Zo reached into his pocket for the letter but fell over panting. He watched her slim figure gliding away from him up the stairs and managed to get enough breath to say, "I've never wanted a woman so badly *after* lovemaking."

Anaya turned to see him, naked and pitiful, clutching his pants in one hand and a pink envelope in the other. She had planned on loving him once, curing his malaria, and forgetting about him forever. But she came back for the letter.

"Don't read it now," he begged.

She stood on the step above him so that when he managed to stand they were the same height. Behind them, the moon teetered in the peaks and then crested them all. The strand appeared under the light like a white road along the coast. She put her cool hand on his flank and his cock sprung to attention between them like a sundial.

"Where did you learn to move like that?" she asked.

They made love once more standing, with his hands around her arms so he could move her like a machinist at his trade. He pulled her evenly over himself with unvaried rhythm, and each time was an effort to find some seed in her, and each time they separated, their hot parts were cooled momentarily in the spring sea breeze.

Zo walked back after midnight feeling like an outcast angel in the reefs. His erratic footprints in the sand betrayed his enchantment. He stopped to wash his hands and face in the surf and marveled at the wonder of the world.

They staggered to their separate sleeps, Zo to his pallet in the fourth-grade classroom and Anaya to her princess's bedroom on the second floor of her father's house. Yet of the two of them it was only the poor man who slept.

Anaya went trembling up the stairs, closed her bedroom door, and locked it. No man had ever pursued her with such nakedness of purpose, and none of the three boys who'd made love to her before had done so with a fervor or skill approaching that of the laborer. Everything about him had been lean and hungry. Anaya grew hot just remembering it. She stashed the unread letter in her night table and lay in bed, but it was impossible to sleep. She opened the drawer and took out the scented papers.

You are like one of the fevers of my youth.

Anaya flushed again. She was afraid of her own body in the sheets. She traced her thighs with her fingertips and measured her breasts one at a time as if to rekindle the magic the laborer had awakened, but none of it thrilled as his caress had.

I haven't slept since I met you.

What followed was a brief account of a hard life in the islands. He'd been raised in the cane to fight and work, and that was what he set about doing.

I cut cane and fought for dollars.

She thought of the turmoil in the poor man's soul and how helpless he must have felt in the face of those new and overwhelming passions, realizing he loved her while at the same time knowing he had nothing to offer.

When I met you everything changed. I knew I couldn't go on living that kind of life.

She read about Anse d'Hainault, the westernmost town in the country, and the house he'd build for her there, and the sunsets they'd watch falling over Cuba. The letter concluded with an accusation.

You said you would cure my fevers. But I'm afraid it's the other way around now. You are the very thing making me ill.

Anaya let herself read to the end before crumpling the letter and allowing it to fall from her hand. She laughed at herself. He was describing a life she could never live. She had never washed her own laundry, and here was a man offering to make her into a fishwife.

Anaya felt better. She considered it resolved. She fell asleep and didn't wake until the cook knocked on her door for breakfast. Then she realized it hadn't been resolved at all.

"I'm not coming," she called. "I don't feel well."

She didn't get out of bed until midmorning. When she finally did stand she was shocked by a soreness that reached so deep into her womb she thought it was an emotion. A closer examination revealed a bounding pulse and a slight temperature at 38.1. She picked up her cell phone and called her friend Lovanice.

"Can you die from a fuck?" she asked.

"What do you mean? Like AIDS?"

"Something terrible has happened."

"Are you pregnant?"

Anaya went to the window and was shocked to find the world outside so dull and static. She had expected the sea to be in flames. But there was the strand, as always, and the surf stretching out under the afternoon, and the hummingbirds going about in the potted plants.

"I slept with a poor man."

"It's *Ayiti*," Lovanice said. "They are all poor."

Anaya climbed back into bed and pulled the sheet to her chin and looked about her childhood bedroom. She felt like a stranger. So that almost as soon as they made love Anaya was thinking of ways to end their affair, while at the very same time Zo was downcoast thinking of ways to make it last.

Paul's crew was back at work in Leconte's yard the following Sunday. Anaya regarded them all morning from her bedroom window while they went about in the rising heat. Zo was shirtless before the sun even rose, and Anaya perspired just watching him work. He carried the cement six bags at a time, stacked them at the edge of the yard, and stood again in a cloud of gypsum haze and sunshine. There was a fundamental difference between Zo and the other laborers. Zo seemed to go everywhere and do everything with great purpose and deliberation, as if he were at work on a holy church instead of a staircase.

When Lovanice came over at noon she found Anaya in a desperate state. The two girls walked out to the second-floor balcony and stood overlooking the yard just as the laborers sat down to lunch. Lovanice pointed at the workmen one at a time and spoke about them like fish she was planning to buy at the marketplace.

"I hope that one's not yours." She pointed at Bos-T-Bos. "He's so short and ugly. Look at that one." It was Boss Paul. "How many teeth does he have in his head?" She told Anaya to describe him.

She started with his shoulders, then mentioned the leanness of his hips, the confidence of his gait, and the circumference of his thighs.

"All you had to mention were his thighs," Lovanice said. "I see him down there right now."

Zo was drinking so lustily from a bucket of water that Lovanice was sure he'd drain the whole five gallons in a sip. He looked like he was accustomed to drinking a river down his mouth every day of the year. She was staring at him and Zo was looking back. "When you're through with him," she said, "maybe you should send him my way."

"You wouldn't like him," Anaya said.

"What makes you so sure?"

"No cell phone."

Lovanice had a long-established policy about men without phones. She didn't date them.

"What a shame." She sighed. "In any other country a man that beautiful would be rich."

"What do I do?" Anaya asked. "He's promised to come back every Sunday until the end of time."

"Ignore him," Lovanice said. "It's all you can do, and it's for his own good. Eventually, he'll get bored and go home."

"How do you know?"

"A man is more like a dog than you think. If you just stop feeding him, he'll go somewhere else to eat."

Zo came back that evening just as he had promised, and Anaya vowed to leave him down there all night. She remembered Lovanice's advice and prepared for bed in the dark. She was asleep before midnight, while Zo walked the tide line and waded in the surf, looking frequently and forlornly at her bedroom window.

She woke after two and turned on the bedside lamp before she remembered him waiting on the beach. But it was too late to turn the lamp off now—if he were outside, he would have seen it. It was late, anyway, and she was sure he would have gone home. She clutched a shirt to her chest as she crept to the window.

Zo was standing on the shore staring at her through her bedroom window with a precision and intensity so immediate she had the sensation that he'd been positioned like that for hours. Something about the frankness of his gaze left her unabashed. She dropped the shirt from her chest and he saw her naked breasts in the far light.

Anaya appeared in the yard a moment later, dressed now in shorts and a shirt, carrying a bedsheet.

Zo hadn't moved since seeing her in the window. "I thought you'd never come," he called.

"I feel sorry for you," she said, holding the sheet. "It gets windy down here at night."

"I've slept in colder places. In the orchid jungles of the Massif de la Hotte it rains every afternoon."

She came halfway down the steps and handed him the sheet. "I don't know what you want from me," she said.

"Whatever you give me," he said, taking the sheet.

"How many girls have heard you say that before?"

Zo didn't answer. They sat together in the sand with the sheet around their shoulders.

"Why did you agree to help me with the *filaryoz* campaign?" she asked. "The others wanted money, but you didn't ask for anything."

Zo told her that he grew up poor in the fishing village of Grande Anse, and the only medical care he ever received was from a traveling clinic out of Jérémie. "They gave us vaccines," he said, "and those little blue pills that tasted like mints."

"You think albendazole tastes like mints?"

"I waited in line two times and savored them like candies."

"Do your parents still live in Grande Anse?"

Zo shrugged. "I'm an orphan."

He said it so naturally, brushing the sand from his shins, that Anaya thought she'd misunderstood. His face hadn't changed or darkened.

Zo thought she was upset or wanted him to say more. "It wasn't bad," he said. "Yiyi took me home and put me in her kitchen. I ran ice for her during the embargo, and she fed me meat on Sundays."

Anaya couldn't shake the image of Zo as an orphan waiting in line for his vermicidal *bonbon* any more than she could ignore the raw and magnetic clarity in his eyes.

"Let me tell you something," she said. "One mother, if she's yours and she loves you, is better than a dozen women who are not your mother, no matter how many times a week they feed you meat."

The wind sawed diagonally across the beach, blowing sand in her face.

"Lie back," Zo said. "Let me lie alongside you."

They lay in the sheet with their bodies pressed together and their faces very close.

"Tell me how it is to have a mother," he whispered.

"I only had mine for a short time," she said.

"Did she hold you when you'd wake from a nightmare?"

"Do you have many nightmares?"

"Only when I sleep someplace new."

"Do you often sleep in new places?"

"I've slept in schoolhouses, churchyards, the police stations in Bomon and Pestel."

Anaya imagined the dark nights he'd spent motherless, curled up on the floor of the police *komisaryat* in Bomon. "Yes," she said. "A mother is there even in your dreams. One could have helped you through your nightmares."

"I don't have them anymore."

"What do you dream about now?"

He kissed her and told her what he dreamt about. He whispered it in her ear. Before he finished they were grinding each other into the cool sand. When he said he loved her and she said it back automatically, like a girl in a dream, she knew she was past the point of no return. It was only their second night together, but Zo had inadvertently entered into the most sacred and sympathetic chambers of her heart. Ever since her mother died, Anaya had felt like an orphan. And here was Zo saying he understood that loneliness better than any other.

Anaya's mother, Roselyn, was diagnosed with ovarian cancer at thirty-nine and dead of it ten months later. Even a radical hysterectomy, performed at the premier surgical hospital in Santo Domingo, failed to save her. The cancer had spread beyond her pelvis and the prognosis was grim.

Until her diagnosis, Roselyn had been the senior midwife at the

St. Antoine Hospital on Avenue Émile Roumer, in Jérémie. But when the illness finally drove her to bed, it was Anaya who became her nurse. She brought ice for the sores in Roselyn's mouth and rubbed the cramps from her legs. She finally stayed home from school altogether and moved into the big bed upstairs so that she could take better care of her mother. From then on, they were like inverses of each other. As Roselyn's skin grew duller, Anaya's grew more brilliant. As her mother tired, Anaya became more insistent on their walks. And as Roselyn became less capable of caring for herself, Anaya became a more competent nurse.

Her mother schooled her in the basics, beginning with a simple lecture on the body's systems. That was how Anaya learned the medical realities of her mother's condition, from Roselyn herself explaining the female reproductive organs and their possible disorders. She explained how the cancer started in the epithelial cells of the ovaries, where eggs were made. "Two fists at the end of the fallopian tubes." And she admonished Anaya quite desperately, taking her in both arms, to have regular screenings for the rest of her life.

"Don't wait too long to have kids," she said. "And listen to your father when I'm gone."

Anaya was thirteen years old and so angry with her father that she didn't like to talk about him. He had just left for the Pan American Health Organization conference in Washington, D.C., even though Anaya had begged him not to go. She rode with him to the airport because he forced her to come, but refused to kiss him goodbye.

"Just think," he said, "your father is delivering a lecture to delegates from fifty-five countries. If we can convince them to support our initiatives, we can save thousands of lives."

"I'm only worried about saving one," she said.

Those six days were the climax and culmination of Anaya's childhood. She took over her mother's care, auscultating her blood pressure using a sphygmomanometer and a stethoscope placed in her elbow pit. She used a hypodermic needle to give her intramuscular injections, cleaned out her bedpan, and bathed her by hand. But all her efforts were to no avail, and Roselyn died in the big upstairs bed on June 13, 2002, two days before her husband returned home from his conference. Her last words to Anaya were one and the same with her last lesson on nursing.

"Give me your hand," she'd said.

Her mother died a week before Anaya's first period, as if her body had been waiting for it. She had no one to turn to then, and it was the cook who finally sent her to Soulyan, a neighborhood widow who served as a counselor about these things. She told Anaya both stories, the one about the eternal period, which never ends, and the one about the girl who never had a period at all but died of old age in the body of a twelve-year-old.

"You are more fragile now than you have ever been," Soulyan told her. She explained that if Anaya had sex with one boy, even if it was the first time for both of them, she could become pregnant. Afterward, they went together to the market and bought a basketload of citrus fruits—lime and sour orange, pink and white grapefruit—and Soulyan made her eat everything. No sugar and no ice.

After that, Anaya was rebellious and contrarian. She and her father lived like two antagonists in the one house. Anaya opposed Leconte's every opinion on subjects ranging from the AIDS epidemic to the leadership of President Boniface Alexandre. If her father wanted fish for dinner, she wanted beef.

Leconte grew cold and cynical toward his daughter. He became a disciplinarian, or tried to be, far too late in Anaya's life. When he hit her with the belt for the first time, Anaya was already sixteen years old, and it was a disaster. The neighbors heard them shouting through the afternoon. Anaya didn't speak to her father for two weeks after that. He bought her a pair of caged Antillean mango birds as a way of making up to her, but Anaya showed them so much love and affection that Leconte felt more miserable by contrast.

Anaya's graduation from the government secondary school,

which should have been an occasion to celebrate, was just another reason to fight. She had long wanted to attend nursing school at the national university in Port-au-Prince, from which her mother had graduated, but Leconte refused. She was only eighteen years old, he said, and unprepared for the challenges and dangers of life in the capital city.

Leconte finally prevailed. Anaya stayed home and attended nursing school in Jérémie, at the École d'Infirmières Notre Dame du Perpétuel Secours. An uneasy peace settled between them, maintained by a set of conditions to which they both agreed without ever speaking of them. Anaya was allowed to come and go as she pleased, without curfew or permission, and she received a generous allowance. They avoided each other most of the week but had dinner together on Sundays, during which they talked about school, work, and politics. Anaya treated her father like a roommate, and he tried not to be a nuisance. That cold understanding had sustained them through the first three years of her training, and only the appearance of Zo in the spring before her senior year upended the delicate balance.

Zo lived for Sunday evenings. His preparations began the moment the laborers returned from their work in Leconte's yard. First, Tiken dry-shaved him with a razor blade, contouring the beard to the angle of his jaw and cutting the mustache back to reveal the line of his upper lip. Then Zo washed himself with the meticulousness of a surgeon going to operate. He scrubbed underneath his nails, splashed cologne at his throat, and borrowed two swipes of Bos-T's American deodorant.

The crew argued over his errand as soon as he left. But only Bos-T knew where Zo actually went each week because he was the only one who'd asked.

"You go every week?"

"Sundays."

"What do you do?"

"Wait for her."

"Like a good dog?"

"Exactly."

"And if she doesn't come?"

"I wait longer."

When a jealous Tiken finally asked Zo if he really thought this girl loved him or even liked him at all, Zo couldn't give him a good answer. "You're a game to her," Tiken submitted. "A toy to pass the time. Here you are spending your last *gourde* on a girl whose panties cost more than you make in a month."

Zo got up from his rice and red beans and towered over the other laborers. "What do any of you know about her panties?" he challenged. A hush fell over the others and they looked down at their dinners. Zo went reeling into the dark and Bos-T followed.

"What's wrong with you?" Bos-T asked.

"For the first time in my life I am not just trying to make love to a girl," Zo said. "I am trying to make her love me." He held his jaw like he had a toothache. "And it's true. Her panties are very expensive."

In May, protests against high fuel prices closed the highway at Ti Gwav and construction was delayed for a week. Zo spent his days with Daniello, pearling the neglected waters off Grande Cayemite. They took turns diving, one sitting in the boat watching for sharks, while the other sunk with a ten-pound rock into the coral depths. One day Zo surfaced with a *zwit* that, when pried open, contained a single misshapen pearl.

Daniello washed it in turpentine and held it to the light. "It's cloudy," he said. "And I've never seen a color quite like it." It was pinkish blue, and Daniello finally appraised it at $200 U.S.

If that were true, Zo said, it was the most expensive thing he had ever held in his life. "But I'm not selling it," he added. Instead, he told the fisherman he wanted to rent his skiff for a romantic cruise of the bay.

"Romantic cruise with who?" Daniello asked.

They shipped out of Daniello's yard a week later, Zo in the prow and the fisherman in back at the outboard engine. The sea was calm in the summer afternoon, and Daniello took them in close to the coast at the government college.

"Look at those girls," Daniello said. They were sitting on the seawall in their uniforms, white blouses and plaid skirts. Some of them were drinking Cokes from long straws. "They look like they're waiting for us."

"Just keep us off the rocks," Zo said.

They came in parallel to the stretch of white sand that ran under the bluffs of Chabanne and could see the two- and three-story mansions of the wealthy perched in the seagrass with the black mountains behind them.

"That's the one." Zo pointed.

It was a two-story white house with every light turned on against the dusk. They could hear the roar of the diesel generator.

"That's some spread," Daniello said. "You sure he doesn't have armed guards or a little navy?"

Daniello threw his fishing lines and they floated offshore until Zo saw the sign: a match lit and flared briefly in the bluff. By the time they beached, Anaya was standing in the sand just where Zo had said to meet them. Daniello whistled when he saw her. She boarded the boat with a bottle of white wine from Chile. She said it was the only wine you could buy in the whole city.

Zo helped her into the prow and welcomed her to the *Tribulation*. He pulled the cork and gave her the first sip, and she drank it cold and sour in the sea spray at twilight. They passed the bottle up and down the boat, Daniello taking long swigs in the stern and Anaya drinking in the prow.

"Where are you taking me?" she asked.

Daniello set a course for the headland at Mount Tapion. When they reached it, he cut the motor and they floated in open water opposite the long, clean beach. Zo produced a small zippered purse from the boat's catch box and showed Anaya his meager treasures.

First was a picture of himself that was all he had to prove his childhood. He was thirteen, and the photo had been taken in the lot where they had boxed him. He had his fists raised, play-fighting, as if someone had asked him to pose for the camera. Besides the photo, which Anaya pondered for a long time as they rolled in the water, Zo presented her with a little more than $100 in U.S. bills, his savings over a lifetime. He passed it to Anaya and insisted that she count it.

"There is the money," he said, reaching into the purse. "And Daniello says this is worth much more." He placed the misshapen pearl in her palm.

"Shouldn't you be more careful with this?" she asked.

"Throw it back into the sea if you want. It's yours."

"Is this why you've taken me here? To give me your pearl?"

Zo stood in the boat and steadied himself by setting his feet far apart. "Not my pearl," he said. "My heart." He began to deliver the monologue he had been rehearsing for days, in which he declared his love for her and promised to work for her all the days of his life. His voice was low and trembling, barely audible above the water slapping the boat.

Anaya interrupted. "You must think I'm one of your school-girls, who'll throw away everything on a few sweet words," she said. "I suppose you expect me to gut your daily catch and sell it in the marketplace, too? Look at me, Zo."

She held his chin and turned his eyes to her.

"I am never going to be your poor fishwife," she said. "Not for you or any other man. I will never live in a hut without electricity or plumbing. And my father would die before he saw his only daughter selling salt fish out of a bucket in a provincial town. He would tell me once again about Great-Great-Grandfather Cincinnatus Leconte. Do you know who that is?"

Neither Zo nor Daniello could say.

"He was a president of Haiti," she said. "From president to sell-ing salted *kong* is a long way for a family to fall."

Then she said Zo's name in such a way that he knew it was over. He pitched sideways so violently that Daniello had to reach out with the oar to keep him from falling overboard. Anaya crept forward, put her hand on his, and prepared to deliver the death blow. But something stopped her. Maybe it was Daniello sitting at the motor pretending not to listen, or maybe it was the picture of Zo as a boy or the gravity of him as he made promises with the night coming on over the world. Maybe it was the white tern that flew so close to the boat they could hear the beating of its wings. Whatever it was, Anaya held her tongue. She squeezed his hand while the wind blew hard off the cape and the swells grew deep and troublesome.

"If you say another word," she finally said, "about our future together and what you will do for me and how you will love me, I will jump off this boat. And then you will lose me for good, because I can't swim."

"How can you live on an island and not know how to swim?" Daniello asked.

Anaya's admission that she couldn't swim was the very thing Zo had been waiting for. All this time he had been looking for a way to make her need him, and he was convinced he had finally found the one thing he could give her that no one else could: swimming lessons.

Anaya agreed to take a lesson each week at the beach outside of town named for the Indians who had once lived there. It was so far away they had to engage a mototaxi to take them, the two of them and a driver going all together up the national highway on one bike. The driver sat almost in his handlebars and Anaya was between the men, so that when Zo whispered in her ear that she was a beautiful woman, the driver turned his head and said, "It's true."

Taino Beach was a long white strand that angled through turquoise swells toward a point in the east. On the other side, to the west, between the beach and the town itself, was the green flank of Mount Tapion. Smooth boulders called Les Poissons had tumbled from the cliffs into the shallow surf.

Anaya wore a white bikini and entered the water slowly, with her shoulders thrown back and her face turned away from the water. She thought that tendrils of seagrass were eels and every fish was a shark. Zo coaxed her into the shallow surf, but she refused to close her eyes or put her face in the water.

"It all begins by lying on your back," he said.

"Is that what you say to all the girls?"

"Try to touch your belly to the sky," he said.

Anaya lay on her back in the water and put her arms out. Zo fit his palm under the small of her back, lifted her midsection, and led her about the shallows like a toy boat.

For their second lesson, he borrowed a pair of snorkeling goggles and fitted them to Anaya's face. Like this he got her to put her face in the water and blow bubbles. He pointed out the black anemones with their long venomous spikes and the sunset-colored brittle stars splayed in the sand. In the lee of the reef they saw a school of queen triggerfish feeding on brain coral. Anaya was so excited that she forgot about the dangers of the sea.

The third afternoon was windy, the water warmer than the air. The beach was deserted. They took their clothes off and ran into the surf together, and he stood holding her in his arms as they kissed under cloudy skies. She lay on her back and put her arms out like a little girl. She was cold where her skin came out of the water and she bobbed there with her eyes closed.

She called his name but there was no answer. His hand wasn't beneath her. She opened her eyes and choked on the salt water. Zo was sunning himself on the beach, his shoulders shining in the heat.

"You didn't even miss me," he said.

To celebrate they bought *lanbi* and beer from the fishermen who worked the beach. They were three lanky teenagers who sat roasting fish on half an oil barrel in the sand. An older man sat apart from them, working the knots out of his tackle. The sun slipped behind Mount Tapion. They shared a single towel in the sand, Zo tracing the contours of her body with his eyes open and then with his eyes closed, as if he were memorizing her for a test.

"What would your father do if he found out about us?" he asked.

"You would definitely be off the job," she said.

"The job's not much."

Anaya watched the high white clouds change shape over the sea while Zo traced circles at her collarbones.

"What about the police?" she said. "My father has friends in many places, and you never know with Doktè Leconte. He's very jealous. And even if nothing happened I'd still be living in that house with him day after day. That could be unpleasant."

"Not if we go away."

"Ki kote?" she asked. "The slums of Pòtoprens?"

"America," he said. "Florida. I'll row you myself."

"Wi." She laughed. "In poor Daniello's boat."

The fishermen returned from the sea with a netful of *lanbi* and a bucket of beers on ice. They seated the shells in the hot coals until they cracked and grew brittle. Then one of the boys split them open with a stroke from his machete. Another pulled the meat out with a fork and cooked it with the flair of a culinary expert, keeping the flesh briefly over the open flames and turning it just once. He halved two lemons and squeezed the citrus liberally over the meat, and the acid hissed in the flame. There was a sharp, pure incense in the twilight.

Then Zo and Anaya fed each other the shellfish one at a time. The *lanbi* were the size of ears and chewy, and the lemon was sharp in the smoky flesh. The beer was cold and crisp and they drank two apiece. The fishermen laughed and pointed through the flames at the *damoukles*, lovers, while they ate. But as the sun fell down the coast and the terns dissipated in the darkness and they smelled the endless ebb tide of the world, the evening grew thoughtful and the fishermen demure. The horizon deepened and then grew endless.

"There is something holy about a woman who doesn't know, or is too young yet to know, how beautiful she is," the old fisherman said, sitting apart and wrangling his tackle.

5

THAT DAY ON TAINO BEACH was the beginning of the end of their affair. They were spotted there in the afternoon by one of Leconte's employees. Officially, Claude Juste was a special secretary at the Department of Public Health, but he also served as Leconte's chauffeur and tended bar at all of his parties. He was parked in the lot when they came up from their lesson, the two of them sharing one towel, and Zo with his arms around Anaya's shoulders.

The very next morning, Anaya woke to find her father in the room with her. It was Monday, and he should have been at the main hospital. She stirred in the sheets.

"I thought you were afraid of the water," he said.

She opened one eye. There was yesterday's bathing suit in plain sight, where she'd hung it over the chair to dry. "We live on an island," she said. "Don't you think it's time I learn to swim?"

"You're not a little girl anymore, Anaya. You're going to be twenty years old."

"*Vingt et un*, Papa," she said, turning over and rubbing her eyes. "I'm going to be twenty-one."

"All the more reason not to go sneaking to Taino Beach with this *travayè* of yours."

"He doesn't work for me."

Leconte took the chair from her desk and turned it toward the bed. "No," he said, sitting in it. "He works for *me*, along with dozens of other men. Can you imagine how it looks to have him sneaking into my house when my back is turned?"

Anaya made a strangled sound and closed her eyes against the accusation. "He's never been inside your house," she said.

Leconte said that was only right and that it must stay that way. "You have, up till now, done everything out of my sight," he said. "That was considerate. But now it is taking place before my eyes, before everyone we know. It must come to an end."

Anaya lay there with her eyes closed. "I wish you would go away and let me sleep," she said.

She heard him sigh. "Believe it or not, I didn't come in here to argue with you," he said. "I came to give you this."

Anaya opened her eyes.

Her father held a package wrapped in brown paper. "I know you're still a year away from graduation, but I thought you should have this."

She took it from him and drew the long box from its wrapping. It was a stethoscope with black tubing.

"I've had your name inscribed on the chest piece," he said.

"I love it," she said, sitting up. "Thank you." She fitted the buds in her ears and put the chest piece over her heart.

"What does it tell you?" her father asked.

She raised her eyes. "That I should learn to swim."

"Then let me find you a proper instructor."

Anaya told her father to come sit on the bed. She moved aside to make room for him and then pressed the chest piece over his heart. The room was silent. Her father heard the sea below the bedroom window.

"What do you hear?"

She took the buds from her ears. "Mama," she said, "telling us to get along."

Her father laughed. "We waited six years for you to be born," he said. "Don't misunderstand me. They were not long years. We enjoyed ourselves. But something was missing and we both knew what it was." He took her hand up from the bed. "When you came, you were a tremendous source of pride and joy to Rosy and me. And I promised her that I would take care of you and protect you from the dangers of life on this island."

"He isn't dangerous."

"Maybe not," he said. "But he's certainly not the kind of man you should be spending your time with."

"Who should I spend my time with?" she asked, and immediately regretted asking.

Leconte stood up and smoothed the front of his pants. "What about André Douyon? There's a serious boy. Someone worth your time and attention. I saw his father last week."

Anaya groaned and fell back on the bed.

"What happened between the two of you?" he asked. "Didn't you used to date?"

Anaya turned toward the wall. "I was fifteen," she said.

Her father said André was coming from Port-au-Prince and wanted to see her on her birthday.

Zo had learned from innumerable disappointments in his youth that it was better to say nothing in a negotiation. Whoever spoke first usually lost, and Zo found that in the face of absolute silence his adversaries would negotiate themselves down to new lows. So when Anaya took his hand that Sunday evening and told him it was over, he fell quiet not out of heartbreak or shock, as she thought, but out of long practice at bargaining for lost causes.

A slack tide hung far down the beach, churning under a colorless sky. Zo kept his peace so long Anaya was afraid he was crying. But when she asked him to say something, his voice was staid and calm in the dark.

"Whoever talks first is lost," he said.

"My father knows," she said. "We can't possibly continue."

The only argument Zo could make was a kiss, and he made it there on the beach. He took hold of her, laid his mouth upon hers, and then walked off without speaking. Nor did he look back. It was heroic.

But then the next week, he was back on the beach as always, as if nothing had changed, armed with a resolution that made her giddy when she saw him from the second-story window. She was getting ready for her birthday celebration—the Carimi concert at the Louco Night Club. The young doctor André Douyon had come in from Port-au-Prince and would be joining her and her girlfriends.

Anaya called Lovanice. "He's here," she said.

"What's he doing?"

Anaya watched him out her window. It was a blustery evening and the clouds spit long threads of rain across the sea. "Standing in the rain."

"Poor dog!" Lovanice said. "He's sick for you."

"What do I do?"

"Give him one last taste. Consider it an act of charity."

"What about André Douyon?" Anaya asked.

"Who cares about André Douyon!" Lovanice said. "Tell him you lost his ticket."

Anaya looked out the window. Zo was very still in the rain on the pale beach. Then she called André Douyon.

André and Anaya had the long and fluid relationship that sometimes develops between children whose parents are friends. Dr. Douyon, André's father, was a well-respected physician and a friend of Vincent Leconte's long before Leconte became the deputy minister of health. The children were childhood adversaries and played all the games children play while their parents talked late after dinner. Though they were five years apart, and André the elder, Anaya always seemed more mature. When she was only eight and he thirteen, she'd scared him into crying while playing hide-and-seek in the bananas after dark. They saw each other often: at the Catholic church on Sundays, at local volleyball tournaments, promenading in the public park, and, later, at the government school, when she was in *troisième* class and he was in Philo, the last year of secondary school.

That was the year they officially dated. Anaya was fifteen and André twenty, working toward medical school. He took her to the cinema and bought her vanilla ice cream, which she ate walking along the seawall. Like many couples in the city, they had their first kiss under the crumbling lighthouse.

Before he left for medical school in the autumn, he took her on a date to a fancy hotel restaurant up Avenue Émile Roumer and told her his plans for the future. They did not include, as he put it, "a lifetime spent giving vaccines to children who are already too old for them." He wasn't content to be a small-town doctor like his father, paid in eggs and honeycomb. He wanted to be on the policy side of things, like Anaya's father, to work internationally and see the world. All this was a preface to him asking if she would wait for him until he was out of school, at which time they could be married. "I'm sixteen," she'd said, which André understood to mean, correctly, that no, she would not wait. However, she did accompany him to a room upstairs, where she lost her virginity in an unspectacular session on the hotel bed.

André left for the capital a week later and never returned to Jérémie without bringing her some treat: candy from America, a box for her pencils, and, finally, jewelry, which she wore whenever they were together. Though André had other girlfriends in the city, they never succeeded in replacing the younger, precocious girl from his youth. As he told her each time he came to visit, she was getting more beautiful every year.

He'd last kissed her when he was home on summer vacation. She was eighteen then and he was twenty-three. He saw her at the Louco Night Club dancing with another man and, growing jealous, took her outside. He was drunk and kissed her when she least expected it. Anaya slapped him afterward so hard he never tried again.

André graduated from medical school two years later, in May, and expected that achievement to make some difference, if not in Anaya's heart, then in her calculations for the future. Full of confidence after the graduation ceremony and the newfound respect that came with being called "Doctor," André planned on making a grand display of his affections for Anaya on the night of her twenty-first birthday. When she called to cancel, it bruised his ego without her knowing it.

"Why don't you pick us up from the show afterward and bring us to my father's house for cake and champagne?" she offered.

"Nothing ever changes here," he said. "Even though I'm a doctor now, I see I'm still to be nothing but your chauffeur."

Anaya showered, fixed her hair, and drew red lipstick over her mouth. She stepped into a dress patterned with black and white stripes, and wore a wide red belt with a studded buckle across the narrowest part of her waist. Then she opened a pint of cinnamon-flavored rum and took a brief, sweet drink. She went out into the yard and called down to Zo from the bluff, fanning the tickets in her hand.

"Little orphan," she said, "do you want to come to the Carimi concert or don't you?"

They walked to the show holding hands. Anaya offered no explanation, and Zo didn't ask for one. He had no leverage and didn't want to press his luck. When they got to the Louco Night Club he waited back in the shadows. "Go with your friends," he said. "I'll come afterward."

But she pulled him into the parking lot. "What's the use? Lovanice has a big mouth. I'm sure she's already told them everything."

Then Anaya abandoned her friends to spend the entire evening with Zo in a corner of the club. They sat just off the bar at a table for two, drinking cold Heineken, while the band played endless *konpa*. Zo was content just to watch her drink her beers, one after the other, but then she came over and danced in his lap. She was an affectionate drunk, taking his hands and placing them over her hips and then inside her dress. When the show ended and her friends came to tear her away, she lingered in Zo's arms even under the big electric lights.

"It's my birthday," she said. "I'll do what I want."

"What do you want?"

"Bo'm," she said. But when he leaned in to kiss her she turned her face. "Not here."

She walked him out of the club, away from the milling crowd. It was drizzling along the coast and she wet her lips with her tongue. She let him kiss her there in the cool, high grass with all her friends for an audience.

"Why didn't you tell me it was your birthday?"

She touched his nose with her fingertip. "I didn't want my poor man spending his last pearl on me."

Her girlfriends were calling from the road. "He's here!" they said. "It's time to go."

A sport utility vehicle was coming down the long dirt track toward the dance hall.

"Who's that?" Zo asked. Anaya was drunk, and he kept a persistent hand at her back to keep her from falling away.

"He came all the way from the capital just to see me."

"Who?"

"Monsieur le Docteur André Douyon," she said with a grand French accent. "The promising young physician from Port-au-Prince."

When her friends came down to collect her, they called her Madam Douyon.

"Are you engaged?" Zo asked. "Do you love him?"

"Don't follow us," Anaya called to him drunkenly while her friends dragged her up the street. "I won't look for you on the stairs. I won't."

Zo stood in the roadside weeds while they packed Anaya into the front seat. Then he walked the tide line in the spitting rain. To reach the schoolhouse where he and the other laborers spent their nights, he'd have to pass underneath Leconte's castle. When he arrived beneath the house, he turned away from the bluff to look at the mournful sea. The rain slashed across the surf. The fire in his heart went cold as ash and a sour taste climbed up the back of his throat from all the beer and jealousy. When the wind blew he felt the weather in his chest, as if he had no flesh at all but only naked ribs to cage his organs.

He finally fought his way up the stairs, against an ominous wind that rushed down from the hills.

The two-story bungalow loomed brightly across the yard. Even from a distance he could see the party clearly through the lighted windows. They sat in the living room on white leather couches and chairs. There were Anaya's girlfriends with plates of cake. Her father sat to one side, a flute of champagne in his hand. On the other side was André Douyon, the doctor who had come all the way from the capital to be with her on her birthday.

To Zo, he resembled an overgrown baby. His face was perfectly round and his head was shaved. The fleshy tops of his cheeks obscured his eyes when he smiled, which was often, and a pair of dimples framed his mouth. He had small, healthy white teeth and a thin mustache clipped neatly to the line of his lip.

Zo came close enough to the window that his breath clouded the glass. He could see the make of André's clothes, a yellow polo and expensive American jeans. His arm was cast casually around Anaya's shoulders as though he didn't know what a miracle it was to be allowed to do so. Zo saw his well-manicured nails and determined from them and from the perfection of his hands that he'd never done a day of manual labor in his life.

When Anaya finally came for him it was very late. The rain clouds had blown out to sea and sat languid and golden over the whitecaps.

"Why did they call you Madam Douyon?" he asked.

She exhaled a breath of sweet liquor in his ear. "My father wants me to marry him."

"Don't you?"

"*Pòv* Zo," she whispered. "Don't you believe I prefer you?"

"To who?"

"Anyone."

"Why?"

"Don't you know by now?" She kissed the back of his neck. "I'm the kind of girl"—she put her fingers in his hair—"who thinks the only thing that can make her happy"—she turned him around to face her—"is the one thing she's told she cannot have."

That was the night Anaya finally invited Zo into her house. She didn't walk him through the front door and declare him her lover, as Zo had hoped. Instead, they snuck in through the back door like burglars, while her father slept in his bedroom upstairs, and kissed in all the dark corners of the house. She stood on his feet in the living room and they stumbled like one clown into her father's study. She kissed him under the medical diplomas. She sat him on the leather couch and drew her tongue down his neck. Then she marched him out of the office and into the kitchen, where she took a piece of ice from the freezer. She lifted her shirt and held the ice against her chest, and Zo sucked her frozen nipples standing up in the kitchen because she ordered it done.

"Tell me you love me," she demanded.

Zo told her.

"Tell me I'm the only one you ever loved."

Zo told her that and he meant it, too.

She took him to the bathroom and sat up on the countertop next to the sink. She flipped the lights on and they saw themselves in the huge mirror.

"After we made love the first time, I thought you had killed me," she said. "Do it that way again."

She pulled her skirt up and wrapped her legs around him and they fucked in the small, hot bathroom with their naked bodies exposed from two angles. Afterward, she put her head on his chest and told him about her mother, and how she had first learned that her mother's cancer treatments had failed.

"I came home from school one afternoon to find all these cars in the driveway. The front door was open, and there were strangers inside the house. Some of them I recognized from church. It was one of the ladies from the choir who told me. She took me into my father's office and sat me down on the couch. I thought she was going to sing.

"My father always wanted me to be a doctor," Anaya said. "And all these years later, he still thinks I chose nursing school because it was the thing that would frustrate him most of all. But that's not true," she whispered. "I'm not like him, Zo. I don't want to be rich or powerful."

"What do you want?"

"I want to be of use, like my mother." She passed her finger down Zo's face. "I want to give albendazole tabs to all the poor orphans, so they can grow into handsome young men."

Leconte disrupted them thus in the sweetest and most profound moment of their affair. Not in the act of lovemaking, but in its precious aftermath. Anaya in her gold hoop earrings, the lipstick kissed off her lips and her dress twisted, telling Zo stories of her mother; and Zo listening closely, in a perilous state of satisfaction, with his pants at his ankles and his wasted cock lying across his thigh in the home of his greatest enemy. Luckily, the stairs were built over the bathroom, and they heard Leconte coming down.

"I'm not afraid," Zo said. "Let me meet him."

Anaya straightened herself up in the mirror as best she could. "If he finds you here, he'll call the police," she said. "I'll never see you again."

The bathroom was at the front of the house, across the foyer from the front door. Zo made it out before her father appeared, but that door was carved from a single panel of solid ebony wood and didn't shut all the way behind him. He heard Leconte's voice booming from the foyer.

"What happened to you?" Leconte went to the door and stepped outside, but it was too late.

Zo had crept around the corner of the house and squatted behind a potted bougainvillea. From there he crossed the yard in six tremendous leaps, bounded down the staircase, and landed two-footed in the sand like a man marking his distance in the long jump.

It was only then that he realized he'd forgotten his sandals.

Telling as few lies as possible, Anaya let her father believe that it had been André Douyon with her in the bathroom that night. As she expected, he was less upset to think of his daughter involved with the doctor than with that laborer off one of his own projects. The problem was the flip-flops—their size and make and state of disrepair. The thongs had fallen out and been melted back in so many times that a lump of rubber had formed under the toes. The backs had been worn away so that the wearer's bare heels were practically in the street. Dr. Leconte couldn't imagine that a man as fastidious about his appearance as André Douyon would ever leave the house in such footwear, much less wear them to a party. He called André and got right to the point.

"What size shoe do you wear?" he asked.

André answered with a number that was three sizes too small for the disastrous footwear Leconte had found in the bathroom.

That was the end of their secret lovemaking at the coast. They had thrashed on the beach like fish abandoned by the tide. They'd made love on the stairs and in the grass. Once, Zo had set her in a wheelbarrow and made love by moving the contraption back and forth on its lone wheel as if Anaya were a load of sweet cane. But the night that Zo left his sandals behind was to be their last.

They tried to meet once more, but it was hopeless. Claude Juste surprised them at their clandestine rendezvous and stopped them before they could begin. When Anaya had been sent inside, Claude came down to the landing and regarded Zo gathering his things.

"How long have you known?" Zo asked.

"From the day you started," Claude replied.

Zo walked the coast like the sole survivor of a shipwreck, threading the tide line, casting mournful glances out across the sea. He looked back once to find her bedroom window dark. She never came to meet him again.

The summer ended in a heat wave. The sea blistered under white skies. The laborers sweated where they slept. The floors had been laid by then, and the laborers went about on high scaffolding to finish the cinder block walls. The tin roof was arriving in sections, and Paul thought they'd have it raised by the end of August. Then there would be nothing but the finishes—plaster, paint, and window fittings. He thought they'd be through sometime in September.

Zo worked through the end of August like a *zombi* raised from the dead and made to work for his rest. He sweated all afternoon as if it were penance for bad behavior and cooled off at twilight in the nearby river. The local girls stood by their laundry and watched his body steaming in the clear water. His nights were sleepless, and he took to wandering the school halls and drinking too much rum.

One Friday they had a celebration: *banan fri* and *griot* pork fried in its own fat with a side of shredded cabbage salad soaked in lime juice. They ate with their hands at the roadside while the long-haul trucks blew past toward Port-au-Prince. Boss Paul had warned them in the morning to have soap and clean underwear because, he told them now, they were going to the nightclub and he was paying.

"For one round," he clarified.

"How many stars?" Tiken asked. It was customary to rate rum by a score of stars, one star being cheap and harsh and five stars being smooth and fine.

"One star," Paul said, "and be thankful for it because it's all you're getting."

He bought them a tall bottle of the cheap Dominican Bakara one-star rum and they passed it back and forth, swigging from the cap. Boss Paul would have no one shave him but Tiken, who took a razor and scraped the hairs from the foreman's grizzled throat with the focus of a professional barber.

Sonson said it was a good club, and Bos-T asked if he had been there before.

"They have a girl there who will put it in her mouth for *soixante gourdes,*" Sonson said.

"In her mouth?" Boss Paul asked. "What do you want with her mouth?"

"Ti Son is confused." Bos-T laughed. "He's not sure where to put it."

"I can't help you with that," Paul said. He leaned back again and lifted his chin to be shaved. "Maybe Zo can find you a woman and show you how it fits."

But Zo didn't go to the club with the others. He sat on the schoolhouse gallery, talking with Terez while she crushed roasted coffee beans with the bottom of a tin cup. She prescribed lime for his heartache, rum for his sorrow, and another woman for his bed.

It hurt Zo to even think about that. He reached for the heap of roasted berries and began to tear away the husks. Then he crushed the beans until he had a small heap of grounds and forced these grounds through a piece of window screen. But he was so brutal on the beans that Terez had to intervene.

"I want coffee grounds," she said, "not coffee dust." She took the beans back. "You need to see someone," she said after a while. "A *manbo* or a prostitute."

Zo said that wasn't the way to a woman's heart.

"You'd be surprised if you knew what roads could take you to a woman's heart," Terez said.

"If we could only have five minutes," he started, "I'd tell her everything. I'd make it clear."

"What would you say?"

"That I know what it's like to grow up without a mother. And that I'd take care of her if she'd only let me."

A mototaxi came up, idling at the gate to the schoolyard. Terez thought it would be one of the drunken workers. "My money's on Bos-T," she said. But it wasn't Bos-T-Bos or any of them, it was the Lovanice girl. She waited at the highway and sent the driver to fetch Zo.

Lovanice was the daughter of one of the wealthiest men in town. She was famous for her complexion and for the trips she took to America each year and the dresses she brought back with her and sold at a profit. Zo had met her briefly the night of the Carimi concert.

She was standing at the national highway, beside the shop that sold patties and roasted sweet potatoes during the day. It was closed now and there were only the benches and the fire pit and a half bag of charcoal. She didn't sit down. Trucks honked and the riders shouted from the roofs of the buses when they saw Demwazèl Lovanice in that midnight-blue dress, with her lemon-painted fingers at her hips.

"Did she send you?" Zo asked.

"I'm not her messenger," Lovanice said.

"I've been back to the beach every day," Zo said. "Her window is dark."

"What did you think would happen? Did you think she'd run away with you?"

"We'd been talking of Anse d'Hainault," he said.

"Don't make me laugh," Lovanice said. "Did you really think Anaya Leconte was going to sell your salted fish in the marketplace?" Lovanice considered her nails. "She's moved on. You should, too."

"I can't," he said, holding his neck with his hand. *"Mw remen li."*

Lovanice revealed her pointy little teeth. "I heard a little about the things you do when you are in love," she said. "The bathroom, the beach, the staircase. Couldn't you at least take her to a hotel and do things properly? I mean, how poor are you?"

There was no good way for Zo to answer that question.

"I can see why she would want you once, maybe twice," Lovanice said. "But for so long and so many times?" She reached for him, squeezing his wrist. "I know you are very confident. And I saw at the concert how well you could move. But what else can you do?" She looked him clear in the face and held up an envelope. "Can you read?" she asked. "What does this say?"

Zo took it from her and unfolded a letter scented with the perfume he had bought for Anaya from one of the market stalls. The cloudy, misshapen pearl that he'd presented to her in Daniello's boat fell out in his hand and broke his heart before he even saw the words.

Cheri doudou,
I didn't have a chance to say goodbye.

He read the letter there on the shoulder of the national highway, with the rich girl standing in her blue evening dress and the long-haul trucks going on to Les Cayes and Jérémie. Anaya had been sent away to finish school in Port-au-Prince, at the Hôpital de l'Université d'État d'Haïti. Her father had suspected them for weeks. *But after all that sneaking around,* she wrote, *it was your sandals that did us in.*

Zo staggered back and put his palm up to his forehead.

I should have run away with you to Anse d'Hainault, where all the houses are made of wood. We could have watched the last sunsets on the island. I would have loved you, Zo. I think I already did.

"What are you going to do?" Lovanice asked.

"*M pa konen.*" Zo put his hand at his throat. "I feel sick."

"Forget her." Demwazèl Lovanice stroked his palm with her painted fingers. "If you need help, I am the one to give it to you."

6

THE BRIEF DREAM of loving her was followed by the unwavering conviction that there was now a place in him scorched so black it would never green again. The tradesmen did everything they could to cheer him up, but Zo drew deeper into despondency. Sonson bought a bag of marijuana off a Rasta called Laurelien, who rolled them a cigar-sized spliff of weed so delicious even Boss Paul puffed on it. They sat in the classroom afterward listening to Lucky Dube on the radio, but Zo got even worse. He was driven from the schoolhouse and finally sought Medsen Fèy for deeper relief.

When Fèy saw him, he came out from behind his cart. "What happened to you?" he asked. Zo's eyes were red-rimmed and Fèy asked if he'd been crying. He asked only as a joke but then worried it might be true.

"They've sent her away."

"I should have guessed," Fèy said. "Did they send her away from you? Or did they send her to go and do something else with her life?"

Zo put a hand over his eyes. "I don't see a difference," he said. "Either way she is gone."

"But there is a difference," Medsen Fèy insisted. "In the one case, they are desperate to keep you from the girl. In the other, they've only sent her off to complete her education. In that case you are not their enemy."

Zo uncovered his eyes and Fèy was sure he'd been crying. "I am their enemy," he said.

"What about her?" Fèy asked. "Does she want you to follow?"

Zo took the letter out, unfolded it, and started to read in a tremulous voice that seemed out of place in his mouth. " '*Cheri doudou*,' " he started. " 'I didn't have a chance to say goodbye.' "

Fèy took the letter and read it himself, stroking his chin. "Come back after dark," he decided. "I have one last treatment to offer you, one last chance at a cure. But it isn't pretty."

Zo couldn't keep away. He showed up at dusk and Fèy made him wait. Only when the sun had set and the last bit of daylight had been drained from the sky did he reach under his cart and produce a potion so foul it had thickened in the jar.

"What is it?" Zo asked.

Fèy unscrewed the lid and scooped a measure into a wide glass. It shook like gelatin. He passed a lit match over the top and the liquor caught fire, blazing and popping in the glass. Fèy pushed the bubbling potion across the cart toward his customer.

"What do you want me to do with that?"

"Drink it."

It gave off an evil black smoke like a petroleum burn.

"How?"

"Shoot it back."

"Won't it burn?"

"*Egzakteman*," Medsen Fèy said. "It will burn her right out of you. Run her from your heart and uproot her from your tongue. It will burn so bad you won't be able to speak her name."

"Not aloud," Zo said.

He brought the boiling cup to his lips and tossed it back. The flame disappeared down his mouth, and they stood again in the quiet off the sea.

Days afterward Zo had a smoker's voice. His burps tasted like char. He sought out the rum dealer and told him what the cure had done for him this time. "I still think about her," he said in a strained whisper. "I just can't say her name."

"You're helpless," Fèy said.

"What do I do?"

"You need an eight-day blow. Something like the storm that wrecked the *Pinta*. Or a lengthy prison sentence, like the one that kept Oswald Durand from Choucoune."

"He wrote her the love poem from prison," Zo said.

"Jesus. You're like a horse with blinders," Fèy said. "There's nothing but you and her in the whole wide world." He put a hand on Zo's shoulder. "There's only one thing for you to do."

"What's that?"

"Go find her."

"I don't know where she lives."

"But you know where she's studying!" Fèy said. "It says so in the letter. You can't miss it. The postscript is clear as day. The nursing school is just west of the government house." Fèy took Zo's arm. "That's the great and terrible thing about these islands. You really can't get off without some trouble."

Fèy told Zo of a ship's captain from Jérémie called Boston who'd be sailing up the coast sometime after midnight and who would be docked in the bay until the early-morning hours. If Zo could be on the wharf before then, Medsen Fèy would get him aboard and he could sail all the way to the capital. "For free," he added. "You might even get paid if you do some work for him. He'll put you ashore in Pòtoprens with cash in your pocket."

Zo went to settle the rest of his affairs. There were the few articles he'd loaned to various laborers, and he spent the first part of the night collecting them: a tape measure and a flashlight that worked on crank power and a pair of work gloves. Terez took every article of clothing he owned, save for what he wore on his back at that moment, and washed them in her tub and rinsed them and hung them to dry on the line at her house. Zo took them down in the dark and folded them and packed them away.

He was owed a fair amount of pay. Not just for a full August of work on the health center, but also for the ten consecutive Sundays he'd spent stacking and mixing cement in Leconte's backyard. They had yet to be paid even a penny for that job, and Tiken had taken to referring to it as their "volunteer opportunity."

Zo found Boss Paul sitting on a desk in the schoolhouse. It was raining outside and Paul was smoking a hand-rolled cigarette, looking through the bars on the window. The foreman offered Zo a smoke and they sat beside each other on the one desk, regarding the rain slashing through the leaves of the mango tree. Zo asked the foreman for his pay and the older man laughed.

"From how far back?" the boss wanted to know.

Zo calculated while the rain rattled the tin roof. "Twenty-one days of August and the last two weeks of July, at two hundred *gourdes* a day. Plus the ten Sundays of work at the doctor's house."

"How much were we paid for that?"

Zo shrugged.

"It's still under negotiation," Paul said. "How can I pay you for work if I don't know the final price?"

They sat for a moment, smoking.

"You know if I had the money I'd give it to you."

"I know."

Paul stuck the cigarette in his lips and motioned to a pair of blue jeans tossed over a desk. "Give me those pants," he said.

Zo handed them across and Paul fished his wallet from the back pocket.

"Look." He opened it and went through the bills, counting aloud with the cigarette hanging off his bottom lip. He folded the bills and passed them to Zo. "It's the best I can do."

"I'm not taking your cash."

"It's all the same."

"No, it isn't." Zo shook his head, and Paul put the money away. "So, who has it?"

"Are you serious?"

Zo did nothing but draw back on his smoke.

"Listen to me," Paul said. "It's harder to ask money off a rich man than it is to squeeze juice from a dry lime."

"The doctor?"

"And you want to go demand the money from him. Why? Because he's sent his daughter away from you and now you are going to follow her?" He lowered the smoke and looked Zo in the eye. "You think I can't guess what you're planning?"

"He doesn't have to know."

"You think he can't add?" Boss Paul said. "You fuck the girl, she starts to fall in love with you, they send her away. Now you want to go see him, demanding all kinds of pay. Special projects plus daily wages and maybe a tip, too? Even to a rich man, two and two make four."

"To a rich man," Zo said, stubbing out his cigarette on the cinder block wall, "two and two make eight."

Zo put his hand out.

"You're owed some severance," Paul said, shaking his hand. "Take one of the shovels."

"The Brazilians?"

"You know what I always say."

"A man with a shovel is a business," Zo said.

"*Bon bagay,*" Paul said. "Ask Tiken to let you into the storeroom." He dug into his wallet, drew out a wad of notes, and passed them across without looking. "Take my advice, Zo. Stay clear of the doctor."

Zo got to the storeroom and chose a shovel with a blond wood handle and a steel blade stamped BRASIL. Then he went off under the stars after the rain cleared with the shovel balanced on his shoulder and everything he owned packed into his bag. He had two thick slices of the *dous makòs* cake from the girl who lived next to the schoolhouse and who had been in love with him from the day he arrived.

Zo walked down the river to the sea and turned up the endless strand. The water piled away under the horizon. He wasn't going to see the doctor for his money. That had been an excuse he made even to himself. Zo had the vague idea that he would introduce himself to Vincent Leconte, admit that he was in love with Anaya, and ask for his permission to pursue her in Port-au-Prince. All the way up the strand he rehearsed different approaches, revising his speech and considering his chances. When he reached the beach under Leconte's house, he left his pack on the landing, laid his shovel across the bag, and climbed up the stairs.

When he finally stood before the house, Zo realized he had never entered through the front door before and hardly even recognized the public face of the building. He climbed onto the raised porch and approached the forbidding black door. He knew from his long labors in the Caribbean heat that it was unwise to hesitate with a great load upon your shoulder and, following that simple principle, without considering exactly what he was going to say when he finally stood before the doctor, he went up to the grand wooden door and pounded on it.

Leconte's man Claude Juste answered, wearing a polo shirt and the black loafers he wore when he was driving. "Using the front door for a change," he said.

"Is the doctor home?"

Claude leaned over the threshold and looked both ways. "Where are the others? Did they put you up to this?"

Zo looked past Claude into the tiled foyer, furnished with a sofa table and a brass floor vase. The door on the left led to the bathroom where Zo and Anaya had once made love. He could see through the whole house and out the rear windows to the sea.

"I've come to speak with Doktè Leconte," he said.

Claude stepped over the threshold and closed the door part-way behind him. "I don't know what you think you're doing here, but you've made a grave mistake," he whispered. "She's been sent away. There's nothing here for you."

From deep inside the house, they heard the doctor's booming voice.

Zo and the driver exchanged a long look. "It's no one, Doktè," Claude called over his shoulder. "The wrong house. They're looking for Commissioner Cledanor."

They heard the doctor's voice again, much closer this time, from the end of the hall.

"What do they want with the commissioner?"

Zo leaned past Claude and pushed the door open.

Vincent Leconte stood barefoot at the end of the lighted foyer. His shirt was unbuttoned and his belly fell out over the waistband of his shorts. Everything about him was substantial—his voice, his girth, the house behind him. His features, too, were heavy and generous. His forehead was fleshy, marked by three deep lines, and his brow shaded his eyes from the overhead light. He had a toothpick in his mouth and he chewed it.

"What do you want with Commissioner Cledanor?" Leconte asked.

"I haven't come for the commissioner," Zo said. "I've come to speak with you, Doktè."

"Are you ill?"

Zo shook his head. "I'm one of Paul's men."

Leconte raised his face for the first time. "Paul sent you?"

"The foreman doesn't know I've come."

"What is this, Claude?" Leconte said, working something from his front teeth. "Is something wrong with one of the crew?"

All the way down the beach, Zo had been preparing to tell the doctor how he felt about his daughter. But now that they were face-to-face, he faltered. "It's our wages," he said. "We haven't been paid since July."

Leconte took the toothpick from his mouth and pointed with it. "That's the problem with this country," he said. "Everybody wants to be paid when he wants to be paid. I suppose you'll decide when and how much, too."

"The wages were fixed by you and Paul."

"And Paul should have spoken to you," Leconte said. "The funds have been held up in Port-au-Prince. It's out of my hands."

Not knowing what else to do, and feeling as if the conversation were coming to a close, Zo drew the folded time sheet from his pocket. To his surprise, Leconte pushed past Claude, pulled the door open, and took it.

"I'm not an ATM," he said, "that you can come to at all hours of the night." But he looked over the hours anyway. "You were on the Sunday crew, at my house?" He looked at Zo with greater care than before. "Yes. I remember you now. You were quite impressive under that load of cement. How many bags was it?"

"Six," Zo said. "Three on each shoulder."

"How much weight is that?"

"National brand comes in eighty-pound bags."

The doctor made a whistling sound. "Yes, I remember you well. *Le bourik,*" he said. "The donkey. What is your real name?"

Zo knew at that moment that he'd miscalculated, and Terez and Paul had been right. Vincent Leconte would never give Zo his blessing, and once he spoke his name, even the illusion of courtesy would come to an end. Zo said it as if he hated to say it, as if he'd been marched all that way against his will just to say it now, like the confession of some long crime of poverty and unworthiness. Once out between them, it was heavy and immovable as a sack of National cement.

The portico was lit by an electric chandelier, and it was so quiet Zo could hear the bugs swirling overhead.

Leconte pulled the toothpick from his mouth. "You're the swim instructor from Taino Beach."

Meeting the doctor's gaze, Zo was struck with the same jolt he felt when he saw a shark while diving for pearls—he was out of his depth.

"*Rete la,*" Leconte continued. "Stay a minute. I may have something for you after all." Half turning, he told Claude, "*Al cheche sak la.* Go and get the bag."

When it was just the two of them, Zo and Leconte, standing on the porch under the ornate lighting, the doctor grew conspiratorial. "We both know you're not here for your wages," he said.

It was the closest they had ever been before, and Zo couldn't help but see Anaya in her father's face. It was his mouth, identical in shape and even color, a shade of ripe eggplant. Except where Anaya's mouth had seemed so mobile, capable of doing tricks in her face, Vincent Leconte's mouth was hard and fixed as stone.

"It's true," Zo said. "I've come to talk about Anaya." Her name felt odd in his mouth, like a foreign word he was speaking for the first time. As soon as he spoke it he wished he could reach out, grab it, and put it back in again.

The doctor's eyes were clear and white, his face taut with emotion. "You have a lot of nerve coming to my house, talking to me about my own daughter as if I didn't know her."

"I have done everything backward," Zo started. "I should have come to you first. I know I'm not what you would have wanted. I'm not rich. But I have worked hard all my life. I am honest and dependable."

"Those are qualities one looks for in a donkey," Leconte said, "not a man."

"I was raised in the cane to fight and work," Zo continued. "And that is what I set about doing. I cut cane and fought for dollars behind the gas station of Grande Anse. I won't defend that kind of life to you for the same reason a fish doesn't defend itself for swimming the sea. It was all I knew. And I would have gone on living that way if I hadn't met her." Anaya was between them as palpably as the scent of bougainvillea in the potted planters. "After I met her everything changed. I knew I couldn't go on living that kind of life. She made me see that I wasn't just here to work for my food. I was here for much more than that. For the same reason as the rich men in Pétion-Ville and New York City."

The doctor hadn't expected Zo's monologue and was put off by his frank display of honesty. "What reason is that?"

"To have a family," Zo said. "To make my children into something better than what I have been."

"And what have you been?"

"They told me when I was young"—Zo raised his face—"that I was the poorest man in the Western world."

"Just tell me this, *travayè*." Leconte was tall as Zo and as heavy, but his shoulders were shapeless under the fabric of his shirt. "How do you expect to care for my daughter and this family of yours on the dollar and sixty cents American you make each day?"

"Two hundred *gourdes*."

"Two hundred *gourdes* wouldn't buy you a gallon of gasoline in Port-au-Prince," Leconte said. "It wouldn't buy a cup of coffee in Brooklyn! Did you think I wouldn't find out? That I don't know what goes on in my own house?"

Claude returned from his errand with the kind of plastic bag that can be purchased for a penny in the marketplace. Zo knew what was inside without having to look, but he took the bag and looked anyway. There were the battered, greasy sandals, like the last vestige of his pride. He heard the doctor from a great remove.

"I'm going to keep you on because you work hard and because Paul says you're one of the best. But one more infraction, no matter how small, and you're gone." He folded his arms across his chest and regarded Zo from the high vantage of a life well lived. "No doubt they are fine arms for lifting block and hitting people," he said, "but that won't feed my daughter. It won't provide her the kind of life she's used to, the kind of life she deserves. Running water. Electric lights. My advice to you is to go find a girl who's used to squalor," he said, shutting the door, "and give her more of the same."

· Book Two ·

7

ZO GOT TO THE WHARF after midnight. An open boat from Grande Cayemite had come in late to avoid the harbormaster's tariff and they were unloading a week's worth of salt fish alongside. Zo sat under the only working light on the wharf and waited for Medsen Fèy, who appeared a little later with a hand wagon, accompanied by the rattling of glass bottles.

"Forty-four liters of rum," he explained when he arrived.

Zo tossed a cynical spit at the water. "I went to speak with her father," he said.

"What for? Her hand in marriage?"

"For money he owes, on work completed."

"My poor boy." Medsen Fèy slapped his hands together and lowered his gaze. "You may be honest, but you're no diplomat."

The rum bottles had been wrapped in newsprint and packed in old fruit crates. "I've been obliged to nail the boxes shut," Medsen Fèy explained. "Otherwise the crew drinks half my stock in transport." He pried a case open and took out a bottle. "I get diminished returns depending on the duration of their doldrums."

Zo took a long drink of clear rum to calm his nerves. Then he walked to the end of the dock, took his battered sandals from the bag, and cast them into the water. The September sea steamed under the night sky, and he could hear the eerie chugging of an outboard motor long before he could see a boat.

"That'll be the *Rekin II*," Fèy said. "I'd know that engine anywhere."

Zo peered out at the fog. "What happened to the *Rekin I*?" he asked.

"That's a sore subject, and I advise you to stay clear of it," Fèy warned. "Boston's as good a seaman as any. Better than most." Fèy took a small flashlight from the waistband of his pants and flashed it on and off. "But he had a run of bad luck once, and he's temperamental about it."

The boat appeared out of the fog. It was a traditional transport dory in the spirit of West Indian banana boats, with a wedged bottom and sheer gunwales. The twin outboard motors were pulled from the water and the sails were stepped forward and furled. The mast was cut from a single tree. One of the crewmen tossed the lanyard ashore, and Zo, trying to make an impression, walked the vessel into the pilings.

Close up under the light, it looked too old to be afloat. The paint was peeling and it's taffrail had broken amidships. One of the sailors was caulking the deck, driving plugs of red putty between the planks. The rigging was handmade, and the rotten ropes hung from the crosstrees. But the pilothouse was worst of all.

"It looks like it's off a sunken ship," Zo said.

It was covered with barnacles, and there were no running lights or radio antennae.

"It is," Fèy answered. "Boston had it salvaged from a tugboat scuttled off Les Cayes. There he is now."

The captain stepped out of his salvaged pilothouse. With his sunburned complexion and salt-colored beard, Boston looked like a typical sailor of the Haitian coast. He was barefoot, wearing shorts and a windbreaker that hung open over his wide stomach.

He shouted a series of commands as he approached the port rails, already haggling over shipping costs with Medsen Fèy. "You may brew one of the finest *klerens* in the southwest," he admitted, "but you don't know a damn about the hazards of shipping."

One of Boston's crewmen vaulted onto the dock to board the merchandise and Medsen Fèy put Zo forward, introducing him as the greatest lover in the Antilles.

Boston regarded Zo as if he were goods for transport. "Can he work?" he asked.

"All he knows is work," Fèy said, clapping a hand on Zo's shoulder. "He can't do anything else."

"That's good," Boston said, "because there are no passengers aboard the *Rekin II*. We run like privateers, under no flag but the flag of commerce."

"The flag of profit," a crewman seconded from the boat.

"You have any questions?" Boston asked.

"Just one," Zo said, leaning across the water. "What happened to the *Rekin I*?"

A quiet descended on the wharf. The crewmen quit bustling on deck and the man caulking the waterlogged planks looked up from his oakum. Boston dropped his foot from the gunwale and straightened up. He took the hat off his head and wiped his brow and then began a low belly laugh that shook the whole vessel underneath him.

"That's the right question!" He slapped the meat of his gut. "The only thing worth knowing of your new captain is what happened to his old ship!" He reached out to shake Zo's hand across the water. "Allow me to welcome you aboard the *Rekin II*," he said, "with third-class service continuing on to Corail, Pestel, Miragoâne, and Pòtoprens." The captain reeked of fish and gasoline. His hand was hard from tugging line all his life. "You'll ship as an able seaman, first class," he told Zo, still holding his hand. "That means you do what I tell you to do. You have been in a boat before, haven't you?"

Zo had been in the canoes handmade by the coastal fishermen

from a single tree trunk. He had ridden in Daniello's fishing sloop while the fisherman puttered around the bay with his lines. But he had never ridden in a long-distance trawler. And though he knew how to swim and was comfortable among the reefs and mangroves near shore, he had never been so far at sea he couldn't see the shore.

"I've been on plenty of boats," he said.

He took his shovel and pack and passed them across the gunwale. Boston laughed again, saying only a true landsman would bring his shovel with him on a boat.

"Unless you use it like an oar," Medsen Fèy offered.

Zo proved himself a poor sailor. Boston told him to sit back at the sternpost and vomit away from the ship. They tacked into the bay and unfurled sails under heavy fog. "Loose sails!" Boston called. "One point off the wind." The *Rekin II* was rigged like a sloop, except that the main mast was farther aft, so that several headsails could be rigged at once. The crew went expertly about the hawsers, and the jib slid up the stay on oiled hanks. The sails bellied out above them, and Zo saw that they'd been mended with rice sacks and bedsheets and, in one instance, a pair of Levi's jeans.

When Zo could stand it, a crewman called Solomon came forward to give him a tour of the ship. There wasn't much to see. The main deck ran from stem to stern. An uncovered hatchway opened into the cargo hold amidship. Solomon showed Zo the boat chest. There was an ax, a hammer, a flare, a chisel, a boat caulking set, brace bits, a marlinspike, lead sheet, yarn, and lamp wick.

Boston had no bridge and steered blind from behind his mast, on the stern quarterdeck. To get a good view of the waters ahead he climbed into the crosstrees or sent one of his sailors up to look for him. There was no wheel or wheelhouse. Instead, the boat was directed by a long wooden tiller painted red and blue. The galley was in the forecastle, where a cut oil drum served as a barbecue.

The cargo was piled five feet high against and above the gunwales, mostly bags of charcoal bound for the cook fires of Port-au-Prince. There were no lifeboats and no life jackets. There were three hammocks strung up between the pilothouse and the mainmast. A man was sleeping in one of them and Solomon slapped his feet.

"This is Colibri," he said. "You'll usually find him here."

"This hammock is my post." Colibri saluted.

"Colibri doesn't believe in hard work."

"Colibri believes in the lotto," Colibri said.

"He doesn't know a thing about sailing or the sea."

"I hate the goddamned sea," Colibri confirmed.

"But he can fix anything that runs on gasoline," Solomon said, "so we keep him aboard."

They sat in the boat with their backs against the merchandise and lit cigarettes and opened a bottle of *kleren* and drank. The rum was hot and clarifying in the dark. They floated east on smooth seas, taking turns at the stern sheets or the outboard motor. The moon was far behind them and reaching for the west when Boston came out of the pilothouse smoking his pipe.

"The Indians could find their way from Curaçao to Florida with nothing more than the moon for navigation." He pointed with his pipe stem. "But most modern sailors can't make passage down a river without radar and depth charts."

Zo asked Boston how he had earned his nickname, and the captain told him the story of his sea life. "As a boy, I'd go about the local waters in a leaky canoe. But the first time I really went to sea was with my uncle, Despero Metelus," he said. "Despero made a fortune running guns and drugs from Jamaica, but it was dangerous work, and he was lucky to get out with his life," Boston said.

He took a long draw from his pipe and told Zo how Uncle Despero bought his own deep-sea trawler. "A beautiful ship, with real diesel engines and a proper wheelhouse, a covered deck and galley. That was the *Rekin I*," he said. "The only thing she had in common with this heap," he added, stomping the deck, "was the name."

"What happened to the *Rekin I*?" Zo asked.

"Despero retired and sold it to me."

It seemed as if Boston would leave it at that. He tore a piece from a fresh tobacco leaf, packed the plug into his pipe, lit it, and blew a long stream of sweet smoke. "It was 1985," he said, "the height of the boatlift. I thought I could make two trips in one season. Craft were shipping from Port-de-Paix, and I left for the second voyage in June. That was my first mistake. It was early in the year for a hurricane, but it wasn't impossible. I knew that. But I had the idea that I could get the better of the easterly trades by sailing against Cuba."

He drew a map in the air with his pipe stem, leaving a trail of tobacco smoke to mark the ephemeral coastlines.

"Here is the northernmost port of Haiti." He pointed. "And here is the coast of Cuba. Normally, a captain will make for the Bahamas and cut toward Florida from the east." He slid the pipe across his face. "But I thought I could fool the U.S. Coast Guard and come up from Varadero, to the south."

He sucked his pipe and the tobacco lit his eyes from underneath. "She was doomed from the start," he said. "A cold front blew up from Venezuela and, fool that I was, I thought it was a good omen."

"It wasn't?" Zo asked.

"We were being chased by Hurricane Bob," Boston said. "Sixty-knot winds. Winds that could blow the hairs from your head. It caught us in open water between Cuba and the Florida Keys. We tied ourselves to the mast." He told Zo that the *Rekin* fought gallantly for sixteen hours, until her engines died. "She was a good ship," he said, looking off into the distance as if he were conjuring the old craft from thin air. "She outran the storm for two days, but it was a weeklong blow. Both engines burned out in high seas and the main mast was cracked. She carried us through the storm, but now we were at the mercy of the open ocean. We had nothing but the forward jib and a cracked rudder to steer with."

"What did you do?"

Boston took a long pull off his pipe and the sweet smoke rose over his face and blew behind him into the sea. "The only thing we could do," he said. "We drifted. So far to the east I was afraid we'd pass Great Abaco and float into the Atlantic to be lost for good. But we were saved by a pleasure cruiser in the Keys. A Bahamian yacht hitched us to it and tugged us to Freeport."

There was a long silence.

"I thought maybe you had sailed all the way to Boston," Zo said.

The captain reached out over the gunwale and knocked his burning pipe tobacco into the sea. A small smoke went up from the water. "When the customs officer in Freeport asked us what our port of call was to have been, this kid who'd been on board began yelling 'Boston!' He had family there, and it was probably the only place he knew of outside the village he'd come from. That made the Bahamian port authorities laugh. They impounded my boat and called me Boston."

Zo lay back against the bags of charcoal while they cut through water and across the tree line of his entire life. He could see the small rivers rushing down out of the hills in the moonlight and the wide gravel fans in the beaches where the rivers emptied into the sea.

In the morning, they voyaged through a country of hard white cliffs under clear sunshine. The water sparkled to thirty feet. Fires burned on Grande Cayemite, and Pestel sat clean and bright in its hills. They coasted by harbors that were nothing more than running boards put out to sea like pirate planks. There were ruined cement pads half submerged, like the wreckage of ancient ports of call. Others were pebbled beaches left unimproved since the day of creation where naked children swam in the surf. They drifted by a graveled sandbank under troubled afternoon skies, and a hard, cool wind blew against them out of the southwest. Boston ordered the sails be placed against it, and Solomon went expertly about the hawsers.

In the light of day Zo saw that the crewmen looked like stowaways on their own ship. They went about barefoot, in boxer shorts and windbreakers. But their teeth were hard and white, like pearls in their mouths, and they were ruddy and good-humored. The captain's beard was loose and shapeless, like shrubs on a hillside, springing from his chin in every direction.

Boston took them to a cove in the sheltered Bay of Baradères, where Solomon stripped naked and dove into the turquoise water. Zo undressed and swam alongside him. So clear was the water that he could see the black shadows of their cocks swinging on the sandy bottom. A school of yellow triggerfish fed under the boat. Zo swam to the mangrove coast and walked in the shallow water. Inland of the other trees, on a small promontory above the sea, he found a white mangrove blazing with new flowers pure as snow. He picked four of the bell-shaped blooms, thinking that someday, when he saw her again, he'd give them to Anaya.

They drifted into the south channel on heavy seas, running between the island of Gonâve and the peninsula. Small fishing boats plied the coastal waters and a red tanker turned ponderously under the horizon. In the evening, they dropped anchor in a marsh of mangroves and calm water. Boston's anchor was four car batteries wired together and strung from chain-link. Solomon couldn't lift the thing alone, so Zo heaved it up off the deck and tossed it over the gunwale like a shot-putter. They waited for the chain to run out, drifting for a long time in the quiet without their engines.

"There's nothing but sand down there," Boston explained drowsily. "It takes time for the anchor to catch."

A laziness settled over the estuary as the sailors readied themselves for bed. A proud bittern crossed the foredeck looking like the blue grandfather of the mangrove coast. Boston, Solomon, and Zo took to the hammocks while Colibri reluctantly took first watch, complaining all the time that Boston was the only captain in the Antilles who required any watch at all.

"You're not an admiral in the Haitian navy," he grumbled.

Nights are short at sea, and they were soon under sail again in an endless blue predawn. They stopped in the port of Léogâne to take on a load of jarred honey, a few cases of late-season mangoes, and a dozen bags of charcoal. They bought six beers to be shared among them and drank the first one ice cold out on the water, every one of them feeling like a ship's captain out on the waves, free from the curses and steaming poverty of the island.

Zo was lovesick in the prow. He talked of nothing but the girl and how he wouldn't make the same mistake twice. Last time, he'd made an altogether unfavorable impression, dressed in his work clothes, complaining about fevers. This time, he imagined himself like a paramour from an older age, wearing a new shirt, a wristwatch, and a splash of cologne.

They came abreast of Carrefour in the afternoon heat and saw the tumbled chaos of the capital in the distance under the colorless sky. The pink apartments and yellow restaurants and white churches of Port-au-Prince smoldered in the hard heat. Grand trash fires burned along the coast and the hills were obscured in the haze. Zo took Anaya's letter from his pocket and read it for the hundredth time, trying to determine the cut of the nursing school from the jumbled skyline.

He imagined their future in the city. A house with a wooden door, a roof to hold against the rain, a garden of corn and Congo peas. They wouldn't need running water because he would cart her buckets fresh from the creek. Zo thought of the kerosene lamp smoking in the dark and the body of his lover in the shuddering light. They wouldn't need gas or electricity and so could live for almost nothing at all. He imagined them waking late on Sundays in the winter, Anaya in his arms as if they were in paradise instead of poverty.

In all his fantasies before these Zo had remained poor. Even in his wildest dreams he couldn't entertain the possibility of attaining wealth. But now he saw himself in a painted house, with a gallery overlooking the sea. "I know how it works in Pòtoprens," Zo said to the sailors. "The poor stay in the hot swamps down below, where the crocodiles used to live. And the rich"—he smiled and cast his eyes on the heights—"they live in the clean ocean breezes. The higher you are, the richer you are."

"So I assume you'll be staying in the swamps," Colibri said.

"I'll be up there." Zo pointed at the mountains. "A small place in the hills."

"That's the fucking HASCO factory dump." Colibri laughed. "You'll sleep in seagull shit."

"Neither of you know a thing," Boston interrupted. "You're pointing at Mòn Nwa."

That was Zo's first look at Black Mountain, but he wasn't listening anymore to either of them. He dragged his eyes across the coast and the ragged skyline and tried to pick her building from among all the others.

"That's where she goes to school during the day," he said.

It was a tall cement block, and he counted three stories.

"At the penitentiary?" Colibri laughed. "What was her crime, fooling around with you?"

Boston looked up from his inventory and regarded the laborer in his prow. Zo was holding the forward mast with one hand, to keep his balance, and in the other he held the girl's unfolded letter, consulting it as frequently as the navigator of a dangerous and unknown coast consults his depth charts.

"When's the last time you were in Port-au-Prince?" Boston asked him. "Ay, that's right, you've never been before. Well, zanmi m, it would take you three hours to get from there"—he pointed downtown—"to your little castle in Black Mountain."

Zo looked on that city like the first conquistadores looked upon the New World. To sack it, to burn it, to destroy every last soul, would be nothing in pursuit of the treasure and the dream.

There were ports west of the city at Kafou and Mariani, and there was the deepwater cargo harbor administered by the government. But Boston bypassed them all to disembark as always at Waf Jérémie, the illegal marina off of Cité Soleil, really just a collection of rotting flotsam caught up on a spit of land between the airport and the seaport. But the tariffs were reasonable and the stevedores cheap.

Colibri and Solomon offered their farewells from the ship's deck, but Boston followed Zo onshore.

"What do you have in your pockets?" the captain asked.

Zo pulled a sorrowful wad from his work pants.

"From what you've said, the girl you're after expects certain comforts." Boston dug into his torn shorts, took out a roll of bills, and peeled off two thousand *gourdes*.

On board the *Rekin,* Colibri shook his head. "It doesn't matter what you give to this fool, Captain," he shouted. "Even Medsen Fèy called him a hopeless case."

"No, Colibri. Fèy called him a hopeless romantic, there's a difference." He turned back to Zo. "You know how to work," he said, "and that's as much as any man can say. Go and get yourself a job, put some food in your stomach. Don't be too much in love that you can't tell when it's raining."

Zo left the wharves and started up through the bustling capital. It was hot and bright in the afternoon, and he wished for the tranquility of the sea. Traffic was stalled on Boulevard Harry Truman, and he made his way between the bumpers of stalled *taptaps* and transport trucks. He went through the lowland markets and up the broken roadways into the hills. Boston was right—it was a long walk to that place in the hills Zo had chosen to homestead, the community of Black Mountain.

Zo took the whole thing on foot with nothing but a bag of clothes and a box of soap and the round-point shovel Boss Paul had given him out of the construction stock. The smoothing trowel and hard hat were tied to the outside of his pack. At every crossroad he asked how to get to Mòn Nwa, and they told him up, pointing higher and higher into the hills. He walked to Kenscoff Road and stood under a stand of Caribbean pine in the evening mist. When he asked if it was Mòn Nwa, a woman finally pointed back down.

"You've gone too far," she said.

8

Judge Desmond Tessier lived below Pétion-Ville proper, in the leafy suburb of Juvenat. He was an amateur botanist of tropical plants and well-known for his exceptional garden. Besides the familiar spreading mango and breadfruit trees, Tessier kept fruiting Georgia peaches, three varieties of avocado, and a flowering cashew. He had imported ornamental shrubs from Brazil and Venezuela, and there was a stand of rare Caribbean pine he'd transplanted from the heights of Kenscoff.

A long brick drive wound through the tropical woodland to the house itself, which the family liked to call Kay Jardin, or Garden House. A square villa with a flat cement roof and a wide front porch, Garden House backed up against a steep ravine and had views all the way to Gros-Morne.

Judge Tessier knew about Zo and Anaya before Zo ever came to the capital. Dr. Leconte had called ahead to say he was sending his daughter to him not so much to complete her studies at the university there as to get her removed from some kind of badness rooting at the coast.

"Is there malaria?" the judge asked.

"No," Leconte said.

"Typhoid?"

"No."

"You talk of it like some kind of pestilence."

"It's worse," Leconte insisted. "A worker here has . . . Imagine your own daughter . . ." He couldn't find a way to say it. "I caught them together in my own house. But I couldn't just confront her then. No. I gathered evidence. That is how it is with girls these days, Desmond. You must come at them with a case already prepared. Convict them before you begin."

"What kind of case did you bring?"

"Airtight," Leconte said. "My man Claude saw them on the beach, wrapped up in the same towel. He claimed to be giving her swimming lessons."

"What did you do?"

"Offered to find her a new instructor."

Tessier laughed.

"I asked her to stop seeing him and thought that was the end of it. Then I found his sandals."

"His sandals?"

"After all their painstaking secrecy, the *bourik* left his sandals at my house. I had him then, believe me. And I had her, too."

"How did she take it?"

"That's the thing with these girls. She does something wrong and somehow I'm the one who ends up making concessions."

"What sort of concessions?"

"She practically had me giving him a raise."

"For the swimming lessons?"

Leconte sighed. "The man was working for me, Desmond. For the Department of Public Health. A laborer on our new clinic."

"What sort is he?" Tessier asked.

"As a laborer, you couldn't find a better specimen. A hard worker, with arms like *kalbas* gourds. But as a boyfriend for my

daughter?" Leconte had to think. "There are womanizers, revolu-
tionaries, gangsters. These things can threaten your peace, Desmond. But a man like this, with nothing to lose?"

He made a sound through his teeth and left it at that. Then he
told Tessier how he'd arranged for Anaya to finish her schooling
in Port-au-Prince.

"A couple of phone calls to the dean, a letter of recommenda-
tion from Dady Malebranche. Her grades spoke for themselves.
I've asked them to provide me with her schedule," he said, "and
will forward it to you as soon as I have it."

Soon after that conversation, which ended in Leconte's admonition that his daughter was capable of incredible duplicity, Anaya
arrived at the judge's house with all of her things.

She came in the evening. It was August and the overripe mangoes
were rotting on the lawn. The judge and his wife, Marie Michelin;
their daughter, Nadine; and the cook called Atamise all came out
to the veranda when Leconte's Land Rover pulled up alongside
the house. They heard Anaya and the driver arguing. A moment
later, the chauffeur appeared around the back of the car with the
suitcases. "Demwazèl wishes to see Miss Nadine first," he said,
carrying the bags into the house.

Nadine went down to the car, opened the back door, and
climbed in. She was two years younger than Anaya and enthralled
by what she saw as her older cousin's recklessness in the name of
love. She made her decision before Anaya even finished the story
about Zo and André.

"Forget them both," she said. "One is poor, and the other is
boring."

"To be poor is not the worst thing you can say about a man,"
Anaya said.

"What's worse?"

Anaya put her hand on her cousin's knee. "That he doesn't

mean what he says." She took Zo's letter from her bag and showed it to her cousin. "I cured his fevers with chloroquine," she said.

Nadine read the letter and then asked Anaya about the sex. Anaya fell back on the seat, threw her arm over her eyes, and bit her lip. Zo was ferocious and docile at the same time, she said. Making love to him was like taming a lion. Moving her arm and looking her cousin in the eye, she told Nadine what she had only come to understand during the eleven-hour drive from Jérémie to Port-au-Prince.

"I'm in love with him," she said.

It was the first time she said it aloud. The only other person she'd ever loved with such fierce unreasonableness before had been her mother. And then Roselyn's death had fortified her, making her impervious to easy loving, so that ever afterward she seemed impossible to reach. Her father most of all had battered himself against that fierce exterior for years without success, in a decade-long siege to enter her affections. It was Zo who had scaled those walls and found some egress at the windows. Who had established, by fervor and revelation, that very sentiment Anaya had attempted to hold off by reason and calculation. What she felt was the first yearning of her life. Zo's embrace was a country that she missed, a country she belonged to, and this new life in Port-au-Prince felt a lot like waiting.

Ever since Leconte had first called to say that Anaya was coming to stay with them in Juvenat, Desmond Tessier had been prepared to take his niece in his arms. She was the only daughter of his youngest sister and had always had a special place in his heart. But when she climbed out of the car, something about the way she stood there, nonchalant and aggressive at the same time, the very same way his sister Roselyn had looked at that age, dissuaded him from trying. He put his hands in his pockets and walked down to meet them in the gravel drive.

"What were you girls laughing about?" he asked.

III

Nadine turned to her cousin. "Didn't I tell you?" she said. "He's the most annoying man in Port-au-Prince. He absolutely must know everything."

"It's the bad habit of an investigating magistrate," Tessier said, but they weren't listening to him any longer.

Anaya had gone up to the veranda and taken her aunt in her arms. Marie Michelin was a petite woman with a heart-shaped face—her chin ended in a point and gave her, even at fifty-five, a girlish appearance. Marie was so short she had to stand on her toes to talk in her niece's ear.

"I hope you're going to stay with us for a while," she said.

Anaya's arrival was like a holiday. Atamise cooked her favorite street food, a salt fish patty served with lime sauce, and Anaya kissed the cook on both cheeks. Tessier offered her a drink and Anaya asked for rum with ice.

Nadine asked for one with lime and soda water.

"What do you know about rum and soda water?" Marie Michelin asked. "Anaya can have whatever she likes. You'll drink grapefruit juice."

Anaya sat on the cream-colored leather sofa with impeccable posture, her legs crossed at the knee, sipping rum from a clear glass. Tessier was shocked at how much she looked like her mother and said so. Anaya asked if her mother had been the kind of daughter who often disappointed her father and Marie Michelin said of course.

"It was impossible not to disappoint Meletus Tessier," she said. "The man was a tyrant. Tell her what happened when Roselyn decided to go into nursing."

Desmond was drinking a cold Prestige from the bottle. "She applied to school without telling any of us and showed up to dinner one night with the acceptance letter in her hand."

"What happened?" Nadine asked.

"It was an awful scene," he said. "Papa threatened to cut her off financially."

"It was much worse than that," Marie Michelin said. "And I

should know. Desmond and I had just been married, and were living at his father's house. Meletus told Roselyn that she'd end up destitute and sick with tuberculosis. He promised not to lend her a dime." She gave her husband an accusatory look. "Shouldn't they know what kind of man he was?"

They ate a half plate of patties. Marie Michelin went to bed. Anaya drank another rum and then a glass of water at Tessier's request. He thought she'd want to get settled before starting school, but it was just the opposite. The semester had already begun, and she didn't want to fall behind.

The night ended with the girls recalling the trip they'd taken to see Citadelle Laferrière, the revolutionary fortress in the north of the country. It was summertime, and the Leconte and Tessier families had traveled together from Port-au-Prince, visiting the beach at Labadie and staying at a hotel in Milot. In the morning, they'd gone to visit the citadel at the top of the mountain. The girls rode on a donkey whose name they couldn't remember.

"You were six and eight years old, and rode together in the same saddle," Tessier said. "The donkey's name was Sheba." He left them with a warning to get some sleep, and the two girls finally went up to Nadine's room and lay side by side in the bed.

"How many times have we begged your father to let you come?" Nadine said, kissing her cousin's forehead. "And here you are at last."

Nadine told Anaya about the apartment downtown, where she'd spent most of the last school year, living with one of her classmates. It had been the best year of her life. It was close to the academy, and there was a boy who came to visit her there after school. But when her classmate's visa to the United States finally came through and she left for New York, Desmond Tessier forced her to come home.

"He couldn't bear the idea of my living in that apartment alone," she said. "But now you're here." Nadine saw her cousin's arrival as the opportunity she'd been looking for, a way for her to get back to her independent life. "My father wants me to a have a roommate, someone he trusts. We'll be living on Rue Monseigneur Guilloux by the end of the week," she promised.

Judge Tessier came down to breakfast the next morning wearing cream slacks and a peach-colored shirt. Both girls were already at the table and they laughed as soon as they saw him.

"I call the style 'Nouveau Caribbean,'" Nadine said.

"She means it as an insult," Tessier said, taking his seat at the table, "but I rather like it. The fact is I'm the best-dressed judge at the Palace of Justice."

"That isn't saying much." Nadine laughed. "Didn't I tell you he looked like a sorbet?"

They were served thin omelets with slices of grapefruit and hot coffee.

Nadine put half the omelet in her mouth. "We better hurry," she said. "It's a long commute and the traffic is awful."

After breakfast, they climbed into the car and the driver took Avenue Lamartinière straight down the mountain. Nadine complained about the traffic jam at Avenue Henri Christophe. She cursed the traffic light at Gaou Guinou and Delmas 33. "It's the only traffic light in the whole city," she said, "and we absolutely must find it red every single morning." She complained about potholes, bicyclists, mototaxis, and vendors selling cornbread.

"You're worse than a fussy magistrate," Tessier said, turning to face the girls from the front seat. "And your point is well made. It is a long commute to make each day."

"Twice a day," Nadine corrected. "One must return, after all."

Nadine went to school at the Carrefour-Feuilles Wesleyan Christian School. They dropped her off on Rue Becassines behind the St. Gerard Cathedral. She asked her father once more to let Anaya stay with her at the apartment, blew them both kisses, and started toward class.

Tessier pulled his glasses forward over his nose and rubbed his eyes. "You see what I have to put up with?" he said. "Ever since she heard you were coming, she's talked of nothing but that apartment." Tessier slid the glasses back over his eyes and looked at his niece. "I can see she's already gotten to you and you've fallen right into her trap. Just like her mother. I don't see what's so great about that apartment. The bedrooms are small; the air conditioner is broken. You would both be much more comfortable with Marie Michelin and me in Juvenat."

He offered a smile. "But for now, I am just happy to have you with us. And I'm glad your father had the good sense to let you complete your schooling here in Port-au-Prince."

Anaya finally spoke. "This has nothing to do with Vincent Leconte's good sense," she said. "It's about his reputation. At the first sign of my doing something he doesn't approve of, he's sent me away like a *restavek* to stay with some relatives. Finishing school is only an excuse."

They hit a pothole and the driver shifted hard to the left. "God knows it isn't easy raising a daughter in this place," Tessier said. "Any man might make a mess of it, even with a wife to help. To do it alone?" He shook his head. "Your father has done about as good a job as could be expected, under the circumstances. You know he loves you, Anaya, more than anything. He just wants what's best for you. I'm convinced that the smallest, most insignificant sign from you will bring him tumbling into your arms."

"That's exactly it, Uncle," she said. "Imagine what you say is true: he wants me to come begging for his forgiveness. If I were to do it, just as you say, without willing to capitulate completely, it would only make him more bitter."

"You're not willing to give up the boy?"

"I shouldn't have to." Anaya shook her head. "All this time I thought I knew about malaria—the red blood cell, the protozoa, the chloroquine cure—but I never imagined the fevers or the hallucinatory dreams. He taught me what it really feels like to be sick. I must have distributed a thousand albendazole tabs without knowing what they tasted like! Don't you think that's odd, *tonton*? Here he was telling me they tasted like mints, and that he was so poor as a child he used to wait in line two times and savor them like candies."

Anaya had inadvertently ventured into the most delicate and convoluted regions of her feelings for Zo, where they resided alongside her love for Roselyn. Her mother had spent her first few years at St. Antoine Hospital with the traveling clinic—the nurses who voyaged by boat and donkey to deliver vaccines and anti-vermicidal treatments to vulnerable children. Anaya could not shake the conviction that somehow, twenty years ago, a young Roselyn had distributed those albendazole tabs to the little orphan Zo in Grande Anse, and she ventured this private thought to her uncle. "It's as if Mama is giving us her blessing from the afterlife," Anaya said.

"To what, exactly, does your father object?"

"Vincent doesn't like him because he is poor."

"Is that all? Well, it's an unfortunate fact that in this country, it is often a lack of money that best attests to a man's honesty," Tessier said. "I've certainly tried enough cases as a prosecuting magistrate to know what the faces of the real criminals look like. I'm afraid they are not often our masons and farmers."

"What's the point?"

"Only that it is sometimes difficult to know the true villain from the convenient one. It's often just a matter of perspective." He turned to look out the window. "There it is," he said, pointing. "Nadine's beloved apartment."

They had come out behind Stade Sylvio Cator, where the national soccer team played, heading down Rue Monseigneur Guilloux. It was a busy avenue, with merchants selling on both sides of the street. Tessier was pointing to a pink four-story building wedged between a Unibank with black glass windows on one side and a squat, drab apartment complex on the other.

"Which one is Nadine's?" she asked.

"Third floor, on the right," Tessier said.

Anaya saw the balcony with its filigreed ironwork.

Five days later, on September 2, the girls moved from the house in Juvenat to that apartment on Monseigneur Guilloux.

9

TONTON OZIAS disliked Zo as soon as the laborer appeared on Black Mountain with nothing but a shovel and a change of shirts. Zo found quick work with a clearing crew, and Ozias watched through his binoculars as they went about cutting drastic flats into his mountainside. "No doubt making way for more illegal shacks," the old man mumbled to himself. Then he counted every stroke as Zo murdered a young mango with one hundred measured whacks of a dull machete without rest. "If I don't give him something else to do, he'll chop down every last tree on the island."

The old man took his crutch down from the hook it hung on and made the journey around the hill to where Zo worked in the newest illegal development. "You there, *siklòn*," the old man said, calling him "cyclone." "What will it take to make you stop?"

Zo considered that proposition. "No one's ever asked me to stop before," he said. "I guess I would need steady work, at guaranteed wages."

So Ozias offered him both and a place to sleep. "Just to keep you off the trees," he said.

Ozias was wearing shorts, and Zo could see that he was an amputee. His right leg had been taken below the knee and he gestured with the stump when he spoke. Despite having only one foot, Ozias was an expert crutch handler and Zo had to hurry to keep up. He was amazed to see the old man pole-vault across a four-foot ravine and conquer a whole flight of stairs with two elegant maneuvers.

"Before it was a *bidonvil* and a refuge for the poor and criminal," O said. "Before you put your trash in my backyard and pissed in the stream we drink from, this place was a paradise. Caribbean pines taller than palm trees." He pointed down among the sloppy cinder block houses. "There, by that shack of children without a father, was a grove of sour orange and patches of wild manioc. Wood ibis and flamingos in the lowland. Wild grape winding up those fence posts and you couldn't stop it from growing. Now there are not enough trees in this forest to string up a hammock."

Ozias had been on Mòn Nwa a long time and he had a good thing going. His plot was prime real estate. Besides a view of the city and the bending coast, there was a lime and a mature avocado tree that gave huge fruits. Tomatoes grew rich on their vines under shade trees. Best of all, there were two separate houses on the property.

The smaller one was built forward on the slope, toward the sea. Ozias said he'd built it fifty years before to be his bachelor's palace. It was constructed in the traditional mountain style, with posts of local hardwoods and walls of *klis,* coconut palm leaves woven together and covered in light plaster. Because of the naturally red earth on Mòn Nwa, the plaster had a bright pink finish, and the gypsum flecks glowed in the afternoon sun. The only door opened toward the sea, and Ozias said he'd set it just so to cultivate the onshore breezes.

"You'll have them all summer," he said. Then he threw the shutters open and they considered the dim *kay.* It was twelve feet square, with dirt floors and an outdoor kitchen positioned at the side of the house so that the cook could watch the sea 1,800 feet below. Zo embraced the old man and told him it was everything he needed to start his life.

"What about the job?" Ozias asked. "You haven't even asked about wages."

"How are the wages?"

"Miserable," O said. "Unless you have true commitment. Then it depends entirely on you." Ozias told Zo that in the old days, when the American ships docked along Boulevard Harry Truman, he used to make a small fortune carting merchandise to market.

"You have a truck?"

"A truck needs gasoline, my boy. Where would I get the money for that?"

"A donkey?"

"You are looking at the greatest *brouetye* in Port-au-Prince," he said. "Before I was forced to retire, that is." Ozias shook his foreshortened right leg.

A *brouet* was the simplest form of ground transport, a flat wagon balanced on two truck tires. The *brouetye* was what they called the man who pulled the contraption by brute strength alone. Ozias referred to his work years as his "beast-of-burden days" and complained that all he'd ever gotten out of it were cataracts and the single stout calf of a weightlifter. He offered his remaining leg as evidence and waited for Zo to feel the contours of his muscle.

"How did you lose your foot?" Zo asked.

"In the worst way," O said. "Stuck it running a load of rotted *kokoye* across Canapé Vert. I didn't know it was so bad. Wrapped it in an old shirt but it stunk to high heaven. By the time I went to the clinic it was too late, I could see through to the bone. They took it at the charity hospital, and I woke in the ward for amputees." The old man clucked his tongue. "Losing it ended my career."

Though Ozias had spent all the days of his life laboring for others, besides the crutch given to him in exchange for his foot, the wooden *brouet* he'd dragged across the city for thirty years was the only thing he'd ever owned outright.

O's wagon had been salvaged and halved and rigged a dozen times. The only thing unchanged was the iron chassis that served as the frame. He'd retrieved it from the undercarriage of a wrecked Ford motor truck. The battered side rails were nailed in at their bases and closed in three sides of the cart. The floorboards were solid wood planks of various sizes and shapes that had been puzzled up and then drilled and grommeted with brass rings and woven together with metal tape. They were fixed onto the perpendicular truck axle with rusted bolts lifted off a cargo ship that had done a decade beached in the shallows.

The chassis was the jewel of the wagon, a single piece of soldered American steel that ran like an H-frame underneath the entire cart. The line of bolts was driven through the floorboards into the cross of the *H*, and this cross was extended to serve as the wheel axle. The wagon was six feet wide all through the carriage and sixteen feet long and had a floor space of ninety-six square feet. It was powered by one runner positioned at the front of the cart, who pulled the contraption by means of two long poles fitted in his armpits.

They set about negotiating a usage fee on O's cart. The old man suggested they do it by percent of daily wages and Zo agreed. He offered 10 and Ozias asked for 20. They agreed to the following terms: Zo would rent the cart at 20 percent for the first three months, 15 percent for the next three, and then 10 percent thereafter for as long as the arrangement lasted.

Ozias fitted Zo out with a few old pots and utensils, but the laborer never cooked. They ended up eating together like eternal bachelors in the old man's house or sitting in the yard between the two houses on plastic chairs that O took from his dining room table. At night after supper he and Zo would sit in the yard watching the city soften in the dark and the great long ships light up at anchor in the bay. They'd sip scalding coffee black from tin cups.

Ozias was fanatical about two things, his *brouet* and his coffee. He bought the green berries by the sack from Darleze, a broker with exclusive access to farms in the mountains behind Belle Anse, on the south coast. Ozias insisted it was the best coffee in the world. He wouldn't buy the berries from anyone else. He roasted the beans himself in an heirloom copper pot, just long enough for them to blacken and sweat. Zo's task was to crush the roasted beans with the bottom of an aluminum cup, pass the coarse grind through a section of window screen, and then crush it again. Only then did Ozias go about brewing his famous Ayisyèn Bleu, a coffee dark as spilled oil in the cup.

Ozias didn't believe in electronics, he hardly owned any. He claimed that the cold wind from a freezer caused cancer and cancer caused a slow death, and he knew that because his wife had died of it. That Madam Ti Klis had served cold drinks from a freezer for fifteen years was the sole proof he needed to condemn all electronics forever.

"They called her Mrs. Small Seed because she was so tiny," Ozias said of his wife. "Four feet tall and lighter than a twin bed." He separated his thumb and forefinger an inch. "But my God, you wouldn't want to fight her. No, sir." Ozias told him how Madam Ti Klis had become famous all over the mountain for arguing with the pastor while he was bathing, naked and covered in soapsuds.

Ozias and his wife had started their married life in the small house where Zo now lived. "But the roof leaked," O said. "Then there were termites in the *potos*. Madam Ti Klis wanted block, she wanted children. She thought that if we just built some rooms for them they'd arrive in pairs to take their places."

The newer house was just as O described it, built of cinder block and set close against the road. There were three rooms, but no children had ever come to claim them. A small addition at the front had served as Madam Ti Klis's drink shop. "She liked to be close to the road so that she could sell things from her living room window and gossip with Madam Zulu all afternoon," he said.

Madam Ti Klis was dead six years, but Ozias still consulted her regularly, insisting she made all the major decisions. "Who do you think it was gave me the idea to offer you work?" he asked. "And a place to stay? You think I want you around? No, sir. It was Madam Ti Klis."

Zo did the toil of a three-oxen team in the noontime heat, hauling mattresses and junk iron and the wares of illegal ships through the portside alleys and out to the satellite markets. They came to respect him at the crossroads and let him pass in the traffic. They marveled at him in the hills. His chest was an advertisement, the steadiness of his labor a proof, and the hugeness of his load on the incline a miracle.

Zo arrived in Port-au-Prince at the beginning of September and was running like a professional two weeks later. The *brouet* was the transport of choice for the poorest merchants, who couldn't afford the fuel premiums of the big *camions*. He picked up regular business from an importer who sold donated grain. He ran boxes of *pepe*, used clothes, through a back channel at customs. He contracted to cart the plantains of a Mòn Nwa farmer who was lucky with his plantation. Like this Zo grew the trade threefold in two weeks.

The nursing school hung over the skyline like his North Star. He learned to recognize it from all the other buildings in the city, yet avoided it with meticulous detours. Ozias finally asked Zo what he was afraid of.

"I don't want her first image of me in the city to be of me at the head of your wagon," Zo said, "sweating like an ox before his cart."

"A beast of burden has no shame."

"I don't want to be this girl's donkey," Zo said. "I want to make her my wife."

Ozias laughed so hard he spit the coffee from his mouth. "Tell me, *mon konpè*, because I'm dying to know." He wiped his lips with the back of his wrist. "What kind of man does she want to marry?"

Zo didn't answer.

"A rich one, no doubt," O said. "Even for you, that will be the work of two lifetimes."

"I'm not afraid of hard work."

"If work were so good, the rich would have grabbed it all up long ago," O said. It was his favorite proverb and he used it often.

Zo finished his coffee and tossed the grounds in the grass. "I thought we were going to plant your winter vegetables," he said. He went out into the nighttime garden and was already weeding the melons when Ozias appeared. The old man was carrying the woman's purse in which he preserved all the keepsakes of his life. He'd already shown Zo a set of his wife's old nightclothes, and Zo hoped he wouldn't do it again.

"I can see that you're serious," O said. "Look at this."

He handed Zo a red button that had been hollowed out to make a ring.

"That was Madam Ti Klis's engagement ring," Ozias explained. "Back then it was tradition for the prospective fiancé to make the ring himself. It showed commitment. I used a button because my older brother worked as a tailor and that's what I could find. But I've heard of them using raw cotton when nothing else could be had."

Zo tried to return it, but Ozias refused. "It's for you," he said. "To give to her."

It was Zo's turn to laugh. He got up from the melons. "*Granmoun*," he began, "you may know how to run a *brouet* cart, you very well may have been the greatest *brouetye* in Port-au-Prince before your accident. But you don't know a thing about modern women. There isn't a woman on earth who'd marry a man who gave her a ring of raw cotton or a red button."

Ozias dismissed Zo's protest with another proverb. "A woman is like a chicken," he said. "She sees a good kernel of corn and runs for it." He squatted in the vines, finally selecting a hard young melon the size of a *kenèp* fruit. "This is an old farmer's trick," he said. "A surefire cure for cold feet."

Ozias bored a hole into the skin with a corkscrew and drew out a cork-shaped piece of melon. He placed the ring very carefully at the bottom of the hole and replaced the cutaway plug. Then he caulked the cracks with gobs of brown shoe polish.

"You have eight weeks before she ripens," he said. "Ten if you like it terribly soft and sweet, which by the look of you might be your thing. But the melon will be ready whether you are or not."

"What do I do with it?" Zo asked.

Ozias looked at Zo with great sympathy. "My boy," he said, "you give her the melon. When she cuts it open, you have your proposal. You share the sweet meat and then your lives together."

But even two weeks after Ozias had planted that red button in the winter melon, Zo still felt he had nothing to show for himself. His back hurt and his boots were wearing thin. "Even if she consents to come with me," he told Ozias, "I have no place to bring her to."

"What's wrong with your house?"

"Dirt floors," Zo said.

"I've slept on dirt floors for fifty-seven years!"

But Zo couldn't disregard Vincent Leconte's counsel that Anaya wouldn't be happy without certain comforts, like running water, electricity, and maybe even a porcelain toilet. So he took nighttime work on a cement crew and asked to be paid in kind. For three nights' service he walked off with a half load of sand, two measures of clean rock from the river, and a bag of National cement.

He hardly slept that night and finally gave up trying. At three in the morning he stood in the seaside breeze laying out his materials: crushed rock, sand, cement mix, water. He recalled the proportions Boss Paul had used. Four shovelfuls of rock, two of sand, and one of the limestone mix. Then he poured the water and turned it with the blade until he had reached the desired consistency.

The floor was laid before the sun was up, and Ozias could only watch Zo pass the smoothing trowel over the rough edges, thinking of Anaya's toes. That morning Zo declared himself ready.

"What's changed?" O asked.

"The wagon, a regular income, a house with cement floors," Zo considered. "I finally have something to show for myself."

At last he went into the city to find her. Zo sat outside the university every day for a week, waiting for classes to end, dressed in his best jeans and a blue denim shirt with bright flowers embroidered up the chest. So beautiful was he in his best clothes, perfumed, waiting patiently for her to come to him, that one by one the sellers of sunglasses and shoes and yellow corncakes began to fall in love with his constancy. They made him little gifts of cakes and sausages.

Zo was in the capital six weeks before he found her, walking with some girls from her pharmacology class. He did not call her name but waded into the crowd of students and stood among them like a rock in the middle of a river. All the lady merchants had left their shops untended to line the street and see. Zo put himself square in Anaya's path and she came to him as sure as a leaf carried by a current is taken in the eddy. He couldn't believe he had forgotten the exquisite shape of her mouth or the high bracing of her neck. He held her two arms in his hands and she inclined her face.

"What took you so long?" she asked.

That first afternoon was a dream. They kissed with mouths like mingled fevers and hearts like hives of bees. The wind climbed down the cordillera smelling of coconut palms and the rich insect cane of the bottoms. The city was dazzling white against the bay.

"I've been waiting for you since August," she said.

"I wasn't sure you wanted me to come."

"Idiot," she said, taking his hand. "Didn't I tell you just where to find me?"

They walked to the wharves, where the Guyanese sailors gathered on their boat deck and made catcalls in their bad Creole. They asked Zo where he'd found such a girl, and Zo invited them down off the boat to fight. Of all Zo told her of his hardships without her, of his near-terminal heartbreak and his attempts to stem it by hard work, Anaya was most amazed that he had actually gone to her father's house and demanded his pay.

"What did he give you?"

"He sent me here to collect from you."

"I'm not responsible for my father's debts," she said. "Besides, what do I have to give you?"

Zo gave her a hard look. She passed her hand beneath his mouth and he kissed her knuckles.

"Is that enough?"

"Yes," he said. "But what else?"

She gave him her palm and he kissed it.

He looked up again and said, "What else?"

"You are hungry."

"Starving to death."

"Didn't they feed you in the schoolhouse?"

He pulled her into the shadow of a discarded shipping container and took her face in his hands. "Nothing worth eating," he said. They fell to kissing and, once begun, could not easily stop. The kiss went on and on until the pedestrians stopped in the street to see it and the cars slowed so the drivers could watch. Their hands fumbled between them and a warm wind climbed off the sea.

He bought them cold beer, and they shared the bottle while walking into the hills like a couple on the promenade. She held his arm and told him about her life in the capital. Without him the days had been pale and thin. They lacked immediacy.

"I felt like I was waiting," she said.

"For what?"

She turned and kissed him hard on the mouth, in the middle of the street.

When her feet began to ache Zo offered her his back, but she refused to ride him like that in public. They ended up taking a *taptap* through the streets to Pétion-Ville. Zo sat her in the circular park outside the police station and gave her the four small white flowers he'd taken from the mangrove coast at Baradères. He'd pressed them and had been carrying them in his coverall pocket all the weeks he'd been without her.

"Why didn't you come to me sooner?" she asked.

Zo lowered his face. The bones were broad across and his skin was bright with youth and red from the sun. He told her how badly he'd wanted to come that very first day, as soon as he disembarked from Boston's ship. "But I only had a few thousand *gourdes* in my pocket," he said. "And couldn't forget what your father said when I went to see him."

"What did he say?"

"That you're accustomed to certain comforts."

"Like what?"

"Electric lights. Running water. I don't have any of that, no. But I do have a little house on Black Mountain." He gestured behind him to the hill. "It's not much, Anaya, but it's ours, yours and mine."

Anaya admitted that she'd grown up with certain comforts. A car and driver, annual trips to the Dominican Republic. She asked him about the house.

"How many windows are there?"

"One window and one door," he said.

"How do you light it if there's no electricity?"

"Kerosene lamp," Zo said. "And candles."

"Where do you cook?" she asked. "What do you eat?"

Zo told her about the outdoor kitchen, with views as far as the island of Gonâve. "A good place to wait for your rice to boil." He told her about the old man's garden. "He's famous for his fat eggplants."

"What about furniture? Where do we eat once we've made the meal?"

Zo hesitated. He said there was no table, and only one chair. "But we often eat with the old man, and he has a proper dining set."

"You do sleep in a bed, though, don't you Zo?"

He looked crestfallen and admitted that he didn't have one.

"I'd give up a lot for you," she said. "Electric lights, running water. But you don't really expect me to sleep on the floor?"

Zo shook his head.

"I'll come to Mòn Nwa when you get a proper bed," she said. "With a frame and mattress."

Zo got up, saying he'd go and get one that very instant.

"No." She took his hand and pulled him down. "I want to pick it out."

Their love in the city began that way, with Anaya asking for a bed and Zo going to work to get one. He hauled his wagon in the streets all week with a work ethic akin to divine purpose, running heavy loads for long hours. He kept every *gourde* in a purple Crown Royal bag. When the weekend came he woke early to brew coffee from fresh roasted beans and served it to Uncle Ozias strong and black in his favorite cup.

O took the coffee and swung out of bed. He grabbed his crutch and ambled out to the yard, where he stood on his bare foot with the cup at his lip.

"What is it you want?" he asked.

"Money."

"What percentage?"

"All of it."

"One hundred percent?"

Zo kept quiet.

"Those aren't the terms of our deal," O said. "Was it a big take?"

"The biggest we ever had."

"You pulled longer hours because you knew you were keeping

it for yourself." The old man was not asking, and he took a sip of hot coffee. "What do you need it for? Or is that a stupid question? The girl, of course."

"For a bed frame," Zo said. "Anaya will sleep here if I have a real bed."

"*Toujou.*" The old man's eyes lit up. "You young men will do anything to fuck. Buy a bed or betray your brother."

"There are certain things you need before you can start your life with a woman," Zo said.

"Foolish men say things like that. Lonely men. I had a friend once who thought he needed a house before he had a girl. Then he needed furniture. Then cookware and a car. He died in a house full of crap long before he ever got to the girl. And what is it that you need so bad?"

"I told you. A bed. Five thousand in the bank would also be nice."

"Then forget about buying mattresses and go buy a shotgun. That's the only way for a poor Haitian like you to get that kind of money."

Ozias talked tough, but in the end he gave Zo the money.

Zo and Anaya ran their first errand as a couple that afternoon, going to buy the bed frame in the salvage market downtown. The vendors stood out in the street before their merchandise. She chose a wrought-iron bed frame painted white, and after long negotiations they paid market price at three hundred *gourdes*. Zo loaded the frame in the wagon and told Anaya to sit in the back, but she refused. She walked beside him through the streets of downtown in the waning afternoon with the sun tilted over the tropics.

He bought her a cold bottle of orange soda in lower Delmas and she drank it with a straw. When he invited her into the back of the wagon the second time, she accepted. She climbed up and sat on the bed frame, and Zo called her the Queen of the Caribbean. She

watched the work of his broad back and shoulders under the sun
as he went without rest up all the long kilometers of Avenue John
Brown. The people who saw him carting the girl and the bed up
the hill together shouted about the wild things a man will do for
love.

"Look at this," they called. "He takes the girl and the bed at the
same time!"

"You got to be prepared," a man called from under the bundled
cane on his back. He gave Zo the thumbs-up. "You got to take
your bed and your woman wherever you go."

A middle-aged shopkeeper told Zo to set the bed by the road
and go at it. "You're wasting time," he said.

An old woman walked with them for a while and spoke with
Anaya. "I think someone wants to make love with you," she said.
"He's working pretty hard for it, too. He takes you with your bed,
cheri doudou? If I were you, I'd keep that man."

They reached the house on Mòn Nwa and Anaya met Tonton
Ozias for the first time.

"Tell me, *ti fi*," O asked, "do you like winter melon?"

Anaya said that she did.

"It just so happens I have the sweetest in the city growing in
my garden." O pointed. "The kind of melon that will change your
life."

Zo started to take her away but Ozias asked if she would check
on his foot.

"Is something wrong with it?" she asked.

"It's the only one I have left," he grumbled. "And I have to be
extra careful."

"Don't worry about the old man," Zo said. "He has the skin of
an alligator."

He took her down the slope to the bare yard in front of the
house.

"Close your eyes," he said. Then he carried her over the threshold like a husband carries his new wife into their first house and

set her down again. He lit a kerosene lamp with a rich wick and she smelled the smoke. "Open your eyes."

Anaya saw the simple bachelor's house: the chair of woven straw, the bare gray walls, the shovel in the corner, the calendar on the wall.

"The floors are new," he said. "I poured them for you."

She kissed him in the dim room and said she loved it. She loved the house and the old man Uncle Ozias, and she loved Zo for what he had done. "I never knew a man could be so steadfast," she said.

They went outside and stood body to body in the last light with their bare feet in the grass. A wind rippled the hillside wildflowers and Zo nearly cried. He fell to his knees and held her body against his face. He kissed her stomach and her hips and thanked God. Then he put the bed frame in the middle of the room, lay the mattress atop it, and they made love for two hours and slept for two more in each other's arms like man and wife.

They woke to the old man clattering pots and pans, calling them to supper. He served them *sos pwa* in his own house. They drank a sweet juice of papaya, canned milk, and vanilla extract. Then Zo took her back on foot to the Pétion-Ville hills where, on weekends, Anaya stayed with her uncle Desmond Tessier, a judge who served on the highest court in Port-au-Prince.

The state health complex occupied an oblong block downtown. Avenue Lamartinière marked the northern end, and the angle of Rue Oswald Durand with Rue Monseigneur Guilloux marked the southern. Rue Saint-Honoré bisected the campus, running through a manicured park just beneath L'Hôpital Général— Lopital Jeneral.

Besides the main hospital, which was the largest referral clinic in the country, each of a dozen specialties had its own building on campus: orthopedics, pediatrics, the eye clinic, the office of dental surgery. The buildings were painted white and green, and with the pink bougainvillea vines winding up the walls and the well-kept Caribbean gardens, the campus was a refuge in the middle of the crowded city. The college of medicine, the nursing university, the only pharmacy college in the country, and a school for laboratory technicians were scattered among the other buildings.

Zo arranged his wagon routes so that they'd end downtown, near the nursing school. Then he'd haul his cart to the shady side of Oswald Durand and wait for her. One afternoon she found him lying in the back of the wagon and invited him to see her classrooms. Taking him in through Rue Saint-Honoré Gate, she pointed out a white building in a grove of *bwa mombin* trees. "That's the college," she said. "Every day, we walk from there to the hospital for our rotations." She took Zo's arm and led him down the path. "They have every specialty you could think of."

"What will you go into?"

Anaya told him that Haiti had the highest infant mortality rate in the Western Hemisphere. "I'd like to do something to change that, if I could." They were interrupted by a nursing student who told Anaya she could still catch Miss Cacquette in the maternity ward if she hurried.

Miss Cacquette was a legendary midwife. She was fifty-two years old and already an accomplished *fanmsaj* when the school hired her as an adjunct professor to teach an advanced topics course of her own design. It marked the culmination of a distinguished career that had begun decades earlier in the slums of Bicentennaire.

Cacquette was nominated for the teaching position by a faculty doctor who'd shadowed her in her busy midcity OB ward. He'd watched her deliver twelve newborns in one day, using the women's husbands and sisters as first and second assists. In his nominating remarks, the doctor wrote that Cacquette had "single-handedly raised the population of Bicentennaire 1 percent in a fortnight," and that he had watched with his own eyes as a clinically dead infant was brought back to life with an ice cube and the nurse's breath.

Cacquette taught an elective called Advanced Midwifery that was considered essential coursework for anyone wishing to pursue a career in labor and delivery. As a transfer student, Anaya needed her permission to enter the course. They hurried to the maternity ward, and Anaya left Zo outside with the expectant fathers. He watched them pacing on the lawn. When Anaya came out he rushed up and took her by the arm.

"They thought I was waiting for you to deliver our baby," he said.

"A boy or girl?" she asked

Zo thought about it. "A girl," he said. "So she can look just like you."

Anaya took his hand. "Miss Cacquette gave me a seat in her class this spring," she said. "We start in January."

When Anaya told her cousin that Zo had followed her to Port-au-Prince, Nadine insisted he come to the apartment so she could meet him herself. Anaya protested, claiming her father, or Claude Juste, or even Uncle Tessier, was watching, but that only made her cousin laugh.

"Desmond Tessier and Vincent Leconte are not exactly the National Police," she said.

Nadine arranged to meet Zo on a Wednesday afternoon in broad daylight. He was to come on a commission, hauling a minifridge that Nadine had just purchased from an appliance store on Rue Derencourt. "The best part is," Nadine said, "your boyfriend will get a job and my father will be the one paying him for it."

The next time Anaya saw Zo, which was in the afternoon following her classes, she presented him with the folded order form. "Do you want to see where I live?" she asked.

Zo ran the *frijidè* as ordered, from Derenoncourt, on Wednesday afternoon. He called up from the delivery entrance at the back of the building. Nadine came down dressed for the dance hall, wearing a miniskirt and a sleeveless top. She was thick all through and old enough to know men liked it. She hooked her fingers around the bars and talked to him through the gate.

"Do you like this kind of work?" she asked. "Delivering packages in the city?"

"It's a refrigerator," he said, "for Miss Nadine Tessier."

"I know what it is," she said, unlocking the gate. "I'm the one who ordered it."

Zo took the fridge from the cart, set it on his shoulder, and followed her up the stairs. She stopped on the landing and looked at him like she wanted him to speak, but it was Zo's habit to keep quiet on the job.

"I hope you know my father is a judge on the federal court of appeals," she said. "I'm only telling you so you know what you're getting into. If you hurt my cousin." She snapped her fingers.

The door of the apartment swung open before he could answer, and Zo straightened under his load. Anaya was in the doorway, wearing the white pants that drove him crazy. He forgot about the appliance and Nadine and her threat about the judge. Striding forward under the *frijidè*, with one arm around the appliance and the other around Anaya, he kissed her.

Nadine had arranged a dinner for them, ordering food from Épi d'Or, the American-style restaurant on the road to Pétion-Ville. It was the first time Zo had ever eaten pizza or seen a chicken nugget.

"Like this," Nadine demonstrated, dipping the chicken in mayonnaise and holding it to Zo's mouth.

The couple sat sipping Coke from the same straw, holding hands under the table.

"At first, I wasn't sure what to think of you," Nadine admitted. "After all, one hears so much about men who cheat and lie, but so little about ones who are loyal and decent."

"That's because loyal and decent men are so boring," Anaya said.

Zo and Anaya enjoyed the anonymity of Pòtoprens. There were three million people in the city and few proper addresses. Anaya pretended to be from an ordinary family in the provinces come to complete her schooling, and Zo pretended to be her upstanding boyfriend already beloved by the family. They met in broad daylight and kissed in the crossroads at noon.

They spent evenings strolling the streets as the shops were closing, stopping at the lighted bakeries to buy hotcakes. In November, when the harvest started, they bought young corn roasted over coals with the kernels hot and hard on their teeth. Zo took her dancing at the Mikamax Club and kissed her on the dance floor. One night, passing through the closed fruit market, Zo bought the last apple from a merchant's basket and they invented the game of apples. Anaya would peel the red flesh with her teeth, spit the peel into Zo's mouth, and eat the sweet part inside.

They visited the Cathédrale Notre-Dame de l'Assomption, famous for its pink buttressing. It was dark and cool inside after the Caribbean daylight, and the lovers sat in the pews half blind, whispering sweet things in each other's ears. Anaya made him wait for her at the altar while she walked the aisle slowly, pretending to be his bride. Zo waited for her with a feeling he'd never had before, something akin to fulfillment, and knew when she reached him that the time had come.

They went back to her apartment near Stade Sylvio Cator. The homes in that neighborhood were squat and uneven, so that Anaya's building, though only four stories tall, had unobstructed views all the way to the sea. The couple liked to sit on the roof when it was cool, especially after the rain, when the diesel had washed out of the sky and the air was clean.

A scattering of palms and a few streets were all that stood between them and the sparkling bay. They could make out the national highway in the dark by the lights passing up the coast. In the other direction was the high, dark mountain that sealed the city from the south. Zo told her it was Mòn Nwa, and he showed her how to find the exact spot they'd made their own by triangulating from the communications tower.

"Poor Ozias is up there right now," she said. "All by himself."

"Speaking of O," Zo said, "this is fresh from his garden."

It was a winter cantaloupe with smooth skin. Anaya asked if he'd been carting it with him all day, but Zo didn't answer. He gave her a knife to cut it with. She set the melon between them and drew the blade through. It halved neatly and fell open. There in the meat, like a mismade seed, was a red button. Zo dug it out with his fingers.

"I have loved you since I first saw you sipping cherry juice from a glass," he began.

10

Ozias's closest friend on Black Mountain was Ti Papa Pikan, a neighborhood healer known for his *coco makak,* a walking stick that performed miracles behind his back. It was unpredictable, just as likely to beat its owner in the ass as to fetch water from the well for his cooking, and Ti Papa used it most often to make children laugh. Pikan was a name he'd earned because he removed illness from the sufferer as quickly as getting a vaccine needle, a *piki,* in the arm. It wasn't that his cures didn't hurt; it was that they were mercifully fast.

In his youth Pikan had been an adept of Lenglensou, a spirit that sometimes got drunk and ate glass. If you brought him rum and cigarettes, Lenglensou might tell you something from your future, or he might make jokes at your expense. But Pikan had mellowed in his old age, and he was famous now for his eternal good humor, because he was the blackest man on Black Mountain, and because he claimed to know the real history of the tribes of Africans brought to Haiti as slaves. For a small fee he would tell whether you were Fon, Dahomey, Yoruba, or of some other extraction, by a thorough examination of your molars.

Pikan's place wasn't far from O's plot in the hills, and the two old men were cantankerous adversaries. They spent whole afternoons lounging in the elephant grass, arguing whether the Dominican dictator Rafael Trujillo had been better or worse than Haiti's dictator François Duvalier.

"Trujillo may have stolen much and killed many," Ozias said, "but at least they have electricity from the dams."

"Ah," Pikan waved his hand. "You don't know what you're talking about. The peasants there are as poor as the peasants here."

Zo kept clear of their endless debates. His yearning for Anaya was a favorite joke between the two old friends, and whenever he came near enough they accused him of dreaming about her.

In addition to playing the cockfights and working as a neighborhood *ougan*, or vodou priest, Pikan was a well-known pica, a taster of dirt. Twice a week he would set up a stall at the Kwabosal market downtown and ply his trade. On those days Zo would transport the *ougan's* strange merchandise down out of the mountains for free, letting the old man ride in the back among his things.

Once pitched in the marketplace, Pikan would sample dirt brought to him from anywhere on the island and tell his client the nitrogen content and the prevalent minerals in his plot. He gave advice on the possibility of growing cane versus banana on a small holding. Then, slowly, he began to taste a change in the island.

A rice farmer brought him a cup of earth from the Artibonite plateau that tasted like iron ore. A truck driver, looking for sellable gravel, offered a sample that gave him sulfurous belches. The normally acidic dirt in the scrub country around Môle-Saint-Nicolas tasted alkali and made a stubborn clay in his mouth that he had to rinse with 7UP. "Bauxite in the north. Phosphorus at Léogâne. It's like the island is remaking itself."

The customers just wanted to know what to plant in their gardens.

"I don't know," Pikan admitted. "The whole island tastes like it's been turned over in ashes."

Zo found him sitting at his empty stall in the Kwabosal market. For a month he'd been predicting upheaval and disaster, a world-wide shift in the distribution of minerals, a collapse of the central plateau, and now he had no customers. Just a spoon and a few samples of dirt on a plate set out before him.

"Some lunch," Zo said. "Why is business so bad?"

"Because people don't want to hear the truth," Pikan said. "They want to hear that the new plot is good for banana, or that there is pirate treasure underneath their house."

"What have you been telling them?"

"Banana or cane, it doesn't make a difference. The whole island is about to capsize like a ship."

"What should we do about it?"

Pikan shook his head. "Shouldn't you be running the Bèlvil circuit?" he asked. "Does Ozias know you're here?"

"That old man may own the *brouet*," Zo said, "but he doesn't own the *brouetye*."

"You came all the way downtown to tell me that?"

Zo said he'd come to ask Pikan to officiate at a wedding.

"Yeah? You and who else?" He paused. "Not possible."

"I asked, and she said yes."

Pikan got out from behind his stall and stood close enough to Zo that he could smell the vetiver shampoo the old man made for himself. "She agreed to be your wife?"

"Yes."

"Are we talking about the same girl?"

"Will you do it or not?"

Pikan rubbed his chin. "I thought it would take whole worlds to convince her."

"Maybe I promised her the whole world."

"Then you lied."

"Just tell me what you charge," Zo said, "and if you'll do it."

Pikan wanted two pounds of O's fresh roasted coffee. "Don't tell him I told you this, but O's brew is the best on the island."

When Ozias heard what Pikan had said about his coffee he was disdainful of the compliment. "That fool spends his afternoons eating dirt in the Kwabosal market," he said. "What could he possibly know about flavor and taste?"

"We're to be his first couple of the year," Zo said.

"What year is that?"

"De mil dis."

Ozias counted on his hands. "That's fifteen days from now! He's crazy."

The first person he turned to for help was his fat, asthmatic neighbor, Madam Zulu, who said outright it would be the biggest party Mòn Nwa had seen in years.

"A wedding on New Year's Eve is one thing, and bad enough," she said. "But don't forget that the next morning is Independence Day." Madam Zulu believed it was bad luck to turn anyone away from a celebration and promised to prepare a dozen pots of the traditional pumpkin soup. "We'll need a whole goat," she said. "And two dozen *joumou* squash."

Zo's friend Sabala Lafortune agreed to loan them his truck for various errands as long as he paid for gas. "No one drives but me," he added. Sabala ran a *taptap* on the Pétion-Ville circuit. Each day he drove from the hill district to the city and back again as many times as he could before dark. His pickup was called the Cheri Doudou, or Darling Sweetheart—an ancient Datsun with a half million miles on the body—and Sabala loved it inordinately.

They started before Christmas with imperishables: cola, candy, liqueurs they hadn't even heard of before, bottles of rum by the dozen, and *joumou* by the load. They bought a dozen flats of beer, paid a deposit on the bottles, and drove as carefully as if they were transporting eggs.

Paul and crew arrived on December 30 and proceeded to get drunk. They'd taken the long-haul bus from Jérémie.

"A rough ride, too," Paul said, "especially for Bos-T and Sonson."

Bos-T rubbed his backside. He looked windblown and sore. "We rode on the roof," he said.

"Eleven hours holding on to the luggage for dear life because they're too cheap to pay for a seat," Paul said.

The crew looked just as they had when last Zo had seen them except for Boss Paul, who'd lost another of his prominent front teeth. Bos-T said he'd taken a fist to the mouth.

"Fighting over a woman?" Zo asked.

"No," Paul said. "Fighting *with* a woman." He pushed the tip of his tongue through the gap in his teeth. "A big, lovely woman."

Sonson proposed a toast of cold beer to big women. They drank to that and then they drank to Paul's lost teeth: "To the multitude, wherever they might be." Toward the end of the night, with fifty empty bottles in the grass and Boss Paul smoking his last cigar, Bos-T-Bos took Zo by the arm and walked him down the terraced garden. He told Zo how happy he was and how proud. His wedding meant that good men could still triumph in the world and that money was not the foremost indicator of a man's potential.

"It's not so much what you say or how you move," Bos-T said, clapping Zo on the shoulder. "It's about knowing what kind of love she wants and giving it to her."

The workmen bivouacked in O's yard after the old man shooed them out of his garden. They strung their hammocks between the slender papaya trees, laid their bedding on the clipped grass, and took their rest. They would be up again before dawn, hungover but with good dispositions, cutting wood for the cook fires and splicing electricity from the main line to the makeshift dance floor.

·   ·   ·

On the last morning of the year, Ozias woke early, opened his coop, and took the chickens out one at a time. He stroked them, said goodbye to each by name, and handed them over to Madam Zulu, who broke their necks and laid them aside.

"Man can eat bird but can't bear to see it killed," she scoffed.

Sabala Lafortune ran his last errand alone, driving the Cheri Doudou to Juvenat to fetch the bride and her bridesmaid in the afternoon. They were waiting for him at the Union School, and he made a grand spectacle of his duties, going around the car and getting the door for Anaya and her cousin.

"*Byenvini nan cha w*," he said. "Welcome to your chariot."

But the truck rattled so badly in the potholed avenues that Nadine worried they wouldn't make it to Mòn Nwa. Lafortune admitted that he left more of the Cheri Doudou in the street every day than he returned with in the evening. Then he let up on the clutch and they blew past a belching transport *camion*. "But she can still ride," he said, grinding up the gears.

The couple wasn't allowed to see each other until the wedding. "It's the worst kind of luck," Madam Zulu said. "And for an endeavor as long as marriage, you would do well to put your best foot forward."

She installed Anaya across the street at her own house, where a half dozen neighborhood ladies were busy cooking the wedding feast. "Same fire," Zulu said. "Same bird. But everyone makes the sauce by her own recipe. Do you understand what I'm saying, baby?"

Anaya shook her head. "Not exactly."

Zulu led her out of the house and into the yard. She reached into one of the cauldrons of boiling water with her bare hand and held up a steaming chicken carcass. Then, sitting Anaya in the grass, she demonstrated how to pluck the feathers. "One at a time. As close to the skin as you can get."

Anaya broke a few feathers in two.

"Like this, baby," Zulu said. "Just like with a man. Don't be too timid, but don't break the shaft, either." Then she grew contemplative. "All men have hearts, but hearts differ. You've found yourself a good one."

"I know."

"If you took sixty more years looking, you wouldn't find another."

"*Wi,*" Anaya said.

"One who will love you with such intention, such constancy."

The day was full of smoke from the cook fires, women squatting with ladles, men coming with wires and ice. Toward evening, Zo found Ozias over a steaming cauldron in the yard, seasoning the water with orange leaves, nettles, and stars of anise.

"I thought Zulu was making the New Year's soup," he said.

"This is your bath, boy," O answered. "And you better get into it, too. The ceremony starts at dark, and I still have to finish mending a pair of dress socks."

"What do you need with a pair of dress socks when you only have one foot?"

"You speak boldly for a man who's never been married before," O said, tossing in a bunch of *asosi* grass. "But you'll soon learn what a real pair is, and why one does not go without the other."

He brought the bathwater to a boil and adjusted the temperature by adding measures of cold water. Then he gave Zo a new bar of the American soap he liked and followed him behind the bathing screen.

"That's what a marriage is, after all," he said. "One lone man trying like hell to make a woman happy and failing at it most of the time."

He poured the hot water over Zo's shoulders, and the fragrant steam rose from the cool grass. It left Zo's skin fresh and clean, and he dried himself in linen pulled off the line smelling of the tradewinds. Then he dressed in the tuxedo Ozias had found for him in the back closet of a Bwa Nam morgue master.

When he first saw it, Zo protested that it looked like Baron Samedi's funeral ensemble. It was an heirloom suit of a much older cut. The double-breasted waistcoat had long tails that reached to the backs of his knees, and the trouser outseam was lined with the same grosgrain as the peaked jacket lapels. Zo complained that the shirt was too long and baggy in the wrong places, cut more for a buccaneer than a modern man. He thought the buttons had fallen off the sleeves and even Ozias panicked when he saw them, but Madam Zulu came over and explained that they were called "French cuffs." She doubled the sleeves and pinned them with her dead husband's links. "You do make a beautiful groom," she said, fastening the cummerbund around his waist.

Ozias was still giving last-minute advice about marriage and Zulu sucked her teeth disdainfully.

"Listen to him, talking like an expert," she said. "His wife complained about their marriage every day for twenty-two years. Let me tell you something. Marriage is like the buttocks, Zo. Even though there is constant friction between them, they still love and live together." Her granddaughter appeared with a bottle of eau de cologne and poured a puddle into Zulu's palm. "Do whatever your wife tells you," Zulu said, running her fingers in Zo's hair. "And when she's pregnant, act like you have two babies."

Anaya washed at Madam Zulu's house, and Nadine helped her into the dress. She was flustered by the endless lace at the back. The sleeves were separate and had to be tied on afterward. When they finally succeeded in getting her outfitted, Nadine looked at her until the tears spilled out of her eyes.

"It's only that you look so beautiful," she said.

A local hairdresser put the finishing touches on Anaya's braids, piling them up on the right side of her head, pinning them in place, and drawing out the ends. She put a red hibiscus behind Anaya's left ear, opposite the knot of high braiding, and held a mirror for her to see.

Pikan appeared at twilight dressed like an undersized businessman, his shirt so billowy on his thin frame he looked like a mast wrapped in its topsail. He had ruined his eyes turtling in the famous Strait of Tortuga and was led about by an old fighting cock he called Ti Zom, or Little Gun. As soon as that rooster entered the house, it went straight to Anaya's side and sat there tranquilly throughout the preparations.

Pikan told Ozias it was a good sign. "Ti Zom is a good judge of character," he said.

Bos-T-Bos and Tiken decked the yard in Christmas lights. At dusk, when they plugged into the main-line electricity, the hillside glittered over the city. The guests clapped at the sight of it. From the slums underneath, Ozias's plot blinked green and red and white on the shoulder of the mountain. Someone had commandeered the aisle runner from the Methodist church and laid it in the grass. There were chairs on both sides, of motley age and quality—cracked plastic, heirloom mahogany dining sets, the miniature wicker seats made by hand in the mountains. The audience sat on them in various poses and waited patiently, in funereal silence, for the ceremony to begin.

The wedding party took their places at nightfall in triumphal pairs, including Pikan, who went with his rooster. The bird's ankle bells opened the proceedings. Ozias and Zo went together, the old man dressed in the same suit he'd married his wife in back in 1981—brown polyester with an orange wool tie. His crutch was decorated with white and red streamers and he went with style, passing up the whole length of the aisle in six fluid sweeps.

Madam Zulu's granddaughter played the flower girl, scattering white frangipani petals for the bridal party, which Nadine led, and then Anaya in her wedding dress. Madam Zulu stood in for Anaya's mother, wearing all neons: an orange dress and green hoop earrings.

Pikan started the ceremony with the story of Tezen that begins, "There once was a girl who fell in love with a fish." He gave a brief history of the island, telling how the Taino had lived on it with their canoes and music, then the Europeans with their sugarcane and whips, and now the Haitians who never left it and never would. He told them they had a dual lineage of African blood and Taino earth, and they must do something to unite these things if they wished to continue. He spoke of love in the world at large and love on the island in specific, and said it wasn't much different from place to place. Before starting the ritual, Pikan asked if there were any objections, and Zo himself spoke up.

"Her father doesn't approve," he said.

"To what does he take exception?"

"My poverty," Zo said.

"How poor are you?"

"Even that wagon and this small house don't belong to me."

The audience looked from the wagon to the house.

"Let me see your hands," Pikan said.

Zo held them up.

"Are they yours?"

"Of course."

"And your legs?"

"Yes."

"Your life is your riches," Pikan concluded. "If anyone offers you more than that, they are lying." Then he had them hold hands and perform a long chant pledging fidelity of their souls forever.

The newlyweds received their gifts in the *kay*. Boss Paul and crew brought a box of salted *kong*, a dish of dried eel that was a specialty in Jérémie, and a full case of the white wine Anaya loved so much. She thanked them and said anything left over from the party would be drunk during the honeymoon, which was scheduled to go through the rest of her winter vacation.

Madam Zulu's granddaughter presented them with embroidered handkerchiefs. It was an old tradition and Zulu still believed in it. They were white with lace borders, and the embroidery read: *A & Z. January 1, 2010.*

Ozias came shyly, at a loss for words. He wished Madam Ti Klis had lived long enough to meet them, he said, because she would have loved them both as if they were her own children. He said they were welcome to stay with him as long as they liked and that he selfishly hoped they would stay forever. Then, as if it were an afterthought, he reached into his breast pocket and presented Zo with a one-hundred-dollar bill, U.S. currency, thereby doubling the laborer's net worth.

Afterward, they joined the party as man and wife and fell to eating. There were vats of rice and red beans and *pwa kongo,* and there was *légume* stew with goat meat and the eight chickens in eight unique sauces. There were buckets of *kremas* on ice and two loaves of *dous makòs* and a dozen bottles of rum. Ozias stood on his crutch, raised his glass, and made a speech.

"My father was a root farmer. Potatoes were his trade. He taught me to plant manioc, yam, *malanga* root. But he broke his back at it. Now Ti Klis, when I met her, she grew coffee bushes, high above here"—he pointed—"in the flats behind Chapatio. She had *veritab* and mango, *kalbas* and coconut. She called me an imbecile, and my father, too. Why plant roots every season and harvest them three months later when you can plant a tree just one time and reap the harvest for twenty years?

"The truth is, I didn't like Zo at all the first time I saw him. Fresh from the provinces, cutting down every last tree on the island. At first, I gave him work just to get him off the trees. But he grew on me." When he started again his voice was high and tight with emotion. "I have loved very few men in my life," he said. "My father. My brothers, when they were alive. Ti Klis and I never had any children." He choked. "But Zo?" He raised his glass. "Zo is the son I never had but always wanted."

The couples danced to *zouk* and *konpa,* kissing in the dark. Ozias danced alone with his crutch and then he danced with Madam Zulu, throwing the crutch aside and clinging to her like a boy to his mother while she turned him on his lone foot like a top in the grass.

Boss Paul offered Pikan a cigar, and they smoked at the edge of the dance floor.

"I hear your couples never get divorced," Paul said.

"Only because they can't afford to," Pikan answered.

Nadine was bridesmaid and photographer. She took pictures of everything: Paul and Pikan smoking cigars, Zo and Anaya's first kiss as husband and wife, Bos-T-Bos breakdancing in O's pumpkin patch. No one slept. At dawn on New Year's Day, Madam Zulu and her granddaughter served the traditional pumpkin soup for breakfast, and the exhausted revelers took their steaming bowls of stew and ate on the grass.

The wedding was over. Zo and Anaya were man and wife. There remained just one last ritual to complete. Ti Papa Pikan was famous for prophesying the futures of his wedded couples. His accurate predictions on number of children to be expected were legendary. But when Ozias went looking for his friend, he found him packing up to leave.

"Aren't you going to see them before you go?" O asked.

Pikan consented reluctantly and went to join the couple at their house. The wedding guests followed, slurping their soups and looking in through the window and door. Pikan burned orange ambergris he'd collected himself from the desolate beaches near Faligon. It smoked scarlet, and the musky stench chased Ozias from the doorway and all the other spectators from the windows. Everyone scattered save the lovers in their globe of sperm whale incense.

Pikan drew a *vèvè* on the floor with white chalk, took a set of teeth from his *pakèt kongo,* and rolled them out onto the board. The incisors fell against the molars in a way that seemed to give him concern. He asked for an *adokin,* a dollar coin, and somebody handed one across. "The engagement ring," he said.

Anaya slipped the red button off her finger.

He gathered everything and rolled again, like dice, carefully studying the angle of the button to the coin and the coin to the teeth and the teeth to the button. The further he read into these things, the more apprehensive he became, until his face was dark with foreboding.

"You are no Adam," he told Zo. "And you." He touched Anaya's arm. "You are no Eve. It is not a new world you are coming into but a very, very old one."

Lin de Myèl (Honeymoon)

THEY SPENT A WEEKLONG HONEYMOON in the hills above Port-au-Prince. The traffic passed beneath them in the streets a thousand feet below. The sea drove against the coast. The sailboats traced the horizon. But entwined in the bed they'd bought from the salvage market, they were oblivious to the world.

They made love with the leisure and fascination of the world's first lovers, burning candles through the night so they could watch each other's bodies. Zo wrote a love song using his thigh as a drumhead and her name as the refrain. They ate cold barbecued pork at midnight, counting the ships in the bay by their lights.

They didn't wake early or late because those seven days were an extended dream of sex and sleep and the naked body of the other in the sheets. They made love before getting out of bed each morning and drank hot coffee afterward in the doorway, calling each other husband and wife. They left the shack only to pee, and even then they went together, stumbling over the kitchen implements into the yard like a drunk woman and her shadow. Zo staked a shower curtain in the grass so that they could wash in broad daylight. He knelt before her like a servant girl to soap her thighs and the soft hair between her legs. Then he washed her feet one at a time, with great care.

They drank a bottle of wine every day, remainders of the gift from Boss Paul and company. They kept the case in a dark corner of the house and drank the wine straight from the bottle, pretending to be connoisseurs who knew about vintage and acidity. By careful planning, their neighbors had arranged a communal bed-and-breakfast, every meal provided by nearby street chefs and housemothers. The neighborhood children ran the hot dishes to Zo's door, where, as Jean the Deportee taught them, they called, "Room service!" as he had once done while working for a Bahamian resort. They brought barbecued pork and delicate fish dinners with plates of macaroni and beet salad.

The night they had *pwason boukannen*, Zo dug through the flesh of the white fish and withdrew every last bone before feeding Anaya small spoonfuls and wiping the grease from her mouth. He piled *pikliz* salad on a fried plantain, turned the morsel to her mouth, and admired the mark of her perfect teeth.

They spent the afternoons imagining an idyllic future, even babies' names and the furnishings of a house. Anaya liked the heavy wooden furniture of colonial France, while Zo preferred the lighter wickerwork of the mountains. He teased her for her expensive tastes. Sometimes the talk grew serious, and they spoke of Anaya's father and what they would do after her graduation. They agreed to stay in the capital until Anaya completed her nursing degree and took her license. Then they would be free to go anywhere on the island.

By the last days of their honeymoon they had truly become husband and wife. Zo worked in the garden weeding a patch of peas, while Anaya squatted at the side of a sudsy washbasin with his dirty shirt in hand. It was the first time she had ever done laundry before, much less someone else's, and she found the act of scrubbing the sweat out of his collars like another kind of love.

· Book Three ·

11

THE RUMBLING CAME OUT OF THE SEA and went into the roots of the mountains and came back again like a rumor of itself. O's chickens stood in the grass; his peas shook on the vine. A haze of exhaust and tropical heat bloomed up from the jammed neighborhoods at Carrefour, where the long brothel sat like its own city of sorrow between the national highway and the strand.

The horizon was pulled taut and held tremulous as a thread of glass. Then a hammer struck from somewhere and a cosmic boom rose up from the core of the earth.

Ten thousand birds lifted off the island as if they were beaten from the trees, not only seabirds but great white birds the color of salt. The welders' torches blazed and blew out. The rivers turned back on themselves.

The archbishop of Port-au-Prince was killed on the balcony of the papal nunciature.

The chief of the UN Stabilization Mission died in his office at the Christopher Hotel.

Nadine Tessier was killed in the kitchen of her apartment on Rue Monseigneur Guilloux, still dressed in her school uniform, eating a cassava cake and peanut butter.

At Terminal Varreux, where petroleum transshipment storage was adjacent to the electric plant, a hundred tons of unrefined fuel ignited when a Panamax crane tipped into the transformers. The flames burned hotter and brighter than a star. Students at their evening classes in the hills ran to the windows and died there trying to see.

The ten-story Teleco building broke in the middle and tumbled serenely against the bay.

The federal penitentiary broke open and four thousand of the most dangerous criminals in the country streamed out thanking God for their manumission.

It lasted thirty-eight seconds. Then it stopped. The sun was in the salt and the salt was in the sea. The sour oranges shivered in their leaves.

Ozias was knocked off-balance in his *militon* squash. He cried out and put his ear to the garden rows as if listening for the squash to come up. Zo was seized by a vertigo so extreme that the sky and sea switched places, and he fell twice retrieving the binoculars from O's house.

"What is it?" O asked. "What do you see?"

A fine dust was lifting up from the bay to hang shimmering in the afternoon light, so thick it obscured the lower districts of the city. Above the smoke, Zo saw the crooked cathedral steeple and, farther on, the petroleum burn that marked the disastrous coast.

"Ki sa w gade?" O begged.

The dust blew apart to reveal the National Palace. The great dome of the republic had crashed down into the offices underneath. By following Rue Monseigneur Guilloux west from the government square, he was able to find the medical campus but couldn't locate the nursing school. The dust was too thick. He tried another way, following Rue Oswald Durand to its angle with Guilloux, but where the school should have been there was only a wreck twisted under a pall of smoke. The roof had pitched forward and was angled steeply against the horizon. The cigarette fell from Zo's mouth, but when he bent to retrieve it he forgot what he was looking for.

"It's the things you love that'll kill you," O said. "Those cigarettes you smoke. Or the sea on a sunny day."

Zo laced up his work boots.

"I'm fifty-seven years old," Ozias said, struggling to get upright with the crutch, "and I have never seen a disaster such as this. If you go down there now, alone, into all of that"—he looked out over the cul-de-sac plain as if he didn't want to see it—"you will never come back."

Zo fastened the loose strap of his coveralls and left the old man dejected in his winter garden.

"The roads are impassable!" Ozias shouted. "Do you hear me?"

Zo entered his house. The interior was dim and torturous because it smelled like Anaya. Her bedclothes were folded on the chair. He surveyed the impoverished scene of his brief and unlikely joy. The meager cookware, the shovel from Brazil, the sagging bed where he had loved her as if he had known the end was near. He took his life savings from under the mattress, his shovel from its place in the corner, and went out into the tumbled afternoon.

The cart was parked in the lawn between the road and the house. Zo tossed the shovel in among the everyday goods—the grease can and tire jack, the tarp and load lines—and squared himself to the *brouet* without ceremony. He fitted the poles into his armpits, leveraged the cart to its tires, and stepped it into the street.

Ever since he had started running the wagon, Zo had been developing his own unique style of work. It was based on a step

of medium stride and strong finish, so graceful and light at the
heel that Ozias liked to watch him work. "Look at that pull!"
he declared. "That reach!" Zo maintained a severe and precise
posture, responding by degrees depending on the grade of the
roadway. By holding nearly perpendicular in the flats, and leaning forward or back in proportion to the incline or decline of the
roadways, he worked to preserve his knees, which, according to
Ozias, were always the first thing to go and the last to recover. Zo
carried on like that now with beautiful precision and style, even
at the end of time when it could no longer matter.

Half of Mòn Nwa was standing in the street. Madam Zulu had
run from her house in her nightclothes, shouting for her granddaughter. Jennica Pierre and her five children watched from their
porch like a crowd of catatonics, their collapsed house smoking
behind them. The young kid Marvins, who sold all kinds of light,
stopped Zo and outfitted him with a battery flashlight, a stack
of candles, and three matchbooks. The pharmacist at Labatoire
Immacule gave him a dozen bandages, a suture set, and a bottle of
iodine. Even the small-time liquor man, who'd never given away a
free drink in his life, gave Zo a bottle of Bakara one-star rum and
said, "You'll need it."

By the time he started down into the capital to find his wife,
Zo had a jar of the hard candies and bubble gum that sell for a
gourde at every street corner in the country, two covered buckets
of drinking water, a bar of Fitso soap, a trial bottle of perfume, and
the good wishes of everyone on Black Mountain.

The first thing Zo saw in the Pétion-Ville flats was the last thing
he had left on Mòn Nwa. There was Uncle Ozias, already at the
bottom of the Kenscoff Road, respiring hotly into a white kerchief
and nursing a cut over his left cheek. He had come by a dangerous shortcut across half the brushy face of Mòn Nwa on foot and
crutch, and his clothes were torn. There were leaves in his hair.

"*Brouetye!*" he called when Zo came into sight. "*Brouetye!*" he
hailed him out of the dust like an everyday passenger.

Zo looked sidewise at the old man without stopping. "You look like you've fallen off the mountain," he said.

"Bring your back up," O said. "You're too low to the ground."

"You came all that way to tell me how to work?"

"I've pulled in this city for thirty years," Ozias said, hobbling after the cart. "You'll never get to Canapé Vert like that."

"Who said anything about Canapé Vert?"

"It will be the only way to go."

"If you want to come, get in the back of my wagon and don't ask me to stop," Zo said.

"Your wagon?" Ozias scoffed.

"I'm the one pulling it," Zo said. "I guess it will go where I do."

O put his hand on the cart. "If there's one thing I know in this world, it's the roads of Pòtoprens," he said. "Delmas will be impassable, I could see that from home."

"I'm not taking Delmas."

Ozias scribed a map of the city into the dirt with his crutch bottom, beginning with the outline of the Bay of Gonaïves. He drew the coastlines going west and north. He arranged the hills and then marked the various zones, Canapé Vert in its valley and Frères on its hills.

"There are three major roads that will get you to your objective," he said, drawing an *X* downtown. "Delmas zigzags through all one hundred and eight precincts of an overcrowded suburb." He traced the crooked route through its neighborhood.

"I've already decided on Lamartinière," Zo said, taking the crutch and drawing the route himself. "It's the fastest."

"No," Ozias corrected. "It's the steepest, there is a great difference." He wiped Zo's route with his foot. "Leaving first isn't the same as knowing the road," he said. "Lamartinière curves and bottoms out along the side of a steep hill. There will be rockslides everywhere. But there is a middle way." He dragged a line between both roads. "The only way. Avenue John Brown."

Zo told the old man to take his seat. "We will take John Brown," he said. "But we will take it by storm. If I never run a *brouet* again for the rest of my life, so be it. Today we will run like Damballa in Gine."

Ti Papa Pikan and his battle cock, Ti Zom, came up out of the dust and ruin looking like undertakers with bad news. Pikan wore his straw hat folded in a style from the revolution. He carried a *macout* sack over one shoulder and wore a long black tank top that went past his knees.

"We went in for a cockfight," he said, "but found other things."

The speckled fighting cock was fitted with copper ankle bells and led Ti Papa by means of a leash tied around its leg.

"What did you find?" Zo asked.

Pikan took his cap off to wipe his brow, but it wasn't sweat. The top of his scalp had been torn away and he was bleeding from his hair. "We came down for the cockfight. A red Goliath." He burped like a terminal dyspeptic and wiped his lips with the back of his hand. "A red Goliath versus a beautiful Dominican."

"He was at the stadium," Ozias whispered in Zo's ear. "And must have fallen through the bleachers."

There was a piece of aluminum rebar sticking a full six inches out of Pikan's belly, level with his navel and two inches to the right, which put it in the midst of every vital organ in his body. Zo had seen the anatomical drawings in Anaya's nursing textbooks, and he thought of the red kidney and fat purple liver and pink intestines.

"We can't leave him here," O said, "with no company but that rooster."

"That rooster is the only company he's ever had," Zo said, fitting the poles under his arms.

"Not so fast. Wait." Ozias opened one of the buckets and dipped a cupful of water. "At least give him a drink."

Zo eased back on the poles and came off the wagon. "I didn't come to play nurse," he said, but he took the cup anyway and carried it to Pikan. The rooster grew more agitated as he approached, even as Pikan remained oblivious. He didn't reach for the cup or even seem to see it, so that Zo was obliged to hold it to his thorny lips. Then the old man trembled so mightily half the water ran down his chin. He choked and spit in Zo's face.

"Dammit, Papa," Zo said. "Where did you learn to drink?"

Pikan wiped his face. "Would you mind watering the bird?" he said. "He works up a mighty thirst when he's nervous."

His breath was sour, and Zo thought of the stomach acid and blood mixing in the dark of his abdomen and the terrible bitters rising in his throat. Ozias dipped some water for Ti Zom, too, and Zo reluctantly set the bowl in the road for the rooster.

"Please," Pikan begged. "Don't leave me."

"There's no room," Zo said

Pikan looked dazedly from Zo to Ozias. "Where are you going?" he asked.

"To the health complex," O said.

"Lopital Jeneral?"

Zo put the poles under his arms, prepared to run. "You just sit tight, old man," he said to Pikan. "Just sit and wait here like you've done all your life and you'll find that not everyone is dead."

"I always lived with so many people." A pink froth boiled from Pikan's lips and he wiped it away. "I'm scared to die alone."

Zo looked at Pikan and back at Ozias and knew they couldn't leave him. He didn't like to add weight, but he finally helped get Pikan into the cart. They set him gingerly amid the donations from Mòn Nwa, where he stirred uncomfortably, clucking for his bird like an ugly hen to her chicks.

"Zom," he clucked. "Ti Ti Ti Ti Zom."

"He wants the rooster," O said.

Zo passed the flapping cock into the wagon. "That thing is a menace," he said, wiping his hands across his shirt.

"I thought you'd understand each other," Pikan said. "He's a fighter, after all, and works for his feed."

"I don't work for birdseed," Zo said.

"I bet my last dollar on the fight," Pikan said. And he offered Zo a hand-rolled beanie, sweetened with clove and sprinkled with *boz*.

Zo put the cigarette in his lips and tasted the tobacco leaf and the hint of dark marijuana. He had the matches from Marvins and he got the thing lit. It was thin and hot even in that heat, and it seared the dust out of his lungs and cleared the strangeness from his head. The smoke came blue and spiced from his mouth when he exhaled, and he passed it to the others. Ozias hit it nimbly, while Pikan took a massive pull and held the smoke forever.

"En ale," he said, puffing smoke. "I'm ready."

But then at every pothole in the pitted street he gasped and burped and coughed and begged Zo to go gently, but Zo did not slow down. He set his back straight and pulled against traffic, going toward the ruins downtown from which everyone else was fleeing. The white dust lifted up behind him and spiraled into powder, and the powder carried off across the face of the hill.

12

ZO COULDN'T HELP turning his transport wagon into an ambulance. It started with Ti Papa Pikan and his rooster, but more were soon added to the load. In Morne Hercule he picked up Wens and Exandieu Noel, brothers who'd been in class at the Nouvel Institut Emmanuel when the school tried to kill them. Wens had pulled his younger brother from the classroom wreckage, and he didn't look very good. When Ozias saw them at the roadside holding hands, aflame in their own blood, he couldn't stand to leave them behind.

"What do you want me to do about it?" Zo asked.

"Take them to Lopital Jeneral."

"It's too far."

Pikan lifted his head up from the wagon boards. "Obin's clinic isn't far from here," he said, pointing. "He'll know what to do."

"Jesus Christ," Zo said. "I should have left you two in the road."

"Pa di sa," Pikan said. "Don't say that."

"I didn't come to play ambulance and *taptap,*" Zo said. "I came to get Anaya from the nursing school and bring her home. The only reason I brought this damn cart was to have something to bring her back in."

Obin's place was a miracle in the city, a clear quarter hillside in lower Nerette he'd inherited by squatting on it for twenty-seven years. There was a long view of the city, from the airport to the Cité l'Éternel slums and the trash fires at the coast. The yard was green with high guinea grass that flashed its silver backside when the wind climbed up from the bay. There was a stand of acajou and a rosewood tree with bark that smelled of cinnamon. There was an Antillean oak with a low crown and a Caribbean pine native to higher elevations. The main house was in a copse of lime and *chadèk* that had fruited twice that winter. The green and pink citrus hung heavy in the leaves.

Obin worked all kinds of potions from his fruit trees and the herbs in his garden. One juice slowed the growth of goiters due to thyroid enlargement. Another aided old men with their incontinence. He'd gone on a long journey and returned with a rare coffee bush that he had planted in the shade. He harvested and roasted the berries each week in a brass basin. He was particularly admired for a tincture of roast coffee and eucalyptus that, taken every morning, was said to cure envy.

Obin himself was six feet tall and broad across, a chain-smoker who believed in the restorative power of West African bitters. He was an accepted master in closed fracture reduction and the treatment of chronic arthritis, and he had delivered lectures to the students of orthopedic surgery at the medical university. His knowledge of inflammation and bone setting was so vast and unique there had once been talk among the faculty of creating a chair for traditional medicine at the university and seating him in it.

Obin was out in the grass, working, with a cigarette in his teeth. He wore a long chef's apron with KISS THE COOK written across the chest. The front was stained with a mix of blood and plaster. A young apprentice followed him through the yard, wearing a white lab coat and carrying a carpenter's box of splints, plaster, gauze, and cotton padding and the jeweler's goniometer the bonesetter used to measure the angles of fractures and repairs.

Obin didn't seem overwhelmed by the work, but his eyes were red-rimmed, even from a distance. It may have been the rum in the cup he drank from. He crossed the grass, pulling the dish gloves off his hands.

Zo pulled the cart onto the lawn and leaned between the poles. They shook hands. The bonesetter drank from his bitters and offered Zo a sip. "It does wonders for steadiness of hand," he said.

Zo took the cup and drank and passed it back.

Obin examined Ti Papa Pikan and the Noel brothers. "I'm not the man for head injuries," he said, nodding at Exandieu, "or for impalements. I set bones and ease fevers." He pointed to a pair of lime trees. "Look at my pediatric clinic. They are scared to death and most of them should be. They need transfusions, and all I have are herbs." He looked around his yard like a captain surveying the deck of his wrecked ship. "They need to get to the hospital," he said. "How many could you take?"

Zo shook his head. "I didn't come to play ambulance."

"Listen," Obin said. "You are already a miracle, whether you want to be or not." He grabbed Zo's arm and shook him. "You have strength in your legs and space in your wagon. It's as simple as that. You are a man with a purpose among those with none." Obin's breath smelled of the bitters he'd been drinking; his hands were pink with blood and plaster. "Most of these will die even if they get to surgery," he continued. "But there are a few who stand a chance, if only you can get them there." He looked Zo full in the face. "I'll ask you again, how many can you take?"

Zo considered the cart. He counted up the wounded, noting their shapes and deformities. "Eight, if there are some children," he said finally. "Nine if they are underweight. But I'm warning you, they won't fit well."

"They don't need to be comfortable." Obin sucked the smoke at his fingertips and tossed it over the grass. "They need a modern hospital, and you are the only one who can get them there."

"They need a doctor," Zo said. "I'm only a *brouetye*."

"That is much better," the bonesetter said. "I have seen plenty of bad doctors but very few bad *brouetyes*."

"You haven't looked. There are those who steal and those who overcharge and those who lose things on the way."

"You will be sure to lose a few of these no matter how fast you pull," Obin said.

The first patient Obin chose for the wagon was Frances Beauge, who'd been carried in on a door. Her pelvis had been fractured, and when Obin gave her the urinary catheter nothing but blood came out. There was a puncture in her lower belly where a splinter of her iliac crest had broken through the skin, and when they lifted her the first time the white tip reappeared like the mast of a sunken ship. She begged to be put back.

Ozias was up in the cart complaining about floor space and cubic packing capacity. "These are not a load of *kokoye*," he told Zo. "They won't stack vertically. And the weight of five would be too much to haul for any kind of distance. Even for you."

He kicked through the donated goods, throwing rags overboard, tying the jack, shovel, and spare tire to the side rail like blacksmith's tools. He slung the water buckets over either side like saddlebags. Only when he announced that he was ready to begin did they start to lay the patients up in the cart one at a time, carefully and closely, as if packing fish in a salt box.

Frances Beauge was first. Obin had her fixed into a makeshift harness to stabilize her midsection. They packed her as snugly as possible with linens and secured her to the sideboard with rope.

Next came Myer Cassagnole, a third-year law student at the university in Gonaïves. He'd been home on break when his head was broken by a piece of ceiling.

There was a police officer among them, a high commandant in

full uniform. Both his legs were crushed in their pants. He'd been at the office of the UN Stabilization Mission and claimed the entire Chilean detachment had been lost. "They were on the third floor," he said, "and didn't stand a chance."

Sabina d'Ayiti had been in labor for five hours already when the earthquake struck. Fòlibète, where she lived, washed away around her like a dream, and she was left alone with her contractions in a bedroom without walls. Her parents were gone. She walked to Obin's clinic, plugging her vagina with her fist, and now the baby wouldn't come. "I think he's scared to come into the world," Sabina said, "and I don't blame him." Obin put her up on the wagon because he didn't know anything about delivering babies and because there were two lives at stake.

O kept a small notebook tied to the cart that served as his teamster's manifest. He took it up now with the half-sized pencil and wrote the names and diagnoses of each passenger as they came aboard: Frances Beauge, fractured pelvis and internal bleeding; Commandant Jonjak, two broken legs, femur to fibula; Myer Cassagnole, skull fracture and cerebrospinal fluid leak; Sabina d'Ayiti, complicated birth. Eleven-year-old Wens Noel and his little brother, Exandieu, who was bleeding from the head, were laid up last. Then there was the old cockfighter and prophet of Port-au-Prince, Ti Papa Pikan, with his sour breath and his proud rooster, suffering from a puncture wound in his lower left abdomen.

Ozias estimated the weight of each passenger and then worked out a weight in total. It wasn't impressive, it was insane. He marked the number on the bottom line and circled it twice. He fixed the destination as Lopital Jeneral. He wrote the time of day—5:43 on the afternoon of Tuesday, January 12—and estimated the time of arrival—8:00 p.m. Then he added his own name to the list as the retired proprietor of the wagon itself and signed underneath.

Zo's passengers moaned and spit and bled on the rocking cart. The ones who could talk discussed their chances of survival. With Zo at the helm, they thought they might make it. He hauled with a pride and confidence that was beautiful to behold. The passengers liked the unbelievable circumference of his thighs. They took his silence for concentration and his steadiness for skill and determination.

"Pull, goddammit, *brouetye*. Pull for all of us. If we don't make it, we'll die just like everyone else. It's in your hands now," they said.

Ozias leaned forward to assure them. "They are wide hands and a good head on his shoulders, too. Look how graceful, look how clean. Zo is the greatest *brouetye* in the city."

Ti Papa Pikan talked about cockfighting. He held forth on the glory of the sport and its meaning. He liked the honesty of the good cut and the eagerness of the bird and the clarity of the work. He claimed that the nobility of the rooster was often overlooked, and he touted its virtues as a national bird. He said the cocks knew before the fight began who'd win and who'd lose, but they still went to do battle.

"It is the same with men," Pikan said. "There is a winner and a loser, and every spectator knows the one from the other. Sometimes it is only about the opponent," he added, "the good and right match. A rooster doesn't know he's a champion until you set him in the ring with an opponent he can kill and kill well."

He explained what went into making a winning bird.

"Have him eat the eggs of his own harem. Feed him figs and cockroaches and the hearts of goats. Dress his wounds with turpentine." He stroked Ti Zom as he spoke. "And send him in like a soldier."

He spoke so long and with such swagger of the clean cut and the honest kill, of the talon marks in the dirt that were like some kind of cuneiform that could be read after the fight, that the police *kòmandan* couldn't take any more. His voice was thick and brutal when he spoke, and he had a lisp from a pair of broken teeth.

"What are you, anyway?" He raised his head up and looked meanly at Pikan. "What kind of old fighting cock are you? Winner or loser?"

"It's enough that I was in the fight."

"Bullshit," the *kòmandan* said. "The fight is over for you. You've got that aluminum paling in you. That's what you got. You telling me you're the winner? *Byen, Granmoun.* What have you won? Where is your treasure? And what about him?" The *kòmandan* gestured toward Zo, laboring at the head of the wagon. "Does he win or lose?"

The passengers who had the faculties to do it regarded Zo's sweating back before them in the avenue like a cut of granite.

Pikan regarded the laborer's steadiness of gait as if he could calculate the probabilities from this. "You're asking if he finds his love?"

"Is that what he's looking for?" Sabina d'Ayiti looked up over her belly. "His love?"

"It is," Ozias said. In a hush of rubber tire and a drift of blown smoke, he told Zo's story. "He was raised as an orphan and a *restavek* and did what must be done to stay alive. Twelve days ago, he was married to the love of his life, a student at the nursing school."

The passengers looked on exhausted, mesmerized by the motion of the cart.

"Why is he so good?" Sabina asked.

Ozias considered his answer while the chassis rocked beneath them. "Because he wants very few things and he knows what they are. He wants to deliver you to a doctor," he told her. "And then he wants to find his wife."

"What are the odds on that wager?" Jonjak asked.

"What's the bet?" Pikan inquired.

"You a betting man?" the officer asked.

"I would bet against my own chances of living out the night if the odds were good and I knew someone would collect my winnings."

"The bet is that he never sees his wife again," Jonjak said.

Everyone in that wagon had an opinion. Those who believed in love were sure Zo would find her alive in the rubble. Among these were the little boy Wens Noel and Sabina d'Ayiti, now suffering from ten hours of unabated labor pains. Others knew for certain that Anaya was dead already and Zo would find her thus or, more likely, never find her at all.

"He'll spend the rest of his life looking," Frances said.

The *kòmandan* agreed. "I, for one, know she is dead and dead again and will take anyone's bet to the contrary."

Ozias abstained, but Pikan took it. He sat up as best he could and accepted the terms.

"Yes," he said. "I'll stand to that. They make a beautiful couple and he will find her."

But they never got to wager a *gourde*.

All at once the wind from nowhere swelled and they had a last vision of the ravaged coast. Far and away, through the endless haze at twilight, the neighborhoods were wrecked in their hills. Yellow fires burned through the low country even to the seashore. But off to the east and north, against all odds, the coastal range had not toppled into the bay. The hills still stood bare and black above Lafiteau.

Zo had run the route Ozias prescribed, taking John Brown through Gros-Morne and Nerette, skirting the thirty-eight tangled districts of Delmas. They'd cruised by the fallen embassies of Panama and Mexico and passed the ruins of the Sunrise Supermarket, where the buried shoppers could be heard shouting for help. The darkness increased by degrees as they dropped in altitude toward the city on the sea plain, as if the night were engendered from below. The twilight thickened around them and had the flavor of pulverized cement.

They made steady progress until the traffic jam at Delmas 12, where John Brown crossed Canal Kayiman. Zo maneuvered up the deadlocked traffic until he couldn't get any farther. He left the cart and its passengers under O's care and walked up the traffic with Wens running after him.

The auto bridge over Canal Kayiman had broken into sections, and the twisted spans lay two hundred feet below on the scrubby river bottom. Hundreds of people stood along the ravine looking down. There was no way to cross from one side to the other.

Canal Kayiman, or Alligator Canal, was all that stood between Zo and the center of downtown. If he could get them across the river, they would emerge a half mile from the health complex, just beneath the nursing school. Both Zo and Ozias knew of the route that led down through the valley, as every taxi driver and deliveryman knew of it. A brutal shortcut that could rip out the underside of a truck. They called it Impasse Kayiman, Alligator Impasse, really just a pack trail made haphazardly by a century of women carting water up from the stream.

Zo returned to the wagon looking grim and ignored the inquiries of his riders.

"What is it?" O asked. "An overturned truck?"

He hauled them to the old mule trailhead and pivoted the wagon to face it. The trace descended through the bush by a series of steep switchbacks before cutting out of sight.

"Don't even think about that," O said. "That's not a road but a mudslide."

Zo told the old man to keep his advice to himself.

"I've run in this city thirty years. I ran when Duvalier was still boss and Delmas only numbered to fifteen. I was running when half the ships in the bay were still made of wood and ran on wind power."

"You're the one who told me to take John Brown," Zo growled. "Now I have no choice."

"A *brouetye* may not be able to choose his load or the time of day at which he runs it, but by God he can always choose his route. Anaya and the nursing school," O said, pointing away from the ravine, "are that way. Destruction and failure"—he pointed at the ravine—"are down there."

Zo bent to retie his boots. "There's no time for another one of your detours," he said.

When Ozias realized that Zo would not be dissuaded by reason, he got down from the cart and stood on crutch and foot to implore him. "Even if you manage to get us down there," he said, "and I'm not sure you can without overtipping, how will you get us across the river? You can't make a wet stream crossing with so much weight on the axle. And what about the grade?"

They regarded the opposite slope.

"Pulling up that degree of incline will kill you, Zo. Not just you but any man at all, no matter his age or ability. We both know about your knees," Ozias added. "And a man has no second gear. You're going to tear them to pieces braking us down the hillside."

"I'm not going to brake," Zo said. "I'm going to coast."

He described a downhill route that would get them to the bottom of the ravine while preserving his knees and labor. The idea was to use gravity and slalom the path like the downhill skiers he had seen in the televised Olympic Games, with the *brouet* poles up under his armpits and his feet actually lifted off the roadway.

Zo rubbed his hands in the dirt and worked it into his palms. According to his theory, if he could gather sufficient speed at the steep beginning of the old mule trace, he'd be able to kick his feet up and coast all the way down to the glittering river.

Ozias didn't like it. "I'm a traditionalist," he said, "and hold that a man should run with his legs. I've seen carts flip on inclines much less severe than this one. And let me remind you, brother, these are not a load of coconuts you're hauling. Besides, the right tire has been punctured and repaired so many times it could blow at any moment, especially at the speeds you intend to reach." He gave a furtive look at the wounded in the wagon. "Are you really going to make this run?"

Zo didn't know how to answer. His body had never betrayed him before. Of all the things he knew on earth, his body was the most trustworthy and sound. There were no vagaries about his bones or the weight they could carry. It was a careful intelligence cultivated from years of being paid for physical prowess and that alone, because Zo had always been paid for his body but never even once for his mind.

Before casting off down the incline, Zo measured himself against the load like a sprinter before a great race, squatting and stretching his hamstrings and feeling the balls of his feet underneath him. He would need to know where to find the fulcrum and leverage in an instant.

"You'll need to know exactly how much to accommodate the drift," Ozias said. "You'll have to steer like a motorcyclist, leaning into the turns." He massaged Zo's thighs and rubbed out his knees. He was gentle with the tendons and he spoke so low no one could hear him save Zo.

"We're ready," he said. "Take us wherever you're going. But remember the tire, Zo. Don't pull too close on the right."

The journey to the bottom of Canal Kayiman was a run of great beauty and smoothness, the likes of which neither Ozias nor any passenger in that cart had ever seen before. Zo set the poles under his arms and started out with a long, measured step. He accelerated steadily, into a trot, and then he had them on the slope, increasing momentum like an airplane on its runway. When they reached critical speed, he slid down the poles, kicked his feet up off the trail, and, just as he'd said, they coasted. The cart shuddered and lurched to the right. For a moment, every rider braced for disaster. Then the wagon found its footing and settled as smooth as a tram on tracks.

"There she goes!" O shouted. "My God, Zo, I knew you could do it."

Wens Noel directed them with his feet girded in the cart against the jostling of the wheels in the pitted grade. "*Gòch, dwat, vit, vire,*" he shouted. "Left, right, fast, turn!" He hung out over the wagon board and advertised their approach like he'd seen people do from the windows of the long-haul buses, slapping his palm against the cart and shouting their destination. *"En ale, en ale, en ale!"* he cried. "Pòtoprens, Pòtoprens, Pòtoprens. Come out, come out, come out!" he yelled. "You wounded, you broken, you sick."

The survivors appeared by the scores, holding their phones aloft to take pictures while the wagon crossed their vision and went down into the valley forever. Zo was a man with purpose among those with none and so an oddity and a hope in those obscure hours. By leaning on the poles and kicking his heels into the dirt, he kept them on the rutted path.

They descended into the darkness of the valley. The red bore of the sun grew cold and blue and was finally lost for good behind the clouds of pulverized cement. The air was hot and sulfurous, as if the ocean were boiling in its rims, and the cinders ran up from the bay plain like ash from a furnace. Zo took the hot blow to his face and narrowed his eyes against it.

He soon had them at the valley bottom, coasting on the sandy river road. The tin and wicker shanties had slid down the steep grade, and a slurry of trash had washed out as far as the riverside. The massive spans of the fallen auto bridge sat in the bushes. Toward downtown, the Salesian religious institute, founded to aid poor children, had collapsed with all five hundred of them at their prayers.

At the bottom of the ravine, Zo turned to face his passengers. He looked like a man come home from the fields, stooped and beaten, a black stripe of engine grease drawn under one eye and blood running where he'd bit his lip.

"How will you get us across?" O asked. "The cart will be too heavy in the mud with all of them in it."

"If we get stuck down here, we'll die," Sabina d'Ayiti said.

"I said I'd do it." Zo wavered on his feet. "I'll take you across one at a time if I have to."

He started with Exandieu. The schoolboy had fallen forward during the downhill run, and Zo scooped him up off the wagon and splashed out into the stream. The people on the hillside had watched the fabulous descent, and now they watched Zo splashing across the water with that wounded child in his arms. A distant shaking came up the valley, rippling the water in its banks, but they remained quiet all along Impasse Kayiman. No one shouted, no one ran. Zo placed the boy on the far side of the stream and came back for another passenger.

That was the last proof the spectators needed. They came out of the hills to help one by one and then by the dozen. The Seventh-Day Adventists came out of their church as one congregation. They formed a line across the river and passed the passengers from one bank to the other. Frances proved to be the most difficult of all because of her broken pelvis. Every time someone touched her she screamed. Zo finally used a crowbar to drive the rim from the spare tire and then, removing the inner tube from the tread, they were finally able to float her across.

Zo took Ti Papa Pikan himself. The old man's blood had run out and dried and stopped running. He'd been quiet so long that Zo was afraid he was already dead. He scooped the old man up in his arms and found he hardly weighed a hundred pounds. Pikan opened one eye. His pupil was obscured beneath its cataract like glass at the bottom of a muddy stream.

"Are we there?" he choked out.

"We're close."

Pikan fell to a fit of coughing and doubled up in Zo's arms, clutching at his neck like a child afraid of falling from his father's arms. They stood like that in the middle of the river, with Pikan shivering around his neck.

"Put me down," Pikan gasped. "I'm too tired."

Zo laid him gently at the riverside, close enough that the old man could reach out and feel the water with his fingertips. He lay back slowly and with difficulty, opening his mouth and closing it again.

"I've put my money on you and the girl," he said, wiping his lips. "It looks to be my very last bet, so make me good."

"I don't even know if she's alive," Zo said.

Pikan was seized by the last conviction of his life. He grabbed Zo's arm and pulled himself up as far as he could manage. "Old men's mouths may stink," he wheezed, "but inside here is wisdom. Go to her. Get her out of this damned place."

Pikan's head rolled back and his chin angled up into the dark like a frail recrimination of the day that killed him.

Zo didn't say his body could stand no more of the brutal inclines or trashed crossroads of the capital. He didn't need to. His passengers knew it from the way he dragged his feet in the grass like rocks, from his knees that were bruised and swollen where the tendons ran. He hated to leave the old man there like a sack of coal, but neither could he afford to haul that extra weight once they started up the incline. He asked Ozias for a sheet of paper and wrote a brief obituary:

Here lies Ti Papa Pikan,
the prophet of Port-au-Prince

and pinned it to the old man's shirt.

It was pitch-dark in the bottom of the ravine, and Ozias supervised the reloading by flashlight. He fixed some of the patients to the running board to make them as comfortable as possible under the circumstances. They tied Frances into the inner tube because it cushioned her pelvis.

Then Zo took his place and hauled them through the shanties lining Impasse Kayiman to the trail on the far side of the ravine. They stood at the foot of the incline and studied it up to where the trace disappeared in the dark.

Ozias pulled out his ancient clinometer, a device like an oversized compass that measured the inclination of slopes. He took it to the foot of the long trail and held it against the angle of rise to measure the incline. "Twenty-two degrees and four minutes," he pronounced to everyone in the wagon, as if they should have known it to be a significant figure. "I've run in this city thirty years and I have never seen a *brouetye* pull straight up a mountain, even with an empty cart. Even young, with legs of iron. My advice is to go farther down, find other ways out."

But Zo was both captain of the vessel and its engine. He leaned forward into the impossible incline, breathing deeply through his nose and burying his head until his chest was parallel to the slope. He turned his head just once, looking back past the wagon, and Sabina d'Ayiti raised her phone and took his picture. After Ozias saw the cast of his eyes, leaden and brutal and fixed like forlorn bullets, he shut his mouth and said no more of Zo's bad knees or Zo's bad choices. The laborer turned savagely toward the incline like a man facing down his destiny.

"Lower your back," Ozias warned, "and go sweetly, Zo. It is no easy run."

It would not have been an easy run in the early morning under good clean skies with no load at all behind him. Zo was a professional and he knew how it went. First went the breath, and not long after went your legs, and then you were finished. A man could not run a thing without his breath. On level road at an even pace, Zo could pull endlessly as long as he held measured breath. But put him on an incline and everything changed.

Zo elongated his steps to lower their frequency and save his knees, but this increased the strain on his thighs and they began to burn. The wagon shuddered and stalled behind him, but he pulled them on. The trace was poorly maintained: there were boulders in the trail and monstrous potholes. Halfway to the top Zo wanted water and called out for it. Ozias checked both buckets.

"It's over, Zo. All the water has been drunk. Lie down and take your rest."

Both Zo and Ozias knew that if he stopped at that moment he would stop forever. To quit his steady workmanship at midincline this late in the running was to quit hauling for good. He would never be able to start again. In his last moments of clearheadedness on that dusty hillside, Zo was thinking of Anaya. How she had loved him despite his poverty or even for it, how she had taught him new ways to kiss, how she had taken her shoes off on the dance floor.

His passengers felt it when his steadiness began to go. They could feel the desperate contractions of his muscles translated up the poles and into the cart with every step. He'd lost the persistent and even beauty of the stride that had marked the earlier part of their journey. Now they rocked and jerked and stopped completely, advancing by narrow degrees. He pulled forward one wheel and then the other.

Ozias was tossing equipment off the cart as if it were a sinking ship, and Wens Noel lent a hand. They rolled the spare tire off the back and tossed the carjack. The neighborhood residents emerged from their toppled shanties to see Zo at the head of his wagon. A man who didn't know their destination yelled, "Pull for them, son. You don't have far to go."

A group of youths ran up behind them and took their places at the back of the wagon. Together they leaned in against the load. The incline had reached thirty degrees and Zo felt as if he were lifting off into the air. A half dozen men and one woman pushed from the sides while a few others pulled from the front. Someone said it looked like that *brouetye* would get them right to heaven. "He will haul them bareback into paradise," she shouted.

Zo hauled the cart up the incline in a dizziness of sweat and heat and a mayhem of calls from the dying. The burning in his thighs diminished until he no longer felt their pumping in the street and then he no longer had his legs beneath him at all. There was a tumbling blackness in his brain and he could go no farther.

The sensation of falling was familiar from his fighting days, when he'd sparred behind the gas station of Grande Anse. He never let go of the *brouet* poles, but they finally overwhelmed him and he lost the fulcrum of the cart. It tipped back on its tail, and the poles slipped out from under his armpits. He pitched forward into the street. Swinging upward past his face, a pole cut him above the eye. The passengers howled and gnashed their teeth. The youths rushed forward and shouldered the load to stop it from backsliding.

13

HE COLLAPSED at the rim of Canal Kayiman and was loaded
into his own cart by bystanders. It took three grown men to lift
him from the street and set him among the other riders in the
cart, where he lay delirious with exhaustion. Then, under Ozias's
coaching, a team of volunteers pushed the wagon that last half
mile to the clinic.

It took six men to do what Zo had done all afternoon alone:
two on each of the hand poles and two at the back who shouldered them forward. Even then they went shudderingly, in fits and
starts. Someone had set red flares in the road to light the way to
the hospital, and by those flares they could see the ruins looming
up on either side. The dust blew off the buildings and stung their
eyes like the atmosphere of another planet, where the air was not
made of oxygen and light but calcium oxide, pulverized stone, and
cement glue.

Wens Noel and Sabina d'Ayiti were obligated to dismount and
walk alongside. Sabina's feet were tender and swollen. She hadn't

been able to fit into her shoes for weeks but neither could she go barefoot in the street, so Ozias untied Zo's boots and she stepped into them.

"These are his prized possession," O said, tying the laces. "He's always polishing them and making small repairs."

The boots were six sizes overlarge for her, and Sabina stomped those last blocks in an increasing fever of contractions, holding on to the wagon board on one side and Wens Noel on the other, wailing at regular intervals. Her birth pains had returned with a vengeance and they were an omen of their imminent arrival. In the hospital yard, they heard her coming long before she appeared.

They crossed Avenue Magloire Ambroise into Rue du Docteur Dehoux and pushed across Oswald Durand. The street was black in both directions and a cold wind ran under the dark. It was not the soft night of the tropics, but a thick and mineral darkness, tasting of gypsum and stone, like the darkness inside the earth. The cries of the wounded were ubiquitous and paramount, coming from everywhere at once like the sounds of the sea. Ozias lit candles and distributed them to the riders.

"Eyes front," he told the volunteer *brouetyes*. "Even strides."

They passed beneath the faculty of law and came at last to the health complex. The volunteer *brouetyes* got the wagon up the circular drive, set one wheel off the pavement into the grass, and dropped off sweating.

Lopital Jeneral looked like a battleship run aground in the plain. The building had cracked in the center and the two wings leaned upon each other in the middle. The orderlies had dragged the salvageable equipment from the first-floor surgeries, and a makeshift trauma center had commenced under the mango trees. Scores of IVs hung in the low branches, and doctors were operating in the open like surgeons in a war zone.

That last half mile of walking proved decisive to Sabina's endless labor. It was as if the baby had only been awaiting their arrival. As soon as they reached the yard she was felled by unbearable contractions. She climbed on all fours and pulled up the hem of her nightgown. There was her bulging vagina, near tearing, the little phlegms of blood and mucus hanging like ornaments. She was hot and frightened, suffering from insomnia and twelve hours of unabated labor pains.

She stood again in Zo's huge boots, her braids falling down her face and her feet set wide apart. Then, with a final shuddering effort and a single cry that pierced the dark, she gave birth standing up like a warrior in battle. Wens Noel hadn't left her side. He crouched between her legs and caught her son like a slathered football, cradling him against his chest.

Zo woke when the wagon quit rolling and climbed down into the grass. He was dazed, barefoot, and badly balanced. The handcart was tipped back on its tail in the grass, and the volunteer *brouetyes* had taken the riders down and placed them on the lawn. They were haphazard and looked back at him with a terminal grimness about their eyes, as if they had gone beyond fatigue into a more spiritual exhaustion. They looked ready to die.

Zo saw the tops of his bare feet in the grass. "Where are my boots?" he asked.

Wens Noel took them back from Sabina d'Ayiti and carried them across.

"She's going to name the baby after you," he said.

Zo took the boots but couldn't keep his balance long enough to get them on. He finally sat on the lawn and pulled them on one at a time, struggling to make satisfactory knots out of the laces.

"Did you hear?" Wens asked. "She's going to name him after you. Alonzo. Zo for short."

Zo concentrated on making a knot with his trembling fingers but finally gave up and leaned back. *"Mare yo."* He pointed down his legs. "Tie them for me."

Wens crouched at his feet and made wide loops.

Ozias appeared and, laying his crutch aside, bent down beside the little boy. "I swear I've never seen anything like it and don't expect to ever again," he said. "A run of such beauty, such grace!" He clapped Zo on the leg. "You've proved me wrong, boy. And under pressure, too. I wish the whole world could have seen it. I wish it could have been on *televizyon*."

"Wagon running's not exactly an Olympic sport," Zo said.

Ozias felt Zo's knees. He rubbed the tendons above and below. "How does that feel?" he asked. "How are those quads? Don't think I didn't see. You abused that knee to control the wagon on the downhill slope."

Zo batted the old man's hand aside. "Get me up, Ozias. There's no time to waste."

Ozias looked up Zo's body. "I know how it feels," he said. "Believe me, I know. When I lost Ti Klis, I didn't want to wake the next morning. But in the months that come, you find other joys."

"It's not like that for me."

"That's because you've never been old," O said, "and don't know the meaning of compromise."

"I'll find her," Zo said. "If not here, then in the next world."

"Maybe some other country?" Wens offered.

"Or some other life," Ozias said, "where men are not men and Haiti is rich."

Ozias knew him well enough to know that further discussion was futile. Setting his crutch at an angle and using it as a fulcrum, he took Zo's hand and, by rotating off the point of his foot like a counterbalance, raised the laborer from the lawn in a single fluid motion, like the work of a machine pulley.

Zo stood for just a moment. Then the horizon tilted and ran away from him. Ozias bucked up behind and beside him, holding him aloft. "This is stupid, Zo. Now is the time to use this." He touched Zo's head. "Instead of this." He touched Zo's chest.

Zo couldn't tell what time it was or even what direction he was facing. There was no moon in the sky or any stars, no marker at all by which to fix the time or location. "Which way is Rue Honoré?" he asked. "She took me through Honoré Gate."

The generator started up and the yard was awash in light from the ruined wards. The hospital had been evacuated, and the patients lay in the grass among the dead in a line so long Zo couldn't see the end. They were in the flowers, under the trees, on the front porch, in the doorways.

"That's the pharmacy and orthopedics," he said after a moment. "There." He pointed. "In the *bwa mombin*. That's the nursing school."

Ozias raised his face in that direction and cried out. He drove his crutch into the grass and stopped them cold. Where the mountains should have been black and solid in the south there was only a pall of smoke hanging from the horizon and, under that smoke, the uneven line of the nursing school. The classrooms had crashed into the administrative offices, and the roof was angled to the earth.

"You can't go in there," O said. "Wait and rest. Until morning at least. Things will look different in the light of day, and we can come at it then. Like reasonable men."

Zo pulled Anaya's schedule from the bib pocket of his coveralls, but he didn't need to. He'd looked at it so often that afternoon he could recite her courses and their hours from memory. Tuesdays and Thursdays, 4:00–6:30 p.m. with Professor Cacquette. He even knew the course number. Women's Health 0743. Advanced Topics in Midwifery.

"That is not a plan," O said. "It's a funeral announcement. Look at the building, Zo. Look!"

They stepped back and gazed arm in arm at the ruined nursing school. It had been three stories high and built in the shape of an L. The long side of the L, containing the classrooms, had been driven into the shorter wing of administrative offices. The back half of the building was tilted upward like the tail end of a crashed airplane, while the front end had been driven at an angle into the bureau of the superintendent.

"How do you expect to get inside?" O asked. "There are no doors, and that shovel of yours is about as useful as a toothpick."

Zo's head was spinning and his vision had been reduced, but he was following an older compass in the blood that needed no lodestone. All the desires of his rough life had been distilled to one single desire, to find Anaya and bring her from the ruins.

The *zouti* were impromptu work crews that joined up after the earthquake to dig out as many survivors as they could find. Some were out for fortune and others for charity, and that mostly depended on the captain's heart. Zo found a crew from Delmas captained by a bearded workman named Delbarth.

"Pòtoprens born and Pòtoprens raised," Delbarth said when Zo came up next to him. "From Delmas sixty-two to thirty-two, a falling man."

"Born by the sea." Zo's voice was raspy and burned from exhaustion. "Raised in the hills."

"*Originel Ayisyen,*" a second laborer called.

"That's Brino," Delbarth said. "He was born in the Dominican and raised at the cockfights."

Delbarth and Brino were roadworkers for the municipality of Delmas and looked like professionals. Delbarth sported a highwayman's hard hat with a working headlight, turned off now, but which he demonstrated for Zo. Brino was shirtless, wearing nothing but an orange reflector vest and transverse tool belts across his chest that looked like the bandoliers of a Mexican revolutionary.

They had between them an arsenal fit to hang a suspension bridge. Machetes and brush hooks and fine-toothed hacksaws graded to cut through steel. A sledgehammer wide as a medieval bludgeon and a crank star drill without the crank. In the sled behind Brino was a mess of braided steel cable, a block-and-tackle set plus rigging, even a stack of orange work cones. On top of all that, Delbarth had a gas-powered jackhammer, which he carried over his right shoulder. It looked like a relic, bitten and evil.

"Does that thing work?" Zo asked.

Delbarth put his arm around the jackhammer and patted it gently, looking like a hangar gunner with a missile to load. "Juiced and ready to go." He gave a thumbs-up.

"How much to rent it for the hour?"

"No one uses it but me."

"How much?"

Delbarth considered. "Fifty," he said, "for the half hour."

"*Gourdes?*"

"I'm a businessman, not a French charity." Delbarth made the money sign. "I work for dollars."

Zo remembered the money he'd taken from the house that afternoon and checked the bib of his coveralls. It was still there. He showed Delbarth the one-hundred-dollar bill that was the savings of his lifetime but didn't yet drop it into Delbarth's hand. "What's it run on?"

"Bar oil and gasoline."

"You have any?"

Brino lifted an aluminum can from their accoutrements and sloshed the contents to prove they had it.

Zo was satisfied and gave the hundred-dollar bill to Delbarth.

"What's the job?" the roadworker asked.

"I need you to get me into the nursing school."

"Get you in?" Delbarth leaned toward Zo and regarded him closely. "No. Take it back." He passed back the hundred-dollar bill. "Just look at the building. There is reinforced concrete, and steel rods placed to support the load vertically." He stood his hands upright. "But with movement of the ground side to side"—he moved his hands back and forth to illustrate shear—"the superstructure can't hold for long. Take my word for it," Delbarth said.

"I've been in these all afternoon. That is no longer a schoolhouse but a house of cards. A strong wind"—he made his lips into an O and blew—"would toss this mess right over. And there are aftershocks coming all the time. No, we don't get people in. We get them out."

Zo's throat was dry and his head was pounding. He asked what time it was, and Delbarth checked the glow dial of his watch.

"Four a.m."

Zo reached into the chest pocket of his coveralls and took out the second hundred-dollar bill, the one Ozias had given him on his wedding day.

"Who's in there, anyway? Are you trying to get yourself killed?" Delbarth asked. "The *prezidan*? Of the United States?"

"My wife," Zo said.

Delbarth took both bills and folded them in half. "I hope she's the kind of woman who appreciates a fool," he said. Then he went ahead to make a reconnaissance of the damaged building while Brino gathered the hand tools into a wheelbarrow. He and Zo started across the campus afterward. Radiology was past repair: the front wall lay in the garden and the MRI and CT scanners had been blasted out the windows. Orthopedics, pediatrics, the eye clinic—all had great cracks running in the foundations. They arrived under the nursing school to find Delbarth in conversation with a second-year student who had agreed to assist with the rescue.

"All Cacquette's classes were there"—she pointed up at the back half of the building—"in the Fatima Maternity Annex, where they keep the obstetrics and maternity equipment."

Like many other flat-slab constructions on the island, the nursing school had no internal hallways. Access to the classrooms was from an external gallery that rimmed the perimeter of each floor. The third-floor classrooms had been forty feet off the ground, but now Brino, who was just six feet tall, could reach up and touch the third-floor gallery with his fingertips.

Brino was the best climber and he went first, pulling himself over the uneven parapet nimble as a cat. Once he had his footing and was sure that the gallery would hold, he leaned over and took up the tools. Zo and Delbarth climbed up afterward and found themselves on the canted third-floor gallery. From up close they could see that the walls had imploded and the roof, where it had held, was borne by naked metal uprights. The furniture had been blasted through the windows and blue electrical flames climbed in the walls.

Yet Delbarth studied the layout and claimed to like their odds. "The roof is fairly high at the back half of the building," he said. "There is still a good chance of finding survivors there." The problems were twofold. First, the structure was completely unstable. "One bad footfall"—he clapped his hands together—"and you will fall through the floor." Second, the rooms are like Egyptian catacombs, confused by false vaults and filled with tons of rubble. To go in that way, through the walls, would take days. They didn't have days. "The only option is to dig you in through the roof and drop in from above," Delbarth said.

Brino went first again, scaling the roof with the expertise of a mountaineer. Delbarth came up after, and together, each taking one of his hands, the roadworkers hauled Zo up to the roof. He was so thirsty he could no longer sweat and reached down his legs, waiting for the world to quit reeling. When he came to, he didn't look surprised. He opened his eyes on that ghastly scene like he had expected it all along, as if somewhere in his darkest hours he had dreamt it. The smoking horizon and the petroleum burns at the coast. The dead in the grass and the two workmen preparing to dig him in. The green dawn breaking over the city.

"*Mwen preparé*," Zo said, getting to his feet. "I'm ready."

Delbarth bent to the jackhammer, demanding space. He checked the bar oil and tightened a bolt with his fingers. He wound a crank and checked the fittings around the drill bit.

"Is that the first jackhammer they ever made?" Zo asked.

"Prototype 1973." Delbarth spun it to show him the nameplate—WAUKESHA. "Made in America," he said. "When you use it you really got to crowd around and hold to, or else she'll spin away and bite you in the foot." He warned Brino and Zo to stand back, then dropped the sunglasses over his eyes.

Delbarth pulled on the cord and snarled it. He unloosed the clutch and flooded the carburetor and pulled again so fiercely that the old beast chugged to life. Once started it could not be stopped. It roared with the energy of twenty generators and there was that thumping sound when the metal bit into the block. Delbarth went slowly at first, then faster, his bones shaking in their sockets. Red iron filings tailed off in the smoke. He smashed and pummeled like a tinsmith with a measured and clangorous stroke, the whole dismal dawn becoming his workshop.

It wasn't the racket of the jackhammer that woke Ozias but Pikan's rooster, crowing practically in his ear. He'd fallen asleep in the cart, among the cast-off equipment, and the rooster was tied up beside him.

"What is it?" O asked. "Who's there?"

There was no one but the anxious rooster and, on the far side of the wagon, little Wens Noel, who'd been watching all along.

"They're trying to get into the school," Wens said.

"*Ki es?*"

"Zo and the *zouti* crew."

Ozias remembered everything at once. He could see the workmen in the distance on the crooked roof, silhouetted against the odd hour, one hugging the jackhammer and the others standing back under the sparks. "My God, Wens, is he going down there himself?"

He pulled himself up and stuck the crutch under his arm. On the far side of the wagon, he was stopped short by the ghastly tableau of the little boy sitting against the wagon tire with his dead brother's head in his lap. Exandieu had expired hours earlier and was stiff in the chill air.

Ozias offered his hand and Wens took it. They went toward the university, while Ozias talked about what a fool Zo was and how stubborn. "The kind of man who would cut down every last tree on the island and then look surprised when he couldn't find a mango to eat."

"Don't you think he might make it back?"

"One small aftershock"—Ozias snapped his fingers—"and he will be lost forever." He swept the tears from his eyes. "He has no concept of that which poverty demands most of all."

"What's that?" Wens asked.

"Compromise. Half measures. Zo knows exactly what he wants, and on this cursed island, where all enterprise and effort come to naught, that is a mortal sin." He hung his head. "The man I love most in the world is going to get himself killed."

"I loved my brother most of all, too," Wens said.

Delbarth claimed to have rescued twenty-three people the previous evening and gave Zo a brief course on the principles of search and rescue as he had learned them. "There are plenty of ways in but only one way out." Drawing a long rope from their equipment, he crouched at Zo's ankle and tied him to it. "There is sixty feet of line here," he said. "If you have to go any farther, you're doomed. Follow this back whether you've found her or not." He warned Zo that the school had become a three-dimensional maze. "It's not just right and left you have to contend with, but up and down, too. Stay close to the walls."

When that was done, the roadworker took the orange hard hat off his head, retrieved a rag from underneath it, and wiped his face. Then he handed the safety helmet to Zo.

"You'll need it more than I do," Delbarth said, "where you're going." He showed Zo how to turn on the headlight, placed the helmet on his head and tightened the ratchet. "Bring it back," he said.

Zo said he would. But then the very first thing he did upon lowering himself into the understory was disobey Delbarth's specific injunction to stay at the walls. The problem was that the simulation laboratory was two rooms and they had punched Zo into the wrong one. He needed to get to the maternity annex, on the far side of the wall. The only way through was a narrow passage shaped like a keyhole, round above and narrow below, where the roof and walls had fallen together. But when he came up against the back wall of the laboratory he found that there was no passage. The way was closed by a section of ceiling.

By lying flat and feeling underneath, he discovered a false floor. The wall did not join neatly with the ground here, and there was a space between just wide enough for him to pass if he lay flat on his stomach. The cement dust stung his eyes and tasted like chalk in his mouth. But he carried forward on his elbows, with the crust scraping along his back. Great fires were burning where the gas pipes had burst in the first-floor kitchens, and the heat carried up through the cement so that Zo could feel the warmth on his hands when he crawled that narrow passage.

By passing beneath the wall, he came into the dark zone, where there was no light from the surface. The farther chamber had its own climate, small and hot and hushed. Live electric wires sparked in the walls, and a chemical fire burned green and blue along the floors. He turned on the headlamp.

It was more like a crypt than a classroom. Zo could see that a number of students had been killed there. It had been the very first day of class and the course syllabi were scattered in the debris like leaflets. Zo read the title by the light of the headlamp: "Advanced Topics in Midwifery." He had climbed at last into Anaya's classroom, but had used all sixty feet of rope to get there. Ignoring Delbarth's warning to stay tied in at all costs, he reached down his body and undid the knot. He found a piece of block and tied it in his place using the Brazilian sailor's knot Ozias had taught him, the one the old man called a bowline on a bight. Leaving the block and rope behind, he carried on untethered.

There on top of the rubble, looking as delicate as a love letter after a bomb blast, Zo found the handkerchief Madam Zulu had made and presented to them on the day of their wedding on Mòn Nwa. He read it in the light of the headlamp.

A & Z. January 1, 2010.

Zo lay on his back and said her name. He said it over and over again, louder with every iteration, until it was a talisman and an elegy and, finally, a terror in his mouth. The air had grown poisonous with carbon monoxide and Zo's arteries pounded in his neck. He could hear the blood rushing behind his ears when he fell quiet, and then he swore he could hear her breathing. He recognized it from the even respirations he'd heard beside him in the bed on Mòn Nwa during their honeymoon. Pulling himself toward that sound, using his arms, he called again. This time, she called back.

"Zo," she said. *"Cheri doudou."*

"It's me," he said. "I'm here."

"Where are you? I can't see you."

Using the light on his hard hat, Zo surveyed his position. It wasn't promising. He was blocked on three sides, and a thick piece of concrete lay between them.

"I'm cold," she said.

"Don't think about that." He could hear her teeth chattering. "Think about Taino Beach," he said. "Remember how warm the water was?" Anaya's voice was coming from above him, on the far side of a slab of roof, which had crashed down like a plate through the middle of the classroom. Zo was on the wrong side, but if he could only get through he'd be able to touch her. "Do you remember the queen triggerfish?" he asked.

"The black and white, with spotted bands."

"That's the spotted drum," he said. He felt the concrete with both hands, seeking a weakness or a beginning. "The queens are purple."

"Tell me about the anemones," she said.

He'd found a fissure in the concrete, something to start with. What he needed now was a tool to drive against it. "You have to be careful of the anemones," he said. "The tines are poisonous." He broke off a piece of twisted furniture, the metal leg from a chair, and, sliding along the rubble on his back, came up against the slab.

"What color are they?"

"Black," he said. "But they sit out in the white sand so you can see them."

"That's nice of them."

"Isn't it?" He found the fissure and struck there, bringing the implement up as hard as he could. The dust fell in his face. "I'm right below you," he said. "Can you see me?"

"No."

Using the chair leg like a crowbar, Zo succeeded in prying free a chunk of concrete.

"Oh Zo," she said. "I can see your light."

Zo wiped the rock from his eyes. His headlight was shining straight up into his work. He'd succeeded in breaking out a sizable chunk of concrete from the slab that separated them. But he could clearly see the net of rebar was still intact and stood between them like a gate. He grabbed it with both hands.

"Can you move?" he asked.

"I don't think so." Bits of rock fell through the dark when she tried. "Something's lying across my legs."

"What is it?"

"I can't see."

Zo turned the lamp into Anaya's narrow chamber.

"It's an ultrasound machine," she said. "Miss Cacquette had us working with them."

"Does it hurt?"

"I don't think so. I mean it did. But it doesn't hurt anymore." They could hear water running, and voices calling from classrooms below. "I'm scared," she said.

"Think of Taino. The water, the sand, the starfish. The boulders they call Les Poissons."

"I'm closing my eyes," she said. "Not because I'm tired, but because it's easier to imagine it that way."

Anaya must have fallen asleep. She woke to hear Zo speaking.

"Even if I could get through the concrete, there is still the rebar between us. I need something to cut through it."

"Like what?"

"A saw, maybe."

"Where will you get one?"

"The *zouti* are outside."

"No," she said. "You can't leave me."

Zo jammed himself against the concrete. By reaching his hand out, he could get it through the net of rebar into the far side, where Anaya was trapped.

"I can almost reach you," he said. "Can you turn toward me?"

"I can't move."

"What about your hand? Can you reach your hand toward my voice?"

Anaya reached down her body as far as she could. "Say something else," she said. "Say something."

"What should I say?"

"Tell me you love me."

"I love you."

"Tell me I'm the only one you ever loved."

"You're the only one I ever loved."

Zo's touch came just in time. It was like passing a flame from a live wick to a dead one. Zo felt it too. That sentiment coursed through them simultaneously with the immediacy and heat of electricity, obliterating everything in its path except that piece of concrete between them. Zo closed his eyes against the dust.

"I have to go," he said. "It's our only chance."

"How will you find me again?"

Zo was lying on his back. The ceiling was six inches from his face. Reaching his free hand into the pocket of his pants, he found a one-dollar coin, an *adokin*. Passing it through the rebar, he held it out with his fingertips.

"*Pran li*," he said. "Take it."

By working her index finger over her middle, Anaya was able to grasp the coin in a pincer grip and, like that, transferred it to her other hand. "What now?"

"Find something metal," he said. "Can you find something?"

He could hear her panting, trying to move against the weight of the roof. "There's something here. I think it's a bedpost."

"Can you touch it?"

"Yes."

"Beat it with the *adokin*."

He heard the faint sound.

"Harder."

"Like this?"

"As hard as you can."

She beat the metal post once, twice, three times.

"Do it like that and don't stop," he said. "If you do that, I'll know where to find you."

He took his fingertips from hers and immediately felt cast adrift.

"Wait, Zo, before you go. What was the name of that other beach? The one from the letter you wrote me. The beautiful beach with the white sand, where the water is clear to thirty feet and you can see the lobsters on the bottom of the sea."

"Are you talking about Anse d'Hainault?"

"I don't want to stay in Port-au-Prince anymore," she said. "I don't want to go back to Jérémie. When I get out of here, I want to go to Anse d'Hainault."

.   .   .

Zo went out the way he came, on his back this time because he couldn't find a place to turn onto his stomach. He was looking for the rope and cinder block he'd anchored under the wall. But in that dark labyrinth he took a wrong turn. One wrong way led to another, and he ended up in a dark cul-de-sac far from his destination. He could hear water running out of the pipes. Then he felt a pressure down his leg.

Sighting the headlamp down his body, Zo saw Anaya's professor, Miss Cacquette. He had arrived at that very spot from which she'd been delivering her lecture on the use of an ultrasound when an entire plane of the roof had turned at an angle and driven into her midsection. She was pinned on her stomach, with her arms stretched out before her, her bladder so full of blood that she would feel like she had to urinate until the end of her life.

Miss Cacquette clawed his leg. Her breathing was rapid and shallow, and there was blood in her teeth. When she finally spoke, it was only to recite the midwife's prayer that she'd addressed to every newborn she'd ever delivered into the world.

"While yet all you know of this world are my hands," she said, squeezing Zo's leg, "let them tell you what is hard, and what is paired, and what is the temperature of the blood. And how badly we want to love you without knowing how." Her voice was eerie and thick, and when she spoke she looked right at him. "I am the one who drew you from your mother's womb," she whispered, "and I can't put you back."

An aftershock slammed into the island. It rattled the warehouses at the port and barreled inland under the mountain. When it reached the flatland downtown it upset the already precarious understructure of the nursing school. There was a booming echo coming up from the earth and then a high-pitched crack as the floors gave way and he tumbled below.

Brino and Delbarth lost their footing on the canted roof and fought to stay upright. They were like miners in a collapsing shaft, blind under the dust and shouting not to let go of the rope, because to lose that was to lose Zo forever. They set their boots in the deranged ceiling and drew the yellow line from the collapsed hull of the university. They didn't speak but sweated and strained in silence, hauling the frayed cordage foot by foot and coiling it at their feet, until finally they had pulled out everything except the very last section of rope and then they pulled that free, too.

It was not looped to Zo at all but to a piece of shattered cinder block he'd tied in his place.

· Book Four ·

14

A SLIGHT TREMOR on Tuesday, January 12, sent Leconte out of his office and into the lobby. It was 4:53 p.m. The wooden shutters were closed over the windows and the great ceiling fan revolved in the heat. His colleagues were gathered around the secretary's desk. Dr. Beaujolais, one of the deputies, pointed at the secretary.

"Sandra thinks the Americans are doing weapons testing."

Sandra smiled. "Bikini Atoll," she said. "They are not kind to the islands."

Leconte went back to his paperwork but couldn't get anything done. He was relieved when Beaujolais appeared in the door.

"You've got to come hear this," he said.

The radio was on in the lobby and Sandra shushed them. "There was an earthquake in Port-au-Prince," she said.

The newscaster's voice was like an SOS from a sinking ship. Frantic and muted by static, it sounded a thousand miles away.

"They're broadcasting from a church in Bolosse," Sandra explained. "It's the only station coming out of the capital."

They heard the newscaster again, begging for help—from the Dominicans, the Cubans, the Americans, and then God, in that order. A burst of static interrupted the broadcast and then the voice again, asking people to go elsewhere for care because Lopital Jeneral had been destroyed.

Leconte was affected by that statement as if it had been from Anaya herself, in her own voice.

"What's wrong?" Beaujolais asked.

Leconte looked without seeing. He was thinking of the university building with its exterior hallways and heavy cement roof. "Anaya goes to school in the capital," he said, "on the campus of Lopital Jeneral."

He went back to his office to call her and, when he couldn't get through, Desmond Tessier. The same ominous static on his brother-in-law's line set his heart racing. He stood up and walked back to the lobby. Sandra and Dr. Beaujolais, seeing his face, asked what was wrong, but Leconte didn't answer. He couldn't.

A constriction in his chest set his arteries pounding and made his eyes feel like they were bulging from his face. Coupled with a ringing in his ears, he could hardly find his way through the corridor and finally dragged himself into the daylight guided only by habit. But there was no relief in the sunshine. The world without was bright and terrifying because it hadn't changed at all, while Leconte felt as if he'd shed his old life and all its habits in an instant.

It was the precise sentiment he'd had upon first learning of Roselyn's death. Then he'd been a thousand miles from home, at the Pan American Health Organization conference in Washington, D.C. He'd left the convention center and walked into the foreign city to be overwhelmed by the monuments and clean, bright streets. Nothing seemed real. Not the conversation with his colleagues, or the taxi ride to the airport, or the sea beneath him on the long flight home. Nothing was real until he saw his daughter again and took her in his arms.

"Anaya," he cried. "Anaya!"

The lament that escaped his mouth caused the nearby merchants to look up from their wares. He wanted to scream at them. How could they go about buying rice and beans on Rue Stenio Vincent when his daughter had just been killed in Port-au-Prince? He looked up the street to the right and left as if he didn't know which way to turn.

Leconte found his car, climbed into the back seat, and shut the door before Claude, his driver, was able to get over from the shady place under the trees where the chauffeurs sat waiting for their charges. Then, hardly speaking, and with a face that was terrible to see, he ordered Claude to take him home. The car rolled along those familiar streets in a city he didn't even recognize. The commissariat where the police played carom, the buses idling at the station, the red cathedral he'd known all his life—all were without depth, like two-dimensional drawings.

Claude watched him in the mirror. The doctor could not sit still. One moment his head was in his hands. The next he'd flung it back over the headrest and produced a kind of anguished sigh the driver had never heard before. Leconte clawed at the knot of his tie, pulled it loose, and undid his collar. Then, contrary to ten years of habit, he rolled down the window and ordered Claude to do the same.

He sat in the wind thereafter and it even seemed to calm him. But that lasted only a moment. Reaching underneath him on the seat, Leconte found an envelope that sent him into further paroxysms of regret.

"It's the letter you were expecting," Claude said. "It came this afternoon."

It was the official record of Anaya's registration for the spring semester. The logo on the university's stationery swam and flashed surreally: it was damning evidence. He himself had sent her away to be killed in the capital.

He recalled their last conversation together, in August, when he had tried, at first, to be reasonable. "I don't oppose you to force my will or be heavy-handed," he'd said. "I just want what's best for you."

She sat across from him with that icy expression, refusing to speak or even look him in the eye, so that he finally grew resentful and ended up saying all those things he would come to regret. Ungrateful, spoiled, foolish. Calling her *bouzen,* a whore! Leconte cried out when he thought of what had come next. How, like a magistrate with a legal ruling, he'd raised his hand and banished her to Port-au-Prince.

And then he was foolish enough to feel relieved! Tensions had been so high between them for so long that the relationship with that laborer from Paul's crew had seemed just the pretext he needed to send her away. He thought of the laborer for the first time since he had appeared at his door demanding back pay for two months of work. Then Leconte had laughed in his face, and sent him away with the admonition to find a woman who was used to squalor and give her the same. Now the worker seemed insignificant and even innocent against the great disaster in Port-au-Prince.

They reached the outskirts of the city and turned toward Chabanne. But the calm landscape of leafy mangoes and tall *kalbas* trees that had always soothed Leconte's spirit only made him more wretched. He played his final meeting with Anaya over and over again, looking for something kind or good, but found nothing. The fever, which had subsided somewhat since he'd rolled down the window, redoubled behind his eyes.

He'd used his connections in the government to secure Anaya's transfer to the national nursing school, and since then he'd had more contact with the dean or the dean's secretary than he had with his own daughter. He'd received her final grades for the fall semester and had a glass of red wine in celebration. When he called Anaya on Christmas Day, she had been distant and dismissive, telling him only that she was going to spend the holiday with her cousin Nadine at the Royal Decameron Indigo Beach Resort where, she warned, cell phone reception was spotty. Spring semester started on Monday, the eleventh of January, she said, and she would call him then. That was the last time they spoke.

Without knowing exactly how he got there, he found himself standing in Anaya's old room. He was struck by an irrevocable stillness there like the stillness inside a shrine. He knelt on the pink carpeting that she had chosen and regarded her things through a mist of tears. The photos of her and Roselyn, the stuffed bear from a valentine long ago, the red gilt box he'd brought back from St. Vincent and the Grenadines. They no longer had any practical application at all, as if they were nothing but keepsakes and Anaya were already gone.

It was then, in the depths of despair, that he realized he was still clutching the envelope from the nursing school. Tearing it open, he unfolded the paper and looked at it blankly. It took him some time to decipher Anaya's spring semester schedule and find where she'd be on Tuesday at 4:53 p.m. That location was as galvanizing as a purpose. For the first time since he'd heard the news of the earthquake, he had a clear idea of what to do next and had that kind of ecstasy that follows a period of extended indecision. The emotion that had blinded him, the pounding in his arteries that had made him giddy, was replaced by a new sense of urgency. To stay a moment longer, he felt, would be a betrayal not only of his daughter, who might be trapped under the rubble, but also of her mother, to whom he had sworn the solemn promise to guide their daughter safely to adulthood.

He packed haphazardly, emptying her drawers, wondering later why he'd brought so much. He checked his watch and was amazed to find that it was only 5:45; less than an hour had passed. When he found the driver and told him they were going to Port-au-Prince, Claude protested. Not because it was too little notice, but because he had heard from the other drivers that the roads were impassable in much of the Ouest Department.

Leconte walked next door, to Commissioner Cledanor's house, wheeling the suitcase behind him as if he were off to board a plane. There in the doorway, refusing refreshment or even to relinquish the bag, he asked the commissioner about conditions in the capital.

Cledanor said the airport was damaged. The highway bridges were out at La Digue, Thozin, Mayombe, and over the Rivye Momance. "If you go by car, you'll have to walk from Petit-Goâve," he said.

"How far is Petit-Goâve?"

"Seventy-two kilometers from Port-au-Prince," the commissioner said.

Leconte returned home and told Claude to get in the car.

"Where to?" the driver asked.

"The wharf," he said.

There was only one ship at the dock when they arrived, a gaff-rigged cutter called the *Rekin II*. The name was painted in silver lettering. The ship looked like it had been put up for repairs. The mast had been removed from the capstan, and a pair of ship-wrights were driving wedges and pouring hot bitumen. The captain was called Boston. He oversaw the work from a stool he'd set on deck, drinking rum and leaning dangerously, pointing out the shipwrights' mistakes. "You fix her like that and she'll blow over in a cool breeze," he said.

The principal advantage of the *Rekin* was that it was there when Leconte needed it. There were no other ships at port and none due until tomorrow and Leconte couldn't wait. He asked Boston when the ship might be ready to sail. "Don't let her present state fool you," Boston said. "The *Rekin* is always ready for work." He bragged of her service on rough seas, naming the tropical storms she'd passed through.

"But can she get us to Port-au-Prince?" Leconte interrupted.

"She may not be much to look at," Boston said, "but she has been leaving from this very dock every Wendesday morning at seven a.m. for the last fifteen years, and she always manages to make her destination."

"Wednesday morning?" Leconte shook his head. "I can't wait that long."

"This isn't a mototaxi service," Boston said. "It's customary to fill the ship before sailing it. I'd go broke if I took single passengers."

"How much do you make, running a full ship one way?"

Boston considered the possibilities. His customer seemed desperate. His shirt was sweated through and open at the throat, but his shoes were a testament to his means, and his demeanor was that of a man used to getting his way.

"Forty-eight passengers at three hundred *gourdes* a head," Boston figured. "Children at half price. Cargo by weight. Double for livestock." He considered deck space, gasoline, docking fees, motor oil—then quoted a price so reasonable Leconte agreed to pay it without making a counteroffer. Boston almost added ancillary costs—labor, navigation, wear and tear—but something about the doctor's manner, the quiet desperation in his speech, the conviction in his face, convinced him to settle.

Leconte left the wharf through the customhouse and came out on Stenio Vincent. Claude was waiting in the car. Leaning forward through the seats and taking his driver by the arm, he said, "St. Anne's."

"What are you planning?"

"I'm certain they could use some medical assistance in the capital," Leconte said.

Hardly two hours had passed since he'd first heard about the earthquake, but it felt to Vincent Leconte as if he'd entered a new age. He was a different man and the world was a different place. He believed in different things. A need to be near his daughter pulsed in his body like a new organ, imbuing him with energy and clearheadedness.

He found Dr. Beaujolais at the clinic and dispatched him to the wards. "See Lamartinier in orthopedics, and Dodard in the OR. Take whatever they can spare."

When the nurses heard that Dr. Leconte was planning a medical relief mission to Port-au-Prince, they came off the floors to help. Those who knew Anaya and knew she'd been attending school in the capital understood the minster's haste. A few of the older nurses even remembered Anaya's mother, Roselyn Leconte, and had worked beside her. That was how Dr. Vincent Leconte ended up organizing the first indigenous relief mission to Port-au-Prince. He set out to save his daughter but wound up trying to save the city.

They arrived at the wharves two hours later with an ambulance full of medical supplies, including ultrasound equipment and units of blood. Beaujolais supervised the stowage of everything into the underdeck hold, ordering ice for the blood and wrapping the crates in plastic.

Word had gotten out that Boston was departing ahead of schedule, and a queue of travelers gathered at the dock. Leconte climbed aboard and addressed them from the level deck. He said it was not a business trip or pleasure cruise they were taking but a medical mission to Port-au-Prince. "We won't be taking any passengers."

"I don't think those are passengers," Beaujolais said.

An old woman in a red bandanna, with a red sash tied around her waist, finally called from the wharf. "*Nou pa vin achete*," she said. "We haven't come to buy and sell." Leconte noticed that they hadn't brought the usual market wares. There was no livestock or bundled vegetables. The men carried all manner of *zouti*— shovels, hammers, pickaxes. With their somber faces and down-turned chins they looked like a party of gravediggers. The women had blankets, rice, candles, and flashlights. They were as solemn as funeral mourners. There were no children among them, nor any fight cocks. They weren't playing music or telling jokes.

It was only then that Leconte realized they were just like him, mothers and fathers with loved ones in the capital and no way of knowing if they were living or dead. They had been drawn together by the same sad and urgent business. Grabbing the gunwale for support, he told the captain to take as many as he could.

"I'll pay their passage," he said.

They loaded the ship in the brief blue twilight of the tropics, shipping sixteen brokenhearted passengers and their baggage. The old woman in the red bandanna kissed her donkey goodbye, called it Boustabek, and warned it to keep out of the pigeon pea. She was the oldest among them, a widow named Misulu who'd spent her entire life in the mountains behind Bomon and had never even been to sea. She stood uneasily at the capstan, holding the mainmast with both hands when the ship cast off from its moorings and drifted into the harbor.

Boston ordered all engines in and the crew dropped both outboards. The powerful Yamahas smoked in the steady sea at dusk. Leconte sat amidships with Beaujolais, who had refused to stay behind. The surgical team sat in the prow amid their equipment, taking inventory of the anesthetics. Claude Juste was there, too, with Leconte's and Anaya's luggage. Leconte looked back to see the headland black in the gray tide and the lights of Jérémie pooling under the mountain.

The widow Misulu had brought a bottle of tafia. She started out drinking by the capful but ended up drinking straight from the bottle. "I'd rather die in a city I've never seen, among people I don't know"—she drank—"than return to where I was born"—she drank again—"as childless as I was when I first came into the world." Misulu only ever had one daughter, and she had been working as a maid in Bel Air. Misulu was afraid she'd been crushed at one of those mansions doing someone else's laundry.

Beaujolais turned her down but Leconte accepted when she offered him a drink. He took the bottle, raised it up, and took the longest pull of *kleren* he'd ever taken, swallowing to the dregs and then deeper, to the bitters and powders and poisons. His mouth burned as hotly as his head, and when the ship rolled he fell back into the old woman's arms.

"I'm like you," he said. "I only have one daughter and won't return without her."

The lights on the coast were impossibly few and distant, and Leconte felt as if he'd been cast adrift from nowhere forever. The alcohol and sorrow, the sky without horizon, the stars shimmering beneath him, made the journey vertiginous, like crossing the river of death. The sea was rough beyond the Baradères and the boat pitched and fell. Leconte could hear the Yamahas straining and smell the burning gasoline when they came clear of the water. The barefoot crewmen went intently in the rigging, while the captain never left his post at the tiller, stoic in a windbreaker and straw hat. The passengers raised a song against the sea and didn't stop singing until they reached calm waters at Miragoâne.

Leconte woke at dawn in the bow of the ship without knowing how he'd gotten there, with a sickness in his gut and the feeling that he'd talked all night. The passengers lined the gunwales, peering out over the gray sea. A pall of smoke obscured the bay and the bay plain, but above that he could see, like an ancient Greek city, the ruined neighborhoods of Port-au-Prince in the silver light. Whole mountainsides had washed out overnight and the homes lay tumbled in the slopes. The fuel refinery burned at the coast, the hot pure blue of a diesel fire, shimmering like a mirage under its own black smoke.

Scores of bodies were floating in Port-au-Prince Bay, drifting on the tin-still water. Some were faceup and their faces eaten off by fish. Others were turned into the sea, away from the colorless sky and the world they had come from.

The Grande Anse medical mission, under the command of Dr. Vincent Leconte, was the first medical team to arrive by boat and had to discover for itself the desperate conditions at the national port. The cement pad as long as an ocean liner had broken in the middle and was half submerged in the sea. The pair of lifting cranes, millions of dollars apiece, had fallen across the shipping lane and the containers had spilled into the water.

They disembarked instead at the illegal wharf in Cité Soleil, where Boston had connections and where there'd been no heavy infrastructure to damage in the first place. The shirtless stevedores appeared from the alleyways, and Leconte rented trucks from a local transport service.

The island seemed like a vast shipwreck in the sea. Parliament, the Finance Ministry, the Ministry of Public Works, the Ministry of Communication, the tax office, the municipal building, City Hall, the Ministry of Justice, the National Palace—all were destroyed. The telephone lines were canted over the avenues like a world drawn in bad perspective. A man went by pushing dead children in a wheelbarrow as naturally as if he'd been doing that work every day for a lifetime. A street cook stood on the curb holding her pan like a drum and beating a doleful tattoo with a soup ladle. "It's killed us in our kitchens!" she wailed. "It's killed us in our kitchens!"

The medical campus, which Leconte had known since his student days and to which he had returned at least once a year for the last twenty years, was as unfamiliar as if he'd never seen it before. Lopital Jeneral was devastated, but a few heroic surgeons were still at work there, operating by daylight and headlamp under mango trees, hanging IV bags from the lower branches. The medical director, Alix Lamothe, was with them. A gastroenterologist by trade, Alix had trained at the Faculty of Medicine in Strasbourg, France. Now Leconte saw him trying to run an operating room without walls, lights, narcotics, or a sterile field.

"We're out of everything," he told Leconte. Desrossiers, a general surgeon who usually performed hernia repairs, had just tried an amputation. He asked how far the earthquake had reached.

"Jérémie wasn't affected," Leconte said. "And I saw Anse-à-Veau from the sea."

"Are the roads that bad?"

"There's not a bridge over any of the rivers between here and Petit-Goâve."

Alix rubbed his eyes. "I never thought I'd see a disaster such as this," he said. "We'll be set back a hundred years, and we were already a hundred years behind."

"What have you heard from your family?"

Alix's eyes were red and glassy. "My wife and children live abroad."

"I'm not so lucky," Leconte said. "My daughter is a fourth-year student at the nursing college. What news have you had from there?"

Alix put his hand on Leconte's shoulder. "The only advice I have for you is not to look," he said.

Leconte's first view of the nursing university turned his blood to ice. The roof, which had been square before the mountains, now made a sinuous line beneath them. He'd never seen the hills from that angle before because the school had always stood in his way. But the university had been brought low, the floors driving down until Leconte could see over it all to the mountains behind.

"You can't tell anything from the outside," Alix said. "The only thing to do is go over there and find out for ourselves." He took Leconte by the arm.

The stretch of grass that had once been the central plaza of the country's premier medical facility had been turned into a chaotic field hospital. The patients who'd been carried in on doors and bedsheets now lay dying in the gardens. The neat paths had been overrun, and Leconte navigated the bodies as carefully as if he were walking through a minefield. He didn't raise his head at all, and only knew they were approaching the nursing school because he recognized the uniforms of the young women lying on the ground.

At first, he was able to marshal the disaffection he'd mastered as a medical student in the cadaver labs. But that hard-won dispassion soon gave way to the weary presentiment that his daughter was there among them somewhere, and then he couldn't help but look. Soon, he saw Anaya everywhere, in every face and every uniform, no matter the year. Some were bloody and ruined, like victims of a shark attack, while others were as pristine as if they were only sleeping and Leconte expected them to open their eyes.

The less grievously wounded nursing students had stayed on to take care of their more grievously wounded classmates, and Alix left him with a student named Yonise. She'd been in Cacquette's course when the earthquake struck, and she knew Anaya and where to find her.

Leconte could hardly understand what she was saying. Though he'd set out from Jérémie twenty hours earlier with the sole intention of finding his daughter again, he still wasn't prepared, when the moment finally came, to see her again. His senses were dull, as if preparing him for the worst shock of his life, and he heard Yonise from a great remove.

"We were in the Fatima Maternity Annex when it happened."

He followed her onto the flagstone courtyard that had once marked the entrance to the nursing school, and felt as if he were standing at the bottom of the sea. All the sounds—the words of the nurses, the calls of the wounded, the barking dogs—were muted and distant. The sunlight was diluted, like light underwater. Even the air had thickened and offered resistance, as if he were in the sea with the tide against him.

Yonise stopped talking and knelt beside one of the girls on the ground.

She was turned away from him, facing the school. But even from that distance, at that angle and under those lights, Leconte knew it was his daughter. He could tell from her profile alone, which had the precise cut of his late wife's profile—her jaw angled forward so that her mouth was primary and paramount, both the first thing you saw when you looked at her and the last thing you'd ever forget when you finally lost her.

His approach was like swimming. He held his breath and

seemed to float over thousands of pages of medical textbooks that had been blasted from the university library. Anaya looked like a figure of unfired clay—soft, already broken. Her hair was plaited with dust and her face was caked with it.

A tremendous weariness overtook him and he fell to his knees. It was not what he thought he would do when he finally saw her again—he'd imagined himself with a stethoscope or instrument, doing something useful—but he was overwhelmed. With trepidation, as if he didn't want to disfigure her, he placed two fingers against her jugular notch.

The steadiness of her heartbeat at that moment, just when he had lost all hope, moved him to tears. Everything came back in a roar, like a wave crashing on the beach. He heard the dogs and the Christian choirs in the hills and the nursing student giving report.

"Blood pressure ninety over seventy-two. Pulse weak and thready. Tachycardic at a hundred and ten."

Anaya's left clavicle had been fractured in the middle third, and a large bruise over her left flank made him fearful of internal bleeding. But her stomach was soft, and when they placed the catheter it filled with urine, not blood. Her left leg had been broken through both bones and the foot was turned against the knee.

He brought his medical bag forward, opened it, and reached through the instruments. Purely from habit, he chose the stethoscope, fit the buds into his ears, and put the bell against her chest. He remembered that morning in Jérémie when he'd presented her with her own stethoscope and she'd listened to both their hearts.

"What do you hear?"

"Mama, telling us to get along."

Now, in Port-au-Prince, her machinery never faltered but battered away, while her breath rushed in and out like a breeze to cool his fiery disquiet.

Yonise brought one of her classmates from the shadows. "This is Verna," she said. "She was with us in Cacquette's class."

Verna looked like the ghost of a fourth-year. She was thin, shivering, and covered in dust.

"The roof broke into plates," Yonise said, "and crashed down at an angle, this way." She moved her hand in a chopping fashion. "Verna and I were able to pull ourselves free, but Anaya was trapped."

"This is how we found her," Verna said. She brought out a one-dollar coin. "It saved her life."

"An *adokin?*"

"She used it to call to us," Yonise explained. "Like this." She struck the IV pole with the coin—once, twice, three times.

The clear, harsh ping, which had been his daughter's cry to the world, made Leconte uneasy. He closed his eyes. The girls told him how they'd found a group of students at the Faculty of Law and convinced them to come to the nursing school. By following the sound of that *adokin,* they'd found Anaya and helped the *zouti* crew to pull her free. Climbing to his feet and taking them both in his arms, Leconte thanked the girls for saving his daughter's life.

It might have been days before the international relief teams arrived; it might have been hours. Leconte lost all sense of time. He slept beside Anaya in a white lab coat, feeling as he had in the early days of his medical residency, when he had been both overwhelmed with and fortified by the task of protecting a life from the onslaughts of a hard world. He finally spoke to a doctor from Quebec and, together, they got Anaya into one of the makeshift surgeries.

"Is she urinating?" the surgeon asked. "I'm worried about her kidneys, and crushing syndrome." The Canadian had wide forearms and dark hair under his throat.

"She would need dialysis," Leconte said. "We don't even have electricity to run the machine."

The Canadian paused and looked at Leconte. "I'm sorry. Who are you?"

"I'm her father," Leconte said.

The surgeon was stout and haggard, an orthopedist with curly black hair and dark discolorations around his eyes from terminal sleeplessness. "Jesus. I thought you were her doctor," he said. Then he took Anaya's splint down and inspected the wound that ran a transverse angle to her shin. He used his fingers to explain that she'd suffered a complex comminuted fracture of both bones of her lower left leg. In the model, his middle finger was the tibia and his index was the fibula and they bent in opposite directions at the knuckle.

"At home, we might stand a chance. External fixation, a series of surgeries. But here? I'm sorry." The doctor spoke an odd French that Leconte would never forget. "I cannot save her leg."

Leconte was finally driven from the surgery by news of his daughter's impending amputation. He couldn't bear to see them take her leg. He called for a car instead, thinking that a hot shower and a good night's sleep were what he most needed. Darkness had fallen outside, and entire families were sleeping under the tamarind trees in the hospital yard. Their candles flickered in the grass.

The driver took him up Avenue John Brown through a darkened city.

"Where are we?" Leconte asked.

"This is it."

Leconte looked out the window. The hotel that he had long considered his sanctuary in the capital—the bar where he'd drunk with his wife, the veranda where he'd taken coffee—had been destroyed. There was nothing now but a bare hillside with palms nodding along the slope and a thousand stars above the lightless city.

"Is there somewhere else?" the driver asked.

Leconte didn't answer immediately. Then, in despair, with nowhere else to go, and feeling like the city was as unfamiliar as if he'd never been there before, he told the driver to take him to Kay Jardin, in Juvenat.

Tessier appeared in the doorway of his house as detached as a ghost in its mausoleum. He stuck a pinkie finger deep into his ear. "This low pressure causes me all kinds of discomfort," he said.

Inside Kay Jardin it was as if the earthquake had just happened. The marble floors were cracked where chunks of the roof had fallen free in the shaking, and heaps of broken china had been swept against the wall.

Tessier said, "I've dismissed Atamise."

"Why?"

"One needs solitude and uninterrupted quiet to grieve properly."

Leconte's breath stuck in his chest. "Nadine?" he said. "Are you sure?"

"I went down to see the apartment for myself," Tessier said. "Perhaps that was a mistake. Now I see that pile of rubble every time I close my eyes. I can't sleep. I see her there that last afternoon, in the kitchen when she hears the rumbling, running onto the balcony, dying there trying to get a better look."

Leconte had come to understand that location was practically all that could be said of those who'd been killed in the earthquake. Where they died had come to stand in for why they died and even why they had lived; it was part obituary and part epitaph.

"Marie blames me for everything, of course," Tessier continued. "And she's not wrong! I was the one who gave in and let her move to that damned place, after all."

Not knowing what else to say, and discomfited by the grief that was even more profound than his own, Leconte asked after Marie Michelin.

The judge waved his hand. "She took the first flight out and swears she'll never return."

"To Kay Jardin?"

"To me. Port-au-Prince. This country. I don't know. She's gone to live with our son in Pompano Beach."

As he'd driven away from the hospital, Leconte felt that he had to tell someone about his difficulties or die of them. But now, in the ruined foyer of his brother-in-law's house, in the face of his enormous and irreversible grief, Leconte felt guilty for his relative good fortune.

"Anaya was trapped in the nursing school for twelve hours," he said. "Some students from the Faculty of Law finally got her out. But she is alive." Reaching into his pocket, he came out with the dollar coin. "She bought her life with this."

Tessier took it. "An *adokin*?"

Leconte explained how she had used it to tap the post of the medical cot until help arrived. "The orthopedist says they cannot save her leg."

Tessier gave a grunt, whether of derision or sympathy Leconte couldn't tell. "Once I thought a father could hope for all kinds of things for his children," he said, taking Leconte by the arm. "But now I see that there is only one thing we can reasonably hope for on this godforsaken island."

"What's that?" Leconte asked.

"That we die before they do."

Dady Malebranche, the old doctor in Jérémie, retired from the Department of Public Health a week after the earthquake. It was the disaster that did him in. He told Leconte that a catastrophe as big as that was too much for a man as old as he was, and he asked Vincent to come back to Grande Anse and take the position. "There's no one else I have any confidence in."

"What about Beaujolais?"

"I've been director longer than Beaujolais's been alive," Dady said.

It was the very position Leconte had worked his whole life to achieve, yet he turned it down without the slightest hesitation. In fact, he used that opportunity to resign from the Department of Public Health once and for all. Saying that he couldn't properly execute his duties under the present circumstances, considering his daughter's grievous injuries, he asked to step down in order to spend more time with her.

Dady Malebranche begged him to reconsider. "We need you

now more than ever," he said. "Even as a ship needs its surest hands in a storm."

But Leconte refused to leave his daughter's side.

"I thought you might say something like that," Dady said. "And I've come prepared with another offer. Something we've made up just to keep you." He finally offered Leconte the post of interim director for medical relief in Port-au-Prince, and Leconte promised to think about it.

15

TI PAPA PIKAN SAID they were no Adam and no Eve. The world was already old and paradise spent when they came into it. Now it was earthquakes and the end of cities. Black smoke rising from endless gas fires. Ten thousand families squatting under their tented bedsheets in the flat country.

The afternoons had no measure. There was neither dawn nor dusk. Just white flashes of pain and heat, a bad taste in her mouth, and the confusion of an endless hour. Her feet were swollen, the mottled green of weathered copper. They were like someone else's feet, because she couldn't move them. For a long time it was dark and she lay in the grass. Then she was alone under a bright light. Her leg was infected and the surgeons wanted to cut it off.

She dreamt of a perfect Port-au-Prince, where the earthquake had not been a destruction but a miraculous recovery. Zo was there in a city of clean white buildings, carrying a briefcase, saying things he never would have said with a diction and vocabulary he had not possessed. So that when her fever finally broke, and

Anaya woke in that long, hot hospital tent, she was even more devastated than she would have been had she not dreamt that alternate beautiful city where red suspension bridges spanned the rivers and pink flamingos nested in the estuaries, and she wished immediately to fall back into the dream.

Instead, whenever she closed her eyes, she returned to Advanced Topics in Midwifery. It was the first day of the semester, and Miss Cacquette untied her head scarf and laid it open on the desk.

"This is all you'll ever need to work a birth," she said.

The students sat up in their seats to see a razor blade and a box of dental floss.

"Just remember to tie the cord." She held up the dental floss. "And cut between the knots." She exhibited the blade.

Cacquette taught her course in the Fatima Maternity Annex, really just two rooms at the rear of the third floor where they housed the ancient electrocardiogram and ultrasound machines, of which only one was working, and which the university called a "simulation laboratory." There was only one ultrasound for the twelve students, and that first day they took turns, coming up in twos. One girl was the patient, and she lay on the exam table with her shirt rolled up while her partner passed the transducer across her belly according to Cacquette's instruction.

When Anaya and Yonise took their turn, they passed the quietest moments Anaya ever remembered in a classroom. She was the patient and lay on the exam table with her shirt pulled up, while Yonise lubricated the probe and drew it across her belly.

"Not too much gel," Cacquette coached. "Just enough to reduce static and form a tight bond between the skin and the transducer."

It was so quiet Anaya could hear Yonise breathing as she drew the probe across.

"Approximately three to four percent of neonates arriving at term will be breech," Cacquette said, "meaning the buttocks or feet, not the head, will be the presenting part." Pointing at the television screen, she explained that the thin white wash in the corner was Anaya's uterus. "If you look closely, you can just see the tendril of the fallopian tube."

Anaya's womb floated on-screen and the class seemed to hold its collective breath. Cacquette took the probe herself and drew it across Anaya's belly. It was so still Anaya thought she could feel the sonar sounding in her organs. Cacquette described the uterus, the ovaries, the fallopian tubes, and Anaya lifted her head from the table to see it.

The girls were watching the television screen like spectators at a miracle, speechless. Anaya's womb was vibrating like a struck bell. That was how they saw the earthquake coming before it hit. It manifested itself to them through Anaya's body and up Miss Cacquette's ultrasound wand to be broadcast onto the miniature television screen.

Then the cupboards swung open and the contents flew out like enchanted objects. Metal bedpans clattered from the closets. The walls tipped and righted and tipped again so completely Anaya thought she'd fallen into the roof.

On January 25, Médecins Sans Frontières deployed an inflatable operating room on the hospital grounds, and Anaya had the first of the four surgeries that saved her leg. Her father was there above her when she woke. Leaning forward, he pressed his lips to her forehead like he used to do when she was a little girl home from school with a fever.

"You've been under anesthesia," he said. "Your throat must be sore."

Anaya looked down her body as if it were a long country she'd have to cross.

Her father seemed to understand. Lifting the pillow so that she could see for herself, he said, "You woke just after I'd left and refused permission." He was almost smiling, in fact almost laughing, at the serendipity of it all and the willpower of his daughter.

He brought her X-rays from a folder and held the oversized films in the light. He showed her the pins running and cross-running in her bones, and explained how they would stabilize the tibia and fibula while they grew back into proper anatomical configuration. The nurse was there, standing in Anaya's blind spot. She'd had one ever since the earthquake, but it seemed so trivial against the other wounds that she kept it a secret.

Anaya lay back and closed her eyes. The last thing she could remember was lying under the lights, begging to keep her leg. She heard the convalescents breathing in their sleep and smelled the wounds rotting in their bandages. She opened her eyes and followed the IV line down the pole to where it ran into her arm.

"Normal saline," her father said, turning the bag so she could see. "They removed the antibiotic yesterday." He told her that she'd been in and out of consciousness for two weeks. "Do you remember any of it?"

"Miss Cacquette," she said.

"The way the school fell." He shook his head. "You were lucky to survive."

Anaya asked if anyone had been to visit her.

That question was too much for Vincent Leconte. His sturdy features quivered and broke apart completely. Holding her hand while the tears fell down his face, he told her about her cousin Nadine.

Anaya listened impassively, her face retaining the imperturbable cast that frightened Leconte whenever he glimpsed it.

"That's the way it was all over the city," he said. "Some lived and some died by the whims of geology and engineering. I think that for you, it might have come down to the will to live." He reached into his pocket and showed her the *adokin*. "Do you know what this is?"

"A dollar," she said.

"Don't you remember?" He placed the coin in the middle of her palm. "Close your eyes. Think," he said.

Anaya was as affected by the cold hard edge of that coin as if it were Zo's own fingertips reaching out to her between the rebar. She rolled onto her side and clutched it in her fist.

Her father leaned over, blowing cool air across her face. "This is the dollar that saved your life."

Anaya felt as if she had fallen down a deep hole and was looking up at her father from a great depth. Though she longed to tell him the truth—that Zo had followed her to the capital, that they had been married on Mòn Nwa, that she was waiting for him and only him—she looked at her father's face, fatigued and anxious, and realized she couldn't hurt him like that, not now, after he had come all that way for her.

Once she had that *adokin,* she never went anywhere without it. It became a charm and a keepsake. She slept with it under her pillow and took it with her when her father pushed her through the hospital grounds in a wheelchair. It distilled her wishes in the world until they became very few and finally singular. She wanted to know Zo's fate.

Vincent Leconte accepted the position offered to him by Dady Malebranche in January. He became the interim director for medical relief in Port-au-Prince. He had an office at the airport and an apartment in Bel Air. He offered to take Anaya out of the hospital, either to stay with him or with her uncle in Juvenat, but Anaya declined. Most of those left in the ward were amputees. Some of them would never walk again. But they were the only people who could understand what she had been through, and Anaya didn't want to leave them.

Her neighbor in the ward was a third-year student named Oberdine, though everybody called her Berdy. Berdy's left leg had been guillotined straight across in a late-night operation without anesthetics or proper lighting. She called the surgeon a butcher, and loved to talk about the money she'd wasted on foot care. "All those pedicures and scented lotions."

Across from them was a girl they called Ti Da, or little Darlene. She was a freshman nursing student and had been in the first-floor auditorium when the earthquake struck. Her hand had been amputated at the wrist. One morning they unwound Ti Da's bandages to find the stump of her wrist split and bulging like rotten fruit and maggots festering on the red wound.

"For God's sake, Ti Da, close your eyes!" Berdy shouted.

But Ti Da couldn't help it. The maggots fascinated and terrified her. She watched them without blinking and then ran a weeklong fever. The white nurses applied ice packs to her neck, armpits, and groin, complaining all the while that if they were in Quebec they wouldn't dream of controlling fevers with ice. Ti Da had never heard of Quebec, and she lay shivering in the meltwater dreaming about cold cities of snow.

Out of the 117 students in the senior class, 81 were killed outright. Of Miss Cacquette's original lecture of 12, there were only 3 survivors: Yonise Brignole, Verna Florvil, and Anaya Leconte.

Verna was from the cosmopolitan north and had grown up in a city once called the Paris of the Antilles. Soft-spoken, well mannered, and proud of her fair complexion, she had an extensive collection of straw hats that she wore against the sun. Yonise was the opposite. Big and gregarious, she had been raised by freshwater fishermen in a sweltering lagoon below sea level. Yonise was so wide that patients who forgot her name sometimes called her *boot miss*, or "stout nurse," but she had no illusions otherwise. She had no illusions at all, which was what would make her, after graduation, such a wonderful nurse.

The girls visited Anaya almost every afternoon. They brought fruit juice—*grenadia,* orange, tamarind, papaya with milk and brown sugar. One afternoon, they brought her sour cherry juice over ice. The cold sharp flavor in her mouth and the smell of the young cherries affected Anaya as strongly as if Zo had appeared in the doorway of the ward. Putting aside the juice and throwing the sheets from her body so suddenly her friends were afraid she'd taken ill, Anaya confided in them the secret that ruled her waking hours and even some of her dreams.

She gestured to the juice with one hand and held her head in the other. "This is how we met," she said. "I was drinking cherry juice. I was wearing my nursing school uniform and he took me for a nurse. He called me Miss." She put the drink down and held her face in both hands. "He told me about his nocturnal fevers and I diagnosed him with malaria."

"Without a test?" Verna asked.

Anaya fell back in the pillows. "That came later," she said. Then, recounting each detail as it occurred to her, she told them about Zo's fevers, his treatment with chloroquine, their lovemaking on the coast, how they'd been discovered finally because of his sandals, and how she had been sent away to Port-au-Prince. She fixed her friends with a forlorn look. "I thought I'd never see him again," she said. "But he followed me here, to Port-au-Prince." Anaya touched her lips and spoke through her fingers. "When he kissed me after all that time, I realized he'd always known exactly how to love me."

"How?" Verna asked.

"Without reservations."

Maybe it was because her friends had never met him, or been to Mòn Nwa or even Jérémie, but Anaya had the unnerving feeling as she spoke that she wasn't describing her life at all but was recounting a dream she'd once had of a man she'd invented in her girlish fantasies. There was a moment in that overheated ward, with the taste of the cherry juice drying on her lips and the smell of antiseptic in her nostrils, that she was afraid their love had been nothing but a hallucination brought on by painkillers and fever. She panicked and reached out for something real. Taking Yonise's hand in her own and squeezing it, she begged them to go to Mòn Nwa.

"Take the coin," she said, reaching into her pocket for the *adokin*. "Tell him I'm waiting for him, and I need him now more than ever."

"What if we can't find him?"

"Then look for Ozias, or Madam Zulu. They'll know where he is."

Sensing her desperation and the fragility of her hope, the girls left that instant, traveling up Avenue John Brown into the foothills. They caught a second *taptap* in the park beneath Pétion-Ville and rode halfway to Kenscoff. They dismounted at the crossroads and found the beaten footpath Anaya had described leading off around the side of the hill.

"Follow it to the old man's backyard," she'd said. "You'll hear it before you see it because of the wind chimes."

Nothing was quite as Anaya had described. That lovely neighborhood of ocean-view villas was more like a mountainside of tarpaper shacks. Though they heard the wind chimes, they didn't find the paradise Anaya had remembered but an overgrown vegetable terrace washed out in the recent rains. There was no tall, handsome gardener. Nor was Ozias up at the main house, where Anaya said they'd find him—he was downslope in the smaller cabin they'd mistaken for a toolshed. They knew he was in there because they heard him talking through the half-open door. But when they entered they found him alone, lying on the bed, talking to a rooster tied to the bedpost. It cocked its head and crowed when the girls opened the door, and Ozias covered his eyes from the daylight.

"*Kite m pou kont mw,*" he cried. "I don't want your eggs or your honeycomb!"

Yonise told him they hadn't come with eggs or honeycomb. "We're looking for Zo."

At the mention of Zo's name, the old man sprung up from the bed and rushed toward them. The half bottle of tafia on the bedside table attested to the state of his drunkenness, but it seemed he'd forgotten even his infirmity. Tripping over his own foot, he fell into Yonise's arms and sobbed into her bosom.

"How dare you come up here to my mountain," he gasped, "talking about him as if he didn't mean the world to me."

Yonise dragged him kicking and screaming into the yard. He lay back in the grass, cursing the rooster and crying for it. *"La zanmi, la.* Here boy, here." He found a kernel of corn somewhere and held it out, talking nonsense. "They don't know any better, baby boy. They don't know what kind of man he was, do they? And how hard it was to lose him." He looked up at Verna and Yonise. "I wasn't thrilled when he first showed up, with his handbag and his machete. I thought he was going to cut down every last tree on my mountain. And he would have, too, if I hadn't stopped him. Believe me. That's why I gave him the job on my cart, just to keep him off the trees." He shook his head. "You girls never saw him run, did you?"

They said they had not.

"It's no easy thing, running a wagon in this city. And I should know. I did it for thirty-three years. But he was born for it! What steadiness of stride. What power! Like something the pastor talks about on Sunday morning. And all that time I criticized him. *Back straight. Even strides. Watch the tire.*" He hit his hands together in summation. "I never even had the chance to tell him how beautiful it was."

O stopped talking. His eyes watered and he got sick in the grass. The rooster ate the regurgitated vegetables from the lawn. *"Li pa gen oken prinsip,"* the old man groaned, trying halfheartedly to shoo the rooster. "He doesn't have any principles."

Yonise explained that they were nursing students and Anaya's classmates. "She told us to come to Mòn Nwa. To find Zo and give him this." She showed him the coin.

O shook his head. "I'm afraid, where he's gone, a dollar makes no difference."

"What do you mean?" Verna asked.

Ozias wiped his lips with the back of his hand. "There is no Zo!" he shouted. "Don't you see? Not on Mòn Nwa. Not in Grande Anse. Not anywhere." He tried to get to his foot but failed and finally lay sprawled on the lawn. "He's dead. Killed by an aftershock! And it's all my fault." He pulled handfuls of grass out by the roots. "I made him drag us through half the city like a donkey in the peanuts."

The girls told him there were camps in the city where he could find rice and safe drinking water, but he waved his hand.

"Some people might still call that a city." He nodded. "Some might even call it a capital. But as far as I'm concerned it's nothing but a graveyard. Every apartment is a catacomb. Every school a mausoleum. No"—he shook his head—"I wouldn't leave my mountain if they paid me good, clean, American money to do it."

Ozias was exhausted by his outburst and wouldn't say another word. They were finally obliged to place him back into the bed he'd climbed out of and leave him there with a glass of water.

"Does he have his covers?" O asked blearily.

"Who?"

"The chicken."

"Sure, old man," Verna said, putting the rooster in its rags. "He's already sleeping."

They found Madam Zulu doing laundry in her yard. She told them, without pausing over the washbasin, not to worry about the old man. "He's been like that for years, ever since his wife died. As difficult an old brat as you'll ever find." She slapped a pair of wet jeans into the water. "But it's really gotten worse since the earthquake. He'd gone around telling everyone that Zo was like the son he'd never had, and here the boy had gone and gotten himself killed."

They offered her the *adokin*, but Madam Zulu refused it.

"Bad luck to take something meant for the dead," she said. "But you tell that girl not to be a stranger. I have a phone now." She told her granddaughter to give them the number.

Then, not knowing what else to do or who else to talk to, the nursing students returned in the evening with the dollar they'd left with that morning, and the heavy task hanging over them all the way down the mountain.

Those were the most trying hours of Anaya's recovery and, other than the hours she spent in the rubble of the university, the most terrible of her life. Sweating and trembling from the pain pills, she was sick all afternoon. She sat in bed chewing ice, awaiting the return of her friends, expecting at any moment to see the shoulders of her lover fill the doorway. She recalled his body and his smell of sun and cement. She recalled that tumultuous series of firsts that marked the course of their early love. Drinking rum out of the bottle, making love on the beach.

She thought of the first night of their honeymoon on Mòn Nwa, drinking white wine in the terraced garden after midnight while Zo described all the classes of love as he knew them. Desperate love, motherly love, starving love. One for comfort, another for affection, one to remind a man of his manhood, and another to make him forget. There was functionary love, as anatomic and automatic as an act of defecation, and about as interesting. When the wind died down and the city was calm beneath them, he'd told her about obliterate love, a love in which to lose yourself without knowing it, like drowning in a sea that is the exact temperature of your blood so that you don't even know when you succumb.

"Is that how you love me?" she'd asked.

Zo shook his head and told her about absolute love, which made you want to live as much as it made you want to die.

Recalling those sweet hours in the overheated ward for amputees, waiting for him to appear, Anaya felt in her heart the strength of that absolute love and the power to carry it through. Until Verna and Yonise returned. Then everything grew vague and dark in Anaya's soul.

She had a scar under her left eye that looked like shattered glass. It bent across her cheek when she smiled. Now, hearing the news that Zo was dead, there was not so much as a flicker of motion. Her face was as still as a mask. Something ceased in her that had been like a vibration in her bones to which she'd become so accustomed she recognized it now only in its absence. It was her love for Zo, which had been as sustaining to her as the medicines she took and the food she ate. Without it, she felt the cumulative weakness of her ordeal and its attendant fevers. For the first time, she felt as if she couldn't go on or she shouldn't, and that it would have been better to have died in the earthquake. She felt that kind of love of which Zo had spoken, that longing love, that aching-for-the-dead forlorn love rooted in hopelessness and grief.

16

FEBRUARY 13 was declared a national day of mourning, and a memorial service for the dead was broadcast over loudspeakers throughout the capital. A Catholic bishop, a *vodou* priest, and a protestant minister held hands outside the National Palace. At 4:53 p.m., the precise moment that the magnitude 7.0 earthquake struck on January 12, a moment of silence descended on the chaotic city. In ruined churches, in tent cities, in parks, and on the sidewalks, women dressed in white and men wearing black armbands bent their heads and fell to their knees.

To Anaya, it was like the moment before the earthquake—still and composed. She was with Verna and Yonise, strolling the hospital grounds. She saw Black Mountain clearly among all the other peaks of the coastal range. But that peak that had once made her think of love and beauty and desire now made her feel empty and windy and rootless and doomed. Zo had confided in her once that his greatest fear was to be forgotten, the way Yiyi had forgotten him as soon as he left Grande Anse. There in Port-au-Prince, one month after his death, Anaya swore she would never forget him.

When the Belgian nurses learned that Anaya had been a student at the nursing university, and in class when it collapsed, she became their cause célèbre. They told the Quebecois, who told the Canadians, who told the Americans; and the Americans told the Spanish, who told the Argentinians, who told the Cubans; and the Cubans sent their best physical therapist to work with her twice a week. He specialized in rehabilitating the victims of auto accidents, and ordered Anaya cut out of the cast.

"Waiting any longer would be a disaster," he said.

He extended his service by two weeks and then two more, promising not to leave until he had her standing.

Anaya was the pride of the amputees. The wholeness of her body came to stand for the wholeness of all their bodies, and the story of how she woke under the surgeon's knife and forbade him to take her leg was their favorite tale. When they tried to transfer her to another ward, the patients erupted in protest. They watched her learn to walk again with the fascination of sports fans, cheering at her physical therapy sessions as if they were important matches. So that when she finally stood again six weeks after the earthquake, the ward erupted with such a clamor of voices that the doctors rushed in expecting a disaster, only to find Anaya standing gingerly in the aisle.

Thirty of the forty-nine hospitals in Port-au-Prince had been damaged in the earthquake. And so many nurses had been killed that new ones were desperately needed. Reopening the nursing institute was therefore a priority of the early recovery. The provisional university was established in the ruins of the old one. The Spanish fire brigade bulldozed a lot clear of debris, UNICEF pitched two galley tents, and the professors started their lessons. As the nurses sat in class discussing the treatment options for *Staphylococcus* infections, they could turn and see the ruins of their old school, where scores of their classmates had been killed.

Anaya had been pulled from that very rubble and she regarded it with contempt. Sitting at the back of the classroom with the other fourth-years preparing for the national exam, she cast disdainful glances at the thing that had almost killed her. "How much money do you think they saved by putting all that sand in the concrete mix?" she asked.

Their final semester was abbreviated so that they could take the national licensing exam in May. Besides the seventeen girls from the national university, the graduating class from Notre Dame was bused in from Croix-des-Bouquets, so that altogether forty-eight nurses stood for their boards. It was hot and stuffy in that tent under the sun, and there were 180 questions in French to be answered. The girls sweated over their paperwork. They broke at noon and took lunch under the mango trees in almost complete silence, because they had been instructed by the proctor not to discuss any of the test questions. Instead, they talked about studying under streetlights because there was no electricity anywhere else and how some had to drink their bathwater and others had to bathe in their drinking water, depending on how close they were to a water checkpoint and whether it was regularly filled. Their conversation was full of acronyms: MSF, WFP, UNICEF, DINEPA, MDM, IOM, USAID. The country had been overrun by international aid organizations, and what the girls wanted to know most of all was who paid best.

Then they went back under the heated canvas, took up their pencils, and completed their exams, while helicopters passed overhead and armored vehicles patrolled the streets. Anaya and her classmates from Cacquette's course emerged together, exhausted. They walked shoulder to shoulder, Verna to one side of Anaya and Yonise to the other. Anaya's leg ached terribly during the exam and her foot had swollen too big for her shoe.

The visiting staff came out of their tents to congratulate them as they passed through the field hospital. Medical professionals from six countries stood cheering in the heat. Anaya's father offered to take them to dinner to celebrate, but the girls said there was nothing to celebrate yet.

"We'd better wait for the results," Anaya said.

They came in June. All seventeen students from the national university passed their boards. They were part of the first class of nurses to be licensed in Haiti after the earthquake, and the smallest graduating class in a century. At the somber ceremony, which Vincent Leconte attended, the director of nursing said, "We need you now more than ever."

The graduates wore white gowns with green sashes and hats with green trim. They held lit candles and sat in folding chairs looking hot and apprehensive, as if they were already aware of the insurmountable suffering into which they would soon be sent with nothing but stethoscopes and blood pressure cuffs.

By the time they received their diplomas, all three classmates from Miss Cacquette's Advanced Topics in Midwifery were living together in Rue Borgella. They had a two-bedroom apartment where the road lifted into the hill. It was simple and bare. The front door opened on a narrow hallway that extended to a small kitchen at the back of the house. The two bedrooms were off the hall. Verna slept alone in the smaller room, while Anaya and Yonise shared the larger room up front.

When she'd first arrived there with her things, Anaya hadn't been able to go inside. She'd stood on the sidewalk, thinking of her cousin Nadine, who'd been killed in an almost identical building a half mile closer to the sea. The other two girls came out together and approached her cautiously. "Look at the roof," Verna said. "It's not cement. It's corrugated tin." They took her by the arms and walked her inside.

There were a thousand camps in the city by then and more than a million people living in them. The Haitians called them *bidonvil,* or Bottle-Towns, and the internationals called them IDP, internally displaced persons, camps.

The tents were staked so close together in some places that they gave away the contours of the land. When it rained in Chancerelles, the residents had to stand up in their bedsheets to keep out of the water. In Pax Villa, near the crematorium, they charged their cell phones from a car battery and held church services under the cinnamon trees.

Anaya, Verna, and Yonise were recruited by International Medical Corps to work in their traveling clinic, with the goal of bringing medical care to the people where they lived, in the camps. Their first medical clinic was held on the grounds of the Pétion-Ville Club. Once the premier golf course in the country, fifty thousand refugees now squatted on the back nine. They bivouacked in the untended greens, shat in the sand traps, and had markets in the fairways.

The medical team worked out of two tents pitched on the seventh-hole tee. The line of patients went down into the the hill and away into the next fairway. And no matter how many people they saw, the line grew longer as the day went on. They screened patients for fourteen hours and found tuberculosis was the least of their concerns. People were hungry and had nothing to eat. Their tents were leaking and hurricane season was on the way.

One of Anaya's patients was Evans Monsignor. According to his own account, he was the longest surviving earthquake victim in human history. Evans had spent twenty-seven days trapped under the rubble of the iron market, living on rotten fruit and drinking from a stream of raw sewage that flowed by his head. He woke in a Miami hospital.

"I thought it was a slave ship," he said, "and the doctors were its captains."

Now he lived under two tarpaulins pitched on the fairway, suffering from night sweats and a hacking cough. He tested positive for HIV and tuberculosis but refused treatment for either one.

"Dying is like taking a shit," he said. "Everybody's doing it and they're doing it every day."

The man who drove them to and from work was a devout Baptist who disapproved of everything, including shortcuts, which was a major setback in the reconstruction traffic of Port-au-Prince. Bulldozers idled in the intersections and armored vehicles from a dozen countries patrolled the streets. But Jeans drove slowly and by the book. Whenever the girls begged him to hurry he'd say he hadn't been hired as an ambulance. The only thing he let them listen to was Radio Shalom FM, a Christian station broadcast from the back office of a church in Bolosse.

Bolosse had the dubious reputation of having been one of the most devastated of all the city's communes. This made the condition of the Église Evangéliste Shékina d'Haïti even more miraculous. It alone amid all that destruction had remained untouched, without even a crack in its paintwork. Jeans, the driver, attributed that miracle to God. "To the right and left, for six blocks in every direction, there is nothing but devastation," he said. "When they finally get around to removing the debris, the church will be left standing alone in a waste of lots where once it had been in the midst of a bustling suburb.

The pastor of the Legliz Shekina was Reverend Garnel Ladoche, who performed mass funerals for the dead over the airwaves. All a mourner had to do was submit a name and a Haitian dollar and the reverend would include their loved one in the public requiem. The dollars raised that way were used to feed people in the local camp. The most popular program ran on Thursday afternoons, when survivors would call in and tell their stories on air. This had led to some miraculous reunions, in which supposedly deceased individuals, hearing the broadcast, were reunited with their loved ones by way of the ministry.

One Thursday afternoon, when the nurses were caught in traffic on their way back from the Pétion-Ville Club, Reverend Ladoche gave a reading from Philippians.

"Finally, brothers and sisters, whatever is true, whatever is noble, whatever is right, whatever is pure, whatever is lovely, what-

ever is commendable—if anything is excellent or praiseworthy—
let us think about these things."

Ladoche told the story of the angelic mechanic, who'd used
his heavy-duty truck jack to raise the roof of the Sunrise Supermarket. And then he told the story of Le Brouetye, the mythical
wagoner who had hauled a dozen strangers to the hospital after
the earthquake.

"Here is a wagon man, the poorest among us, the most
wretched, who makes his living like a beast of burden, hauling
our wares through the streets. Imagine his shanty in the hills.
Imagine his hungry children. No matter how many bananas or
television sets he carts each day, he knows he will never make
enough to feed them. Truck drivers curse him in the street, rich
men roll down their windows and spit, traffic cops beat him with
their batons and call him a nuisance. Even the donkeys must have
laughed when they saw him pass! Going endlessly on just two sore
feet. Can you imagine his beaten shoe wear? The ragged soles?
The laces?

"But at the eleventh hour, when it mattered most of all, it was
not the police or the rich men or the truck drivers who attempted
to save their neighbors. It was this lowly wagon man, powered by
nothing but his legs and aided by that very contraption which we
have all derided as ridiculous and out of date."

He encouraged his listeners to phone in with their own stories.

The first call came from Route de Frères; a woman claimed to
have known the same man before he became Le Brouetye. "He
was nothing but a vagabond in the streets," she said. "Everything
he owned fit in one bag, except the shovel he carried over his
shoulder."

"Not at all," a second caller said. "I saw him in Kafou Fe just
after the quake. He was proud, even angelic, and moved easily
considering that load."

"What was the load?" the reverend asked.

"There must have been twenty-five schoolchildren packed into that wagon and he was hauling them to heaven. To heaven! And not even sweating when I saw him pass."

An impossible journey took shape out of the dark time of the city's demise. There was Le Brouetye, at 5:30, sighted at Kafou Fe in the far western reaches of the city. Later calls contradicted his presence there and had him at Étang Saumâtre at the far inland end of the cul-de-sac plain. But most calls had him coming down out of the hills west of the city. He was sighted in three locations in Pétion-Ville, from 5:45 to 7:30 and possibly again after midnight. He was placed by several callers at a bonesetter's clinic around twilight, and then the bonesetter himself called in.

"My name is Obin," he said. "My clinic is in Nerette. I've had it so long the city council ceded me the property in perpetuity." He said that Le Brouetye's appearance that day was the answer to his prayers. "He took as many of my patients as he could manage, and we secured them as best we could. We made them as comfortable as possible for what was sure to be a long and excruciating journey."

"You say he left your clinic with a half dozen riders in the wagon," the reverend said. "But where were they going?"

"Lopital Jeneral," the bonesetter said. "To seek care."

There was a call from Garde Cote. "He wasn't just engine and captain of that ancient ambulance at the end of time," the caller said. "He also tended his load like a nursemaid. I saw it myself. Every so often he'd lay the wagon down and perform his rounds. There he was, climbing among those wounded and doing a nurse's kind of work."

"What do you mean by 'a nurse's kind of work'?" Reverend Ladoche asked.

"He tended to their wounds, gave them water. He dipped from the bucket himself and poured it into their mouths. He tightened their tourniquets."

A Seventh-day Adventist from the congregation in Kanal Kay-iman called and described how the *brouetye* effected a stream crossing. "He took them in his arms, like his children," he said. "One by one. Going across the stream and laying them on the far side. But he never made it to Lopital Jeneral."

"How do you know?" the reverend asked.

"I saw him collapse with my own eyes," the caller said. "At the top of the incline. I was one of the spectators who got him back up in the wagon."

Then a woman from Mòn Nwa called claiming to really and truly know him.

"Of course I knew who he was," she said. "I helped cook the food for his wedding, after all, and gave him plenty of work when he took over the old man's business. He lived on Mòn Nwa, too, nearby to me and my own children. I thought of him like my own. We all did."

"Sister," the reverend interrupted, "what time did you see him going down to the *lavil* from Mòn Nwa?"

"If the earthquake was at four fifty-three, this was four fifty-four," she said. "That boy didn't waste any time. He never did. We saw him in the avenue fixing to go down there or die trying."

"Other people saw him?"

"Everyone on Mòn Nwa who had eyes!" she said. "You had to be blind to miss him, a beautiful man like that. We all came out to see. There he was in the street with the empty cart behind him, looking like he was trying to get someplace while we were still trying to figure out if it was the end of the world or not."

Anaya was sitting in back with her head hanging between the front seats.

"What's wrong with her?" Jeans asked.

"Turn up the *freez*," Yonise said.

"I don't want her to get sick in the car."

"Then drive faster," Yonise retorted. She cooled her hand at the AC vent and pressed her palm to the back of Anaya's neck. Traffic was at a standstill and Jeans laid on the horn.

"What none of you understand," the caller went on, "what

none of you can guess at because you never really knew him no matter what you say, was why he went to *lavil* in the first place."

"Why did he go?" the reverend asked.

"My name is Madam Zulu," she testified. "I have lived a long time on Mòn Nwa and even longer in Haiti. That was no myth and no messenger from God. That was no mystery at all. It was the *brouetye* Zwazo Delalun, and he was in love."

17

OZIAS THOUGHT HE WOULD DIE with the secret that wasn't even a secret. It wasn't as if he couldn't tell it to anyone, because he told everyone he saw. The sock merchant over her wares, the electrician on his ladder, the fry cook over her bubbling pots. He announced it from his yard in the Antillean dusk, but there was only the purple land swelling toward the sea and the dogs barking down through the hills and his neighbors telling him to shut up and let them sleep.

"She's alive," O pronounced. "They pulled her free."

But people weren't interested in hearing about Anaya any more than they were interested in the self-pitying old man. What they wanted to know was where Zo was, if Zo had made it. Madam Zulu asked him point-blank five days after the girls left.

"We hear you, old man, every day we hear. We got our grievances and losses, too," she said. "We tired of you moping up the streets. Half of us scared to walk alone at night. 'She alive! She alive!' Well, all right, Ozias, good for she. But we alive, too. And what we want to know and what you not telling us is is Zo alive? Did Zo make it? I haven't seen Zo."

That struck O silent. He understood then that it wasn't that he had a secret he couldn't tell; it was that the only man who needed to hear that secret was gone.

The visit from the nursing students had given Ozias a new and crazy hope. He thought that maybe, if Anaya had survived, perhaps Zo had, too, and one afternoon he set out to find him.

Ozias crisscrossed the plain with a *macout* sack in the early morning like a man with somewhere to get to and something to sell. He walked until his leg ached and his underarm chafed where he bore his weight on the crutch. His whole world lay wasted under the sun. Sixty thousand people were living in Bizoton Park under their bedsheets and O didn't see a single familiar face. They were sleeping along the national highway, camped even into the medians, and gathered in the national square. When the tent camps got too large and mean, he despaired of ever finding Zo or any news of him at all.

The city he'd lived in all his life was like a city he'd never seen before. East was not east and west was not west. Ozias started to get lost. He walked up the wrong avenues looking for the wrong landmarks. He was in Bourdon for hours looking for Bourdon. But it was Fort National that finally broke his spirit. Though he walked Avenue Poupelard from one end and Rue Fort National from the other, he couldn't find any sign of the bustling neighborhood that had been there between those two streets as long as Ozias could remember. He walked under the heat until he grew dizzy and sat down in the street. A young man pushing an ice cart took him by the arm and dragged him into the shade of a building.

"Please," Ozias begged the ice vendor. "I don't know where I am. I've been looking for Fort National."

"Look no further," the vendor said, passing Ozias a chunk of ice. "You're sitting in Rue Fort National. There." He pointed to the naked slope in front of them. "Fort National hill."

Ozias dropped his ice. Fort National had been named for the citadel built on its crest and was famous for its commanding view of the bay. A thousand houses had been built around the slope in warrens of concentric circles, and dozens of businesses had lined the avenue underneath. But the entire face of Fort National hill had come unhinged in the shaking of the earthquake, and the whole neighborhood had washed away like a dream. The hill and the flatland directly beneath it were a cataract of waste with rubble reaching as high as the telephone lines.

"There are neighborhoods of Port-au-Prince that have never been written into the maps," Ozias said. "But now they are not even on the land. They are nothing but old words in the mouths of the people."

He went home and didn't leave for three weeks. He brewed coffee by starlight and pronounced the *brouetye* dead in the world and dead in his heart. Then he lay out in the grass like a man stricken with typhus goes to die alone in the weeds. The neighbors sent their children with eggs and bread, but Ozias chased them away until they stopped coming. They heard the old man talking to someone and he was: it was the rooster, Ti Zom. They argued all day, about house rules and dinner plans. They'd been arguing, and Ti Klis won even from beyond the grave.

One afternoon Ozias finished the bottle of Rhum Barbancourt he'd kept hidden for seventeen years and started conversing with his missing foot. "Where are you, you coward?" He accused it of bad craftsmanship and held it accountable for his gloom. "There he was on that fool's errand, going to find *her*. And there *she* was, waiting for *us!*" He sat in the dark kitchen sipping from the bottle. "If only I had my foot!" he cried. "If only I still had my foot, I would have saved his life. I would have saved them both."

At one time, O's garden had been the pride of Mòn Nwa, renowned for the tenderness of its tomatoes and the fatness of its eggplants.

But when Anaya finally arrived in June, she found the vegetable beds overrun with weeds and the grape growing wild from its trellis. O's fruit trees had once been adorned with driftwood, colored glass, and mirrors, but these lay in the roots now among the fallen fruit. Even the valuable cashew tree had been abandoned, and the fat apples rotted in the dirt.

The guinea grass had grown so high that the tall yellow flowers almost reached to the eaves of the house. Anaya could hardly see it through the overgrowth, much less the old man, but she knew he was there somewhere because he had shouted for whoever it was to go away.

"You don't even know who it is," she answered.

A speckled fighting cock, three feet tall, stood up out of the wild grape. It eyed Anaya menacingly, shaking its copper ankle bells before advancing across the yard. O appeared after it shirtless, dwarfed by his own grass, swinging a long garden hoe.

"Ti Zom," he clucked. "Little gun. Baby. Darling."

The rooster stopped and turned. O reached a hand into his pocket. "You're not a bad boy, are you?" he said, offering a palmful of corn. "You only know that its a bad world."

"That's more of a guard dog than a chicken," Anaya said.

Ozias raised his face. His right eye was cloudy and white as a pearl. "Zom was a real killer," he said. "A true fighter. Papa Pikan's little terror. But he's mine now, and we don't fight anymore, do we?" he asked the bird.

"Where's Pikan?"

"He died in the earthquake." Ozias looked down at the bird. "That's how I came to have his damned chicken." He put his hand out and the bird came alongside. "You proved to be a good friend," he said to it. "You were with him to the end."

"Ozias," she said. "Don't you know who I am?"

"My eyes aren't what they used to be," O said. "The doctor says even my cataracts have glaucoma. But even on this dim hillside, with these bad eyes. Even though you've changed." He finally worked up the courage to look her in the face. "I can still tell it's you."

Anaya showed him the bald spot in her hair. "It won't grow there again," she said. She showed him the long purple scar running down her shin. "I almost lost it."

"I don't mean that kind of change," he said.

"What do you mean?"

O's eyes misted over. "You look like the kind of woman who has done the last of her crying in this life."

Anaya embraced him. She stood in his ropy arms smelling the sweat in his hair.

"I tried," Ozias started. "I loved him."

"I know you did," she said. "I loved him, too."

Ozias walked her into the garden. "We were standing right here," he said, "when the earthquake started."

Anaya felt as if she were standing in Zo's footsteps. She felt closer to him there on that mountainside than she had in six months.

"All he wanted was to find you. He only took the *brouet* to have something to bring you back in. Turning it into an ambulance?" O shook his head. "That was my idea. I made him do it. I made him pull through half that city like a donkey in the peanuts."

They stood side by side, looking out at the twilit landscape.

"You should have seen it," O continued. "That last run of his was a thing of great beauty. His posture, his technique. The way he moved under the last load of his life." He looked at her. "For focus and purpose, for evenness of stride, it may never be surpassed." He told her how Zo had powered them up the Kayiman incline single-handed, with 420 kilograms in the wagon. "I've done the math over and over again," he said. "The angle of incline was better suited to a bird in flight than a man on two legs."

"Did you reach the hospital?"

"Yes."

Mw pa kompran.

Ozias told her about the spectators who, seeing what Zo had

done, lifted him into his own wagon after he collapsed and took him the rest of the way.

"What happened at the hospital?" she asked.

"I closed my eyes for five minutes. Five minutes! And there he was preparing to climb into the classroom after you. Wearing a hard hat like a goddamn fool!" He shook his head. "That place was a death trap," he said. "You know that better than I do. And those aftershocks coming all time."

"Why didn't you stop him, O?"

"Don't you think I tried? You know what kind of man he was! Incapable of compromise. Disdainful of the half measures and constant little defeats this island demands of us. He had your class schedule and believed in it like some believe in Scripture."

A breeze passed through the trees and an overripe mango fell with a dull thud.

"Two workmen from the municipal highway crew finally dug him in through the roof," O continued. "Made a racket to wake the dead. Hacksaws and gasoline jackhammers. *Tut-tut-tut!* Thought they were on a rescue mission, like real heroes. But they were really just digging his grave."

Anaya thought of her classroom before the earthquake. The students gathered at the ultrasound. "Did he die in Cacquette's classroom, looking for me?"

Ozias took her wrist and looked her in the eye. "The aftershocks were coming all the time," he said. "One came."

They passed a moment like that on the hillside. The old man holding her wrist, his eyes fogged with cataracts and tears, and the city below them dark in great patches where the blackouts reigned.

"*Vwa l,*" she said. "His voice was real. All this time I thought it was a hallucination brought on by blood loss and shock."

"You mean he found you?"

"He spoke to me."

The heat was dense with smoke from the trash fires.

"What did he say?"

"He told me to close my eyes and think of the queen trigger-fish, and the warm water off Taino Beach, where he taught me to swim. Did you know that, O? He taught me how to swim."

Ozias led her out of the garden, and sat her in a plastic chair.

"I have something you might like to see."

"What is it?"

"*Kod la.*"

"What rope?"

"The one they tied around his ankle when he went in after you. They thought he'd be able to find his way back with it. The *zouti* crew managed to keep hold of it through the aftershock. They drew it out foot by foot. But when they had it to its full length there was no sign of Zo at all."

"What was there?"

Ozias shook his head. "A piece of cinder block," he said. "He'd tied a cinder block in his place."

That pale bit of cinder block was the thing that tortured Ozias most of all. It appeared in his dreams and even then in strange places. He gave Anaya an example. He'd dreamt once that he was working in his garden on a foggy night when he hit his toe on that block in the *militon* squash.

"The *militon*," he repeated. "Soup or no soup, that boy loved his *militon*."

"You think the block stands for Zo?"

"Who else? Obstinate. Misplaced. See for yourself."

"You still have it?"

"The block and rope both," he said.

Ozias returned with the woman's purse that had once belonged to his wife, and in which he kept all his keepsakes. He drew out the rope they had tied around Zo's leg—a yellow nylon load rope, stained with dirt and frayed where it had been tested.

Anaya let it run through her fingers. "It's just like one of your wagon cords," she said.

"The rope is not the important thing," he said. "What you have to realize is what kind of knot Zo used to tie the cinder block in place. It wasn't any random hauler's knot but a very specific sailor's slipknot. Called a bowline on a bight."

Anaya looked unimpressed.

"It's a kind of clove hitch," he explained. "A complex knot I learned from Brazilian sailors of that country's merchant marine. I taught it to Zo myself, as part of his training."

"What's the point?"

"There's no mistaking the clove hitch," O said. "It takes time, intention, and a level head. I think Zo was trying to tell us something." He reached back into the purse. Farther down, wrapped in wax paper like a cut of meat, he found the square of cinder block. He pulled it out, unwrapped it, and held it in his palm.

"Take it," he said.

Anaya took it.

"Close your eyes."

She closed her eyes.

"Concentrate," he said.

She remembered the classroom, the smell of the laboratory chemicals. She remembered reaching for Zo's hand in the dark.

"What does it tell you."

Anaya opened her eyes. "That I should have been the one to die in that classroom," she said. The block was about as heavy as sand and air, and broke to pieces when she dropped it. "It's no wonder the university collapsed," she said.

Ozias knelt and raked the pieces from the grass. "Don't go," he said. "There is something else you absolutely must see."

"Enough!" she said. "I'm tired of ghosts and relics. I want to go a whole day without thinking I've seen him in some camp, or on some street corner. I want to sleep through the night without dreaming of him."

Ozias went through the purse again and found what he was looking for—a single sheet of notebook paper. "It's a shipping invoice," he said. "From Ozias and Son Transport Company."

He was as solemn and superstitious about that page as he had been about the rope and cinder block, and Anaya took it reluctantly.

"It's Zo's last bill of lading," he said. "Those are the riders from his final run."

18

Zo woke in the back of a municipal dump truck feeling as if years had passed. The moon was in the wrong quarter of the night and Miss Cacquette's prayer was playing in his head. "I am the one who drew you from your mother's womb," it went, "and I can't put you back." His dizziness was deeper than vertigo because it was a dizziness of spirit. Zo didn't know if he was living or dead. He recalled the rope that should have tethered him to the living world and felt for it at his ankle, but there was nothing connecting him to what had come before.

Zo's body had been recovered by an Israeli rescue crew using a hydraulic breaker and a massive jack. He was laid out behind the hospital with the cadavers and loaded into the *camion* at night. The line of trucks threaded the black highway under the moon, angling inland north of the city near the desolate plain of Canaan. The turnoff was marked with a red flare burning on the coast. A lone man with a shovel over his shoulder smoked a cigarette in that desolate crossroads like a signpost of the vodou future.

It was the burial ground at Titanyen. Long trenches bisected the limestone flat, and a backhoe idled under the stars. Clouds of white chalk rose in the headlights. When the truck driver backed his rig to the edge of the pit and activated the elevation cylinder, Zo fell out with the rest of the cadavers.

A pair of gravediggers had been working at the rim of the pit, tossing dirt over the bodies, but one of them quit when Zo resurrected. The cigarette he'd been smoking tumbled from his mouth.

"Are we dead?" Zo asked.

The workman cast his shovel over his shoulder and didn't stop running until he reached the road. But the other gravedigger just smoked on. "You are," he said. He pulled Zo out by the wrists and offered him a cigarette. They smoked with their feet hanging in the grave and the dust rising under the moon, looking across the cindered island.

Zo asked if it were the afterlife.

The gravedigger, inspecting the red end of his cigarette, said, *"Se Ayiri."*

Zo wasn't surprised. It was as if he had expected it all along, had dreamt that very afterworld out of all the other afterworlds that could be. That pit of bodies. The body parts. The dirt thrown across his face. The unnatural wind off the Bay of Gonaïves. He asked for water and drank a liter without cease, and then he drank another. He asked for a shovel and went to work alongside the gravedigger, and didn't stop until his skin was whitewashed with limestone chalk. When the shovel handle snapped in two he worked on with the shortened implement.

The body trucks came all night and the next day in long caravans, bearing schoolkids in identical uniforms. The Malraux School, the Presbyterian mission, the Catholic college. At dusk, a single truck bearing a load of nursing students from the national university emptied its cargo without ceremony, and Zo walked in after them with the nonchalance of a bather going to the sea. He waded through the bodies. The gravediggers came from their excavations to see him turn the girls over, one at a time. Then he climbed out and walked off across the dry plain without looking back.

He walked until he reached the seashore at the village of Lafiteau. The climbing tide and crying gulls mirrored the tumult in his heart so perfectly he was on the verge of drowning himself, and he cursed the impulse of self-preservation that finally drove him inland, up the wide floodplains to Sibert and Moleare. He hardly looked up again until he reached Rue Monseigneur Guilloux. He didn't need to. It was exactly the world he expected without her. Everything was beaten and weary—the horizon sagged, the mountains huddled, the homes crowded, and the people hushed.

The apartment that Anaya once shared with her cousin Nadine was like all the buildings on that street. The floors had been driven down one upon the other until Zo could ascend to the penthouse by pulling at the mangled wall irons. He sat on the roof remembering his proposal; the red ring, the fat slices of melon, the kiss after she said yes.

Anaya was dead and his dreams were dashed. He could never return to O's place on the hill, not to collect his things or to clap the old man on the shoulder and look him in the eye. These things went into the bonfire of his ever having known her or loved her or known love at all.

Zo came through those months like a shipwrecked sailor, swinging his fists and thirsty. Treating his wounds with turpentine like he had learned from the cock trainers and his sorrow with rum and weed and violence. He roved the trashed city looking to destroy himself, with no manager or keeper but himself and his smoldering rage.

There was good fighting in the aftermath. Dozens just like him in every zone of the city who had lost it all and remained submerged in grief, going in to fight like maniacs for one destruction. Zo fought a man whose four sons had been killed at home. He fought a man who had robbed a bank and given the money to his neighbors. Zo fought for sport and blood and vengeance against God and only later for cash. When he finally got some he had no idea what to do with it.

They fought in small yards, or crossroads, or up in the rubble of fallen buildings like actors on a stage so that the whole city could see, declaiming with their fists. They went into the *stade gagers,* where the roosters fought and the bettors laid down their cash and the fighters went at it. Sometimes they matched before the chickens and sometimes after in the blood and feathers with half the audience gone. Zo fought shirtless, wearing nothing but the white wedding kerchief tied around his biceps. He worked as his own ringer and coach, preparing his own hands and treating his own wounds. He bet everything on himself and then fought to win. He fought until his heart felt distant and brutal, like a moon lost from its orbit.

When they put him in the ring he battled like an enigma. Huge, sullen, and explosive, sometimes he wouldn't swing for two minutes. He'd get pummeled, cursed at, spit upon without turning. Every fistfall stoked his rage. They called him names like Rock and Imbecile and Mountain and, finally, Goudou, the first half of Goudougoudou, the colloquial term for "earthquake." That was because of his stillness before the rage. Then in a moment he would turn on his opponent and decimate his jaw with a single brutal combination they came to call the *Goudou*—a jab over the kidneys that opened his opponent up for the death blow.

He was famous for the long reach of his right and the quick, unexpected jab of his left to respond and for the silence with which he battled. He was the only fighter who never bragged before a match, so that when people asked, "Have you heard of that fighter?" the others responded, "*Wi,* his fists do all the talking. His uppercut severs tongues."

Like this Zo made his money, collecting the winner's purse. He purchased rum and ate his desultory lunches of fried meats and plantain cakes. He gave money to the saddest-looking widows, the hungriest children, the most disfigured of the amputees. There was a soreness in his heart where Anaya had been pulled from him like a bone. He refused a tent when the charities came, and punished himself in the heat and chill or rain and mosquitoes of the season.

Zo camped on a hillside too steep to farm—a high and windy incline at sufficient elevation to be in the mists all winter. It was north of the city, in the range that fronted the burying ground of Titanyen, far from the sight of Black Mountain and everyone he knew. He leveled the slope and dug out a shelf to stash his sad bachelor's things. Everything he owned testified to his loneliness, from the unclean cookware to soiled clothes. He had a pack of straight razors for his beard, exactly one cup and one bowl and one fork missing a tine. He had a rusty machete. His boots were stamped MADE IN AMERICA, but he knew that nothing lasts forever.

It was his old friend Sabala Lafortune's idea to fight Zo against the different soldiers who made up the UN Stabilization Mission in Haiti, called MINUSTAH. Since the earthquake, Port-au-Prince had begun to resemble an occupied city that had been at war with the whole world. The Brazilian marines ran airport security and the Jordanian artillery was staked out in the traffic circles. El Salvadoran national guardsmen patrolled Martissant in antitank vehicles, and a regiment of the Sri Lankan air force provided security at food distribution centers. Lafortune even saw a detachment of U.S. Marines exiting a Black Hawk helicopter at the soccer field on Avenue Maïs Gaté.

Sabala had assumed that Zo was dead, the same as he assumed of every other person he had not seen since the quake, until he saw the laborer at the *stade gager* in Delmas. It was a cockfight stadium in the lower reaches of Delmas where Zo had a standing match every weekend in March. Sabala had come to fight his rooster Ti James, who he claimed had Dominican roots.

The birds went first. They were brief and ruthless, leaving their blood and feathers in the dust. After Ti James fought, Sabala picked up his chicken and went over to where Zo sat in the bleachers.

"What was your bet?" Sabala asked.

"I don't play the chickens," Zo said.

"Are you an owner?"

Zo said he was not.

"So what do you bet on?"

"Myself," the laborer answered, carefully wrapping his fists in tape.

Sabala placed the rooster in its cage on the bleachers between them.

"How was he?" Zo asked.

"A chickenshit, as usual," Sabala said. "Though he eats like a king."

"It's not about the feed," Zo said. "It's about anger, vengeance, the love of violence."

Sabala laughed. "If you know so much, why don't you bet on the chickens?"

Zo dropped his fists to his hips and moved his feet. He shook out his shoulders and rolled his neck so it cracked. "It's barbaric," he said.

Then he pulled off his shirt and took the bloody ring where the cocks had just battled. He walked around it and threw a series of shadow punches. He looked like a form for Greek sculptors. The sole blemish of his perfect body was a long scar up his ribs that looked like the slash of a rapier.

His challenger was too slim and Sabala knew it right away. "You'll kill him," the driver said.

Neither contender wore shoes. Zo came into the ring, planted his feet, and put his hands at his sides. His opponent punched and then dodged a phantom attack. He turned and came back, landing a right in Zo's stomach, but the fighter didn't flinch. He made no sound at all. When Zo finally made his move his opponent looked terrified and suddenly very fragile.

"Take it easy on him!" Sabala called.

Zo threw three swift punches, planting them as carefully as a gardener with his most precious seeds. To the right lower ribs, the left side of the neck, and, finally, square on the nose bridge. Zo didn't stand over his opponent or help him up afterward while the kid spouted blood from his nostrils. He went for his cash. Sabala saw the payout and it looked pretty good.

"This is a nice gig," he said. "There's no initial investment. How did you figure it out?"

"I never lose," Zo said.

Sabala Lafortune got the idea for the international matches like this. He still ran his truck, the Cheri Doudou, but had changed his route. Tired of the reconstruction traffic, he'd shifted from the Pétion-Ville circuit out to the west of the city. The ranges were longer, but he actually saved gas because he didn't idle in traffic for six hours daily. He ran the Portail Léogâne–Kafou connection. It was mostly a good road, with predictable traffic patterns and potholes. He mastered the worthwhile shortcuts in the first few weeks.

He stationed himself at the Honduran mission every day from 3:30 to 4:00 p.m. and soon became friendly with the guards. He knew enough Spanish to run their errands, which mostly consisted of buying drugs, American deodorant, and alcohol. They were insatiable for cocaine. Sabala grew especially friendly with Private Antonin Avendado, who'd been a petty thief and a boxer in the mean streets of San Pedro Sula before the police gave him the choice of prison or the army.

"I guess you chose the army," Sabala said.

"You don't know Honduras," Antonin said. "I chose prison. Afterward, they put me in the army anyway."

Sabala asked if he'd fight again and the Honduran said he would. "If my opponent is a worthy one. No cripples or psychotics."

Sabala found Zo two weeks later at a ring off Kwabosal. He had just beaten a father-and-son team. They were local sailors and Zo beat them in the same ring at the same time, one in front of the other, with a fist for each of them. Afterward, he stood in the corner finishing a pint of Bakara one-star rum.

Sabala asked if he'd had to take on the whole family.

"That's how they wanted to fight," Zo said.

"What's happened to you?" Sabala asked. "Where is that girl I used to see you with?"

Zo eyed the bottle for another sip but couldn't find one.

"The beautiful one," Sabala continued. "The nurse. I drove her to your wedding celebration on Mòn Nwa."

Zo roared to life. He took the driver by the throat. "I should have followed her to hell," he said. "I tried." He let go and Sabala half collapsed. "There was nothing in those classrooms. Some dead girls." Zo tore the bandanna from his arm. "And this."

Sabala looked at it. " 'A & Z, January 1, 2010.' " He looked up. "What is it?"

"The last proof."

"Proof of what?"

Zo grimaced and the blood ran in his teeth. "That this is not an island but a ship," he said. "And we are steering into dark music."

Even though Sabala only understood half of what he was saying, he knew he was in the presence of a fortified entity, something forged for dark days. Zo wasn't in it for cash or glory but for the simple and pure brutality. He was in it to battle, and not just to battle but to hurt. It made him invincible in the ring.

"I didn't come to fight with you," Sabala said, wiping the dirt from his pants. "I came with a business proposition." He billed the fights as international competitions, pitching each match as a little World Cup. "An international opportunity," he called it. "No more fighting sailors and their friends. You'll be fighting for the pride of Haiti."

He told Zo about Antonin, the Honduran soldier who had been a middleweight champion in the Central American circuit. For Zo's part, he wouldn't have cared if his opponent were the reigning heavyweight champion of the world.

"The pay is a hundred dollars. *U.S.*," Sabala added, making the money sign with his fingers. "All you have to do is stand there and take the punches until you've had enough. It doesn't even matter if you win."

Lafortune arrived with his truck full of bettors at eight a.m. and they drove onto the national highway. The camp dwellers came out under the rain to shower, stripping naked and soaping themselves in the gutters under overcast skies. There was an endless breadline in Martissant, where an old woman lifted her shirt and grabbed her flaccid belly and shook it menacingly at the UN supervisors.

The Honduran military mission was west of the city, in a soggy plain just under the mountains. It looked like the encampment of a Roman legion in barbarian country: a square of high fencing capped with guard towers and barbed wire. Zo and his contingent weren't allowed inside the barracks, so the fight took place just beyond the main gate of the base.

Lafortune drove up as close as they'd let him and pulled onto the grassy plain. It was wet from days of rain. Spectators came out of the nearby tent camps to see it, and they drew merchants selling fried meats and beer. The Honduran soldiers and even their officers watched from the overlooking gun towers while the Haitians gathered around the fighters. They fought in a bare patch in the grass, between the main gate and the street. The battlers shook hands and posed for pictures before the fight.

The opponents had two different styles. The Honduran, called Antonin, had started in the streets but been refined in the gym. He had the muscles and shape of a man who conditioned with free weights and protein powders. He was explosive but inflexible, his swing foreshortened by the sheer size of his biceps.

Zo had been built and maintained in the streets. He was leaner than Antonin and faster, built for hauling loads up an incline. He had a longer reach and an uneven strength that gave his right the power of two arms. When he connected flat with that hook it would be the end of the match.

He and Antonin boxed it out for eight minutes. There were no rounds and neither fighter was conditioned for such a long match, so the last few minutes were sloppy. They were exhausted and hung on each other to stay upright. Zo took a shot to the side and a hotness blazed in his gut. It caught him in the throat and he came alive like a vengeful beast of sorrow. He boxed Antonin out of the ring and up into the street. Traffic stopped and surged around them; the truck drivers climbed out of their cabs to watch.

Antonin couldn't find Zo to block him, so he shut his eyes and threw his head back. He looked like a man fighting with bees. He couldn't even fall over because the swiftness of Zo's punches kept him upright and stumbling. Zo knocked him from right to left across the pavement—he couldn't miss. The sound was vicious and final when Zo's knuckles cracked home on his chin and Antonin went down.

His officers climbed down off the towers and passed their money through the gate. Zo peeled an American twenty-dollar bill from his winnings and put it in Antonin's waistband. After that, Lafortune went to work all over the city as Zo's promoter. He called Zo the best in the world and boasted of his fearsome right.

"He's never set foot in a gym," Sabala bragged. "Doesn't know what a punching bag is. But Zo will box your man into the Stone Age."

In the weeks that followed, Zo fought a Jordanian lieutenant with a beard up to his eyes, a Peruvian soccer champ with a deadly high kick, and a Filipino private whose style was to come up close and throw as many punches as possible.

The cheap Dominican rums he'd been drinking soon failed his insatiable sorrow, and Zo went looking for the most murderous *kleren* on the island. He drank a brew fortified with the resin of the *bwa mombin* tree that gave him a three-day erection. In the mountains behind Chapotio, he swallowed a concoction of rum and tree leaves that gave him the longings of a pregnant woman for vinegar and sour orange, so that he returned home with a basket of citrus fruit and ate nothing else for two days.

Then he heard about Augusto Quans, a distiller brewing a street drink known as Ti Wo Wo, or Little Tall Tall, because it was rumored to turn the drinker's perceptions upside down and inside out. It was said that under the influence of Ti Wo Wo the courageous were cowards, the timid grew fierce, and the Christians were mounted by *lwas*. It enjoyed such wide renown that they'd begun exporting it to the Dominican Republic and doing brisk business.

Augusto sold his rums in Léogâne, a town famous for its rum distilleries and spiritual practitioners, and because it marked the exact epicenter of the earthquake. Every cement building within the city limit had been destroyed.

Zo found Augusto Quans where they said he'd be, at the junction of the Jacmel highway, but the dealer refused to sell him any rum.

"This isn't water I'm selling," Augusto said.

"I didn't come from Pòtoprens looking for water."

Augusto's cart was a chifforobe on wheels, but instead of clothes, the tall cabinet was filled with bottles of tincture, each preparation specialized for a specific symptom and its concurrent spiritual distress. His infertility treatment for men did more than cure the drinker's erectile dysfunction; it also increased his testosterone production, righted his shaky confidence, and eased his swollen prostate. Augusto powered a light and small radio from a car battery, and his customers were gathered around listening to the music, dazed as opium addicts.

"Ti Wo Wo isn't for the good times," he said.

Zo told the dealer he didn't have many good times. "I lost my wife in the earthquake," he said. "We were married ten days."

Augusto looked up from his bottles. He almost asked if Zo really loved her, but that question would have been an affront to the brokenhearted fist boxer he saw before his cart. Instead, the dealer ducked among his potions and reappeared with a set of laboratory glass.

"I've made a long study of the psychosomatic effects of metals," he said. "Gold for whiskey. Copper for rum. Silver for pure cane liquor." He showed Zo a flask of clear liquid with flakes of metal on the bottom. "The research comes from the mining regions of Venezuela, where they are rich in all kinds of minerals but poor in food." Using an acid burette, he extracted a small amount of potion from a brown bottle and, counting carefully, added twelve drops to the pure cane liquor. A purple current ran like a strike of lightning in the bottle, and the *kleren* seemed somehow clearer than water.

"What is it?"

"The Dominicans call it *manzanilla de la muerte*," Augusto said, looking at the bottle. " 'Little apple of death.' It's what killed Ponce de León."

"What happened to Ponce de León?"

"He fell asleep beneath a beach apple tree and died two days later, choking on pus."

"Is that what happens when you drink it?"

"More or less." Augusto blew across the glass and the potion effervesced. "In varying degrees, of course, and each according to his own nature and ambitions. Ponce de León set out to find the

Fountain of Youth and wound up eaten by alligators, but most of us don't set out for the Fountain of Youth."

"Believe me," Zo said, "I'm not looking to live forever."

He paid for a pint traveler, pulled the stopper, and had a long drink. The lemon verbena helped it across the front of his tongue, but when that fell away he could taste the bitter alkaloid of the poison at the back of his mouth. His tongue burned and his eyes watered.

"Not like that!" Augusto scolded. "You'll ruin your voice."

Zo took another long pull and rocked back on his heels. "I don't have much to say."

The lightbulb dimmed and grew strong again.

"I'm not frightened of alligators."

It looked like an electric rainbow burning in the dark.

Augusto begged him to stop. "Don't think of it as a beverage or even a medicine. Think of it as a poison, man. The pH is about as bad as that of chlorine bleach."

But it was too late. Zo's throat was already torn, and by the time he reached the mango plantations on the outskirts of the city he was spitting bright red blood from his mouth. He walked the fourteen miles to Mariani along the highway, under a deepening intoxication. A Canadian field hospital had been set up in the flatland there and the countryside looked like a military protectorate. Huge camps had been carved from the cane plantations and the residents stood outside their tents like defeated soldiers in the blowing wind.

At the park in Bizoton, Zo held his head in his hands and drank short pulls from the bottle. It was half empty by then and his head was spinning. The Ti Wo Wo upended his perceptions one by one, and finally his judgment, too. He couldn't feel the rain because his skin was numb as leather. Even the rum had lost its bitterness; it was sweet and clear as water in his mouth. He saw the world at a great remove, like one looking through the wrong end of a binocular.

He watched the waves crest the beach at Garde Cote and dreamt he was at sea upon those swells and the water was filled with hungry sharks and his boat was sinking. In Kafou, he stood boxing in the drizzle while the neighbors watched from covered porches. A group of boys playing jacks under the eaves argued his origins.

"A convict escaped from the National Penitentiary," one said. "Titanic block."

"A Miami gangster deported from Florida."

"You're both wrong," one of the boys said. He threw the stone and picked up one. "That's Le Brouetye." He threw the stone and picked up two.

"How do you know?"

"Because I was one of the riders on his wagon," he said.

It was Wens Noel. He was living with his mother at the Bizoton camp and had been sent off to find rice and warned not to return empty-handed. Not one for begging, Wens had paused a while to play a game of jacks.

"There were eight of us in the back of his wagon," Wens said. "The *brouetye* swore to get us to the hospital downtown or die trying. But the bridge was out over Canal Kayiman."

Wens soon had the other players believing in the miracle of Le Brouetye, so that by the time he left Kafou, Zo was followed by a sizable crowd, foremost among them Wens Noel and the jacks players, with their playing rocks in their pockets.

Zo hadn't heeded Augusto's warning that the poison had a long half-life or that it compounded in the blood. By the time he reached the busy traffic circle at Tabarre, he felt like the ghost of himself in the world. What had started in Bizoton as the faint suspicion that his hands were not his own ended there in Tabarre City with the conviction that his heart had stopped beating, his organs were rotting in their places, and he'd been dead since January 12.

He staggered into traffic, waving his knife. The truck drivers honked their horns and cursed him from their high windows, but one look from Zo and they shut their mouths. With his yellow eyes and bloodstained lips, brandishing a machete the size of a cutlass, he looked like a pirate with old scores to settle.

The boys followed him to the break-wall.

"That isn't the Caribbean Sea," he said. "There is no farther shore."

"What about Florida?" Wens asked.

"Florida is a fairy tale the old men like to tell." He pointed inland, toward the hills. "This isn't even Port-au-Prince, Wens. It's *lanfè*! We are not citizens here, but dead men in hell. Listen. *Tande m*. Once people died and stayed buried in the dirt, Wens. But now, so many die at once it's as if the island cannot contain them. No sooner are they buried than they are back again doing ghoulish work."

Wens was the only one brave enough to speak. "How can you be so sure?"

"I was trucked out to be buried in Titanyen."

"What happened?"

He turned on the boys and jabbed the point of the long knife. "I woke up," he said. "The plain there is flat and pale as the moon. The sand is so white and the grain so fine you never get clean afterward."

"After what?"

"There is only one thing to do in Titanyen, Wens. Dig graves. So I dug them. Dug them deep. Under roots and rocks, deeper still. Down into that country under the earth where Goudougoudou has his house."

The term was onomatopoeic—if you said Goudougoudou ten times fast, it would re-create the sound of the buildings shaking.

"What did you want from the earthquake?"

"Just what you want, Wens. You want your brother back, don't you?" He pivoted to face the boy. "And I want vengeance. To make him pay. Blow for blow." He raised his machete and swung the knife in the rain. "One for every man, woman, and child."

His parry sent the audience fleeing, all but the little boy Wens, who stood his ground even when he heard the cut of Zo's blade approaching in the raindrops.

"What did he look like?" Wens asked.

"It was too dark."

"How dark?"

"Dark as Grotte Kounoubwa," Zo said. "I couldn't see him. But I could hear him. Hammering at his forge. Crunching bones with his teeth." Zo bent over the pavement and made three clear cuts with the knife. "Goudougoudou, Goudougoudou." It was so quiet afterward they could hear the rain falling. "I could feel the heat at the center of the world," Zo said. "Just like the heat of the sun but without any light, like fevers that burn you from the inside."

"What did he look like, when you finally saw him?"

"Wide as a rhinoceros, and the same color," Zo said. "I called him Killer of Children and Masher of Bones. You know what he did?" Zo paused. "He took one look at me and laughed, and when he laughed Port-au-Prince shook. The whites call it an aftershock. You know what he told me?" Zo asked. "Three-eighths of iron will not hold a ten-ton roof. And there is too much sand in the block maker's mix."

"But you got him, didn't you? You made him pay."

"I still had my knife," Zo said. "I cut right and left. I was upon him in a flash and had the blade against his throat."

Zo cut an erratic arc through the rain with the knife, up and down. He feinted, stopped, hit, and parried. For a moment it was heroic. They imagined that lone battler challenging the earthquake at his house in the core of the earth, demanding recompense for all of them. Then he slipped in his ruined sandals. He lost his balance and fell to his knees. The machete clattered over the pavement. The rain fell from the sky.

Vincent Leconte had been at his office near the airport until ten p.m. It took him that long to placate the Swiss commissioner, who was concerned over allegations of corruption.

"I felt for him, too. I really did," he told Claude when they were finally in the car on their way home. "They want him to account for every penny. He and I both know a report like that would only prove the corruption is even worse than they think."

Claude got them as far as the roundabout in Tabarre City, where Avenue Toussaint Louverture, Boulevard du 15 Octobre, and Rue Flerio converge east of the airport. There they were stopped in traffic.

"Are we close?" Leconte asked.

"Halfway."

The traffic was backed up on all three highways, including Rue Flerio, where they were headed. The line of cars disappeared under the rain. Claude was contemplating alternate routes to Bel Air when Zo walked out into the street in front of them, drunk on Ti Wo Wo.

"Turn on the high beams," Leconte said. "Run the wipers."

He expected Zo to be washed away with the rain but only saw him more clearly through the clean glass. With the bottle in one hand and the machete in the other, he looked like a *maroon* down from his revolution in the hills. He was gone again almost as soon as he appeared, followed by a crowd of boys throwing rocks and dancing in wet clothes. Leconte opened the door and stepped out into the drizzle even as Claude tried to stop him.

That ugly roundabout, so hot and desolate at noon, was carnivalesque at midnight. The boys who sold sunglasses were still working, and the street chefs sat behind their fried spreads. Zo's machete was long as a cutlass and green with rust, flashing like jade in the headlights when he held it aloft.

Leconte reached the edge of the circle just as Zo was about

to disappear into the chaos of the far shops and, without thinking, shouted his name. The laborer stopped. The ruinous shanties were leaking in the cold. When Leconte called him a second
time, Zo turned monstrously, chopping with the knife and drinking from the bottle. Stumbling, grabbing the cars to keep himself
upright, cursing the drivers, he approached obliquely through the
traffic. He fell once and called out for Wens Noel. The boy was
beneath him.

"*Mw la, brouetye.* Take my shoulder."

The people scattered from him as he came, turning their
bicycles in traffic, pushing their carts up the curb. All except for
Vincent Leconte, who stood his ground until it seemed to be just
the two of them, he and Zo alone in all that wide pavement, like
adversaries come to settle the score.

Zo's eyes were jaundiced and bloodshot. There was grass in
his hair. His shirt was ripped from the armpit to the collar. But
underneath the months of brutal living and those bruises like
blue tattoos on his face, Leconte recognized the features he'd
never forget: the unassailable posture, the granite brow of a dictator, and that light in his eyes that reminded him of Mackandal
aflame at the stake. Zo's shoulders rose and fell with his breathing.

"The drink is killing you," Leconte said. "You can hardly stand
straight."

Zo tipped the bottle up and, holding it three inches from his
mouth so that they could see, drained it to its bitter end.

"That stuff's hardly distilled," Leconte said. "Your skin will
turn yellow. You'll be sick every morning."

"My skin is black," Zo said. "And I'm sick all the time."

Leconte was as rooted to that place by fascination as much as he
was by Zo's magnetic sorrow. "I have my medical bag in the car,"
he said. "Perhaps I could examine you."

"You think your antibiotics can cure what I've got?"

"What's wrong with you?"

"A split lip," Zo said. "A black eye. Parasites. A bruise some place

I can't reach." He swung the machete. "I'm thirsty but have nothing to drink. I'm hungry for something no food will satisfy." He raked the blade through the rain. "I sleep in the dirt because I cannot bear the feel of the walls around me."

"Why don't you put the knife down?" Leconte said.

Zo considered the weapon. "There's nothing wrong with the *manchèt*."

"It's like a gun," Leconte said. "Nothing good can come of it."

"Guns just kill people. But a *manchèt*." Zo raised the blade and chopped with it. "With this *kouto* I can chop a mango in the mountains and make a boat from its trunk. I can sail that boat to America and make my million."

"What would you do with all that money once you had it?"

Zo got to his feet wearily and stood weaving under the rum like a boxer ducking phantom punches. "Burn it at the Carrefour dumps," he said. The faraway look washed from his eyes and he regarded Leconte so directly the doctor could feel where the laborer's eyes fell on him.

"I tried not to love her," he said. "I took all kinds of cures and drank all kinds of potions. They told me to drink bitter melon and I drank it. To bathe in the river after dark, and I did. But these things only doubled my love for her." He looked at Leconte as if he were looking for pity. "I had fevers. I was tired but couldn't sleep. I couldn't tell east from west."

"You're describing idiocy, or delirium," Leconte said. "Typhoid fever, perhaps."

"I have had malaria and I have had love," Zo said. "They are not so different. A fever in the dark. An emptiness in the stomach. A feeling like your blood has been hijacked for purposes other than your own."

When he shouted, it was not a word but the expression of a dark sentiment. He cursed Ozias and his wagon, the foreign soldiers and their worthless right hooks. He undid the handkerchief he wore around his arm and dropped it on the pavement like his white flag of surrender. Then he went in and out among the motorbikes, cursing at the drivers, going deeper into his habitat of heat and ruin.

The crowd broke up soon after. There was nothing else to see. The street cooks put out their fires and the cars started in the rain. Claude Juste was continuing down Rue Flerio when they came upon Wens Noel walking alone in the same direction. They pulled over and Leconte rolled down the window.

"Get in," he said. "We'll give you a ride."

Wens climbed in the back and sat against the door.

"Where are you going?"

"Bizoton."

Leconte gave orders for Bizoton. "How well did you know him, that man with the knife?" he asked.

Wens was shivering. The water streamed down his face. "I guess I know him about as well as you do."

"I don't know him at all."

"Neither do I."

"What did you call him?"

"Le Brouetye."

"Why do you call him that—the wagon man?"

"Haven't you heard the radio shows?" Wens wiped the water from his hair. "He used his wagon to take eight strangers to the hospital downtown."

"When?"

"*Douz Janvye*," the boy said. "The twelfth of January."

"How do you know that?"

The boy lifted his chin and raised his right hand. "I'm Wens Noel," he said proudly. "I rode in Le Brouetye's wagon all the way from Wo Nerette."

19

L'IMPÉRATRICE was Desmond Tessier's favorite restaurant in the city. Serving French-Creole fusion, it was known for its fresh seafood and extensive wine list, and for the lucrative reconstruction contracts often negotiated there. The restaurant itself was a compound behind high fences. The long tree-lined drive wound from the entrance to the top of the hill, where the diners sat at tables overlooking the city. There were stepped terraces beneath, where patrons could stand with drinks in hand and look out all the way to the harbor.

Tessier was already there when Leconte arrived, sitting on the main deck at his customary table. He took one look at the doctor and ordered a bottle of rum for the table. "Five stars, and a bucket of ice," he said.

That encounter in Tabarre had upset Leconte's uneasy equilibrium. "I'm telling you, Desmond. I wouldn't have been more surprised if the statue of Toussaint Louverture himself had come off its pedestal and was walking there among the mototaxis. It wouldn't have been any more remarkable than what I actually saw."

When the bottle came Tessier made two drinks, pouring the rum over ice, and passed one to Leconte. "I don't doubt that you saw something," he said. "But after midnight, in the rain, at Tabarre traffic circle. Can you really be certain?"

Leconte diagrammed the scene on the white tablecloth. In the center was the saltshaker, the statue of Toussaint Louverture. The silverware was arranged around it in a line of spectators. Wens Noel was a one-centime piece, Leconte was five *gourdes*, and Zo was the pepper shaker. "It may have been a year since I last saw him," he said, holding up the pepper, "but I'm telling you, Desmond, it's not a face you can forget." He showed Tessier exactly where he had been in the audience and where Zo had been standing. "You should have seen that knife," he said. "It was so rusty you could get tetanus just by looking at it."

The waiter came and they ordered dinner. The doctor would have the tender beef tips in okra sauce and the judge a whole grilled lobster with macaroni salad. A chanteuse from Martinique took the stage and sang to a zouk accompaniment.

The plates arrived and they ate in silence, listening to the music. Then Tessier took the lobster bib off his neck. "I'm still not convinced," he said. "Who hasn't seen a drunken cane-cutter coming home from the fields at midnight?"

Leconte brought out the handkerchief and placed it on the table between them. "But how would you explain this?"

"What is it?"

"Evidence."

"Of what?"

"That I am less sure of."

Tessier pushed his plate aside. The handkerchief was torn through from edge to middle and embroidered in one corner with black thread. He read it aloud, running his finger over the stitch. "'A & Z. January 1, 2010.'" He looked up. "So what, Vincent?"

"A and Z."

"You can't possibly think that A . . ."

"Who else?"

"Have you asked her?"

"You know how things stand. How could I? I still feel she and I are as fragile as that hankie."

Tessier slammed the table so hard the silverware shook. "How I wish I were like you," he said, "with nothing but an apology between my daughter and I! As it stands, there is an eternity between us, and I am not one of those who believe we reunite with our loved ones after death."

"You think I should give her that thing? And then what? Tell her how a drunk, armed with a machete and bleeding from the mouth, gave it to me at Tabarre traffic circle?"

"Why not?"

"You don't know her like I do, Desmond. The earthquake changed her. It's as if she were a hundred years old and already tired of this life."

"I'm talking to you as one father to another."

"You think I should be the one to bring them back together, after I almost killed her trying to break them apart?"

"She would love you for it." Tessier poured himself another drink, straight. "That should be enough for you. We both know how hard it is to marry off a daughter these days, when most men are penniless," he said. "If they have any well-gotten money they are usually our age or older." He drank. "Let me tell you something I tell everyone who comes into my office, whether they are a lawyer or a criminal. And believe me, Vincent, oftentimes they are both. There is no such thing as justice. Only judgment, punishment, and restitution."

"I didn't come for a lecture on law."

Tessier wiped his mouth with the napkin and threw it over his plate. "Didn't you tell me he had a nickname? Something they called him in Tabarre."

"Le Brouetye."

"The wagon man. Yes. You said he pulled twenty riders from the Dominican Republic to Haute Turgeau."

"I said eight. And that's according to Wens Noel."

"Numbers hardly matter in a folktale, Vincent. That's how ten enemies become a hundred. Mark my words." Tessier gestured with his glass. "It's not the tent camps that will save us, or the internationals, with their conditional loans. But the stories the old people tell, the ones their grandchildren believe in."

"You're much drunker than I thought you were."

"The people must have something other than Bouki and Ti Malice."

"It's one thing to say the stories are good, or necessary even. I can concede that. But it's quite another to say that you believe them. You can't honestly tell me that you believe this vagabond from Jérémie is also the *brouetye* from the story." Leconte shook his head. "He may be something with a bag of cement, Desmond, but I hardly see him as a champion of the people."

Tessier spoke sympathetically, calling Leconte *bon zanmi m*— my dear friend. "You miss the point entirely," he said. "It's quite plain to me at least that the *brouetye,* whoever he is—laborer from Jérémie or mechanic from Turgeau—is a hero of the modern Antilles. As worthy of renown as the Jamaican sprinter Usain Bolt, the fastest man on earth. Maybe he didn't break any world records, but then hauling a foot wagon is not an Olympic sport. And you can't deny certain parallels with our own revolutionary heroes," he continued. "Not Toussaint or Dessalines, perhaps. But Mackandal and Dutty Boukman."

Leconte remembered the light in Zo's eyes that made him think of Mackandal burning at the stake. "Weren't they both condemned to death?"

"Wasn't Zo? Once when he was born poor in a poor country, and again when he hauled his wagon through the tropical apocalypse?" Tessier drank the rest of the rum and set his glass down with finality. "There is no such thing as a good man or a bad one. Not on this island," the judge said. "There is only what he does when asked."

Vincent Leconte was present at the meeting on October 24 at which an epidemic of cholera was officially declared in Haiti. The federal minister of health, a grizzled old physician with a bad shave and purple bags under his eyes, stood at the podium with the report in his hand.

"On October nineteenth the Haitian Ministry of Public Health and Population was alerted to high numbers of patients suffering from acute watery diarrhea and dehydration in the Artibonite and Centre Departments," he said. "Four days later, on the twenty-third, the National Public Health Laboratory in Port-au-Prince isolated *Vibrio cholerae*, serogroup 1, serotype Ogawa, from stool specimens obtained from patients in the affected areas."

The minister from Sud-Est, whose department included Les Cayes and the tourist resort on Île-à-Vache, said it was impossible. "There hasn't been a case of cholera on this island for sixty-five years."

The minister agreed. "It was one of the few things this health service had done well to combat," he said. "Unfortunately, I have seen the results myself." The director was a veteran of outbreaks, hurricanes, and previous political administrations. "This is like nothing we have ever seen before," he warned. "The models are predicting half a million sick and ten thousand dead."

Leconte was a longtime student of tropical epidemiology. As he drove through the lowlands, alongside camps pitched in drained mangrove swamps, he began to grasp the scale of the disaster with which they were faced. Come rainy season these people would be walking about in their own feces. They would die by the thousands in their houses of seashells and bedsheets. In the markets, the vendors of sweets and seeds, vinegar and mustard, brooms, oils, clothes, fruits and meats, would be sickened with and then become vectors of the outbreak themselves.

Leaning forward through the seats, he told Claude to take him to Rue Borgella.

All three girls were at the apartment when he arrived. Speaking gravely, he had them follow him into the kitchen, where he took a map from his briefcase and unfolded it on the table. It was a topographic chart of Port-au-Prince, longer and wider than the table.

"The internationals don't know a thing about the tropics," he said. "Our greatest threat will not be from hurricanes but poverty and poor sanitation." He jabbed the map at Bizoton. "You girls know better than I do how it stands in the camps. There's no infrastructure. The Europeans want to talk about fair elections, but these people don't have toilets or drinking water. They've already had outbreaks of typhoid. When the rains come"—he indicated Pax Villa and Kwa Wouj—"the water will rush into the camps."

Putting his hands flat on the map, he leaned toward them. "Can you girls keep a secret?" he asked. Then, extracting the promise of silence from each of them, he told them about the outbreak of cholera that had just been declared in the Artibonite. If he expected some kind of reaction from them, he was quickly disappointed. Those nurses, who had survived the collapse of their university and had been fighting hand to hand with tuberculosis for four months, were unfazed by news of another epidemic.

"The models are predicting half a million sick and ten thousand dead—before New Year's. Malaria, typhoid, tuberculosis—they're nothing compared to this. Don't you understand, girls? Cholera spreads by handshake and kills quickly. Twenty liters of diarrhea in a day. The electrolyte imbalance sends the heart into a fatal arrhythmia from which it cannot recover." He snapped his fingers. "They won't even have time to get off their mountains."

He looked from Verna to Yonise.

"If I were either of your fathers," he said, "I would want you to come home. Now. Before it begins. And you." He looked at Anaya.

"I've come so close to losing you once. I don't think I could bear to go through it again."

Yonise and Verna took that as their cue to leave. They passed under the curtain separating the kitchen from the rest of the house, leaving Anaya alone with her father. After a moment's silence, he took the handkerchief out of his briefcase and put it on the map between them, in the blue Bay of Port-au-Prince.

"Where did you get that?" she asked.

"Are you A?"

Anaya picked it up and felt the embroidery. "Madam Zulu made them for us."

"If you're A," her father said, "who is Z?"

Anaya retained the immaculate poise that she'd perfected after her injury. "Don't you remember?" she said. "You found his sandals."

Leconte felt hot and dizzy. "The swim instructor?"

Once she said his name out loud it was there between them as inescapable and symbolic as the map of Port-au-Prince. It seemed to stand for all the trouble between them.

"You were wrong about him," Anaya said. "Zo was honest and kind. He was the finest man I ever met."

"What about the handkerchief?"

"It was made by Madam Zulu and her granddaughter."

"*Ki es?*"

"Madam Zulu. She lives on Mòn Nwa." Anaya pointed at it on the map. "The people there may be poor, but they are generous," she said. "I spent the New Year there."

"I thought you spent the New Year at Royal Decameron Indigo Beach Resort with your cousin Nadine."

"That was a lie," she said. "When I told you I was at the Indigo, I was really with Zo on Mòn Nwa. We were married there, on New Year's Eve." She described the party—the dance floor, the high platters of rice and chicken, the soup *joumou*.

After the breathlessness of the initial shock, which had gone off in him like an incendiary device, a kind of weariness settled over Vincent Leconte for which he was thankful. He became languid and subdued, accepting everything she said as though it were a normal conversation.

"Zo followed me from Jérémie," she said, "and proposed at Nadine's apartment. After we were married on Mòn Nwa, we only had ten days together. We had to fit a lifetime into our honeymoon." She told her father that Zo wasn't a vagabond but an orphan, who practically raised himself from the age of eight. "And this was during the embargo, when even the well-to-do had trouble filling their bellies." There was a wet heat rising behind her face and Anaya wanted her father to feel it. "Zo never went to college," she said. "He was never going to be a surgeon, or the director of a federal bureau. But he did what he could after the earthquake." She turned and held the curtain aside. "*Vin ba lo,*" she said. "I want to show you something."

She took her father into the bedroom she shared with Yonise. He'd seen it before but was still shocked by the brutality of it. With walls of unpainted cinder block and iron bars over the window, it looked like a prison cell. The girls had driven nails into the wall to hang their clothes, and besides the mirror in the corner, that was the only decoration.

The beds were pushed to opposite sides of the room. Anaya went to hers and lifted the mattress off the frame. Leconte saw that she kept all her important documents there under the bed: her work contract, her bank account information, her nursing license. She found what she was looking for: a single sheet of stiffened contract paper.

"When Zo came to Port-au-Prince," she said, "he found work on a *brouet* wagon, taking a cart through the streets. He usually ran mattresses, TVs, you know, commercial goods. But on the day of the earthquake, he turned his cart into an ambulance."

If he was surprised, Leconte didn't show it. Saying he couldn't read a thing without his glasses, he took them from his pocket, wiped the lenses, and fitted them over his eyes. The paper was an invoice. A stamp in the corner read OZIAS AND SON TRANSPORT CO.

There were six columns printed across the page: TYPE, UPC, DESCRIPTION, QUANTITY, PALLET, WEIGHT. Under "Type" were names: Frances Beauge, Exandieu Noel, Myer Cassagnole, and five more. Under "UPC" was either an M or an F. The "Description" category read "fractured pelvis," "crush injury," "internal bleed." The "Quantity" was always 1, except for the last entry, where it was 2, and the riders were listed as Ti Papa Pikan and his rooster, Ti Zom.

"What is this?" Leconte asked.

"Zo's last bill of lading," she said. "Those are the riders he took to the hospital."

The invoice was marked an hour after the earthquake, on January 12. The point of issue was Mòn Nwa and the intended destination was Lopital Jeneral. The estimated time of arrival: 8:00 p.m. Leconte looked at the list again, putting it together. Frances Beauge, a forty-seven-year-old female suffering from a fractured pelvis, weighing an estimated seventy kilos, was loaded into the wagon at Obin's clinic in Wo Nerette. Exandieu Noel, a nine-year-old male with a skull fracture, had been picked up outside the Nouvel Institut Emmanuel. At the bottom of the column was a final number, added up and circled twice. It was labeled "Total Estimated Tonnage" and was irrefutable proof of Zo's miraculous deed—420 kilos.

Leconte recalled the first time he'd ever seen the laborer, shirtless under a half dozen bags of cement mix. He was practically heroic even then, in the backyard. What must it have been like for him, with these riders bleeding to death in his wagon, and his legs aching as he dragged them up the incline?

When Vincent looked up again his head was swimming. His daughter, the mirror, the clothes hanging on their nails, all wavered before his eyes. A sob rushed into his windpipe and sat there under such pressure he knew that if he so much as opened his lips to breathe, it would escape irretrievably. He thought of the Fishermen's Union slogan in Grande Anse—"Our Poverty Is Our Fortitude"—and understood Zo better than he'd ever understood him before.

"I don't pretend to know what happened to you during those hours you were under the rubble," he said, "or how you survived that ordeal, which would certainly have killed most others, myself included. The only thing I know for certain is that there is a hardness in you where once there was my daughter."

He finally worked up the courage to look her in the face, and then he saw her as Zo did, a woman to change your life for. Without knowing the full measure of what he said, he told her that he had seen Zo at the traffic circle in Tabarre City.

Anaya had been heartbroken for so long that she was impervious to everything but hope. It was the one attack for which she had no contingency, and it pierced her defenses as easily as an arrow. She felt weak and hot. She told her father he'd made a mistake—Zo had been killed in an aftershock on January 12.

Her father insisted. He described Zo's clothes, his manners, the way he stood and swung the machete, but Anaya wanted hard evidence. There was the handkerchief, but who was to say that hadn't been lost in the ruined city for months? What really gave Zo away in the end was not her father's description of his body or the clothes he wore, but that he had said, there in the rainy streets of Tabarre, "I have had malaria and I have had love. They are not so different." That sentence, repeated now by her father, was as irrefutable as an artifact, and the sentiment so specific to Zo that she couldn't deny it any longer.

Anaya emerged from her apartment into a world much altered because of Zo's living in it. All the things that had once evidenced his death—Mòn Nwa under the sunshine, the wind in the banana leaves, the sparkling Caribbean Sea—suddenly became symbols of hope. She'd felt nothing like it for so long that it made her at first uneasy and finally sick. She collapsed at the end of the driveway under a pair of cinnamon trees.

Verna and Yonise found her in the kitchen after midnight, presiding over the unfurled map of Port-au-Prince. "My father saw him in Tabarre," she said, moving the red marker from Parc Jean-Marie Vincent and placing it over Tabarre Circle. "And I know from the bill of lading that they started in Mòn Nwa." She placed a yellow sticker over the mountain. "And stopped here in Wo Nerette, at Obin's clinic." And another one over Wo Nerette.

The girls stayed with her until dawn, moving the markers around the map, charting the sightings of Zwazo Delalun in Port-au-Prince since the earthquake. It was a different city altogether that was laid out before them in the morning. Zo's wagon route from January 12 was tacked out in yellow, and the sightings of him since then were in red.

They asked her what she planned on doing now and Anaya said she was going to find him—no matter what it took, or how long.

The girls swore to help.

They started a week later at Obin's clinic in Nerette, where Zo had picked up most of his passengers. Anaya was hoping for a lead, but all they found was the bonesetter himself. His hair had gone gray, and a falling-out with his apprentice had left him alone. He lit a match, held it to his pipe bowl, and shook it out.

"Zo was really something to see." He puffed. "At the head of his wagon, with thighs like that. I can see why you loved him. But the truth is, after he left my yard with those passengers"—he blew out a stream of spicy smoke—"I never saw him again."

Anaya went into the camps but they were huge. All the informal systems that had once kept communities intact had been blown apart. "It's like living at sea," one of the residents told her. "Where you go to sleep at night is not necessarily where you wake up in the morning."

She despaired of ever finding Zo again, and finally went alone to see the Reverend Garnel Ladoche. She found him at his church in Bolosse.

"Perhaps you were expecting someone else," he said when he saw her. That booming, magisterial radio voice was apparently produced by a thin, neat little gentleman with a shaved head, wearing round spectacles low on his nose. "But the Hebrews had eight days of light from a single measure of oil," he said, sitting her in one of the pews. "So you see, it's not the shape of the vessel that is important, but the oil inside."

Anaya introduced herself as an avid listener of his radio show. "It's the only thing the driver lets us listen to," she said. She told him she was a nurse in the tent camps, and had lost her husband in the earthquake. "There was a program about him," she said. "You called him Le Brouetye." Anaya produced the last bill of lading. "There were eight riders on his wagon," she said. "But I can't find any of them."

"And if you could find them," the reverend asked, "what good would it do?" He handed back the paper. "My daughter," he said, "when Lazarus came out of the cave, he was tied hand and foot with burial bands. His face was wrapped in a cloth. The people were terrified. Do you know what they did? They put his whole family out to sea in a vessel without sails, oars, or helm."

"*Mw pa komprann.*"

"If one walks during the day," he said, "she does not stumble because she sees the light of this world. But if one walks at night, she stumbles because the light is not in her." He touched her hand. "It has been almost a year," he whispered. "It is one thing to wait for a miracle, but another altogether to wait for the dead."

· Book Five ·

20

THE CHOLERA EPIDEMIC started nine months after the earthquake, in the Latem River valley. A dozen patients came to the
government hospital in the back of a pickup truck complaining of
watery diarrhea. Then it was in the Artibonite River and the city
of Saint-Marc, where the river empties into the sea. From there,
it climbed deeper into the hinterland mountains, where they had
never even seen a UN soldier or heard a white man speak. They
were dying in places that weren't on the maps.

Then it hit some *bidonvil* fifty kilometers south, on the door-
step of Port-au-Prince. It had jumped half the coastal settlements
and no one knew how. The internationals blamed shellfish, the
easy traveling habits of Haitian market women, and a bus that had
made a wet stream crossing. In the precarious makeshift cities of
the lowland, extended families squatted under their tented bedsheets awaiting cholera and loss and the cyclone season.

"Don't drink the water," they said. "Whoever drinks the water
drinks his last."

The international relief organizations turned their attention to the epidemic. Treatment centers went up in empty lots across the capital. Hospital atriums were turned into women's wards and their yards converted to morgues. The International Medical Corps, where Anaya, Verna, and Yonise still worked, quit the traveling *tebikiloz* business to focus on the emerging threat. In November, all three were transferred to the newly operational cholera treatment center in Beleko. They had uniformly rejected Leconte's advice to leave the city and reported to work one Monday morning prepared to combat the new disease.

Their instructor was a nurse called Jeanne-François, who fanned her face with the welcome packet. "The worst part about working here," she said, "is that every time you get a stomachache, you'll think you are going to die." Jeanne-François was a committed Wesleyan and compared the treatment center to the Holy of Holies. "But instead of finding the blessed tabernacle in the innermost chambers, here you will find one of the most contagious and deadly bacterium known to man." She held up an enlarged microscope photo. "Know your enemy, ladies. Gram-negative *Vibrio cholerae*. It's gotten so bad we've built a morgue and begun to fill it up, too."

The CTC was laid out in the car park of St. Catherine's Hospital and had been charged with the impossible task of serving all sixteen precincts of Cité Soleil, including La Saline and Fort Dimanche. Jeanne-François took them on a tour.

"Incoming patients are stripped naked and sprayed with chlorine bleach," she said in the intake tent. "This the Green Zone— kitchen, mess, storage, administration." She led them through the chemical footbath. "And this is the red zone—wards, laundry, showers."

The treatment center had been established by a Spanish organization but was staffed by Argentinians. They all smoked cigarettes except for the country director, who smoked a pipe. He was a retired military physician and went about the clinic wearing combat boots.

"Sixteen precincts? It's preposterous," he said. "Look at the living conditions. We tell them to wash their hands—they can't afford soap! And the Americans?" He made a fist. "They are bringing us beef stroganoff when what these people want is rice!"

The principle of treatment was surprisingly simple: rehydration at all costs. By oral salts if the patient arrived in time or intravenously if they were too late.

"Dehydration, acidosis, electrolyte imbalance—it's of no importance to you because the treatment is always the same," Jeanne-François told them. "Hydration. Hydration. Hydration. Your single concern is to get fluid back into them as fast as you can with as close to the correct proportion of electrolytes as you can manage."

The other principal duty of a nurse in a cholera epidemic was no less heroic: to properly dispose of the noxious waste of their patients. *Vibrio cholerae*'s natural habitat was brackish, and it multiplied tenfold in the warm waste of its victims. Every single load had to be treated with cresol and carried to the proper latrine.

By December, there were ninety thousand cases of cholera in the country, and the nurses were working hundred-hour weeks. Anaya, Yonise, and Verna pulled the night shift through the end of the year. They were there on Christmas Eve, when the electricity went out and then the generator, too, because no one had purchased reserve gasoline. A local pastor, whose wife had been admitted, held an impromptu service in the dark, taking up a collection from the families of the patients to buy more fuel. Meanwhile, the nurses lit hurricane lamps and went about their duties as if they were working under siege.

Anaya and Yonise were working in the pediatric ward when an infant presented early on Christmas Day. The initial findings were bad. He was lethargic, with a dry diaper and delayed capillary refill. His pulse was rapid and thready, and he felt limp as a doll in Yonise's arms.

Anaya had become an expert in the art of finding veins and set-ting the needle, and she was invited to seat the tiny sixteen-gauge butterfly. The lantern cast a troubling glare and the kerosene smoke stung her eyes. They'd already tried his hand, his foot, and his elbow pit, so Anaya chose the only palpable vein in his body, and stuck him there, in the jugular. She seated the needle and fixed the line in place.

Afterward, she stepped out into the miserable Christmas. A light rain was falling and gray waterbirds wheeled over the smoky lowland. She looked toward Mòn Nwa but couldn't see the peak through the fog. Her anniversary with Zo was approaching. She wiped the rainwater from her face and went to check on the boy's mother.

"She's hypotensive," Verna said. "And she has that faraway look they get when there's not much else you can do for them."

The patient's mouth was open and a white rime of spit ringed her lips. Her skin was paper-thin and had no luster.

"How old is she?" Anaya asked.

Verna showed her an ID card. "Eighteen, from Fòlibète. Fabiola d'Ayiti."

Anaya's face went blank. Her eyes clouded over.

"What's wrong?" Verna asked. "Are you sick?"

She followed Anaya through the chemical footbath into the green zone.

"I've read that list so many times I practically have it memo-rized," Anaya said. She entered the mess tent, took her bag from the hook, and unfolded the bill of lading. "Look here. Sabina d'Ayiti. Twenty years old. From Fòlibète."

"The girl in there is only eighteen," Verna said, "and her name is Fabiola."

Anaya didn't leave when her shift ended. She went to the administration tent, lay down on the cot, and slept fitfully through the morning. A day shift nurse woke her at eleven and told her Fabiola was awake now and able to speak if Anaya still wanted to.

Anaya put her feet on the ground and rubbed her face. It took her a moment to remember what she was still doing there.

"What about the boy?" she asked.

The day nurse briefly closed her eyes.

The women's ward was a harsh sight in the morning. The patients lay naked in gold foil blankets. The IVs hung from the roof. The nurse's station was near the entrance, a desk crowded with binders and reference manuals and staffed by a team of tired-looking women.

Fabiola d'Ayiti was sitting up drinking oral rehydration salts through a straw when Anaya introduced herself as one of the pediatric nurses. "I'm so sorry about your son," she started.

Fabiola screwed her face up and hung out over the cot. "No," she said.

"We did everything we could," Anaya continued.

Fabiola burped and wiped her mouth with the back of her hand.

"One of the nurses held him in her arms until the end," she said. "It was as if he went to sleep."

Fabiola spit a mouthful of rehydration salts into the bucket. "No. I'm not his mother," she said. "I'm his aunt."

The protocol for epidemic containment required that a hygiene specialist accompany every body on its return to the community. They were to oversee the disinfection of private homes and supervise funerals so that the dead didn't contaminate the water supply. A stable of motorcycles were on hand for that kind of work, but Anaya convinced them to release one of the ambulance vans. Then she rode in the back with Fabiola, who was exhausted but stable, and lay on the wheeled stretcher as dry as salt fish.

They'd given her a water bottle at the clinic and she drank from the straw. "They promised us a house if we stayed," she said. "But three months passed. Then five. We are still there in Parc Jean-Marie Vincent, in the sun and the rain. They give us a little rice and keep telling us to wait."

Anaya took the bill of lading from her backpack and showed

it to Fabiola. "My husband was a *brouetye*," she said. "Before the earthquake he hauled TVs and mattresses, but that night, after the earthquake, he turned his cart into an ambulance."

Fabiola took her mouth off the straw. "You're the one he was trying to get to? The nursing student?"

"How do you know that?"

"My sister still talks about him," she said. "How wonderful he was. How committed. To hear her talking you'd think he was her husband instead of yours. She even named the baby after him."

"Who?"

"My sister. The baby boy. You didn't know?"

Anaya's breathing was so shallow she could hardly feel the air going in and out of her mouth.

"My sister named him Alonzo but we mostly called him Zo, like the *brouetye*."

The ambulance inclined steeply and came to a stop. A moment later, the hygienist opened the door.

"Welcome to Jean-Marie Vincent," he said.

The camp where the d'Ayitis stayed was a neighborhood cobbled together from the nightmares of many mothers. The shanties were pitched in an uneven lot near the old army airport, and though the tents were tied one to the other for stability, Anaya thought it was likely that the whole establishment would blow away at once in a tropical storm.

Fabiola took them behind the old runway and introduced them to her sister. Sabina d'Ayiti was barefoot and dressed like the other prostitutes there, in a threadbare bra and panties. Her hair was only half done and she held the end of the unfinished braid. She knew her son had died as soon as she saw her sister without him.

"I'm glad," she cried. "I'm glad! I'm glad!" She fell on her knees and the braids came undone. "He's found a way out of this misery while the rest of us are caught in it like fish caught in a net at sea."

The boy had been her only child, but she still had Fabiola and a school-age brother to feed.

Anaya didn't need to ask if they were hungry because she could tell from the way the boy kept looking at her that they were starving. They'd never received a proper relief shelter but lived in an A-frame stitched from their own bedclothes. The walls were sewn together with the dental floss the internationals had been distributing for tooth care.

The hygienist was dressed like a soldier in a chemical war, wearing a hooded jumpsuit and surgical mask and armed with a pressurized spray pack of chlorinated water. When he kicked into the tent, a group of children ran out screaming. He primed the pressurized pack, held the nozzle like a gun, and pulled the trigger. A cloud of bleach-smelling mist ballooned out from openings at either end.

The hygienist appeared soon after, dragging their sad furniture into the sunlight. Everything was scavenged. They sat on broken cinder blocks, slept on salt fish crates, and cooked over three big stones. Anaya sent Sabina's young son to buy charcoal, and they soon had the family's tattered wardrobe boiling in a pot of water.

They buried the boy in an empty salt fish box in the weeds beside the old runway after dark. Sabina spoke first. She said she was in labor when the earthquake started and that the walls came down around her like the walls of Jericho. "But there were no trumpets." After that the contractions ceased. "It was as if he knew what kind of world it was and had changed his mind about coming into it." She wondered most of all why God would let him survive the earthquake only to kill him now with cholera. "What sense does that make?" she asked.

The eulogy was delivered by a prostitute they called Sè Azou, the matriarch and leader of their commune. "God didn't give us these bodies to ruin in prostitution," Sè Azou said. But living on that island was like going up a mountain backward. "One must turn to look every now and then and when she does, the future looks bad. Though we've all earned the right to say, 'I can't help you with your problems, I have enough of my own,' we must never say it. Even though it is a war to get enough food to eat," she concluded, "let it not be a war between neighbors."

After the interment, when the boy had been laid to rest and the dirt thrown across the box, Anaya approached the d'Aytiti sisters.

"My sister told me why you came," Sabina said. "But there are a thousand *brouetyes* in Port-au-Prince. What makes you think we're talking about the same one?"

Anaya showed Sabina her name on the bill of lading.

"There's only one way to be sure," Sabina said. Ducking into the tent, she reappeared with a flip phone. *"Pagen chaj,"* she said.

Anaya followed her up a narrow lane to the corner, where a teenaged businessman charged electrical devices from a car battery. He protested at first because Sabina owed him money, but Anaya paid him up front. He took the phone and matched it to a charger.

Sabina flipped it open. "It takes forever to power on," she said. When it did, she searched the memory. "I took this at the bottom of Impasse Kayiman."

Anaya took the phone and looked. The image was proof of an apocalypse. There in the cheap flash was the collapsed rubble going on like purple hills in the dim. A fire burned in the background and the cinders tumbled across the dark. In the foreground, a figure stood fixed between two poles. He didn't seem to be looking back at the photographer or anything at all, but gazed past them into the thick dust spiraling over the capital.

Sabina didn't need to ask if it was him. She could tell from Anaya's face. Seeing that photo was like putting hot coals amid the dead ones of Anaya's love for Zo. The fire began in her anew, and in that dim street she blazed bright as a candle.

Sabina led her through the alleys into Avenue Haile Selassie, where the surviving wall of a school served as a bulletin board. It was plastered with dozens of announcements, mostly for churches, aid organizations, and people looking for loved ones. Sabina tore one down, an orange flyer printed with black ink. It advertised "The End of the World Party," planned for the one-year anniversary of the earthquake. It promised music, alcohol, entertainment.

At the bottom of the page, in print so small it was hard to read, there was an advertisement for a boxing match. Billed as "The Fight to End All Fights," it promised to be a battle between champions: one a fugitive called Foom, and the other, his opponent and challenger, called Zo.

21

THE FIGHT TO END ALL FIGHTS was Zo's idea. Following his encounter with Dr. Vincent Leconte at the traffic circle in Tabarre City, he'd asked Sabala for harder and more dangerous bouts.

"You want to duel with pistols?" Sabala asked.

"I want to fight the fight to end all fights," Zo said.

Sabala looked at Zo's face, the dull cast of his eyes, his poor posture, and said, "You may have already fought that one and lost." Nonetheless, the promoter liked the idea and went about getting Zo just such a match. "The only thing we need is a worthy opponent," he said.

They found him a gangster who had escaped the penitentiary when it fell open in the earthquake, a famous ruffian with guns and no compunction who now believed he had been pardoned and sanctioned by God himself.

"Sanctioned for what?" Zo asked.

"He claims he summoned the earthquake to secure his own freedom," Sabala said. "Someone needs to show him otherwise."

Everyone called Sabala's money manager Manaje because of the good work he did managing accounts. Manaje's advice was simple. "Don't do it," he said. "You can't win. If you win in the ring, one of his gangsters will shoot you. If you lose, you've lost your first match."

Sabala told Zo it was all set for the one-year anniversary of the quake. "Imagine two stages, live music, beer shops, a proper ring to fight in. They're calling it the End of the World Party, and your fight is the main attraction."

"What's the payout?" Zo asked.

Sabala smiled. "That's the question, boy," he said. He put his hand on Zo's shoulder and gave a number so great they were all hushed by it, even Sabala himself.

"The man you're fighting," Manaje said, "he's no ordinary criminal. He's a murderer. He could kill you by knife or magic, or with a shrug to one of his henchmen."

"Did you have other plans?" Sabala asked. "Did you want to light a candle in the Catholic church, maybe? Oh, that's right," he said, "the cathedral collapsed with seventy-two parishioners on their knees. The archbishop was killed." He looked at Zo. "Beating this gangster is a public service. Do it for the community, Zo. The cops can't catch him. They say he doesn't exist."

"You don't have to convince me," Zo said. "I'll fight."

The morning of the match he woke high above Martissant, in the mists of Leclerk Bidonvil. He'd wintered there, playing dice and dominoes and betting on cockfights. Someone had cut down the tree he slept under and sold the wood for charcoal, so he had no shade. He found his bottle and spent the morning draining what was left of it, sitting on the tree stump and regarding the city under overcast skies.

At noon he made his morning toilet, crossing through the long yard of trash in the rising heat. Though the settlement was on a river that flowed year-round, the residents refused to drink from it because it was known to be contaminated with cholera. A dozen people who drank from it had died. When the shipments of drinking water ceased, they grew so thirsty they dug down to the municipal water pipes and broke into them. Naked children raced under the geyser, singing:

> M pa pè kolera.
> M pa pè kolera.
> I'm not scared of cholera.
> I'm not scared of cholera.

A little girl named Pepel, who'd been in love with Zo since the day he arrived in camp, begged him not to bathe in the stream, but Zo cupped the water in his hands and had a long drink, slurping loud enough that she could hear him. He had supper at four o'clock, at the cart in Delmas where he took most of his meals.

"Komo w ye?" he asked the chef.

"Ah, you know," the woman answered. "Hungry. Broke. Naked."

Her lunch special was kasav cake and a shot of kleren. The cake tasted like the coals it was cooked over, and he ate with his fingers.

Sabala came late as always, driving the Cheri Doudou with eleven passengers in back. "They're all for you," he said when Zo climbed into the cab. "Every last one. A lot of cash in their pockets, too."

"Sure," Zo said, checking the rearview mirror. "They look like high rollers."

Manaje was there, in the middle seat. "Tell him about his opponent," Manaje said.

"What more is there to tell?"

"What was he in for?"

"Murder in the first."

Zo raised his half-taped hand and told them he didn't want to know.

A minor gangster called Iegans commandeered the Cheri Doudou at the Bwa Nef checkpoint in Cité Soleil, and he started by grinding the clutch so hard it hurt Sabala.

"Ride her softly or she won't be ridden much farther," the driver said.

"I've ridden women harder than this piece-of-shit truck," Iegans said, kicking the clutch. A zippered scar running from his mouth to his earlobe made his expression sour. He took them to Boston and Beleko, where the homes were raised on stilts. Iegans never took his hand off the horn or his foot off the gas, but ran dogs and children off the road. The passengers rocked in the back and slapped the roof. He let go of the wheel and closed his eyes.

Sabala reached across and took it. "You might be a gangster," Sabala said, "a real *tonton macoutes*. But if you are going to drive my Cheri Doudou, do it carefully."

Iegans opened his eyes and took the wheel. "Rice costs more in Pòtoprens than it does in Santo Domingo," he said. "Phones are more expensive here than in Miami. Gas, too. That make sense to you?" He sucked his teeth. "We sick of getting slave man's wages and paying international prices. So we built our own wharf, international port of shipping, with our own docks and longshoremen. Our own customs officials to collect the tariff. Belize, Jamaica, Honduras. And they pay tax! *Komès entènasyonal.*" Iegans made the money sign with his fingers. "That's not gangster," he said, "that's business. Motorcycles from Korea and you better believe they run good." He patted his shirt pocket, reached in, and pulled out a small baggy fat with powder. "We middleman on this," he said, easing off the gas and snorting a fingerful of cocaine. He kicked the clutch wide open and they roared up the road in a cloud of exhaust.

"It's too easy to die in this country," Sabala said.

"What's hard is to die old," Iegans agreed. He turned his head and showed the entry scar at the back of his neck. "I've been shot five times." He took his foot off the gas and they coasted and stalled. He showed his ankle, the side of his knee, and then kicked them back into first.

"Just a year ago I woke up in prison. Titanic block, tropical lockdown. No fuck for seventeen months. No trial, no hope of one. Murder charges, gang man, Tonton Macoute," he counted his crimes. "Never getting out and I know it. Then the earthquake. The penitentiary opens and we walk out, every last guilty motherfucker praying to Jesus and thanking God. That's not all," Iegans confessed. "We get here and the Brazilians are gone. Dead in their headquarters. Radios, GPS, body armor like the U.S. Marines. A diesel generator."

Iegans turned onto the wharf road. The shanties fell off on the left to reveal that they were riding along the sea, up the coast of a short peninsula.

"Welcome to the marina at Waf Jérémie," he said.

Zo's fight was to take place in what Iegans called "the boatyard," a lot against the water where wrecked vessels were beached and stripped for parts. The boxing ring had been swept clean of debris, and a fixed jib crane provided lighting.

Criminals allegedly dead for eleven years were in attendance. The *zenglendo* sat under hurricane lamps on plastic seats smoking stogies, looking mean. They were passing an eighty-dollar bottle of Rhum Barbancourt from the president's private stock. Ti Manolo, believed dead since the fall of Duvalier, sat fat and ugly in a fisherman's vest sipping Italian champagne out of the bottle. He was talking about reestablishing lucrative drug routes with an eye toward Miami.

The night was inaugurated by a gangster who called himself Dread Williams, after his long dreadlocks. He wore the blue helmet of a UN peacekeeper and an unfastened Kevlar vest. Pressing a megaphone against his mouth, he said, "One year ago the island tried to kill us. Then *MI-NU-STAH*, with his soldiers and his *ko-le-ra*, tried to finish us off for good. But we are still here." He moved his finger and the microphone chirped. "Tonight is for you. The immortal. The survivors. I give you the party to end all parties. And the fight to end all fights."

The battlers stood at opposite ends of the ring like moody itinerants. Dread Williams introduced Zo's challenger as a latter-day gladiator, sentenced to life twice over because his freedom was that ugly in the eyes of the state. "The roughest and toughest and most savage," Dread Williams said. "I give you Foom!"

Foom came into the ring like an executioner to his scaffold, casting a ten-foot shadow. When he pulled the hood back from his head, Zo saw that he'd been burned over most of his face; the skin was wrinkled like smoked meat. He'd lost the top of an ear to knife or barbed wire. The roman numerals I, XII, and X were tattooed in black ink on his neck, in commemoration of January 12, 2010, the date of his emancipation and the date of the earthquake.

"I don't know how you draw blood from a man like that," Sabala said.

Foom's chest was too broad across for his arms and it made them seem foreshortened, his hands dangled at the waist. Zo noted this short reach as his only weakness. Other than that he looked invincible.

Manaje rubbed down Zo's arms. "Don't go in and slug it out with him," he said. "Play him long. Remember: whoever manages the distance manages the damage."

After his introduction as Le Brouetye, hero of the postapocalypse, longtime fist boxer and work tramp, greatest lover in the Antilles, Zo broke from his handlers and walked out under the light. He raised his arms over his head and fisted his hands. His arms looked like wide pistons and they were oiled for the work at hand. He performed his quick two-step and shadowboxed a crisp combination. The audience erupted. Zo bent down and pounded the dirt so hard a cloud of dust rose up to his knees, and then he stood again, rubbing his palms dry.

Dread Williams declared that the only rules were the rules of the island. "Cyclone. Earthquake. Gunshot. Disease. There will be neither quarter nor mercy."

He raised the Glock into the air and squeezed a single shot into the overcast.

Foom opened the fight with two short jabs, advancing across the lot. When he got close enough he hooked and missed and hooked again. He dropped his head and followed Zo's feet, already every now and then pulling his left shoulder and throwing his right hook.

Zo boxed with a natural ease, prizing coolness and calculation above all else. He carried an open stance with his feet at hip's width and his fists loose and vicious. He held his elbows low and close over his midsection and danced with his face pulled back above his hands.

Foom wanted contact and threw an erratic overhand right. Zo wheeled away from it and came back again on his left leg. He carried most of his strength there from hauling wagonloads up the incline and his hit was clean. His calves bulged and tensed. Then he shifted position and landed a left into the side of the gangster's neck. Foom fell back into the lot and for the first time that night seemed to understand the idea of caution.

When the first bell sounded, Sabala was full of praise for Zo's fight. "You surprised him. Now you ought to tire him out. He won't come out swinging like that again."

"A man is only a lion once," Manaje agreed.

"I don't think he gets tired," Zo said.

"No," Manaje conceded. "But neither does he know defense. Make him learn. Run him a bit."

"He wants to get me up against the crowd."

"Don't let him," Manaje said. "He'll kill you there."

Foom fought without style. He had nothing but a fatal, repetitive right and trusted in the law of probability that he would finally land that brutal right to end the match. He refused to defend himself, but his ability to absorb punches was remarkable. He took them to the ribs and over the kidneys, to the side of the head.

Foom's battle never flagged. He chanted as he squared off. "This is how I die. Rich, hated, happy. This is how I die. And you?" He punched right and away. "This is how you die. With a right and a left." Punching away. "This is how you die." He threw two hard fists, one after the other.

In the third round, the fighters came out under the electric lights like gladiators into an abject coliseum. They were both bruised and had begun to bleed about the face. Foom had quit any pretense of stance or technique. His hands were fisted or open as he remembered them. He held them far apart in front of his body, or down at his sides, or up about his head like moons at orbit. They finally closed in the roadside trash.

Foom lowered his face and advanced under a hail of tossed fists. "Everyone is afraid of Foom." He worked away with his right until he got inside of Zo's defenses, and then he swung up with a foreshortened uppercut. "Everyone is afraid of Foom." The blow caught Zo under the chin and the blood spouted from his mouth. Foom leaned in close and, grabbing the back of Zo's head, spoke into his ear. "Everyone is afraid of Foom," he said, "but Foom himself."

Zo stepped forward through the blood and hurt and threw a surprise jab straight to Foom's mouth. It connected with concise, classic brevity. Foom's head rocketed back on his neck and the spit flew from his mouth.

"When I get through with you," Zo said, "you'll wish you were back in Titanic block at the National Penitentiary." He retreated just as the round was called and watched Foom sitting in the far chair bleeding from the nose. They could hear him huffing like a damaged machine.

"Good answer." Sabala slapped Zo's shoulder.

"Don't let him get away with anything," Manaje said.

Zo watched the dust float up under the lights and blow off across the water.

Sabala had bought oral rehydration salts from a cholera clinic and had Zo swig from the electrolyte mix. "I don't like that cut," he said. Scooping from the jar of Vaseline, he gobbed it over Zo's eye. "How many more rounds can you go?"

"Not many."

"Then you've got to knock him out," Sabala said.

"I don't think he can be knocked out."

When they met again both fighters were exhausted. Zo drew Foom around the perimeter and they went up into the boat parts and down again. When he came close enough, Zo could smell the alcohol on Foom's breath and see the white ring of cocaine under his nose. He boxed Zo back against the crowd, punching without purpose. He hit forearm and elbow and the top of Zo's head. All the while Zo played him loose, feinting and falling back and landing a series of low body shots.

"Come here and face me!" Foom challenged. He landed a blow to Zo's sternum that bent him double. And while Zo struggled to regain his breath, Foom finally landed his brutal right, a tight fist square to Zo's cheek. The world was a hot white flash and then silence, like cotton in his ears. He felt like a child boxing in the cane, looking out for a familiar face where there was none.

Beyond the spectators, out across the black water, Zo saw Anaya Leconte floating over the waves of Port-au-Prince Bay. She looked just as she had the very first time they met, when she was sipping cherry juice under a tree and he was shoveling gravel in the heat. He wondered if Foom's punch had been fatal and if he really stood tottering at the edge of the Caribbean Sea or if he was, as he suspected, standing for his trial at the gates of paradise.

Anaya had been in Cité Soleil since two that afternoon, accompanied by Verna and Yonise.

"We love him almost as much as you do," Verna said. "And wouldn't miss this for anything."

They thought that by coming early, they might catch Zo before the festivities started. But he never showed, and they waited to see if the fight would go on at all. At sunset, a crew of shirtless boys fanned out and cleaned the boatyard. They gathered the trash and carted it off. They passed push brooms across the lot. Anaya couldn't help but think of Zo in Grande Anse, picking up the trash and rebar at the construction site so that she could dispense albendazole tabs. But she didn't speak about it to her friends. The truth was, she was tired of talking.

The music started at dusk, a drum troupe and horns. The crowd got so big the girls couldn't see. They walked out along the wharf to where the Guianese sailors were stationed. The dock went straight out from the mainland for fifty yards before angling up the coast opposite the boatyard, and Yonise thought it would be the best seat in the house. When the battlers did arrive they just appeared, as if summoned by the master of ceremonies with their introductions. The light came on and they stepped into it.

"Is it him?" Yonise asked.

"I can't tell," Anaya said.

The battler closest to them was thick all through and graceless; he was flat-footed and slow. But the far fighter was like a dancer; he bent forward from the hips. He wore black trunks and was sweating all over. They worked in the lighted foreground, rounding each other in the dust. Behind them were the stripped vessels lying at the edge of the light.

The graceless battler came across the lot, leaned forward through the dancer's defenses, and landed a clear left to his chest. Then, while he was dazed, caught him with a brutal right fist to the side of his face. The dancer half spun and spit blood from his mouth. He stood looking forlornly out to sea.

"Look at me," Anaya said. "Look at me."

When he fixed her with a very still and composed gaze, Anaya didn't look away. She couldn't even if she had wanted to. His eyes electrified and froze her down to the bone. There was no love there, only a kind of lostness and a bitter, endless longing.

Zo had boxed men twice his age. He had lost teeth in the cane fields to fighting. He had been hit square in the jaw by men who could have boxed the world circuit if they ever escaped the island. But he had never felt his organs drop so completely out of place as when he realized it really was Anaya standing across the water on the dock in Cité Soleil.

After seeing her, his fight changed. He grew aggressive and unschooled. He fought Foom the way Foom fought. When the next round began he came out bent double, moving inside Foom's fists, catching the convict in his floating ribs. When Foom recovered he threw a blind body shot that caught Zo over the kidney, and one of the spectators said he'd be pissing blood for a week.

The fight had begun high in the boatyard, in a lot swept clean of trash and debris. But they began drifting toward the shore. It was imperceptible at first, but Zo was driving them to the water. By flanking Foom to the right again and again, he drove the heavy battler against the sea. Zo finally boxed his opponent down into the black sand and they fought there, threading the tide line.

"He's tired," the stevedores said. "If he doesn't force it soon, he's done for."

But Anaya knew it was something else. Zo had seen her on the pier and was coming after her even if he had to swim to get there. The audience had come off their seats and pressed the fighters close against the sea. As they came nearer to the water and the docks, Anaya could hear the deadened thuds of the fighters' fists falling in their opponent's flesh and then their panting like tired animals. No further rounds were called and all semblance of order was lost.

There were two cement slipways intended to return repaired boats from the boatyard to the sea. Zo finally drove Foom down one of these and into the water, just to the ankles at first but then to where the water broke about their knees. The crowd followed them at a run, and now they were fixed at the shoreline, holding the fighters to the water. Foom was stumbling in the breakers between Zo and the place where Anaya now stood, not one hundred yards away amid the stevedores on the dock. A fog had rolled in over the harbor and nothing but a warm rain fell between them.

Zo boxed Foom into deeper water, until they stood in the surf to their thighs, hitting like weary machines that weep and gasp, going back and forth as the tide came in and out. When Zo staggered too close, Foom embraced him in an awful parody of affection.

"I have been killed three times," he said. "Burned in a fire. Fed to the dogs." Foom tightened his arms, squeezing the air from Zo's chest.

Zo put a fist in Foom's gut. "Even the earthquake couldn't keep us apart," he said.

He succeeded in breaking that bad embrace and they stood panting in the frothy water. Foom looked like a cyclops. One eye was swollen shut and the blood flowed from his mouth. Zo thought of Anaya barefoot on the dance floor of the Louco night club. He wiped the sweat from his face, dropped his head, and launched himself across the water. He took a hit to the shoulder and one to the front of his chest, but nothing could stop him. He feinted, weaved, rolled, taking blows over the back and shoulders, coming close enough to land his fatal combination. One-two-three-two. Jab, cross, hook, cross. "Left, right. Left, right," Zo chanted as they landed. The first jab opened Foom up wide as a window, and Zo climbed through without hesitating, landing his big right finish.

Foom's lips went loose and his mouth opened up. He looked genuinely surprised before pitching into the sea.

Zo dove into the surf. The salt stung the cut above his eye and a thousand cuts besides. But the water cooled his throbbing face, and the silence was welcome after the thudding fists and roaring crowd. He had trained with pearl divers and did not break form. Shutting out the murky sea, he dove to the bottom, and only then, when he could feel the seagrass, did he drive himself forward with a steady flutter kick.

"Spear the fish, bring it to your belt, wipe the guts," he chanted as he swam.

His arms ached from hitting and his head was spinning. He could hear the blood pounding in his ears. But there was nothing in that dark sea, neither shark nor tide, that could drive him to the surface. He didn't come up for air until he thought his lungs would burst.

He felt the wind on his face and heard the steady meter of the sea as it rushed beneath the boats. Behind him, he could hear the commotion of the gangsters dragging Foom from the surf. Fighting the terror that threatened to overtake him and drive him back to the bottom of the sea, Zo turned toward the dock.

Above him, just out of reach, was the face that had haunted him for so long. Her eyes were bright across the water and the weight of a year was in her gaze. Her lips parted and he could see her perfect teeth. Then she said his name. Zo's strength, which he had maintained all that long year he'd been without her, suddenly failed him. He was incapable of swimming those last few yards.

Anaya seemed to comprehend him perfectly. She begged the stevedores for help, and two of the Guianese boatmen leaned over and pulled him from the water. He lay on the pier battered and breathless, dripping like a clubbed shark.

"I should have known to look for you here," she said.

Her voice, when he finally heard it, was like the secret code against his long defenses. Zo felt as raw and vulnerable as if he'd been punched twice and left wide open for the finishing blow.

"This is where I belong," he said. "At least I know the rules." His voice was untamed. There was a cruelty Anaya had never heard before and a wildness, as if he'd gone to seed. "Even the roosters understand. One hand follows the other. Winner takes all."

"You're not one of the roosters."

"The same men bet on both of us. One hundred on the red Goliath. One hundred on Zo. They only want to see us tear each other to pieces."

"Why give them the satisfaction?"

"I know what I am. They told me when I was young and haven't let me forget."

His honesty, his unexpected vulnerability, his magnetic sorrow—everything was so familiar and so close, but his soul seemed as far from her as Florida. "What are you, Zo?"

"The poorest man in the Western world."

She wanted to touch him, to obliterate that space between them once and for all, but something repelled her, as if they had been too long oriented to the identical poles of loss and heartache. "Don't you remember what Pikan told us the night we were married? Your life is your only riches, Zo. No one can promise more than that. If they do, they are lying."

"Pikan is dead."

"Ozias told me. He told me what you did after the earthquake. How beautiful it was, and how difficult. How graceful you were."

"To sweat before the cart is nothing," Zo said. "It's what I was made for."

"But you got them to the hospital. You saved their lives."

"It was an ox's job," Zo said. "Any dumb beast could have done it."

"No," she said. "Not a dumb beast. Only you. Only you could do it, Zo. Why won't you open your eyes and look at me?"

Zo was torn apart by hope and hopelessness, like a sea ravaged by its own waves. "I'm afraid."

"Of what?"

Zo closed his eyes so tightly the seawater ran from his lashes. "That it will be between us like it was with me and Yiyi," he said. "That you will have forgotten about me, too. And then I will know once and for all that I am worthless as a coconut husk."

She leaned so close she could smell the sea on his skin. "I have loved you since I first saw you shoveling gravel in the work yard

at Grande Anse," she said. "I loved you when I saw you naked at
your bath in the eggplant patch. I loved you again when you found
me outside the nursing university, and kissed me in the cathedral.
I loved you when I married you on Mòn Nwa. But most of all,
Zwazo, I loved you when you found me in Cacquette's classroom,
and gave me the *adokin* that saved my life."

Zo was outmatched at last. Anaya's words accomplished what
no opponent's fist had ever been able to do: they calmed his rage
and brought him meekly to submission. "Remember the queen
triggerfish," he said, "and the warm water off Taino Beach."

It was as if they had crossed that final meridian back into each
other's hearts. The slums melted back into the hills, the gangsters
went home, the Guianese sailors sailed back to Guiana—and they
were left alone on that pier with the wind coming off the bay and
the gulls skimming the tide.

"I saw you everywhere," she said. "Under every load of coal and
cut wood. In every young man who has determination without
means, purpose but no shirt, a machete and no cash."

She took his hand and regarded the split knuckle. "Poor hand,"
she said. "What has he been doing to you?" She ran her fingertip
under his swollen lip. "Poor mouth," she said at last. "Doesn't he
know what you're for?"

She leaned down, placed her lips against his, and drew them
away.

Zo had a face like a shield, impenetrable, battled with and bru-
talized to save his life. But that kiss broke him wide open. She
could see right through him.

"You still love me," she said.

His eyes, when he opened them, were clouded like breath on
a mirror.

"In the beach beneath your father's house. In the grass under
the lime trees on the hill called Black Mountain. In the middle of a
boxing match." Their faces were so close she could smell the blood
on his breath. "I have loved you in all of those places."

Zo was right about Foom: he couldn't swim. He went over in four
feet of water and panicked as if he'd been thrown into the open
ocean. He was finally rescued by spectators, several of whom were
injured in the attempt. They succeeded finally in dragging him up
the beach and left him coughing up brine. He threw handfuls of
sand and raised a raucous, half-drowned challenge for Zo to come
back and finish the fight.

Foom's associates had meanwhile grasped Zo's deception and
were coming out along the jetty to bring him back. A scuffle broke
out between them and the Guianese sailors, who stood in their
way. The foreigners may not have understood a word that was
said between the couple, but there was no mistaking a reunion
between lovers. They comprehended everything perfectly and
knew what side was righteous.

While the Guianese shipsmen kept the gangsters at bay, Anaya
led Zo farther out along the docks, until they reached the outer
gangway. It was a series of pallets tied over makeshift pontoons
that dipped crazily as the couple walked across them. When they
reached the end of the dock, Zo asked how well she remembered
her swimming lessons.

She looked at the lights on the far side of the bay. "Not well
enough to swim to Carrefour," she said.

Behind them, the gangsters had broken through the line of
brave Guianese, and the lovers thought all was lost. Then they
heard the call of the very last fisherman coming in off the late-
night sea. He was standing in a gaff-rigged catboat with his catch
in a basket at his feet.

"*Pwason wouj, pawson ble, pwason sel,*" he advertised.

"*La,*" Zo yelled, waving his hands.

The fisherman changed course and headed straight for them,
calling, "Red fish, blue fish, salt fish!"

A lone lamp hung over the boat and they could see his face by it as he approached—the thorny cheeks of an old sailor. Zo waited until he had come up alongside. "It's not your fish I need, old man," he said, taking hold of the gunwale, "but your boat."

The fisherman heard them out and finally agreed to give them the boat outright. "The truth is, I'm tired of this old tub," he said. "Sick of eating fish, too."

Most of the boats moored off the pier were rope rigged and masted like ancient Phoenician vessels, and many of them listed to one side. The *Mesi Manman* was no different: a homemade skiff with shipped oars and a furled sail that listed awfully in the tide. "I suppose she'll do for you, as she's always done for me." The fisherman pointed out the vessel's features and began a labyrinthine explanation of how to rig the lone gaff sail.

"The outhaul must be made fast to the end of the boom," he said. "And the luff should always be full. The leech and mainsail must always be roached. You see? The curve should be convex, extending outward to the clew."

Zo told the old man they had no time for a sailing lesson.

"*Dakò,*" he said. "Do as I say. Head straight out from here, parallel to the Carrefour shore. There is a breeze there, and you will be comfortable. It'll be a nice ride under these stars, with a woman like that." He smiled. "I almost wish I was going with you."

Zo and Anaya shipped off together in the old fisher's skiff just as the gangsters reached the outer gangway. The pallets were tied to empty oil drums and the dock dipped crazily, throwing the closest ones over. Foom called raucously for Zo to return and finish the fight.

Anaya sat in the prow and Zo at the rower's bench. He saw that it was not a rod fisherman's boat but the craft of a spear fisherman. He noticed the harpoon blade, the chewed swimming fins, the snorkel goggles. Like that the old man went hunting in the reefs. There were coiled nets in the boat bottom and a five-gallon bucket full of stones, for ballast and diving aids.

They went out alone among the moored fishing vessels until

they were past the last of these. Neither of them spoke. Zo rowed steadily until they had outrun every craft anchored in the bay. The oars moved smoothly in the oarlocks, and working in the water felt innocent after the business of his fists in the ring.

"Why are you rowing so hard?" she asked.

"I have with me the only thing of any worth on that god-forsaken island and I don't expect to return with it."

"Where will you take me?"

"Anse d'Hainault."

"In this rowboat?"

"She has sails."

The wind died and the tide went slack. A high swell jumped the gunwale and they were both wetted in the spray. When Anaya laughed, Zo saw the clean cut of her teeth in the moonlight and the narrow *chenèt* that he believed made her kisses more passion-atc. She leaned over the prow and trailed her fingers in the clear night sea.

"What was it like?" she asked. "All those people in your wagon and you their only hope?"

"Same as hauling mattresses," he said. "I did the best I could." He drew the oars clear of the water. "What was it like in Miss Cacquette's class?"

Anaya stood carefully, making certain not to upset the boat. She passed through the coiled line toward him. "Like floating in the surf at Taino Beach," she said.

They placed the fishing nets and furled sails in the bottom of the rocking skiff to make a kind of bed. Zo saw her body sprawled against the clean white canvas and thought he was dreaming. He approached her as if she had been rescued from the sea, with such gentleness and tenderness it was as if he was afraid to wake her. He knelt at her feet and took inventory of her scars as if he loved them, kissing up her legs and arms to the scar beneath her eye.

Anaya begged for more of him and all of him, she wanted to be shattered, dashed. She had been too long intact and she was bursting at the seams. When he finally entered her all the way with a masterly thrust of his hips, the entire boat pitched forward in the waves as though their desire alone was a sufficient engine to drive them across whole oceans.

22

THE BOAT HAD A SMALL FOREDECK and a pair of bench seats. It was steered from a rudder in the stern. Zo fitted the oars into the oarlocks and set a course toward Point Kafou, a passage that would carry them across the narrowest part of the bay. The sea was easy, and when Zo grew tired, Anaya took over at the oars. He lay back on the stern deck and watched the stars passing overhead. Anaya woke him when they were opposite the point. Beaching was difficult because Point Kafou was also the delta of Cold River, a stream with headwaters in the hills above Kenscoff. The current was strong and ran anterior to their purpose, pushing them back to sea.

Zo noticed the high black clouds over the slopes. "It must be raining in the mountains," he said.

By steady oarsmanship, he turned them out of the current and toward shore. The beach was littered with trash carried from the city's interior and crowded with the pigs who lived on a steady diet of it. Zo and Anaya beached in total darkness, dragging the boat up the shore of Styrofoam cups and coconut husks until they had it safely out of the tide. Then they climbed aboard and lay arm in arm in the furled sails.

They woke at dawn in clothes stiff with salt and kissed each other like lovers in a dream. The tide had come up and they were afloat, drifting back and forth in the easy shallows. Anaya was hypnotized and, taking his face in her hands, asked if he was real.

"When I woke in the back of the truck I thought I was one of the dead," he said. "I thought that Port-au-Prince was the afterworld." He took the oars and drove them hard through the breakers. "I'm never going back."

Port-au-Prince Bay was blue and clear under the sunshine, and the rain-washed houses sparkled in the slopes. Looking back at the wrecked city in its cradle of hills, Anaya said, "Everything is beautiful from a distance."

They had the offshore breeze at their backs and tried to rig the sail, but neither of them was much of a sailor, and the old fisherman had an intricate and anachronistic system. There were three long bamboo poles, and the lines were hopelessly tangled. They managed to raise the mainmast by setting it into a dowel on the forward deck, but then the heavy sail hung at the bottom, useless as a sack. Zo tied one end to the prow with the hold-boom rope, but it stayed limp and looked too heavy even for hurricane winds.

Someone shouted across the waves: "Are you rigging your sails or drying your bedsheets?" They were two boys out at sea on a patched inflatable raft. The thing was half sunk in the water and they were partially submerged. One of them sat on the raft in water to his belly, while his partner dove for *lanbi* and lobster. It was the diver who'd called to them, grabbing the pitiful raft with one hand and lifting the goggles from his face.

"These sails don't make any sense," Anaya said. "They're too heavy for the wind."

The boys looked at each other and laughed. Then the diver fixed his goggles again and put his face in the water. By kicking and paddling, he soon had them alongside the *Mesi Manman*. He pulled himself aboard and stood dripping, with the goggles resting around his neck. He climbed about the boat showing them how to rig the bowsprit, a long piece of wood that stuck off the prow of the ship. The butt rested against the footed mast itself, and the body jutted over the front of the boat. By running the hawser out to its end, the young diver made a long triangle and furled the sail to its full length.

When the wind came down from the mountains it filled the sail. The canvas bellied out and the boat came alive in the water. The nose lifted so dramatically they couldn't feel the swells slapping beneath them. It had been hot in the still shallows, but now the breeze of their own progress cooled their wet faces. The diver showed them how to rig the hold boom to the right or left, depending on whether they wanted to go in or out of the wind.

"The offshore breeze blows out all morning," he explained, "and the onshore blows you in again in the afternoon."

They had been towing the raft behind them and the boys climbed back in. They stood in water to their knees and waved, looking like sailors clinging to the ends of a shipwreck.

They ran all day under full sails and favorable winds and were finally driven ashore by thirst at Valou Beach, where the River Momance meets the sea in a wide gravel delta. Zo went over the gunwale in water to his hips and pulled them up the strand. The trees had been cut down on both sides of the stream and the banks were dry and white.

They bought two green coconuts and a sack of fish patties and went back to sea, rigging their jib sheet like expert sailors and coasting alongside Gressier on the wind. They ate sitting on the stern deck, taking turns at the tiller, sharing the salt fish patties and feeding each other pinches of spicy cabbage salad. Anaya brought out a coconut and they swigged from a hole with the cool juice running down their chins. Then Zo opened the nut with a machete and fashioned two spoons from the shell itself, and they scooped out the sweet white meat and ate that, too.

Traveling without haste, they made it as far as Léogâne by twilight and then had no choice but to beach. The onshore breeze had turned up in the afternoon just as the divers promised it would and drove them coastward. They rounded a green promontory full of birds and came into the wide bay. The coast curved widely away and the town of Léogâne lay behind the promontory with the suburbs strung out along the water. Endless cane plantations drew out of the haze, and they could see the huge mango orchard that had been planted under the hills.

The fishermen were racing off the sea with the onshore breeze at their backs, and the *Mesi Manman* was caught up in a fleet of canoes. The fishermen shouted to each other, inquiring over the catches of their rivals.

Zo asked one as he came alongside, "Which way to the wharf?"

The fisherman angled his canoe toward them and grabbed their gunwale. "What wharf?" he asked. "It was ruined in the earthquake, along with the rest of the city. If you ask me, I'd say you're better off going to Miragoâne."

Anaya asked how far it was.

"You'll never make it tonight," the fisherman said. But, giving them two fish from his catch, he told them about a beach up the coast in the direction they were headed. "There's shelter there, and charcoal for a fire."

They spent the night camped out like Taino Indians, cooking *pwason woz* over an open flame and eating it charred in the skin. There was a small hut the fishermen had made but Zo and Anaya slept out on the sand, using the unfurled sail for a bedsheet.

·   ·   ·

They rounded Mount Qulperie late in the afternoon and had their first view of Miragoâne in its rocky gray hills. It was the capital of Nippes Department, and the principal port for secondhand goods from Miami. The downtown was bustling with the merchants who purchased the imports and those who came from the provinces to distribute them.

The harbor was at Trou-Mouton, where the big freighter *Dread Wilna* had been wrecked for a decade. It was fruiting season for mango Francique, and the dock was busy with native craft come to take the fat green fruit up or down the Tiburon Peninsula. Among the barges and derricks and ferryboats going to Gonâve Island, Zo recognized one by its turquoise and yellow paint. Looking up, he saw the patched sail that hung against the mainmast as unique as a flag, and then, as they floated close by, the name painted in silver letters: *Rekin II*.

As they drew alongside, the hatch opened and Solomon appeared.

"I'd know that face anywhere," Zo called.

Solomon hoisted himself from the hold and cried out. He leaned across the gunwale and pulled Zo's little ship hard against the *Rekin*. "Colibri's into me for a thousand large," he gloated.

"Why's that?"

"He bet we'd never see you again."

Boston was ashore, arguing with his mango wholesaler. "What are you going to do, let them sit here and rot for a few extra *gourdes*? I tell you it isn't worth it."

"Why don't you just pay him a fair price and be done with it?" Zo said.

When Boston saw him, he climbed up on deck and took Zo in his arms. "Where did you come from?"

"Cité Soleil."

Boston looked over at the *Mesi Manman*. "You came all the way from Port-au-Prince in that tub? How much farther are you planning to go?"

"To Anse d'Hainault," Anaya said.

Boston turned and looked at her for the first time. "What do you want to go there for?"

"Zo promised to show me the last sunset on the island," she said.

"I've seen it a dozen times," Boston stated.

Zo put his arm around Anaya's waist. "But we want to see it together," he said.

"Mw kompran," Boston said. "I see. This is the girl you came for in September. Yes." He stroked his chin. "I can see why you'd want to get her as far away from the rest of the world as possible." The captain offered to take them most of the way. "At least as far as Jérémie," he said. "Medsen Fèy will be glad to see you. He figured he just about killed you with his bad advice."

"He practically did," Zo said.

They spent the last of their money on a fish dinner—barbecued grouper served with rice and beans and boiled plantains. Anaya made two phone calls afterward. The first was to Verna and Yonise.

"We thought you had been killed, or kidnapped," they said.

"We left Port-au-Prince," Anaya said. "I'm not coming back."

"What should we tell Jeanne-François?"

"Tell her I found what I was looking for."

The second phone call was to her father. Leconte had been waiting for it and knew what she was talking about without having to ask. "Are you together now?"

"Yes."

"Where are you calling from?"

"Cathédral St. Jean-Baptiste."

"What are you doing in Miragoâne?" His voice got away from him.

Anaya told him how they had found each other, and how they'd escaped from the capital in an open boat.

Her father begged her to be safe. "Perhaps I will see you someday soon," he added.

They returned to the wharf to find the *Rekin II* transformed.

The planks had been scrubbed and sprinkled with cinnamon oil. Red and blue streamers hung from the rigging. The forward deck had been rearranged for the privacy and comfort of the couple and looked like the wedding suite on a dilapidated yacht. A hammock was swinging from the mainmast.

Boston welcomed them aboard their honeymoon cruise, with continuing service to Pestel, Corail, and Jérémie. "The *Rekin* is at your disposal," he said.

They set out amid a fleet of old fishermen with cataracts paddling out to the daily catch. Boston had taken on a load of mangoes and the bags were piled past the gunwales. The ship smelled of the sweet fruit and perfumed the sea they floated on so that the birds followed them from the coast and perched in the rigging. They set a route to the west and came to a country of high white cliffs. The people in the mountains were burning the trees for charcoal on the steep sidehills and the smoke rose silently into the high blue sky.

By noon they were anchored at the fabled Kokoye Kay, where the water was clear as a chlorinated swimming pool and the sand fine and white as sugar. The beach was studded with blue shells smooth as pottery. Boston bought three lobsters and had them boiled in a pot of seawater right there on the beach, over a fire of driftwood and coconut husks.

"The meat cannot be improved by lime, butter, pepper— anything," he said.

They pulled them steaming from the pot and broke into the meaty tails. The sweet flesh had been made savory by the thin rime of salt from the seawater it had been boiled in, and they washed it down with cold beer.

Boston postponed their departure so that the lovers could swim after dinner. The water felt warm in the evening cool. They lay on their backs and counted the houses in the hills by their lights as they came on, all gas or candlewick because there was no electricity anywhere along that coast.

They took a bucket of fresh water from the spring and went

aboard with it, bathing on deck while the ship made way. Zo knelt before Anaya to wash her thighs, her knees, her calves. He lifted her feet carefully to wash beneath them one at a time like treasures he'd unearthed on an expedition. At first, the sailors watched with envy, then with fascination. Boston said he'd never seen a man so tender.

"That's how to treat a woman," he marveled.

They were moved to shame and finally looked away, going about their tasks with averted eyes.

The lovers dried out on deck like salted fish, splayed naked on the warm planks under the starlight. They woke to make secret love while the sailors slept, going on like acrobats amid the shipping implements. Zo had her straddled on the capstan, in the piles of fresh mangoes from Léogâne, swinging in the hammock. He pulled himself up by the rigging and they fucked suspended, with their feet hovering over the weather deck like angels at play.

They paused to watch the lights of Petite Rivière de Nippes, and at dawn, Boston pointed out the high spire of St. Anne's Cathedral at Anse-à-Veau.

That homecoming was the most glorious of Zo's life. He felt like he had two years earlier, when he'd come that way in Daniello's boat sick with malarial fevers, only now he was returning with the sweetest prize in the world—not pearls or sugarcane or Inca gold like the Europeans thought, but the love of his life and the time to love her with. Together after that long year of tribulation, Zo and Anaya felt invincible. They stood on the ship and regarded the whole island like something they had already conquered. Anaya had cheated death there and Zo had gone looking for it, yet they had emerged to love each other again. Only now they loved with a kind of burned-through affection, without excess or doubt, a pure love to match the pure coast at noon.

The lonely houses of the woodcutters high in the hills, the shacks of the fishermen beside the sea, the farming settlements in their river valleys—each seemed a little paradise where some man loved the woman of his dreams. For that moment, they forgot about cholera, malaria, typhoid, and earthquakes and thought only of the thousand sweetnesses they would exchange and the way they would enjoy each other with leisurely intent through all the long twilights of their lives.

Boston made the narrow passage at Anse-à-Maçon, where the Grande Cayemite was so close to the mainland they could look to either side and see the houses strung out along the yellow strand. After that, they entered the protected waters inside the Cayemites. Naked boys swam in the coves and the fishermen sailed shirtless under the sun. There was the Grande Anse River, smoking between green hills, and the seaside town of Roseaux crowding its bay. The white church, the yellow school, the green hospital, the pink Presbyterian mission—it was just as they had left it.

Boss Paul and the crew were on the pier when they docked because Boston had called ahead from Miragoâne and told them to be ready. When Zo came ashore, he took them in his arms—Paul, Tiken, Sonson, Bos-T-Bos. Medsen Fèy came with his drink cart and stood them all to a round.

"Hot or neat or sweet or clean?" Fèy asked.

When they had drunk, Zo turned to Anaya and said, "There's someone I want you to meet." They crossed the highway and started up a sandy track beneath the trees. He took her into a small, disorderly *lakou*, fenced in thorny acacia, where an old woman was shelling peas.

"Gran Yi," Zo said, squatting beside her. "Gran Yi. It's me, *kabrit*."

The old woman raised her face and shook her head. Her eyes were milky with cataracts. Only now, Zo didn't care that she couldn't remember him. He took her by her grizzled chin and kissed both cheeks, promising to bring her a fat fish every weekend. On the way out he told Anaya, "That woman was the closest thing I ever had to a mother."

Zo and Anaya never made it to Anse d'Hainault. Their homecoming in Grande Anse was so pleasant that they decided to stay.

Paul found them a house in the hills above Taino Beach, where Zo once taught Anaya to swim. It was a *kay* in the traditional mountain style, with a peaked roof and wicker walls. A narrow, covered porch opened to the parlor through a pair of French doors. The bedroom was behind the parlor, and had windows on the garden. It was a happy place, with fruit trees in the yard—lime and sour orange, a tamarind for shade and juice.

Then they couldn't leave for Anse d'Hainault because Anaya was pregnant. She had her first cravings in March and sent Zo for hot peppers, sour orange, grapefruit, and vinegar. "Remember what Madam Zulu told you," she said. "Now that I'm pregnant you must act like you have two babies."

Indeed, Madam Zulu had said just that, nor had Zo forgotten. When she craved ice he went down to the store and hurried home again before it melted, just as he'd once run ice for Gran Yi's cold drinks. He rubbed her swollen feet in the evening and bathed her in water infused by the leaves of their own citrus trees. He did their laundry, too, squatting over a basin in the yard while she reclined on the porch and supervised.

When it was warm at night and the wind wasn't blowing, they took their plates out to the porch and ate watching the sunset across the water and the lights turn on in town. Afterward, Anaya would lie in Zo's arms under the tamarind tree while the blue sea ran out under the mountain.

"If it's a girl we're going to name her Nadya," Anaya said. "After my cousin Nadine."

"And if it's a boy?"

"What do you think about Ozzy?"

"After Ozias?"

She turned in his arms to see his face. "He loved you like a son. And mourned you like one when he thought you had died. It broke my heart to see his garden like that. You need to call him, Zo."

"He doesn't have a phone."

"But Madam Zulu does."

Zo didn't say anything for a moment, and then he laughed. "I like to think of him up on his hillside, puttering about with the half garden shears he uses for everything."

"You'll call?"

"*Jodi a*," he said. "I'll do it today. If you promise to call your father and tell him."

There had been a long disagreement between them. Zo believed they should do everything clearly, in the open. He was tired of fearing Leconte. Anaya was less sure. She was still skittish with her father. But as the pregnancy went on, she was beginning to change her mind.

Zo spoke to Madam Zulu's granddaughter and then to Madam Zulu herself. The old asthmatic was thrilled to hear his voice. "Myself, I never thought you were dead. A man so vital, and steadfast."

Zo asked to speak with Ozias.

"Old fool's up at the main house now. On the porch. Pretending he's taken up the pipe."

Zo could hear her harsh wheezing over the phone when she crossed the yard and climbed the porch steps.

"Hey, scarecrow! Sit up and take this thing. Someone wants to talk to you."

There was a long, strained silence and then a pattern of breathing that perfectly expressed the intensity of the old man's emotions.

"*Papa m*," Zo said. "*Sak a fet la? Komo w ye?*"

Zo's voice struck the old man like a bullet.

"*Timoun mw*," he cried. "My boy."

There was a crash. Then Zulu was on the phone again.

"He dropped the phone," she said. "We'll call you back."

Anaya didn't call her father right away. She waited for the evening breeze. Then she took the phone out to the porch, leaned on the railing, and dialed.

Vincent Leconte wasn't in Port-au-Prince, like she thought. "I was only ever in that city to be near you," he said. "I left almost as soon as you did." In fact, he was just a dozen kilometers away, in Jérémie, at the house in Chabanne. When he learned that she was pregnant, and just down the coast, he insisted on coming to visit.

He had to go by boat because the bridge was damaged. It was August and the sea was purple. The little fishing boats turned in and out of the waves. He marveled at how different he felt on that voyage compared with the one he'd taken a year and a half earlier.

"It's wonderful how swiftly your life can change," he told the captain. "A year ago my daughter and I were hardly speaking. I thought she had died in the earthquake."

"The sea is never the same two days in a row," the captain said.

The slopes were bare and green, the water clear as air. The sunlight wasn't refracted but shone straight down to the depths.

He could see Zo and Anaya even before he was aground on the tiny beach. His daughter wore a wide straw hat and sundress, while Zo stood behind her and a little to the side with his arms around her belly. They were waiting in the shade of a little boathouse, though Leconte wondered when he saw it up close whether it could really be called that. A shed of sawn *portos* and coconut leaves, it looked more like an afternoon hideaway. Bags of outgoing fruit and baskets of fish were laid aside to be packed into the ship.

Zo was deferential and averted his eyes from Leconte's gaze. He shook the doctor's hand, took his bag, and spoke only when Anaya expected him to or when Leconte put a direct question to him. They took him to their house above the beach and served him a simple supper of boiled fish and yucca, which grew abundantly in those sunny hills.

"What are you doing in Jérémie, Papa?" Anaya asked.

He sighed. "After all those months in Port-au-Prince, I thought I wanted rest and relaxation. But I was wrong."

"What did you want?"

"More work, I guess." Leconte laughed—not the short, arrogant laugh she'd known from before—but weary and complete. "I wanted to be of use," he said. "To leave this place a little better than I found it. That was what I told Dady Malebranch, anyway, when I went to see him."

"You're *Direktè Jeneral?*"

"Since March."

"*Felisitasyon.*"

"Alix Lamothe said it best," Leconte continued. "We were a hundred years behind before, and that earthquake set us back a hundred more. I'd started to think the whole country was like that, one monotonous ruin. It seemed like that on my way back home, all the way through Léogâne—Carrefour, Garde Coté, the burned stacks at Varreaux. It wasn't until Fond de Negres that I had any relief. The countryside was a revelation," he said. "The green cane. The mangos. The enterprising merchants. Life goes on as it always has."

Leconte had come with a handheld fetal ultrasound so that they could hear the baby's heartbeat. And after dinner, Zo cleared the table and did the dishes, too. Then he brought the mattress out to the porch and Anaya lay down and lifted her shirt.

Vincent took the doppler out and unwrapped the cord. "Your mother was the one who taught me how to do this," he said. "She had a way of finding the baby with her hands, and putting the wand exactly on the heart."

Anaya shivered when her father pressed the probe against her belly.

"Is it cold?" Zo asked, and she locked eyes with him.

Leconte slid the wand obliquely. A distant sound punctuated the static—a steady, wet pulse. "That's it," he said. "The heartbeat."

Zo didn't sleep that night but lay beside Anaya in the dark, wondering how he was going to give them, mother and baby both, the life they deserved. In the morning, he walked the doctor back to the ship, carrying his bags.

"You told me once that my wages wouldn't buy a coffee in Brooklyn," Zo started. "And that I could never provide Anaya with the comforts to which she had become accustomed."

Leconte watched his footing in the rocky trail. "Did I say that?"

"You were right," Zo said. "All my life I've worked. Harvesting cane and cotton, dragging goods through the streets. Fighting for hundred-dollar purses in Potoprens. But I've never had any money. Not enough to support a family. I've never even had a bank account."

The bush hens were calling from the brush.

"You're going to be a father," Leconte said. "It makes you think."

"It's something I never had myself."

Leconte stopped in the trail. "You'll make mistakes," he said. "We all do." The sunlight gave his eyes a strange depth. "The important thing is that you love my daughter more than you love yourself."

"I do. Yes. Absolutely."

"What more could a father ask of his son-in-law?"

When Zo returned to the house above Taino Beach, he told Anaya he wanted to go to Jérémie.

"Why?"

"To be closer to the hospital."

"What do you want with the hospital?"

"They have ultrasounds, operating rooms, and an obstetrician who could help us."

"You talked to my father."

"I asked for his advice."

They closed up the mountain house in September and traveled to Jérémie in Daniello's boat. Anaya was seven months pregnant and uncomfortable at sea. She was relieved to see the big white house on the bluff.

The doctor was waiting for them at the top of the stairs. From that vantage point, drinking a cold beer, he couldn't help but approve of the way Zo treated his daughter—he jumped into the water and carried Anaya to shore before returning for the bags. Her belly was big and round now, and she stood barefoot in the sand with her hands behind her back, very much as her mother had once stood. When Zo reached the top of the stairs, Leconte produced a second bottle of beer and offered it to him.

Anaya spent her days on the couch or out in a lawn chair eating fruit and ice. Zo kept her company during the day, while Leconte was at the office. In the evenings, they waited on her hand and foot, passing each other in the hall with pillows, cool compresses, and herbal tea.

Leconte woke one night in October at two a.m. and found Zo rubbing Anaya's feet on the couch downstairs. She was having contractions. Vincent drove them to the hospital and followed them into the maternity ward. The labor was protracted, and he stood by himself in the dim waiting room.

A girl was delivered late in the morning. The midwife clamped the cord in two places and cut between. She administered a shot of vitamin K and rubbed the baby's eyes with erythromycin. Nadya was wiped clean, wrapped in a blanket, and handed to her mother.

When Zo held her for the first time, he knew exactly what to say. The words were there as if he'd written them himself.

"While yet all you know of this world are my hands," he said, "let them tell you what is hard, and what is paired, and what is the temperature of the blood." He dropped his face against his daughter's. "And how badly we want to love you without knowing how."

Author's Note

Zo started with a radio show. I was riding in a car in Port-au-Prince when a woman testified that she'd woken up after the earthquake in a dump truck bound for the burial ground at Titanyen. That was the only word I really understood—"Titanyen, Titanyen"— she said it again and again. I knew what that place was, and I understood her tone. My gracious host, Hughes Desgranges, filled me in on the rest.

As for the pair of lovers who lose each other in the aftermath, that was a story the nurses were telling in a cholera treatment center in November. I had learned enough Creole by then to understand it myself.

I arrived in Haiti in January 2010, two weeks after the earthquake. I was an EMT and thought I might be of some use. I went with the Jatukik Providence Foundation, under the leadership of Father Jean-Claude Atasameso, a Catholic priest from the Democratic Republic of Congo. Father Atusameso normally sends medical supplies to isolated hospitals in the DRC but had rerouted his shipment to Haiti. Before we landed he said, "We have more in our hearts than we have in our hands."

One night I gave CPR to a five-year-old girl on the back of a motorcycle. She'd come in convulsing, and I hoped it was febrile seizures because I had seen those before and knew what to do. But she didn't have a fever. Her father took two glass vials from his pocket. She'd been injected with an overdose of chloroquine, the medicine used to treat malaria. I had no idea what to do. I'd come to do wound care, and here was a tropical disease. We climbed onto the motorcycle and headed for the Wesleyan Clinic—the driver in his handlebars, me with the girl in my arms, and Yamina Armand, our guide and translator, in the luggage rack.

Somewhere on the national highway, just before she died, I guess, the little girl reached up and grabbed my chin so hard I was scared I'd fall off the bike. That was the last thing she did. It was the night I'd hold a dead child in my arms, the night she'd die at five years old. All I could think about was her father: that he had given me a live daughter and now I held a dead one. And ever afterward he'd remember me like a nightmare or a terror—a white man on a motorbike bearing his daughter down the highway and into the neverward, and there's no stopping me or meeting me when I get there.

He gave me a live daughter, and I gave him back a dead one.

I returned to the States, raised money to buy an ambulance, and purchased a used rig in New Jersey. When the seller heard it was for a good cause, he cut the price. A local EMS company helped install suction and a stretcher. It shipped to Haiti from the port of Red Hook, Brooklyn, bound for the Dr. Henri Gerard Desgranges clinic outside Petit-Goâve. I returned to Haiti to see the ambulance through customs just before the cholera epidemic started.

I am not a Haiti expert. Many of the country's native writers—Edwidge Danticat, Dany Laferrière, Jacques Roumain—capture its beauty and depth to greater effect than I ever could. Neither am I an expert on disaster relief. Jonathan Katz, Dr. Paul Farmer, Peter Orner, and Evan Lyon in their excellent collection, *Lavil: Life, Love, and Death in Port-au-Prince,* are more knowledgeable and experienced on the challenges and realities of responding to a crisis than I can ever hope to be. The truth is, I am an unlikely choice to author a story set in Haiti, but I fell in love there, and found when I set out to write a love story I could put it nowhere else.

I first saw Naomi at a cholera treatment center. She was working for Oxfam International, in their hygiene campaign, and I was with the Dr. Henri Gerard Desgranges clinic. But you can't flirt at a cholera treatment center—all that death and diarrhea are not conducive to it. Still, when our eyes met, something happened, and all that was left was to ask for names. We did that, a few days later, at a concert for Digicel Stars.

Naomi's dad did not like me. I was *etranje*, and he couldn't be sure my intentions were good. To be honest, in those first few weeks, maybe they weren't. I was lonely and far from home. But then there was the night I had a bout of cholera-like symptoms and thought I was going to die. Naomi came to see me. She mixed a bottle of oral rehydration salts, put my head in her lap, and saved my life.

No one thought we would last, but we've been married for seven years. We have a son. Sometimes, we look at him and wonder that he was forged by an earthquake and an epidemic.

When I returned from Haiti in 2011, I found the narrative was all wrong. It was said everywhere that foreigners had come and saved the country. But that's not what happened. As is always the case on that island, the people saved themselves. They saved each other. The UN Office for Coordination of Humanitarian Affairs said 132 people had been rescued from the rubble by international teams. I am certain that the citizens themselves rescued thousands more.

Like Klerverna, who walked sixty-two kilometers to dig her daughter from the rubble of an apartment. Or Bouchon, who used a tire jack and a sledgehammer. Or Dr. Joussaint, who worked seven days a week for three months.

It has been ten years since the earthquake. People continue to die of cholera. Jobs are scarce, and the price of commodities like gasoline and rice continue to rise. Political unrest is common-place. Despite the heroic work of the people, and the generosity of the world in the aftermath, Haiti has not been "built back better." Much of the aid money pledged after the earthquake was never accounted for, or was misspent. In my wife's hometown, for example, USAID spent millions building a new prison, which the citizens have nicknamed "the university." It stands empty and well lit with energy from its solar panels, while the rest of the town remains in darkness.

To those who let me into their lives, took care of me when I was far from home, and loved me despite my being *blan* and *etranje: mesi anpil. Mw pa ka repaye w pou tout w te bay m.*

To Mama Myel, a miracle worker and my mother-in-law, who raised seven children to beautiful completion on less than a dollar a day. To Tamarre, Dardd, Emmanuel, Holdschie, Ashitophel, and Nachalie—for letting me be your brother.

To Ti Darlene, who was raised in a police *komisseriat* and killed by sickle cell disease—you are not forgotten.

To Emwa, who went barefoot and farmed blind, and Madam Ti Klis, who birthed fifteen children without a doctor—it was an honor to have known you both.

To Miyomene, for the kind of friendship that stands by your side on a deserted beach at midnight with a broken bottle in her hand, ready to fight. To the real Verna, who survived twenty-four hours under the rubble in Port-au-Prince, and then went back to nursing school as soon as she could walk.

To Yamina Armand, who taught me Creole, and who later moved from Boston to Europe out of love for her daughter.

To the Dr. Henri Gerard Desgranges Foundation and the Desgrottes family: thank you for the trust you put in me, and for the tremendous support and relief you give to the community you serve every day. Special gratitude to Dr. Tania Desgrottes, whose expertise is profound and irreplaceable; to Maryse, who is the heart and soul of everything; and to Dr. Tessier, Jean-François, and Miss Cacquette—who do it every day.

To Jean-Claude Atusameso and his Jatukik Providence Foundation: thank you for taking me along and for the work you do. To Thom Gallemore and Tom Cotter, who continue doing good work around the world.

To Ricki—I am only standing because of your support. To Scott and Florene, for their love of books. To Craig, Joan, and Michael Michaud, for that decisive season on the vineyard.

Thanks to Seth Fishman, for coming out of his wheelhouse. To Robin Desser, for the chance—I will forever be grateful to you for it. And to Annie Bishai, who came to this project like wind to the sails of a ship long caught in the doldrums—you brought us home.

Most of all, to those who died in the earthquake and those killed by cholera: may we be worthy of the world you left behind.

Sunday, January 12, 2020

Xander Miller has lived in Ohio, Washington, Arizona, New Mexico, California, and Pennsylvania. He worked at national parks and monuments, and as an emergency medical technician, before traveling to Haiti after the earthquake in 2010, where he was a volunteer EMT and founded a nonprofit called Ambulance for Haiti. He met his wife, Naomi, in her hometown of Petit-Goâve. He is currently a physician assistant, and *Zo* is his first novel.

A NOTE ON THE TYPE

This book was set in Monotype Dante, a typeface designed by Giovanni Mardersteig (1892–1977). Its first use was in an edition of Boccaccio's *Trattatello in laude di Dante* that appeared in 1954. The Monotype Corporation's version of Dante followed in 1957. Dante is a modern interpretation of the Aldine type used for Pietro Cardinal Bembo's treatise *De Aetna* in 1495.

Composed by North Market Street Graphics, Lancaster, Pennsylvania

Printed and bound by Berryville Graphics, Berryville, Virginia

Designed by Maggie Hinders